# Broken

*Broken Trilogy, Book One*

*J.L. Drake*

*Broken*

Limitless Publishing, LLC
Kailua, HI 96734
www.limitlesspublishing.com

Formatting: Limitless Publishing

ISBN-13: 978-1-68058-071-6
ISBN-10: 1-68058-071-X

# Dedication

For my mother who has followed this story with me from the very beginning. Thank you for the endless support you've given me in everything I've ever tried.

I love you.

# Prologue

Deceit
Deception
Dishonest
Distortion
Fiction
Myth
Tale
Fib

…anyway you say it, it means the same thing…lies.

# *Chapter One*

I don't know how long I've been here—four months possibly five. Time passes in strange ways when you have no means to mark it. At first, I counted time by the meals I received, but after a while they became fewer and less dependable. I know for sure I've been here one full season. The men went from wearing long sleeve shirts to T-shirts.

My prison is a small room with a rusty bed that squeaks anytime I shift position. A tiny wooden table with a small stool takes up one corner and a toilet and sink hide behind a ratty curtain in the other. No windows, no TV, nothing to read but an old copy of *Wiseguy* by Nicolas Pileggi. I wasn't one for reading crime novels in the past, but I can recite every single word by heart now.

I hear the familiar sound of the key retracting the lock and my stomach sinks. I pull at my ratty sweater wrapping it around my midsection a little tighter—like that is going to help protect me from them.

I hear his boots scuff on the hardwood and sweat

breaks out along the back of my neck. *Shit, it's him.* My skin crawls when I see his sausage-like fingers holding a tray of food for me. His hairy stomach pushes out below his T-shirt and bulges over the top of his jeans. As soon as he spots me he gives me his lopsided smile.

"*Hola, chica,* how are you today?" His voice is raspy and his accent thick, but I understand every word. His body language is enough in itself. "I ask you a question," he barks at me.

"Fine," I say through the lump in my throat.

He stands holding the tray above me. Finally I raise my eyes to meet his and he smirks, showing me how much he enjoys having this power over me. I've had enough encounters with this man to know that he won't leave without wanting something in return. Luckily up till now it's never been anything sexual—just more head games. That doesn't mean he's never insinuated it. I feel my body tremble, shaky fingers pulling at the hem of my cotton nightgown that is sitting mid-thigh. I don't need to give him any ideas. His gaze drops to my legs and he licks his lips.

"Beg," he orders, drawing out the word.

My mouth goes dry. He loves this part. I am an animal to him. He calls me his *perra*, which means dog in Spanish. I feel my temper rise as I try to tell myself to stop but I can't help it. I am past caring anymore.

I give him the sweetest smile I can muster. "Screw you." I'd never spoken more than I absolutely had to since I got here; suffice it to say he is blown away by my choice of words. Normally

3

I do what I'm told while secretly fantasizing the many ways I'd like to kill this man. I try to behave, never wanting to relive my first few days here. The incredible pain after they beat me to a bloody pulp when I didn't do what was asked made me wise up quickly.

My present adrenaline high is short lived, however, as I watch his eyes narrow and his jaw tighten. He suddenly tosses the tray across the room, shattering the dishes against the wall.

"No food for you, *lengua de mierda*!" he hisses, taking a step toward me. I cover my ears, tucking my knees up to my chest. This man is large enough to pick me up in one hand and toss me across the room, meeting the tray's fate. He grabs a handful of my hair and drags me across the room, my knees bouncing along the floor like a rag doll. I barely register the pain—I am more aware that this six foot, three hundred seventy-five pound man is hovering over me, enraged. Why did I have to get smart? The only thing I have going for me is they haven't killed me yet. Maybe I am being held for ransom. It's no secret my father has a lot of money and everyone knows his name—he is running for a second term as Mayor of New York City.

I try to force myself up onto my hands but his boot crushes down on my back forcing me down hard. My forehead smacks against the floor making my ears ring. I let out a whimper as my eyes focus on something just out of reach. I hear the sound of him removing his belt and my heart quickens—no, no, no! This can't be happening. If I could just move a few feet to the right…I muster up all I have

4

and launch myself forward along the floor.

"Where do you think you're going?" His voice is calm—oh, so calm. My fingers wrap around the broken piece of plate and I tuck my hand under my chest to hide it. "Come." He bends down, grabbing my feet and flipping me over, dragging me back toward the bed. I scream out in protest. I kick and wiggle but his grip is too tight. "Feisty little thing, aren't ya?" he chuckles. He leans over to grab me and I take my opportunity. I shoot upward, driving the sharp piece of glass into his neck. His eyes go wide with shock and he falls to his side with a loud thud, cursing and digging at the object. I scramble to my feet and head for the open door.

I have no idea what direction to go but I don't care—for the first time in forever I am free of that room. I move as fast as my feet can take me. I'm low on sugar and my head feels light but I keep going—this is my chance. Physical activity has not been a part of my world for so long it is hard for my brain to wait while my legs try desperately to keep up. The hallway is long with lots of doors, the wallpaper is ripped in places, and the lighting is low. It looks like an abandoned hotel, but where are the windows? I keep winding around corners, my hands holding me upright against the walls as my knees grow weak. I have no sense of direction; every hallway looks the same. I can hear voices getting louder and my heart is in my throat. I try pulling and pushing on the closest door handle but it doesn't budge. Stinging tears race down my cheeks, panic is kicking in, and sobs are overtaking me. I fight them back but I feel I'm letting myself down—I have a chance to escape and I can't even open a goddamned door! A heavy click followed by a humming noise makes me freeze. Then the lights flicker and go out.

I cover my mouth to stop the screams as my hands shake violently along with my teeth. I press my back up against the door needing something stable for support. A bright flicker off to the left draws my eye, but it quickly dies, followed by a dull orange glow. Someone is standing about ten feet from me smoking a fat cigar. I close my eyes saying a silent prayer. When I open them again I'm met with a mean set of eyes inches from my face. I am unable to move. I know this man—I've seen him a few times before and I think he runs this place. He puffs away, filling my nose with the nauseating scent of his Montecristo. I'd know that smell anywhere. My father often had parties and they seemed to be the most popular cigar among his guests.

My knees weaken as he continues to stare at me, saying nothing. I hear his shoulder shift in his jacket as his hand comes up and grips my chin tightly. With casual ease he flicks open and ignites his Zippo, holding it up to inspect the growing lump above my eye. The light goes out and I feel his vice-like grip move to the back of my neck and he pushes me to move forward. He obviously knows the building well since it is still pitch black and he directs me without hesitation. All I can hear is my hammering heartbeat and my short, ragged breaths.

Finally we stop at a door and he pushes it open and tosses me inside. I stumble forward, falling to my knees. Suddenly, the lights come on and I come face to face with the fat man whose neck is now wrapped in a white bandage. He holds his belt in his hand snapping it for more effect. The last thing I remember is being pushed onto a couch and the first crack of the belt along my lower back. This kind of pain I'll never forget; it is permanently embedded in my memory. Thankfully I slip away into a blissful place, one I welcome with open arms.

I wake to blinding pain, the smallest movement causing me to sob, which in turn hurts even more. My brain is cloudy. I can barely form a thought—even breathing is tricky. It takes me a few moments to realize I am back in my prison lying face down on the squeaky bed. I let go and allow the tears to flow. I need something to think about, something to focus on. I remember the first day I came here. Christ—it seems so long ago.

*** 

*"Hello my love," I purr to my Keurig as I place my beloved mug that reads "Don't talk to me till this mug is empty" underneath and push the button. My friend Lynn gets a kick out of the fact that I can't function until I've had at least one large cup of coffee in me. She bought this mug for my twenty-sixth birthday. It was tucked inside a basket she had done up along with an airline ticket to Fiji for the two of us to escape my crazy world. Man, what a trip that was. I hear my front door open.*

*"You're in for it now, Savi!" Lynn shouts as she comes into my kitchen. She holds up a magazine,*

*showing the cover to me. As soon as my eyes read the caption I knew I was in shit.*

*"Oh no!" I snatch it from her fingers.*

*"Oh yes," she sighs, passing by and opening a cabinet. "So I take it he hasn't called you yet?"*

*I shake my head no as I study the picture in horror. Us Weekly has a picture of me at a bar last night leaning over a table showing off my behind. The caption reads, "Mayor's Daughter Reveals All".*

*"I was reaching for my purse!" I shout. "It isn't even my butt—this has been Photoshopped."*

*"I know that, but will daddy dearest believe you?" She sips her coffee, eyeing me with concern. "Maybe you should call him first. It might look better if you do."*

*Lynn and I have been friends forever. We met in middle school the day we got stuck in detention for running our mouths and became fast friends ever since. She rode the wave of fame and publicity right alongside me. She is my rock as I am hers and we both consider ourselves the sisters we never had. Perhaps she has a point. I toss the magazine aside, reaching for my purse and pull out my cell. Three rings later I hear his voice.*

*"Dad—how are you this morning?" Silence grows on the other end of the line. "You there?"*

*"Any reason why I'm staring at my daughter on the front cover of yet another popular magazine?"*

*Shit! Shit! Shit!*

*"Dad, look, you know I haven't been out much. I've been so careful after what happened last year. But this isn't what it looks like—"*

"*Save it, Savannah. Do you have any idea what kind of damage you cause me? I have three people working on this, wasting their time on this crap!*"

"*Dad, please let me explain—*"

"*No, Savi, we'll discuss it tomorrow night at dinner.*" The line goes dead.

I toss the phone on the counter and rub my face with both hands. Lynn touches my back gently, giving me a few moments to process everything. I sigh, running my hands through my hair. Lynn moves in front of me, getting me to look at her.

"*Come on, Savi, let's get out of here.*"

After a hot shower I start to come around a little. I pull on my favorite navy blue dress with black boots and a black pea coat.

"*Okay, okay, stop fussing,*" Lynn groans from my door. "*You look fine.*"

"*If I end up looking like I have a hangover and the media finds me, you know they'll have a ball with the story.*" She grabs my shoulders and looks at me in the mirror.

"*Who cares what anyone thinks, Savi? Anyone who knows the real you knows you have a heart of gold...and a quick tongue to put people in their place.*" She grins. "*What's not to love?*"

"*I am pretty great,*" I joke, linking arms with her as we walk out the door. We have to sidestep two painters outside in the hall and as I push the button on the elevator I glance at one of the men. He's wearing a massive belt buckle that reads 'Texas' with a Longhorn head sticking out of the center.

"*He's a long way from home,*" I mutter. Lynn shakes her head at me.

*"Oh please."* She laughs, noting the direction of my gaze. *"They're a dime a dozen at any market."* She hustles us into the elevator. I sigh, not wanting to face the outdoors.

*"Ready?"* she asks, pulling on her sunglasses.

*"I guess so."*

*"Stop worrying, Savannah,"* Lynn says through a bite of her bagel. *"Your dad will get over this. You know how he is."*

*"I know. I just hate disappointing him, especially over something like this, and I've been so careful."* I thought about the last time I made it on the cover of a magazine. I tripped over some drunk and fell flat on my face. It made a great story for the tabloids and made an even bigger stink with my father. Everything is about image in the public eye and frankly I am just plain sick of it all. The idea of another four years was enough for me to run screaming for the hills.

*"You got plans tonight?"* Lynn asks as she tosses her napkin on her plate.

*"Yeah, I have a dinner thing for work I have to attend. We're trying to win over another new client."*

She makes a sour face, *"Sounds…fun."* Lucky for Lynn she works her own hours as an artist in her own studio while I work for a big marketing corporation. Even though I worked my butt off in school for years, I still feel like they use me for my connection to the mayor just to win over clients.

When my mother passed away six years ago after a long battle with cancer I was mentally and physically exhausted. I changed my last name to her *maiden name when my father got more involved in politics. I didn't want people knowing who I was right off the bat. My father didn't understand at first, but now I'm sure he's fine with it. I just needed time and privacy to get on with my life and to get over my grief.*

*Later on that evening, I find myself lost in thought instead of paying attention to the conversation around me. Here I am at another fancy dinner with beyond boring executives who are talking about nothing remotely interesting. They hardly engage me in conversation and never ask for my opinion. I just sit there and try not to show what I'm thinking. Like how Mr. Roth's tie keeps dipping into his soup and how his wife pretends not to notice. She keeps trying to hide her smirk—I take it they don't get along very well at home. At least this was a tad amusing. I shift my gaze out the window and into Central Park—oh, what I wouldn't do to go for a run through the snowy paths right about now.*

*"Wherever you are, can I join you?" Joe Might asks, leaning over so only I can hear him.*

*"I'm sorry?"*

*He smiles. "You look like you were off somewhere else."*

*Oh. I am embarrassed, caught daydreaming by our hopefully soon-to-be client. This doesn't look good for me.*

*"I'm so sorry." I wrinkle my nose, feeling embarrassed to no end. Nice one, Savi!*

*"Don't be." He pulls his hand out from under the table and shows me the phone he's been using to*

*play online poker. I try to hide my laugh; he grins and shrugs. "We all know it's a done deal, right?"*

*"I guess so, huh?" I say with a sigh. "I just wish I could get something stiffer." I point to my glass of Pinot Grigio. I don't drink as a rule, but this dinner is painful. He winks at me before he clears his throat.*

*"Excuse me, gentlemen—but I need to have a word with Miss Miller." Before I know what is happening, he pulls out my chair and helps me to my feet, walking me through the dining area and out the front door. He hands the valet his ticket and moments later I'm sitting on the tan, plush seat of his red corvette. "Now," he grins. "Let's see about getting you something stiffer—to drink, that is." All I can do was nod like a moron.*

*After a few drinks at a Scottish pub I decide I should get back before I get in any more trouble with the press. There is only the bartender and a lone man in the corner, but lord knows they'd have another field day if they find me in another pub after what happened last night.*

*"Let me drive you back to your car, at least," Joe says, standing to shrug on his jacket. He is a handsome man—his gel-styled brown hair and light eyes are a pretty combination. I guess he's in his mid-thirties.*

*"That's not necessary. I can take a cab."*

*"Nonsense. I stole you away; it is only right I return you, too." He gestures toward the door. "Is your car at work?"*

*I shake my head as I slip my purse over my shoulder. "A friend dropped me off this morning."*

*"Home, then?"*

*I nod as we walk outside. The ride is nice, he offers more information about his company, and asks a few questions about my position.*

*"So you'll fax me those samples as soon as you can?" he asks as I duck down to say goodbye through the open window.*

*"Yes, I will. 'Night, Joe, thanks for the fun evening—and the ride!" I walk toward my condo, deciding to grab the necessary file now rather than tomorrow.*

*I prop myself up against the wall in the elevator feeling tired and anxious about how my day started. The idea of disappointing Dad again was weighing heavily on me. It seems to be a weekly event. Either it is the media or something I just say or do around him. God, I really miss my mother! She was so sweet and understanding. She wouldn't have cared if I wore the wrong outfit to lunch or said the wrong thing during a business dinner. Christ, I'm only human. I never wanted to be a part of the public eye in the first place—never once!*

*I step out to a quiet parking lot. Luckily my car is parked close by as my feet are getting sore in my high boots. I open the trunk, reach for my laptop case, and suddenly sense someone is behind me. I start to turn, but a dark cloth is roughly slapped over my face. A hand covers my mouth so I cannot scream. My feet leave the ground as I am flung over someone's shoulder and something cold and hard strikes my shin. Fear courses through my veins; the air is forced out of me as my attacker tosses me roughly into the back of a vehicle. I can feel the movement as we speed away. I can't believe this is happening! I am terrified out of my mind.*

*Someone makes fast work of binding my wrists and ankles together. I can make out only shadows around me, and hear male grunts and heavy breathing. Fear has taken over and I seem to have lost my ability to speak. Someone grips my shoulders, pinning me while another stretches out over top of me, with all my might I buck my legs up and nail one of them in the crotch. His screech is ear piercing as he falls back then I feel the poke of a needle and everything gets fuzzy.*

That's all I remember from the last day I spoke to my father, my best friend, my coworkers, and since I saw the light of day.

# Chapter Two

I attempt to roll off the bed as I have a horrible case of cotton mouth and desperately need water. My knees buckle as I start the trek to the sink. Normally, my prison room seems so small but right now it feels like I am a hundred yards from the wall. I must have taken quite a beating; I hurt everywhere.

Finally reaching the sink, I grab the rusty, tin container. Water never tasted so good. I wet my lips and let it trickle down my throat before collapsing into a painful ball. I begin to sob, knowing I'll never get out of here. I can only imagine how bad my back looks. It feels wet and burns terribly, my head is throbbing, and my wrists feel tender. He must have tied me up during…my stomach drops. I slowly move my hand down to the hem of my nightgown and pull it up. I let out a small hiss of relief when I see that I still have on the same panties as yesterday. My outsides may be damaged but the rest of me remains, at least for the moment, undefiled. But emotionally I am spent. My hands cover my face in sudden defeat as I lie on the floor to think. I've been treated like something less than a barnyard animal for way too long. My captors never seem to tire of their sick power trip over me. I'm sure it brings them endless amusement. I get a bath once in a while, during which they take plenty of photos and videos. I have a toothbrush which has grown disgusting and a bar of soap which is down to a small nub. My food, when they decide to feed me, is some kind of soup and crusty bread. The water is always warm with flakes of dirt in it.

Occasionally a doctor is brought in to check me over; twice I had to get IV fluids pumped into me. I was more concerned whether the needle was clean than what they were putting inside me. Once I tried to ask the doctor for help, but he acted like he didn't understand me. I know he did because when I mentioned home he flinched and wouldn't make eye contact. All I got was a jab in the ribs from one of men and shouted admonishments in Spanish for attempting to talk.

My only choice will have to be starvation. I've decided I'm done and at least my death will be under my control.

I hear footsteps outside my door. At the clink of the lock my body automatically starts to tremble. Sure enough the fat guy returns with my tray of food. He drops it loudly on the table then glares at me. "Sore?" he asks with a laugh. I want to lunge at him and jab another piece of plate into his neck. Next time I'll remember to pull it back out and continue till the fat bastard is dead

"No, you?" I hiss back. Really, what do I have to lose? His face drops and his hand jerks to touch his neck, but he stops himself. He picks up my water glass and pours it out on the floor, and continues to do the same with my soup and bread as he watches me with an insolent smile. A few days ago I would have been heartbroken but today it plays right into my decision and I just smile back. *Fuck you.*

A few hours later I hear the familiar key in the lock. The lights are dim so I can't see very well. Someone brings a new tray of food—I hear it scrape on the floor as he puts it down. He moves toward my bed. I smell the familiar aroma of Montecristo and know it is the man with the cigar.

"You need to eat," he says roughly. I don't move. I just lay there feeling completely defeated. He reaches over and chucks a piece of bread at me. It bounces off my shoulder. "Eat, *perra.*" He leaves, slamming the door behind him.

After some time I finally move over to the tray and nearly vomit when I see the same meal I've been fed for lunch and dinner for God knows how long—a watery beef stew. Knowing these guys, it's probably rat or possum. It helps reinforce my choice to not eat. I take a sip of the water feeling some grit slide down my throat, and I cough, choking down the rising bile, and stumble back to bed.

Five more meals are brought to me, five meals that stayed untouched. Although my body begs me to eat, my willpower is not faltering. Needless to say I feel like shit.

My mother visits me often to whisper words of encouragement. I know it is only my body's way of coping with starvation but on some level it brings me joy to see her again. She is just as I remember—

long, dark hair, perfect teeth, and dark eyes. Her touch is so real I can feel the heat from her hand on my face.

*"I love you, Savi. You know that, right?" she says. "I'm here for you." She touches my chest right over my heart. "My little angel."*

I pull my knees up to my chest and sob as the memory fades.

I wish I was capable of love like that now. Love and trust was something that I'd promised myself I would never give away. I've been tested many times only to be betrayed over and over. It is always a trap. They can have my body but I will be damned if they will get my soul!

I'm lying in bed staring at the ceiling, watching it fade in and out of my blurry vision when I think I hear a popping noise followed by loud shouts. If I was in a clearer frame of mind, I may have understood what was going on but in my present state I don't really care.

A series of events seem to happen all at once. There is a loud bang, my door flies open, and a bright light moves all around the room. A man dressed completely in black with a helmet and goggles draws closer. It takes considerable effort, but I roll my head over to face him. The light flashes over my face making me squint. He pauses for a moment, then shouts something into a radio on his neck. He reaches forward, lifting me out of the bed. I groan as his hand grips my back. I don't know if I am dreaming or not, but I don't seem to be able to take it all in—my brain isn't functioning properly.

The man holds me tightly as he carries me down a long hallway. There are a few other men dressed in the same black outfit in front of us, guns raised and ready to fire. I am so tired, but now I'm wide awake and afraid if I close my eyes I will find myself back in that room again, alone. We travel down a long staircase toward double wooden doors that look to have been blown open. I don't seem to be able to speak; I'm still afraid I'm dreaming.

The air is cold and it is dark and feels like it might rain. This has to be real. I feel moisture on my face and the fresh, cold air is so wonderful. I want to cry with the pleasure of it. Three black SUVs are waiting out front. I am placed in the middle vehicle, followed by the man who carried me and three others: the driver, a man in the front passenger seat, and one in the back facing the opposite direction. I am quickly fastened in and have a blanket wrapped around me. The first thing that comes to mind is how clean the blanket smells. We travel away from the building. I have no strength and my head seems to have a life of its own, bouncing around until it finds a comfortable bump on the blanket. I watch the driver's hands slide over the wheel looking perfectly calm. After we are a good distance away from the house the man who carried me tears off his goggles and helmet. He runs his hand through his black hair, looking over at me. I am surprised to see that he looks to only be a few years older than me, maybe early thirties.

"Savannah? You're okay now; you're safe," he says quietly in a steady voice. I just stare at him. I heard what he said, but it didn't seem to register in my brain. I am still afraid to believe that I am really rescued from my prison. Perhaps this is just a nasty trick. He studies my face for a moment then reaches over. I flinch, closing my eyes momentarily. He pulls his hand back but points at my forehead. "Looks like that hurts. Are you all right? Do you hurt anywhere else?"

I want to tell him about my back, but I am still unable to speak.

"The jet is standing by, sir," the driver says into the rear view mirror. The man beside me nods.

"Good. Tell them we're ten minutes out."

"Yes, sir."

I start to feel dizzy. The lack of food has taken a toll on me. I flop my head against the window and watch as tiny raindrops make paths down the glass. I don't recognize anything. Houses and streets look different and nothing makes sense. I wonder where I am and where I'm going.

Again, I feel the rush of cool air as I am lifted out of the car. The rain is cold but feels wonderful as my head bobs against my carrier's shoulder. I have no strength left. The raindrops bounce off my face, sweeping away some grime.

If this is a dream—it is the best dream ever.

I am placed on a warm leather couch inside an airplane and watch as ten other men dressed in black board the plane and take their seats. They look like SWAT or something. My vision is getting very fuzzy and I feel so tired.

"Stay with me, Savannah." The voice comes from beside me. I force my eyes open to see my carrier looking down at me. His incredibly dark eyes are looking into mine and hold on to me for a moment. A voice sounds over a speaker and, within a matter of minutes, I feel movement and my carrier is gone from sight. My eyes grow heavy again with the hum of the plane. I have fought sleep for as long as I can. I feel myself sliding down into the void and my last conscious thought is how I usually hate flying.

***

The calming sound of rustling leaves brings me back to consciousness. I move my head slightly, rubbing my cheek up against the softest pillow ever. The faint smell of fresh roses fills my nose. Could this be right? My eyes flutter open, blinking a few times to take in the soft sunlight that fills the room. A wall made up of large windows with three doors that open to a balcony is on one side. An ivory curtain flutters in the breeze, wafting the floral scent of the roses grouped together in a glass vase to my eager nostrils. I feel a tug on my arm and realize I have an IV attached to my left wrist. The bag hanging from a pole next to me is almost empty. I take in the queen size sleigh bed with its amazingly red sheets and duvet that feels like heaven. I am overwhelmed and close my eyes, drifting back to sleep.

\*\*\*

When I regain consciousness it's dark, my fluid bag has been changed, and someone has lit a fire in the stone fireplace. The lovely sound of crackling wood almost brings me to tears—it is beyond soothing to my soul. Is this heaven? If so, I'm completely fine with being dead. A creaking sound makes me freeze.

A wooden door opens off to my right. An older lady, maybe in her fifties, wearing slacks and a blouse comes in holding a tray. I start to push myself up into a sitting position but *Oh God, everything hurts.* Sadness washes over her face.

"Oh no, dear." Her voice is soft. "Please, I'm not here to hurt you. I've been taking care of you for three days." My mind goes blank. *Three days!* I pull my knees up to my chest and wrap my arms around them, flinching. The pain is another reminder of the hell I've been through. "Please." She sets the tray down on the table and raises her hands. "My name is Abigail. I didn't mean to scare you. I know you've been through a lot, but you're safe now. I wanted to bring you something to eat and maybe a few answers." She raises her eyebrow, knowing I am interested. "May I sit?" She points to a rocking chair. I swallow past the lump in my throat. *At least she seems nice enough.* I slowly nod and watch as she pulls the chair over, being careful to not make any sudden movements. I know I should welcome her—and this place—with open arms, but instead I want to curl up in a ball and protect myself. I want so much to believe that I'm safe.

"There, that's better." She smiles warmly. "Thank you. Please call me Abigail, or Abby. Everyone else does."

*Everyone? Who else is here?* I look around, taking in the room again with a more critical eye. It is huge and has a large cathedral ceiling.

"I bet you're wondering where you are," Abby says. I turn back to her. "You are at a safe house. No one here will hurt you. You are extremely dehydrated and malnourished, but you are young and your body is healing fast. Your back..." She clucks her tongue and looks sadly at me. "Your back must still be very sore, but it will heal soon. It will take some time to get your strength back and feel like your old self again."

I stare at her a moment, then out the window, wondering where exactly I am.

She smiles, sensing my confusion. "You are in North Dakota, Savannah." She pauses a moment, allowing this information to sink in. *Holy shit! Okay, breathe.* "I know it's a lot to take in right now, but once you feel better I can tell you more. You really need your rest."

*Rest, yes that does sound like a good idea.* Suddenly I'm very tired again.

"But first, Savannah, do you think you could eat for me?"

*Oh God, food.* I not sure if I am truly safe; eating is out of the question.

"You've lost a lot of weight and your body is battered. You really need to help it by eating something." She hands me a small saltine cracker with a nod. "Baby steps." I slowly reach for it.

Holding it in my hand I look up to see her hopeful eyes. I hold it to my nose sniffing to see if it is laced with anything. It doesn't smell funny. I take a small, cautious lick. It tastes normal.

The door suddenly flies open and in strides a huge man. I immediately drop the cracker and pull the blankets up to my chin, turning a terrified look to Abigail. She looks just as shocked as I feel at the sudden appearance of our intruder. She stands and shields me from him. "York, what are you doing coming in here like that? You frightened the life out of us."

He strolls in with a small smirk. "Cole told me she arrived and I wanted to make sure she was adjusting to her new accommodations."

"She's fine. Now please leave." Her posture tells me she's been up against him before. He leans to the side to get a better look at me and issues a wolf whistle.

"My, she's a pretty one! A real step up from the last, hey?"

*The last? Where the hell am I?* I feel sick. I see a bowl on the floor and heave over the side, letting my stomach wretch and twist, removing anything possible that may have been in there.

"Oh no," Abigail moans, coming to my aid. "Here Savannah, let me help you." She pulls my long hair out of my way. When I finish, she takes a cool cloth to my face. It feels lovely having someone take care of me, though I cannot let my guard down. I am always wary of traps and know better than to let someone get too close. There are many questions firing off in my head. Am I safe?

Where the hell is my father?

"Leave. Now." Abigail hisses at York, who doesn't seem to be fazed by my vomit show. "Does Cole know you're here?" she asks, her voice more accusing then anything. That seems to get his attention and for a moment concern flickers across his face.

"Fine." He shakes his head then gives me a smile. "See you later, pretty girl."

This man seriously makes me uncomfortable. Abigail seems to have caught my feeling as she pulls the covers around, tucking me in.

"Don't worry about him. He's not around too much, and when he is Cole watches him carefully." *Cole?* "There isn't a thing that goes on that Cole doesn't know about. That's what makes him so good at what he does."

*And what is that exactly?* I want to ask questions but I can't find my voice or the strength to stay awake for that matter. I am spent. I close my eyes and listen to the comforting sound of Abigail's rocking chair.

\*\*\*

I remain in my bed the next four days, feeling a little better every day. I am helped considerably, I'm sure, by the fluids they are giving me. I haven't had any more unexpected visitors and Abigail has become a constant, comforting presence as she nurses me back to health. She is kind to me but so was Maria; I still keep my guard up. *Everyone has their own agenda.* She tries to get me to talk but I can't—silence is easier for now. She comes and goes throughout the day opening windows and doors, letting the warm sun find its way to me. The air itself is chilly, but I don't care. It is lovely. Sometimes a bird lands outside the window, its song reminding me how much I miss the outdoors.

I am pleased on the eighth day—wow, I am finally able to keep track of days again—to awaken IV free. I test out my body, limb by limb. My back still hurts like hell but at least the throbbing headache is gone. I feel like I need to stand and move around so I slowly slide my legs off the bed. They shake when they begin to bear weight, but they don't let me down. The door opens slowly and Abigail enters with a beaming smile.

"Well, look at you," both hands to her face. "You're standing!" I feel a small smile tug at my lips but quickly chase it away—I can't let myself be too comfortable. I can trust no one. She comes to my side and wraps my arm carefully around her shoulders. I cry out in pain and she quickly drops her arm back down. "Your back?"

I don't look at her. I want to cry on her shoulder and let her in, but I just can't. I know better. Abigail guides me into the bathroom. I surprise myself with how steady I am by the time we get there. She turns me around and gently pulls my button-up nightgown off my shoulders. I let it fall to just above my bottom while I cover my front with my arms still in the sleeves. She pulls my hair up into a clip. I can see her eye me but she doesn't say anything.

"Abby, I wanted—" The voice stops suddenly. I

look up, and in the mirror see the wide-eyed stare of my rescuer taking in my back. Abigail quickly shields me with a towel.

"Please, Logan, give us a moment." His reflected eyes meet mine showing sadness, then…anger? He steps back, retreating toward the bedroom door.

"Yes of course, forgive me," he mutters on his way out. So now I know my carrier's name is Logan.

Abigail runs warm water and helps me into the deep tub. I cry out as the water touches my wounds and she continues to pour Epsom salts around me.

"Soak, darling. The pain will ease in time." She gently washes my hair, helps scrub my body clean, and empties the tub, refilling it with fresh warm water. It crosses my mind—in my earlier life I would be very uncomfortable with a stranger washing me. After my experiences in my former prison, I hardly think of it now.

I hold a piece of my hair in front of me, noting how ratty it looks. My nails are dirty and my feet are in rough shape. All things that I took for granted in the past. I wasn't one of those girls who went to the spa monthly but I did look after myself. But now—I close my eyes, letting a few tears slip. I look and feel nothing like my old self. I am someone else now, and I have no idea who that is. I feel completely lost.

Abigail leaves me to my tears, later returning to dry my hair and tuck me back into bed. I notice she has changed the sheets. It feels wonderful to be clean.

She places a bowl of fresh grapes and

strawberries next to the bed.

"Only if you feel up to it, dear," she cautions, leaving me to rest.

The next day Abigail escorts a new visitor in to see me. She is a tall woman wearing thick, green, trendy glasses. She smiles down at me.

"Hello, Savannah, I'm Mel. Someone told me that you could use a little pick me up." She beams, patting a medium sized polka-dotted suitcase she pulled behind her. I turn quickly to Abigail who also grins happily. She moves forward to help me out of bed and slips a cozy bathrobe over my shoulders.

I am settled in a leather chair in the middle of my huge suite, feet propped up on a stool, looking out at the mountains. I let out a comfortable sigh. *Wow, is this really happening?* It still feels like a happy dream.

"Every woman deserves to be pampered now and then," Abigail explains. "It helps us on the inside even more than it shows on the outside, so just relax and let Mel work her magic." I'm nervous to be alone with someone new, but feel better when Abigail pulls up a chair to oversee the proceedings.

Mel treats me like a delicate flower that will crumble if she is too rough. Little did she know that I have been treated like someone's *perra* for God knows how long. Her actions calm my nerves; I soon relax and enjoy the flow of the comb through my freshly washed hair. She snips here and layers there, not asking how I normally wear it. After my hair is blow-dried and styled she moves to my nails, buffing and polishing. She paints them a deep purple then does the same to my toes. When Mel finishes, Abigail beams at me with delight. She thanks Mel and shows her out.

I sit in the chair looking at my hands and feet. All the dirt and stains are gone and they look pretty. *Wow, they look normal again.*

"I hope that was all right, Savannah," Abigail says, coming back in the bathroom. "I'm not sure if you're tired or not but I need to go start lunch. I'll leave you be. If you need anything just call for me," she says, pointing to the intercom. With that she leaves.

I stand looking in the mirror and my heart leaps—there I am, the old Savannah, hair cut long to the middle of her back, loose curls half way up, natural dull highlights peeking throughout. I reach up, running my fingers through what feels like silk. If only I felt like the old Savannah on the inside. *No, don't sweat it, this is a start.* I look down, remembering the last time someone washed me and did my hair. I shake my head, forcing that memory back down. *Okay, I need to get out of this room.*

I find myself heading into the closet hoping something might fit. To my surprise, everything is my size, even the shoes. Slipping on a pink cashmere sweater perfect for my back and a pair of tan jeggings with flats, I take in how small my waist has become. Christ, how long was I gone? One last look in the mirror and I feel like I just might be able to face people now that I'm feeling a little more human.

I open the door and step out into a long hallway. My hands grow cold quickly when I realize I have no clue where I am going. I take a deep breath and head to my left. Luckily after a few minutes I find a large staircase that spirals around to an entryway. My stomach turns as I hear a low voice speaking. I want to turn around and go back upstairs but I push on. *Breathe, Savi.*

"Must have been about ten to fifteen slashes across her poor back, and she's such a tiny thing," I hear Abigail say. "I think you're wrong about this one Logan—she's as innocent as they come."

*Wrong?*

Both heads turn when I step around the corner finding them both in the kitchen. My carrier—I mean Logan—catches my eye. His jaw drops as he looks at me. I realize he really is a good looking man with his gelled black hair, dark eyes, and broad shoulders. I instinctively lower my gaze—having learned to avoid eye contact from my prior captors. Sensing my reaction is making them uncomfortable, I force myself to look up.

"Savannah," Abigail says warmly. "You look beautiful. I'm glad you found the clothes."

Logan pulls out a chair for me. "Hello again, Savannah, you look lovely. I see Mel got her hands on you. Please have a seat."

I hesitate for a moment but comply. He sets a prearranged plate in front of me with bacon, eggs, toast, and hash browns with a glass of orange juice. My stomach twists but I fight back the nausea. They take a seat on either side of me at the island, sipping coffee and talking about their days. I know they're trying to act normal for me, but it isn't working. Frankly it is all a bit strange. I can't help wondering what is going on here; what kind of place is this? So many questions fill my head, making it ache slightly. I raise my hand and rub where the bump used to be—now it is just tender. I see Logan watching me and his eyes have an odd effect on me; I can't quite place the feeling.

"You really need to eat, dear," Abigail says.

She's right, but somehow I can't find the will to do so. I just want to cry. Perhaps coming downstairs was a mistake. They continue talking as I pick up a slice of toast and smell it out of habit. It seems fine. The first bite is all right, but the second is quickly rejected. Food and stress do not co-exist in my world anymore. I hear Abigail sigh as she sets her cup back on its saucer.

"Would you like a tour of the grounds now, dear?"

I would, but I also have a ton of questions and don't know where or how to start. Seeming to understand my dilemma, Logan turns to me with his mug between his hands. "Savannah, I'm sure you must be confused about where you are and what is happening. We'll get together later this afternoon, say around four. Is that all right with you?" I slowly nod, not sure why he couldn't just talk to me right now. "Abigail will show you where my office is." With that he checks his watch and stands. "Enjoy your day, ladies."

"You too, and I'll be sure to have Savannah there at four," Abigail says. When he leaves, she gathers my dishes. "Come dear, let's go for that tour." She stops and waves her hand, "First, the kitchen." It is larger than my entire condo with a view of a lake nestled in front of two mountains. "It is always stocked with food. Please help yourself. If there's something you want that's not here just let me know and we'll get it." She opens the huge stainless fridge that is packed with everything imaginable.

"There's always at least eleven people working here, plus those who live here full time, so this is what you'll typically find." I shake my head. I'm just glad I don't have to do the grocery shopping. "There's a wine cellar behind that door if you fancy yourself a glass." She winks. Wine, wow that was something I hadn't thought of for a long time, my general menu being mostly water. Suddenly I could almost taste my favorite Chateauneuf-du-Pape. Hmm, I will definitely have to check out that wine cellar. I pull my mind back to the room and note that Abigail is leaning against the marble top island with a little smile on her face, giving me my moment. She continues, "I generally do the cooking. It's pretty exhausting but it is part of my duties, along with making sure you're comfortable here." She smiles again. Another comment that makes me realize I'll be here for a while and my mind once again fills with questions. I really need to start talking but the wall I have built up for my own protection won't allow me any wiggle room.

"Come, let's move on."

I follow her into a grand living room with a view of miles upon miles of land that weaves throughout the mountains. It is hard to comprehend where I am but this place is spectacular. I was born and raised in New York City so all this land is fascinating. The living room has high ceilings with wooden beams and a grand fireplace. Everything is either dark wood or stone. The couches are red with large black blankets draped over top. A huge, tan rug with black thread woven through in a native pattern sits in the middle of the room tying together the decor in the sitting area. Despite how massive the room is it has a cozy feeling. I notice a patch of fluffy white fur on the floor by the couch leg. Someone must have a pet.

We move into the dining room and again face the same beautiful view overlooking the lake as the kitchen. A huge wooden table that looks like it seats at least thirty takes up most of the room with three cast iron chandeliers hanging over top. I also notice a security camera tucked in the ceiling, quickly looking away, not sure who was watching me.

On the top floor Abigail shows me all the bedrooms, including mine. Next we head to the bottom floor, down a flight of stairs near the kitchen. There is a game room, indoor pool, workout room, and an entertainment room. I note how supersized everything is and begin to feel a bit exposed. I want to find a small room and wrap myself up in a blanket.

On our way back to the main part of the house she points to a shorter hallway and tells me this is where Logan works, his office being at the end of the hall.

"He works a lot, but he's around for dinner and most evenings unless he is traveling. If you're afraid you'll be lonely, don't be. This place is always crawling with people. Some are friendly and some don't talk that much. You'll learn who's who.

When you're in this business you see a lot of things, things that can change you."

I wasn't completely blind to the fact that their job must be high risk and dangerous. I just wish I knew if it was legal or not.

"So you take a left out of your bedroom, down the stairs, and another left is the hallway to Logan's office. Remember, your meeting is at four," she prompts, looking for my reaction. I nod, and she smiles. "Well that's great, then. Are you tired or would you like to see outside?"

Outside…freedom…I smile and nod toward the door.

She steps outside and continues to talk about the history of the house but I stand motionless at the doorway. She stops and looks back at me with a sad expression. "Baby steps."

*Right, okay.*

She hands me a pair of tinted sunglasses. "Put these on, Savannah. Your eyes will need some time to adjust to the light. Thankfully, it's cloudy this time of year."

She gently links arms with me and walks me out onto the stone porch that wraps all around the house. I take a deep breath, filling my lungs with the cleanest air I've ever breathed. A gentle breeze moves my hair around my neck and I close my eyes, soaking in all the sounds surrounding me. Birds chirping, the sound of the leaves, water lapping on the shore—it's perfect until I hear the snap of a twig behind me. I jump, gripping Abigail's arm.

"Remember, never far from people," she

whispers, pointing to a camouflaged man armed with a semi-automatic assault rifle and blending in seamlessly with the tree he stands next to. "This is a safe place—one of the best, Savannah—but in order for it to be that way there has to be constant surveillance. Everyone who works for Cole is top notch. Scout Snipers, Navy Seals, Green Berets, you name it if they're Special Forces we've got them."

So does Cole run this place I wonder and when or will I ever meet him? I scan the woods trying to locate more guys but I can't see any.

"Just because you can't see them doesn't mean they're not here," Abigail says, taking in my gaze around the property, then nods for us to move on. "You'll get used to it, in time."

*Time, there's that word again.*

"The lake is cooling off fast, but midday some can tolerate the cool water—not me—too hard on these old bones." She laughs. "There are canoes and kayaks in the boathouse along with anything else you may want—don't forget to wear a life preserver!"

We round the house coming up to the front again and I am starting to grow tired. Walking great lengths isn't something I am used to anymore. Abigail senses this and starts pointing to things rather than actually walking over to them. We stop at the front door. "Later I can show you the rest, the stables, and the hot tub. All this is yours to use whenever you like. We want you to make yourself at home, Savannah."

We walk back inside and up to "my" room.

Before she leaves me to rest she pauses, sitting on my bed. "I'm sure this is a lot for you to take in after all you've been through, but I promise everything will be fine. The sooner you relax and settle, the easier it will be for you to adjust."

I watch her leave trying to process everything she said. It doesn't take long for me to drift off to an unsettling sleep.

# *Chapter Three*

I stand in front of the heavy wooden door to Logan's office admiring the door knob. It looks like a handle from an old sword. Three iron pieces curl around your hand when you grasp it. I know I can't stall any longer and knock gently.

"Come in," I hear him say in a harsh tone, making my hand retreat from the handle. I hate how scared those bastards made me. My mother would be heartbroken to see her once full-of-fire daughter acting like a burned out wick.

The door bursts open in front of me. "York!" he barks, stopping abruptly when he sees me. "Oh, Savannah, I'm sorry. I've been waiting for someone." He steps to the side glancing at his watch. "Is it four already? Please come in, take a seat."

I move inside, taking in his office. His desk stands in front of a floor to ceiling window overlooking the stables and part of the lake. The decor is like most of the rest of the house with its fireplace and couch. Two rifles hang on the wall. I note these almost subconsciously while my attention is drawn at once to the flat screen TV on one wall tuned to a Los Angeles news channel. I can feel Logan's gaze on me but he remains silent. I catch the date from the news anchor—October 26th. I gasp and try to rationalize this date with the day I was taken.

"Yes, they had you a little over seven months, Savannah," he whispers, answering my unspoken question. My eyes dart to his and I feel the tears welling up. Oh my God, I've been gone for over a half a year! As much as it felt like a lifetime for some reason knowing the actual amount of time was soul shattering. It solved the nagging question that's been eating away at me and now that I know I am reeling in shock. My hand flies to my chest.

"Please take a seat." He reaches for my arm and gently pulls me over to the couch. He sits across from me watching me closely. Once I get hold of myself he begins to speak.

"A lot is has gone on since you've been missing, Savannah. I'm sure you have a ton of questions, mainly the one about why you are here and why you were taken."

I nod.

"The men who took you are not just regular kidnappers. They're part of a highly dangerous group called *Los Sirvientes Del Diablos,* which means Servants of the Devil. They are a part of the Cartels and had you hidden well in Tijuana."

*Holy shit!*

"Your father—"

I sit up straighter when I hear his name. *Is he here? When will I be able to see him?* Again

38

nothing comes out.

He raises a hand. "Your father has been making a media storm out of your kidnapping."

*Great…more unwanted publicity.*

"Problem is, Savannah, the two main guys." he holds up a picture. "Rodrigo Heredia." a lump grows in my throat—the Montecristo smoker. He holds up another picture, "and Jose Jorge—"

My stomach suddenly turns violently. I desperately grab the closest trash can and heave stomach bile into it. I sense Logan behind me as he hands me a napkin and sets a glass of water next to me. I wash out my mouth and sit back on the couch, unable to look him in the eye. I feel embarrassed about my reaction, and his poor office being used like a bathroom.

"I'll take it you recognize Jose?"

I nod again fighting the urge to scream. *Yes the bastard made me beg for my meals, whipped my back till it was raw and took every shred of human dignity away from me!* Logan hands me a clean napkin—I didn't even notice I had started crying. "What I was going to tell you is both of them managed to elude capture."

My gaze shoots up in horror. He leans forward, resting his arms on his thighs. "I know, and I'm sorry, but until we know where they are and take them into custody you need to stay here. Your family, friends, nobody knows you're safe yet. That's the way we have to keep it for now, for their sake as much as yours. It will only be a matter of time before *Los Sirvientes Del Diablos* and the rest of the Cartels find out who rescued you and when they do the hunt will resume in earnest. You're worth a lot to them, and I'm sure they're pretty pissed that you're gone."

I stand up, shaking my head, not sure what to do with myself. A knock at the door causes us both to look up. York, the ass from last night, comes in holding up his hands.

"Sorry, sorry, been a busy day—" He catches sight of me. "Hello again, pretty girl." His voice is like velvet.

*Screw you, asshole.*

"York," Logan spits out. "Take this and deal with it."

York grabs the file from Logan's hand and leaves, but not before giving me a wink.

Logan stands in front of me. He is much taller—I only come up to his chin. "You don't have to stay. It's your right to leave but if you do we cannot protect you. I give it one week before you're snatched up again and disappear into thin air. It took us five months to locate you the last time, and we're one of the best there is." He glances at his watch again and I see his jaw tense. "I have a video conference shortly, but tomorrow you have a meeting at oh eight hundred with Dr. Roberts. He's our resident therapist and it's mandatory that you attend."

*Oh, hell no! I will not be seeing a shrink!*

He crosses his arms, sensing my change in mood. "Mandatory," he repeats. "Abigail will see you make it there on time. For now, if you need anything, go to her. She'll be your aide. Feel free to use anything in the house, and know that the house is under constant watch for everyone's safety. Of course the bedrooms and bathrooms are not under video surveillance, but the windows and doors all have sensors so we can keep track of who is coming and going. Please understand that the use of phones to call outside of this area is strictly prohibited, as is the use of the internet for communication. We've worked extremely hard to keep this place secret— only a select few know its location and they know the consequences if they should ever reveal it. I'll give you a week to decide if you want to stay, and if so we'll talk more about the rules." He moves to sit behind his desk. "Any questions?"

*Yes, about a billion.* I shake my head and head back out the door closing it behind me. Jesus, there is so much to take in my mind is reeling. I need to get back to my room and think. Am I really ready to live like this? Trade one prison for another, however posh? Or do I go home and take a chance and risk it all?

***

Dr. Roberts is a tall, skinny man with blond hair in his mid-fifties. His hazel eyes look warm against his crisp navy suit, the thin tie resting over his belt buckle. He repeatedly taps his right heel against the floor while he thinks.

We are in a small room next to Logan's office, the color scheme is yellow and has different shades of green. It is quite pretty.

"Not much of a talker?" Dr. Roberts asks, trying to lighten the mood.

We've been staring at one another for the past forty-five minutes. When I first arrived he asked a few questions but when I didn't respond he just watched my behavior as I did his. I know he is going to go with a shock question to get a response out of me. Oh, here it comes. I can practically smell the smoke from his brain turning gears.

"What's your feeling on Jose Jorge?"

I don't flinch.

He nods, then continues scribbling on his tablet. "Savannah, would you like to go home?"

*Ah, the follow up shocker question. Nice one doc—I've got to hand it to you, using family would have cracked me at one time, but not now.*

He leans forward, setting his tablet on the table. "Well, I guess we're not going to accomplish anything here today." He removes his thick framed glasses and rubs his eyes, sighing. "If you don't let people in, Savannah, how can we help you? Aren't you tired of being alone?"

Okay, that hit a nerve, almost broke my mask. I am terribly lonely but when you live with no one to talk to and no one to trust for as long as I have you almost forget how. People are sneaky creatures. "Can you at least tell me your favorite color?"

I silently watch him shake his head.

"Okay, fine. I'll see you tomorrow, same time." The door opens and in walks Abigail.

"Hello, Dr. Roberts. Will you be joining us for lunch?" She smiles at him.

"No, I'm afraid not. Thank you, though, I do love your chicken pot pie." She blushes a little.

Huh. This is interesting. Does soft-spoken

Abigail have a crush on the snappy-dresser therapist? I think so.

"Ready, Savannah?" she asks, holding the door open.

\*\*\*

I wake in a layer of sweat, my heart still wild from my nightmare, and glance at the clock. It's barely past midnight. I can still smell the foul sheets of my prison room. They had been changed only three times during what I now know was over seven months. I bet they never saw any soap even then— probably just rinsed and dried. Knowing I'll never get back to sleep with the memories of my nightmare still fresh in my mind, I toss my blankets off, grabbing the robe that Abigail left out for me. The cool silk feels amazing against my hot skin. I make my way downstairs to the bottom floor. The entertainment room window overlooks the lake and the space is filled with the glow of the lovely, soft moonlight. A black grand piano sits in front of one of the windows. My hands twitch as memories flood over me. I slide onto the cold bench and lift the cover, running my fingers over the keys and feeling how smooth and familiar they are as goose bumps run along my skin. It has been fourteen years since I've played, fourteen years since I've seen my mother, fourteen years since I promised myself I'd never play again.

*"Sweetheart," my father said coming to my side, "it would really mean a lot if you played for her one*

*last time. Please play her favorite."*

*"I—I can't," I whispered through a sob.*

*"I really need you to do this, sweetie." He nodded toward the press that was gathering in the church. Of course the new up and coming Mayor would have press at his wife's funeral. I looked up at him through my tears. It's always a show with him. He stood, pulling me to my feet. "Now." He took my hands in his. "You can do this, Savi." He gave me a kiss on the cheek and pointed me toward the front of the room. I shook as I passed by the coffin. My dear mother looked so peaceful. As I sat at the piano all eyes were on me. I glanced at my father who brushed a tear away and nodded at me to start. I felt sick as I looked down at the black and white blur. I took a deep breath, not wanting to disappoint. I couldn't bear to sing, so I only played. Leonard Cohen's oft-covered Hallelujah.*

*"Thank you," my father whispered.*

*Still, to this day I don't know if he was thanking me for doing it for mom, for him, or for the media.*

*I shake off the memory and test pushing down, making the first note. I close my eyes, feeling the melody. I quietly sing the familiar opening line, hardly recognizing my voice as the tears drop— feeling my mother beside me, playing her part. This was one of our favorites and she had taught me how to play this same song I would play at her funeral.*

*"Only play if you want to, Savi," she would whisper, glancing over at my father on the phone pacing the kitchen. "If it makes you happy, then play, that's why I do." She kissed my cheek. "It helps me escape my disease. It sets me free." She*

*started to sing again, winking at me, her head*
*swathed with a wrap hiding the fact that she's lost*
*all her pretty dark brown hair that matched my*
*own. Her voice would warm the coldest soul.*

I had maybe had a quarter of her talent for
singing—my skills were in my fingers. I was meant
to play the piano.

I open my eyes to the moonlit room, feeling
cold. Something catches my eye, making my hands
retract off the keys.

"Please, don't stop," Abigail whispers as she
steps out of the shadows, "it's so beautiful."

I close the lid with a snap swallowing a lump in
my throat.

"I haven't heard that song in a long time. Your
voice is lovely."

I push off the bench, not looking at her and leave
the room. I feel strange hearing Abigail's
compliments. I'm not sure what her angle is.

\*\*\*

The next few days are the same. I go see Dr.
Roberts and we'd stare at one another for the hour
long session. I walk around the property with
Abigail trying to build my strength up. She never
mentions the other night and I am happy she
doesn't—that was a raw moment for me. We have
lunch and I nibble on some fruit and vegetables, but
it's something. A nap, followed by watching the
horses run around the stables, then dinner. Abigail
tells me old folk stories about the mountains which

are really quite interesting then I head to bed. Sleep isn't something I enjoy but I know my body needs it no matter how much I protest. Abigail keeps telling me the small amount of food I eat is why I am always so tired. I know I really need to work on that.

The sun beats down on my face, filling me with all kinds of mixed emotions. I struggle with the idea of staying here. Although it is the most beautiful place in the world, it is not my home. If I do go home, was Logan right about me not making it past a week before I would be kidnapped all over again? My head hurt thinking of all the 'what-ifs'…What if they take me? What if next time they kill me? What if they hurt my father or Lynn?

Abigail takes a seat next to me on the patio. She knows it is one of my favorite places to sit and think. "I love how the water reflects the mountains; such a pretty display of colors." She's good with me—never tries to force me to talk. She just fills in the silence when it becomes too much for her.

I notice Logan walking with York around the property line.

"Stepping up security," she says as if I asked her the question.

I nod and keep watching.

After a few minutes she sighs. "He's a good man, Logan; never married, doesn't date—claims he doesn't have time. Men," she laughs.

I smile a little too, that does sound like a workaholic male.

"Always an excuse to not let one's guard down."

I know she didn't mean to direct that to me but I

feel a funny sensation in my gut when she says it. Maybe I need to start trusting someone or I'll be lonely the rest of my life, but trusting people…the thought really scares me still.

\*\*\*

After dinner, I sit on the floor in front of the couch in the living room soaking up the heat from the fireplace. Scoot, the house cat, doesn't seem to mind sharing the warmth with me—I think because he gets a belly stretch from it. He is a fat little thing with an "I don't give a crap about anyone" attitude which strikes me as quite funny. A lot of the guys wear black and I swear Scoot rubs up against them just to hear them groan. Now I know exactly where the patches of white fur come from.

None of the guys pay much attention to me. They are always polite but never speak more than they have to. Right now, that works just fine for me.

"You should've seen Cole. He flipped his gun around and smoked the guy in the face, breaking his nose—spraying blood all over the place," I hear one guy say to another behind me. "Then he clocks him under the jaw, sending him down the stairs, the rat tried to grab for his gun but Cole popped three right between his eyes; he never saw it coming."

Holy hell! The mental image I have from that almost made me gag. Who was this Cole guy?

"I can't believe I missed it," his buddy whines. "So that's what, number thirty-four for him?"

"Thirty-five," the story teller corrects. "Not to mention the six he killed with his bare hands.

47

Dude's friggin' Rambo."

A chill runs up my spine. I've never heard someone talk about killing someone so openly and so casually. Does this Cole guy come around often? I have no interest in meeting such a stone-cold killer. It frightens me to even think about taking someone's life, let alone...how many times was that?

Scoot paws at my hand. Apparently I stopped rubbing. "Sorry, kitty." I immediately make up for it by giving his tummy a good once over.

"I'm going on a guess here, but I'm thinking a 2004 Merlot will make that belly stretch a little more tolerable." A guy grins down at me, handing me a glass of red wine.

I smile with a small nod, taking the glass.

He sits down in front of me, leaning against the opposite couch and stretching his legs out in front of him. He runs his hand through his brown hair, removing it from his green eyes. It seems like something he has to do often. Scoot doesn't like the interruption, so I make even more of an effort to give him attention—greedy little cat. The stranger leans forward. "Mark Lopez." He holds out his hand.

I look at it then move mine into his for a quick shake.

"You're Savannah Miller," he states. "We've already met, but you were kind of out of it."

I look at him trying to recall his face. He is Latino and tall, although everyone seems tall to me, and I'm 5'6.

"I was sitting in the front passenger seat but

never took my mask off so you're off the hook for not remembering me." He grins playfully.

I look down at my wine. I take a sip, letting it swirl around my tongue. *Oh my, it tastes divine!*

Logan quietly sits across from us on the stone ledge in front of the fire. He looks tired and it looks like he is nursing a glass of something strong. *Something strong?* Those words bring me back to the restaurant that night with Joe Might. I feel tears coming; my old life seems so far away. Joe probably thought I was a flake for never getting his samples to him.

"Hey," Logan says softly, "you all right?" His sincerity makes me feel a flicker of warmth deep inside.

I quickly nod not wanting to draw attention to myself.

"Lopez could you give us a moment?" he asks.

"Sure thing." Mark rises to his feet. "Talk to you later, Savi." He grins like we are good friends

It makes me feel good. Wow, that's a strange sensation. I really didn't think that feeling was inside of me anymore.

Logan shifts to Mark's spot beside me on the floor, eyeing me. "I see you made friends with the moodiest one in the place." He leans over and fingers Scoot's ear.

The cat purrs into his palm and his smile grows. I know the two of them have probably spent some quality time together. I take another sip of my wine, not sure what to do.

He is almost painful to look at he is so attractive. His eyes so dark they match his black hair, and his shirt stretches over his broad chest showing just how fit he is.

I run my hand through my hair not wanting to gawk and needing something to do. "So, tomorrow marks one week since we last spoke. I hear you haven't made any progress with Dr. Roberts. That's disappointing."

My eyes shift away from his.

"You really need to talk to someone, Savannah. Dr. Roberts has done wonders for people in the past. I'm sure if you give him a chance you'll feel a lot better. That is if you decide to stay." He pauses, taking a sip of his drink. "It's all right to let people in. You're safe now."

Safe. That's what everyone keeps telling me.

He suddenly turns his head, looking over my shoulder. "Please excuse me." He sighs, hopping to his feet.

I sit, thinking about what Logan said still keeping up my required efforts with the demanding Scoot. My thoughts are soon interrupted by a conversation between two guys sitting near the window. They are talking about the one named Cole again and how he "popped this rat in the face." The other guy then begins to describe another Cole story with so much detail I actually have to get up and walk out of the room. I've decided it's time for bed anyway, and I have heard quite enough of that.

*\*\*\**

I watch as Dr. Roberts glances at me over his glasses. We are forty minutes into our potentially last session. I am having an internal battle with myself and finally a side wins. I breathe in deeply and decide to take a leap of faith—really at this point I have nothing to lose and maybe something to gain.

"Purple," I whisper. I watch as his gaze flips up from his tablet, his eyes narrowing at me.

"Pardon?"

"My favorite color is purple." My hands twist together as I am feeling uneasy with my decision.

"Well, that's a pretty color." He grins, taking a moment to think. "If you could use three words to describe how you're feeling today, what would they be?"

Only three? I think about it carefully before choosing the words and clear my throat.

"Scared, confused, overwhelmed."

"All normal to be feeling after what you have been through," he nods. "How do you like it here so far?"

I shrug. "Fine."

"What do you like most?"

That's a hard question to answer; there are surprisingly a lot of things. I mean who wouldn't love the view, the horses, the lake, the air.

"Lots."

He nods, scribbling on his tablet again. "Could you name one thing?"

"Scoot." This makes him laugh.

"Good old Scoot. I swear that cat runs this house. What is it that you like about him?"

I study the doctor for a moment trying to figure out where this psychobabble might be going.

"He is what he is."

"It's true animals don't judge like people do. They're trustworthy, loyal companions," he tilts his head to the right. "Were there any animals where you were held?"

The hair on my neck stands up.

"I'm thinking something that might have brought you comfort?"

"No," I shoot back quickly, remembering I want desperately for someone to talk to, someone to trust, someone to be my friend, hell someone or something to love.

"Okay." Resting his head on his hand, he watches me.

I see his chest rise and fall heavily.

His lips press together before he speaks. "Can you tell me about the night you were taken?"

I hear a door slam shut in my brain.

"Time's up, Doc," I say, jumping to my feet. I can't go there, I don't want to.

He stands too, placing his tablet on his chair.

"Savannah," he says.

I stop mid-step to the door.

"I've been doing this for thirty years. I've seen a lot of patients and heard a lot of stories. You need my help or this will destroy you. If you leave now you'll be looking over your shoulder going mad waiting for those monsters to take you, and that's no way to live. Take Logan's offer, stay and be safe, take back your life. Only you can make that choice but you have to want to fight. Don't let them win."

I wipe my wet cheeks. His words cut me— everything he says is true and I know it.

"Just think about it." He opens the door for me.

I walk out and make it to a nearby bathroom where I manage to pull myself together. Looking at my red, glossy eyes in the mirror I know what I have to do. I fuss with my off-the-shoulder green sweater, making it hang correctly over my leggings. It's funny how my obsessive need to fix myself in case I am being watched by the media comes right back to me. I wonder what else would surface over time.

# *Chapter Four*

*Okay, okay, you can do this.* I bite my lip and knock on the wooden door, waiting for the command to enter. It comes after a moment and I slide my hand into the sword handle, squeeze and push. Logan is sitting on the couch leaning over the table looking intently at his laptop. I stand, holding onto the door for support. I'm not sure how to even start this conversation.

"Logan?" I whisper.

His head flips up and when he sees me his eyes go wide and soften.

"May I have a word with you?"

His smile runs along his lips as he closes his laptop.

"Of course, Savannah, come in, take a seat." He points to the couch in front of him. "How was your appointment with Doctor Roberts?"

"Interesting."

"I can see that. Have you made your decision on whether you want to stay or go home?"

I let out a long breath. Okay here it goes. "I-I think I'd like to stay."

His face speaks volumes though I'm not sure why he cares so much. What am I to him but some head case?

"That's a smart idea Savannah." He moves over to his filing cabinet pulling out some paperwork which he places front of me. "Like I said before, if you wish to stay you'll need to sign a few waivers, an NDA. That is a non-disclosure agreement."

I nod, glancing at the papers.

"This is a document stating that while you're here and after you leave you will never give up the location of this house. You'll never discuss why you're here with anyone outside of this house. If you leave the property you'll have an escort with you at all times. That's for your own protection as well as ours, Savannah. Someone could be following you and you could lead them right back to us. Know that you can leave at any time but there's no coming back—we will not protect you a second time. Do you think you can handle all this, being under this much protection? This many rules? You will be totally isolated from your past life."

"I've already lost seven months of my life to those bastards. If this is what it takes to gain it back then so be it."

I read everything carefully, making sure I understand every word. "Pen please." He hands me one from his breast pocket and I stroke the pen over the black line—Savannah Miller.

He holds out his hand. "Welcome to our house."

I slip my hand in his, noting how small mine is in comparison.

Something flickers over his face and slowly he

pulls away leaning back.

I hop to my feet, not wanting to take up any more of his time. I need to get some air; I feel like I just signed my life away.

I pause at the door. "Thank you, Logan, for saving me."

His smile reaches his eyes. "It was my pleasure, Savannah."

\*\*\*

I find Abigail waist deep in laundry. She looks beyond stressed and at the same time has a few of the guys asking her a million and one questions, so I leave her be. She doesn't need to babysit me. I am familiar enough with the house and grounds now to be somewhat comfortable. I walk down to the lake and around the shore—it is becoming one of my most favorite places. Everything is so quiet. Not 'empty' quiet the way my prison was; this is different, it's a comfortable, peaceful place. I don't feel as lonely because of all the wonderful soft sounds that surround me. It's funny how this kind of quiet isn't really quiet at all. Knowing that there are men hidden in trees all around also brings a sense of comfort. I miss my father terribly and I miss Lynn even more—I even miss my job, but I think living in constant fear would destroy me more than the prison. Yes, the decision to stay is the right choice for me—at least I hope.

\*\*\*

Poor Abigail was still pumping out laundry when I returned several hours later. She looked exhausted so I decided to help her out.

I make my way into the kitchen and open the freezer pulling out a mountain of steaks. I look at the calendar that Abigail referred to every night and see that there will be fifteen attending tonight's dinner. I set out the meat to thaw while prepping the toppings. I wrap large potatoes in tin foil and chop enough carrots to feed a small army. I cut the bottoms off the asparagus and drizzle oil, salt, and pepper over top. While the oven heats I peel and chop apples, tossing them into three large casserole dishes with cinnamon, sugar, and a little butter, putting an oat crumble over top.

It shouldn't surprise me that the BBQ is so huge—what isn't huge around here? But nonetheless it is very intimidating to light. I manage to fire it up finally and start the potatoes without setting the house on fire.

Within an hour the kitchen starts to smell lovely. I pull out the three apple crisps, setting them aside to cool.

"What is that smell?" I hear someone yell which is followed by heavy footsteps. "Good God, my mouth is actually watering!" Mark Lopez, the guy from last night comes around the corner. "Hello Savi," he grins, looking around. "Are you cooking? Please tell me what that heavenly smell is." He takes a seat on a stool opposite me at the island.

"Apple crisp." I point to the desserts on the counter.

"Well fuck me sideways…she speaks." He raises

a playful eyebrow.

"She does," I shoot back with a smirk. He cracks me up.

"Yes, yes, I'll think of something maybe I'll order a pizza—" Abigail stops short when she enters the kitchen, hanging up her cell phone. "Savannah?" She looks shocked.

Oh no, maybe I crossed a line doing this. Perhaps I should've stayed away. This was her thing to do.

"I'm sorry." I see her lips turn into a smile.

"Savannah speaks now." Mark grins up at her.

She walks by giving a playful smack to the back of his head. Taking in the kitchen with a look of amazement at all the food, her eyes dance over at me.

"You did this?" she asks.

"Yes, I'm sorry if I stepped over a line. I was—"

"Sorry? Oh dear, don't be sorry." Her cheeks flush. "Thank you for doing this, this is so kind of you. You have no idea what a relief it is that someone noticed I need some help around here." She leans in and gives me a huge hug.

I stand stiff at first but can't deny the warmth I feel toward her. My arms slowly wrap around her, embracing the affection. I feel a small chip of cement break off around my heart.

"If you guys need a moment I can leave," Mark laughs. It's such a male thing to joke at an emotional moment.

"Go wash up. I know you boys just came from training," she hisses, shooing him out of the kitchen.

Mark sticks his finger in the sauce, popping some in his mouth.

"Yum!"

"Don't make me come after you." She gives him a stern look.

He laughs all the way down the hallway.

I am starting to see she's the mother of the house and they all respect her.

\*\*\*

I start to feel self-conscious when everyone sits down for dinner.

They all begin complimenting me on how great the food is when they find out that I made dinner for Abigail. Everything is piled on plates in the center of the table and they all take turns helping themselves.

Logan enters and takes a seat, apologizing for being late.

Then York comes in and sits a few seats across from me. He winks at me as he takes his seat. Christ he's unsettling.

Some people make small talk through dinner mostly about the hockey game that is on tonight. I'm more focused on eating, baby steps I keep telling myself. I poke at a piece of potato, feeling full. I know I have to force myself to try to eat more, but my stomach seems to be shrunk to the size of a pea.

"Burke wasn't the psychopath," York says in an argument with his buddy across the table. I know what they are talking about right away.

"Who cares, it's just a movie."

"Tommy Desimone was the psychopath," I interject, making the entire table stop and stare.

York gives me a strange look.

Yeah, that's right, creep—I have a voice. "Umm, Tommy was crazy, not Burke." I look at his friend. "And it was actually a book first—called *Wiseguy* by a crime reporter named Nicholas Pileggi, published in January, 1985. Five years later it was made into the movie *Goodfellas*." I suck in some air. I haven't said this much at one time in a very long time. It feels good.

"Oh!" Mark laughs pointing his knife at York. "You just got schooled!" The entire table bursts out laughing. York watches me while I struggle with the fact I just opened my mouth in front of so many people.

"There was no question. Jimmy could plant you just as fast as shake your hand. It didn't matter to him. At dinner, he could be the nicest guy in the world, but then he could blow you away for dessert." He quotes the book, clearly showing off to me how he already knows all about the novel. I secretly wonder if he is threatening me for embarrassing him.

"Chapter two, paragraph twenty-four," I toss back. "Oh, and we're having apple crisp for dessert. If you could hold off blowing me away until afterward I'd appreciate it."

Logan breaks into laughter first. The rest of the guys follow.

"She's good," Logan shouts over the roar of the table.

York leans back folding his arms watching me. His eyes have a way of making my skin crawl. The noise at the table dies down except for the sound of some of the guys polishing off the last of the food when York pipes up again. Clearly he had been thinking.

"Savannah, you don't strike me as someone who would read that kind of novel." He stabs his last piece of steak.

I hate that I shift. I'm sure I'm giving off an uncomfortable vibe. It doesn't go unnoticed because a smirk appears on his face.

"I'm trying to recall the last time I've seen a copy of that book." He taps his finger against the table dramatically. "Oh, that's right—it was on the little table in your cell."

My hand flinches, making my fork bounce loudly off my plate.

"York." Logan looks up from his plate. I stare at my hands on my lap as images of that room fight their way to the surface.

"Little wooden table right, with a stool?" he adds, making my stomach twist painfully.

"Enough, York," Logan warns in a clipped tone.

I rise to my feet wanting to get away from here but Logan's warm hand wraps around mine. "Savannah, please stay."

I stare down at him hating all the eyes on me. I find myself rubbing my uneasy stomach.

He looks at York and flicks his head to the side. York shakes his head, tossing back his beer then leaves the table, muttering.

"John," Abigail says, breaking the tension in the

room.

The man across from her looks up. "Are you going into town tomorrow?"

Logan still has my hand. I pull it away. I feel like I don't belong here.

"Sorry, I didn't mean to start anything," I whisper so only he can hear.

The corners of his mouth rise. "Are you kidding? It's refreshing seeing someone take on York. He can be an ass sometimes." He reaches for my hand again and tugs. "Please sit."

I sink back down into my chair.

"Abigail, dinner was delicious."

"Thank Savannah—she made it all."

He looks back to me.

"You made this?" he asks, surprised.

I nod.

"Don't forget about the apple crisp," Mark adds. "Speaking of…" He leans over to the table against the wall and picks up a bowl, setting the warm dessert in front us before diving right in.

"Impressive. I guess we still have a lot to learn about you." Logan grins, taking a serving for himself.

Yes—something tells me their background checks wouldn't include culinary skills. Despite my little spat with York I'm feeling happy with myself. I helped Abigail when she needed it and everyone seems pleased with dinner. The guys all thank me as they leave the table.

\*\*\*

"Good morning, Savannah." Dr. Roberts catches me in the entryway on my way down to his office for our eight o'clock session. "I was thinking maybe we could have today's session outside?"

"Sure." I follow him across the lawn and down to a covered chair swing. He sits next to me, which feels odd—normally he watches me face on.

We sit in silence watching an eight-man war canoe race effortlessly across the lake. I wonder who is on it—Mark, Logan or maybe even York? The morning sun feels warm but the clouds wrapping themselves around the mountains tell me it won't last long. Perfect weather for Halloween, I guess. I let out an unexpected yawn and the doctor shifts. I know the silence is about to end.

"How have you been sleeping?"

"Fine," I lie.

He glances over at me and waits.

"Soon as I fall asleep I'm right back in my prison."

"What happens when you're there?"

I shiver and close my eyes. "I'm alone again. I'm cold. I'm in a dirty, white nightgown and a brown sweater that's way too big for me. I smell mold and rotting food. It's making my stomach turn." I rub my stomach. "Sometimes I wake up vomiting, sometimes I can't wake up at all but if I do I feel restless and can't go back to sleep."

"Is it the same dream every night, or does it change?"

"It was the same up until last night. The fat man—"

"Jose Jorge?" he asks, trying to follow me.

"Yes, Jose. He shows up with my tray of food." I pause pushing my tongue to the roof of my mouth. I want to curse and scream but I hold back, something I'm used to doing. "He liked the power he had over me. He was a real bully, for lack of a better word."

"Hmm," he says, shaking his head.

"What?"

"Do you think the change in your dream was because of the situation with York at the dinner table last night?"

I look up at him confused. How did he know about that?

He shrugs with a laugh. "You made quite the impression with the guys. They like you."

I look back out over the water. That's kind of nice to hear.

"Perhaps," I agree.

"Well, I can give you something—"

"No, thank you." I cut him off. I don't want anything to alter my new-found feeling of freedom.

"Well, tell me if you change your mind."

The doctor doesn't ask too many more questions about my prison and I don't offer up any more info. It is quite painful reliving it.

"Tell me about your father, Savannah. What's he like?"

I pull my knees up to my chest, feeling the loss of a parent's comfort. Things weren't always great between us and I have a lot of mental scars thanks to him, but he is still my dad.

"We're close enough." I swallow past the lump. "We did the typical things together that a working parent could do. When I was younger we fished and hiked. We didn't get together much when he got deeper into the political world because he became a lot busier and stressed out. I didn't help his stress level back then either."

"What do you mean?"

"I wasn't used to the publicity that I had as the Mayor's daughter. I hated it; I still do. I was never a party person or a troublemaker but it seemed whenever I'd go out somehow the paparazzi found me and would catch me in some compromising pose and spin an embarrassing story. I'd make the front page of some magazine and my father would have to deal with the repercussions. It happened so often that I stopped going out at all. One time I tripped over a drunk guy at a pub and the story read that I was a drunk and needed AA. It nearly killed me when my father started to believe the lies. I just stopped trying to have a life of my own." I stop talking and swallow again. "It was a year since I went to any kind of pub or bar but one afternoon my friends from work insisted I join them to celebrate the landing of a new client. I did and had a wonderful time. It felt so good to be out. The next day, the day I was—" I stop, finding it hard to say the word.

"Taken," he says for me.

"Yes. My friend Lynn came by with a copy of *Us Weekly* with me on the front showing off my backside. It had been Photoshopped of course—my dress wasn't that short. I was so angry that after so long the media would still peg me as a sloppy drunk. I barely drink as it is!" I shake my head. "Of course my father was furious and told me we'd discuss it over dinner the next night. That never happened." Goosebumps slowly inch up my arms. I take a long breath, trying to rein in my emotions. "I hate that my last conversation with my father was him being disappointed with me again." The doctor hands me a tissue.

"It's hard being in the spotlight when you never asked to be there." He sighs. "Sad that people care more about celebrities than what's going on in their own country. Troops being sent over to fight for our freedom get less media coverage than the Kardashian family." He slowly stands, stretching his legs. "You did well today, Savannah. Try to get some rest tonight. I'll see you tomorrow. Enjoy the sun while it lasts."

"Thanks."

***

My foot leans against a small table allowing me to gently rock myself. I lean my head back and smell the oncoming rain. A low rumble echoes over the mountains warning of the storm that is brewing. It has been a long time since I've watched a good show of force from Mother Nature. In New York we have the four seasons. I missed them terribly in my prison—my time without so much as a window was terrible.

"May I join you?"

I look up to see Logan standing next to the swing holding a blanket, a thermos, and two mugs.

"Sure." I sit up, making room for him to join me,

surprised and a little pleased that he is being so thoughtful. I know how busy he is all the time.

"I love a good storm," he says, opening the thermos. "Abby told me you love your coffee. Seems we have something in common." He hands me a mug and I wrap my chilly fingers around it seeking its warmth.

"Thank you."

He leans back, draping the blanket over my lap. "The temperature can drop quickly in Montana this time of year."

Wait, what?

"Montana?"

He shifts, making the seat sway. "Sorry, but you hadn't signed the NDA yet."

"Now that I have what else can you tell me?" I think I have the right to ask now.

He lets out a long breath. "What do you want to know?"

"Everything," I say without missing a beat. "But first you can tell me who you are." I wave my hand around. "Abigail filled me in some. She said you're top of the line trained, and some of you are Special Forces."

He sips his coffee taking a moment. "We're all Special Forces," he corrects me. "My grandfather was the founder of this group. We're called 'Shadows.' The US government wanted a group of highly trained professionals who could slip in and out of Mexico gathering information on The Cartels, *Los Sirvientes Del Diablos*, and a few other drug and kidnapping rings. At first that's all we did and then they started to use us to retrieve hostages and bring them back across the border safely. That's when this place was built. We needed a safe place to bring the kidnapping victims while we tied up the loose ends. We like to call them our 'guests' when they are with us. As soon as it's safe they go home to live their lives and we move on to our next job."

"Why Montana? Why not somewhere closer to the border, like Texas or California?"

"Because that's the first place they'd check. Who would think to look in the back mountains of Montana? Plus we have a pretty good advantage if attacked." He waves at the view where you can see for miles all around us.

I try to remember back to my journey here but I still blank out after the cabin of the plane. I think about the other people that were here before me and what it was like for them.

"Were there any that didn't make it? You know, when they got back home."

He nods. "Yes. Some refused our help and went back before it was safe and were taken again or were killed. Some couldn't handle what they had been through and ended it themselves."

Lovely. He must have caught my expression.

"We have a high success rate, Savannah. Eighty-five percent go on to live normal lives."

"Who was the last 'guest' who stayed?"

He looks at me carefully.

"York mentioned something about the last one not being as pretty."

He rolls his eyes.

"York," he mutters to himself. "We haven't had a lot of women here; mostly wealthy businessmen.

The two women we did have were in their fifties and they were the wives of some important people. You're the first that's young and, well, pretty."

I blush at his unexpected compliment.

He clears his throat. "Needless to say, the guys were all happy you decided to stay." I don't look up. "Plus you give York shit, and that's just plain fun to watch."

"Am I the only vic—" *I hate that word*, "person like me here? Are there others?"

"Just you for now."

I nod, thinking about what he said. The clouds start rolling in around us. It is a spectacular show—so many different shades of grey change the color of the lake. I wrap my arms around my mid-section feeling my mood shift again.

"He makes me nervous," I confess.

He peers down at me. "Who?"

"York."

"Does he?"

I nod.

"Savannah, look at me, please."

I peel my eyes off the floor, meeting his stare.

"If he does or says anything to you that makes you feel uncomfortable you tell me right away, okay?"

"I'm sure it's nothing." I shake my head, feeling stupid even saying anything.

"Regardless, you tell me. You tell me if anyone here makes you feel uncomfortable."

A loud clap of thunder makes me jump, nearly spilling my coffee. I set it down on the table and pull the blanket over me. I bring my knees to my chest, something I've done to protect myself since I learned to fear that terrible click of the key in the lock. The rain comes down like someone just turned on a faucet full blast. We both shift toward the middle of the swing getting out of the way of the splatter. His arm rests behind me and he turns into me slightly almost like he is shielding me; it must be second nature for him. Although it is a small action, it makes a little bubble of warmth grow inside me. Huh.

"Can you see them?" I ask peering into the trees and forcing the feeling aside.

"I can because I know where to look. That and I'm trained to sense their movements."

"So the whole time you've been sitting here you can feel them around us?" He nods, looking off to my right and pointing into a thick wooded area.

"One there." I squint but can't see anything.

"There." He nods to the right a bit with his head. "Two down by the beach."

"Are you playing me?" I ask with a skeptical look.

He smiles pulling out a small radio and switches the channel. "Beta seven, come into the clearing." Sure enough, a man off to my right, exactly where Logan first pointed, dressed in camouflage comes walking out. "Back to post." The man turns and disappears back into the woods.

"I stand corrected," I say through trembling lips. It is starting to grow very cold.

He stands offering his hand. "Come, let's get you inside. You're freezing."

\*\*\*

After a hot shower and some dry clothes I head down to the living room to my favorite spot in front of the fire. Before I can even sit down Scoot appears out of nowhere, pouncing on my lap. He walks himself around my waist under my open sweater—apparently he is cold or maybe he is marking me with his scent. Either way it tickles and makes me laugh.

"Now that's a sweet sound." Logan grins, sitting on the couch across from me. He has changed into a pair of jeans and a black long sleeve shirt. He looks his age, thirty something? His shirt shows off just how fit he is. No doubt. These guys always seem to be training for something.

"Feels kind of nice," I admit but don't make eye contact. Scoot hears Logan's voice and pops his head out by my side. The little bugger made my pink tank top white along the bottom. "Hey," I pat his head, "I thought we had a truce about the fur." He looks up at me and meows. A bright light fills the room, followed by a crack of thunder that shakes the windows. The rain beats hard against the windows making Scoot run and hide under a chair. I want to do the same. I stand up feeling uneasy; it is growing dark even though it is only two in the afternoon. I look out at the woods thinking about the men out there. "This place is being monitored by cameras, right?"

"Yes," Logan comes and stands behind me, "twenty-four seven."

"Then why aren't you calling in the guys? I

mean its pouring rain out. It's got be freezing for them. Have they even eaten lunch?" I see a smile grow on his face in the reflection of the window.

"They have huts to protect them from the rain and proper rain gear. These aren't mall security guards." He chuckles. "A stormy night is a walk in the park for these men. Besides, it's their job and they do it well."

I twist my face. "But we're not in any danger right? I mean you said only a handful of people know where we are so why do they have to be out there—"

"Just because we can't see danger doesn't mean it doesn't exist," he explains, cutting me off. Folding his arms, he comes to stand next to me. "The men who took you are part of The Cartels, a group who openly kill their own people in broad daylight in the middle of busy streets. The police have no control over them. Shadows has been doing this for almost three generations…just think how many people we've pissed off." He looks down at me over his shoulder. His eyes soften. "Don't worry. I make sure they get fed properly and their shift ends in two hours."

I nod feeling a little better about the guys but not so much about what he just said though. "Abigail mentioned that you are updating the security equipment. Is that just protocol or because I'm here and I bring extra baggage because of who is after me?"

"A bit of both."

I figure since he's on a roll answering my questions, I might as well go for the one that's been eating me alive since I arrived.

"Did my father ask you to come for me?" A crack of thunder makes me stumble over the last word.

"I can't answer that," he says. "I'm sorry."

"When will I be able to speak with him?"

"Soon, when we know it's safe."

"There's that word again," I mutter, jumping at another clap of thunder. Christ, my nerves are shot! I hate feeling so jumpy. I start to grow angry as my emotions twist around. "How much did those bastards ask for my ransom? Tell me—what am I worth?"

"Savannah," he turns to face me, "don't think like that."

I stare up at him point blank in the eye. Now I know I'm angry.

"Fifty thousand," he murmurs quietly. I feel my stomach drop, tuck, and roll over the hardwood floor.

"Nice to know I missed my life for seven months and I'm only worth fifty thousand! So that's what—roughly over seven grand a month." I shake my head. "No wonder they barely fed me." I'm bitter, angry, and sad. I try to fight back the tears but it's no use.

He touches my shoulder giving it a gentle squeeze. He is struggling with something; I guess about having to tell me my total net worth. Suddenly it hits me. "If I was only worth fifty grand, why didn't my father pay it? Why did I have to rot away in that cell for almost a year?"

"It's not as simple as handing someone the

money, Savannah. There are always tricks and schemes and in a lot of cases the victim is killed long before the families even agree to pay to have them returned. They make a fake proof of life video or take pictures before the victim is killed and use them throughout the negotiations."

My blood drains from my face as another flashback plays out in front of me.

He grabs the tops of my arms holding me steady. "Whoa. You should sit down."

I shake my head not listening. "W-why was I spared then? Why not kill me? Then collect. It doesn't make sense."

"That's what we're trying to figure out. When we came for you we planted evidence setting up Rodrigo's brother. There's been some bad blood between them in the past and we hoped to throw them off our trail. We knew it wouldn't stand up for long but it should take the heat off for a while. We need more time to figure out exactly what is going on."

Evidence, fake proof of life, fifty thousand dollars—my head is swimming. Before I know what is happening I'm placed on the couch and told to put my head between my legs.

"Breathe, Savannah." He runs his strong hand over my back. "You're getting too much information too fast. You've been through a lot and your body and brain need time to catch up. I promise I'll answer all your questions in time but that's it for now."

He is right; it is too much. I start to sob.

He pulls me into him holding me close. His

smell engulfs me. It's been years since I had a man hold me other than my father and it feels nice…almost safe.

***

I wake to a booming sound that could restart a heart. I lie on the couch staring at the fire and try to catch my breath. Lightning fills the room, followed by another earth-shaking boom. I sit up, looking around. I'm alone in this very large house in the middle of a freakin' battle-of-the-gods storm! I make my way slowly toward the kitchen. Abigail must have left the light on for me. The clock reads eleven. I glance outside when the lightning flickers illuminating the entire lake. I squeeze my eyes and cover my ears waiting for the next—"Ahhh," I yelp when it rumbles all around me like a speeding train. It is so unpredictable. I hate it!

I hear voices coming from downstairs and follow them hoping to find Abigail. I could really use some company right now. They became louder when I reach the entertainment room. The door is partially open. I take a deep breath, stepping inside the door. Logan, Mark, York, and three other men I recognize but don't know by name are sitting around a poker table, drinking beer.

"Hey there, Savi!" Mark gives me a cocked smile. "Did we wake you?" Everyone turns and stares at me.

I shake my head and jump at another boom. "N-no, you didn't."

"You look a little nervous," York chimes in as he

sips his beer, glaring at me over his bottle.

"Stop," Logan warns. "Everything okay?"

"Umm, yes." I jump again feeling my face blush. "Just looking for Abigail."

"She went to bed a while ago."

"Oh," I whisper, feeling even more anxious about going back to my room, "Thanks."

"Savannah, you want to join us?" Logan asks, giving a flick of the head. I know he is only being nice.

"No, it's okay, you guys enjoy your—" Boom! I jump, closing my eyes for a moment.

Mark stands, making room between him and one of the guys.

I sigh, giving in to myself. Who am I kidding? I'd probably sit outside the door just for the comfort of their voices. "Thanks." I watch Mark deal out a new hand and give me some green chips.

He tells me they play for fun once a week but once a month they play for money.

"Have you even played before?" York asks, fiddling with his cards.

"A few times." My grandfather played once in a while. He taught me the basics—mostly how to bluff. I look around the table at the three other guys. "Hi." It felt wrong sitting without introducing myself.

"Savannah, this was the guy who was driving the night we brought you here." Mark points to the man next to me.

"John." He flicks his cigar off to one side as he offers me his hand.

"This was the man in the back, Paul." Mark

points, Paul gives me a wave. "York was in the Escalade in front of us." York gives me a smirk. "And this is Keith."

"AKA Beta seven." Logan winks at me.

"Oh!" I say, remembering him from earlier in the day. Logan got him to come out into the clearing. Boom! I jump—why did this place have to have so many windows? I stop myself, shocked that I went there. Do I miss my prison walls? No way! Christ, stop! "Umm, well I guess this is a little late but thank you all very much for saving me that night. I owe you."

"It's all in a day's job," John the driver says with a tight nod.

"I know how you can make it up to us." York wiggles his eyebrows. Logan elbows him hard in the side, he grunts cursing out loud. "Fuck, sorry! I was only playing."

"Speaking of playing, shall we continue?" Mark asks, tossing a chip into the center. We play a few hands and I fold twice, mostly to watch the body language of the others at the table. Logan and Mark are hard to read but the others make little slips here and there. By the fifth hand I think I am ready to stay in and I chuck two cards and wind up with a pair of twos. Crap! But I go with it; they don't know what I have, and plus it's fun. Soon it is down to me, Mark and York.

"Come on, Savi," Mark chuckles, "break that poker face."

I remember what my grandfather said…grab at something serious that happened in your life and think about it. Pull that hard face from somewhere.

So I do...not like it's hard.

He thinks for minute then tosses his cards "Fine! I fold!"

Great. One down, one to go. I glance at York who is studying me. I toss two more chips on the table raising the bid.

"Hmmm," York mumbles as he stares at me for a few more minutes. "You haven't played a hand yet, so I think you have something." He looks at Mark. "Her face tells a lot, you just have to look for it." York shakes his head in a cocky manner. "Fuck it, I fold."

I couldn't believe it! We had been at this hand for almost thirty minutes and he's folding! He thinks he's so smart...what an ass. I start looking around the room, behind Mark's chair, then under the table.

"What are you looking for?" York asks, annoyed.

"Oh, um, just your balls." The whole table breaks out in a roar. Paul almost falls out of this chair. Mark flips over York's cards, revealing a pair of tens.

"Well, what did you have?" York barks at me.

I don't have to show him but it only makes this moment so much better. I flip them over and watch his face fall.

He chews on the inside of his cheek.

I catch Logan watching me, he smiles and seems impressed. I'm impressed *and* I'm having fun.

"Next Friday, ten p.m., I'm taking you down." Mark points a finger at me as he scoops the chips into a bin. "I will figure you out." He laughs, standing up. Huh, I feel myself smiling and really enjoying the company of these guys. I think I may be making friends. The idea thrills yet terrifies me. Can I really be easing back into a normal-feeling life so soon?

"Good night, guys." I wave, watching them heading off to their bedrooms. Logan walks me to my room and does a quick check for me. I know he is trying to make me feel safer.

"How long until this storm passes?" I ask, glancing out the window.

"Forecast says this is a big one. Will you be all right here or should I get Abigail?"

I turn, shaking my head. "No, I'll be all right." I watch him light my fireplace. "Logan, thanks for tonight. You didn't have to involve me."

He drops the match stick into the flames and moves to stand in front of me.

"It was fun and I'm glad you joined us." He waits for a clap of thunder to pass by. "Try to get some sleep. Remember, Abigail is just across the hall and I'm two doors down, on your right."

I nod.

"Safest place you can be is in this house." His eyes brows pinch together like he's thinking as his eyes burn into mine.

I'm very aware of my stomach fluttering.

He makes a slow movement—making his actions known, "Can I see something?"

I nod, feeling very comfortable with this man.

He brushes my hair away from my face, running his hot fingers along my temple, stopping at my cheek.

I fight to not close my eyes and bask in the warm feeling that's spreading throughout my body. I let out a small puff of air that I hadn't realized I'm holding in.

His eyes close. He looks like he wants to say something, but stops himself. "Good night." He drops his hand and heads for the door but then stops. "Oh, and Savannah?"

I turn to look at him still feeling the touch of his hand on my face.

"Please call me Cole."

*Wait! What…your name is Cole…Cole Logan?*

# Chapter Five

I toss and turn all night, now having a face to go with the name I've heard so much about. I find myself dreaming about Cole "popping three" into a sweaty man's forehead. How can such a nice, caring man be a stone-cold killer? I know it's their job to take down bad guys but the way the guys talk about him it's as though he doesn't have a soul. Like Cole and Logan are two completely different people. I should have known Logan was his last name—that's how they address everyone here. Abigail does speak fondly of him, and she seems to have a heart of gold. I rub my face roughly. *Why am I so bothered by this? Why do I care about him anyway? All I am is a broken victim worth less than a frigging down payment for a house!* It's not like I can even figure out myself anymore. Finally I give up, kicking off the covers and staring at the ceiling, waiting till morning.

\*\*\*

81

I avoid Lo—Cole for the next four days, mainly staying locked in my room. I'm fine with not being around people—some days I crave it, other times I don't. I love my balcony and I find that if I sit directly in the right corner near the wall no one can tell I'm out there. I ask Abigail if she could have Dr. Roberts come to my room for our Monday session. I don't offer an explanation and she doesn't ask. I can tell she is concerned about me hibernating but I assure her I just need some time alone to "process." It was, after all what I had been doing for the past seven months. At least this time it was by choice.

My thumb rubs around my middle finger methodically while a flashback flickers in front of me then suddenly I am there, reliving it moment by moment.

"Where are you right now, Savannah?"

I can hear the Doc's words but they aren't totally registering.

"Where you are? Is it safe?"

*Safe?* I think, then slowly shake my head no.

"Tell me what you're seeing."

"I'm at the place where they took me. I'm so scared. My knee really hurts. It keeps throbbing and it feels warm and sticky, so I know I'm bleeding." I pause, trembling. "There's an American man here speaking to the others in English." I swallow a growing lump. "Someone throws me to the ground. My knees hit the floor hard—it feels like brick or stone. My hands are tied behind me, and when I fall forward I hit my face. I keep sucking the cloth bag they put over my head into my mouth when I try to breath. They yank me back up to my knees and I can see their shadows moving around in front of me. They keep yelling at each other."

"Okay, you're doing really well, Savannah. Can you make out what they're saying?"

"T-the The American is shouting something about proof—needing confirmation." My breathing picks up and my voice is shaky. "'*Es ella!*' one man shouts. I know what it means. He's saying 'It's her!' The American man doesn't seem to believe him then suddenly the cloth is pulled off my face." I can tell I'm crying but I just can't stop this flashback…can't help the terror that's ripping through me. "It's dark. I can make out small lights, but my vision is blurry. Someone flashes a bright light in my face. They grab my chin to hold me still."

"Can you see the American?"

"I-I'm so scared, my heart's beating out of my chest. I can barely suck in a breath. The light shifts to the side for a moment and I see him."

"The American?"

"Y-yes," I choke out. "His face is covered by shadow but I can feel his eyes glaring down on me. He steps forward, making the other man let go of my chin. He is standing in front of me. My face is just above his belt. He smells like something familiar but I can't figure out what it is. He's asking me if I'm Savannah Miller. I look up at him and I see his cheeks rise—he's smiling at me. I'm begging for him to help me, but he just laughs, and I see at the last minute he makes a fist. I thought he was going to punch me but he ends up slapping me across my cheek instead. I fall with no way to protect my face and hit my head on the bricks. His boots flicker in the dim light; they're so distinctive."

"What's distinctive about them?"

My head shakes back and forth and I break out in a sob. "They leave me on the ground while they continue talking, like I don't exist. I'm crying and pleading for them to let me go, but they continue to ignore me." I'm full-out sobbing now, and hiccupping as I speak. "Who are these people, why have they taken me? Why?"

"Savannah," Dr. Roberts reaches out for me as I heave forward. "Come back to me, you're safe."

I look up at him seeing his friendly face.

"You're safe, Savannah, you're not there anymore." He looks over my shoulder shaking his head at something, but I am too upset to care.

"Then why does it feel like I am?" I cry. "Every time I close my eyes or let my mind wander I go back to my personal hell. Those men took so much from me. How do you come back from that? I hate them!" I curl myself into my protective ball. "How can anyone treat a human the way they treated me? I was nothing more than a scrap of human waste to them."

"You are not a scrap of anything, Savannah. You are a strong woman. You survived for those seven months and you didn't let them beat you down."

"I didn't want to live, though, Doc—I wanted to die!" I admit, gripping my chair and sucking in deep breaths. "I just had nothing to do it with, so I decided to starve myself. It was the only thing I—"

I point to my chest, "the only thing I could control."
I wipe my eyes on my sleeve trying to calm down.
"Tell me, Doc, what does it mean when a person is
willing to give up and die? Even now, after a
miracle happened and I was saved, I still can't eat.
When I do eat I feel guilty, like I'm betraying
myself," I hiss at him.

He takes off his glasses, cleaning the lenses.
"What do you think that means?"

I roll my eyes. "A question with a question.
Classic, Doc."

He leans back, crossing his legs. "I'd say you hit
the lowest point a person can go, you made a
promise to yourself that you intended to keep. Then
you got rescued—something you never thought
could happen—and when you left that room
perhaps you left a piece of yourself behind." He
thinks for a moment. "Savannah, you've only been
free for three weeks. Give yourself a chance to heal,
a chance for your brain to catch up with what has
happened. In time things will go back to normal,
maybe not exactly the same as it was but a new
normal that will feel right."

I nod through a hiccup.

"You wouldn't believe the things that I've heard
when I came to work for Shadows. I have helped
people see that, yes, they've been through
something I'll never understand, but I can still help
them find their way back home." He leans forward.
"Funny thing is sometimes going home is going
backward for them. Some find starting a new life
somewhere else is their ticket to freedom." He
raises one hand to rub his jaw. "Let this place

protect you and also heal you. You are lucky. Not everyone gets to have this privilege. Just keep telling yourself that you are free, you have a voice, and you have choices."

"All right," I whisper. His words make the ache dull momentarily.

"Now," he stands, picking up his bag, "our session ran a little bit long today." I glance at his watch. We have been talking for two and a half hours! "Have you taken the horses out for a ride yet? If not, you should—there's plenty of countryside to see. Enjoy the rest of your day! I'll see you tomorrow."

\*\*\*

Cole checks his watch for the fifth time in sixty seconds, waiting impatiently for Doctor Roberts to finish this session with Savannah. He doesn't have time to waste; he needs to know what the good Doc got out of her this morning. Mark Lopez, his best friend and one of his most trusted men, had overheard their conversion from the patio. He said she sounded really upset and thought maybe the doc had made a small breakthrough. Cole wanted to check on her himself and make sure she was okay.

He hasn't seen Savannah since that night in her room where he had wanted to tell her how he felt. As normal his pride got in the way and he couldn't. He knew better than to cross a line with a "guest" of course. It was totally unprofessional and not like him at all. He knew she was avoiding him, although Abigail assured him that she just needed some alone time. Kidnap victims tended to take one step forward and two steps back, so he was letting her be, but when Mark came to him there was nothing he could think of other than making sure she was okay. He marched right down the hallway and burst into the room. In hindsight he was glad they were out on the balcony—he felt like a Neanderthal with his lack of courtesy. When Cole moved toward the open doors and heard her sobbing, the doctor caught his eye and shook his head for him not to interrupt. Once he saw she was all right, to some degree, he nodded, leaving the room.

What was with this woman? Getting him to drop everything and go find her right in the middle of a conference call? Living with two generations of Special Forces men lends itself to a certain kind of lifestyle. It's a structured, no bullshit do-your-job-and-do-it-well way of life. He had girlfriends before but never had much time for them with the family business. A few women never liked the fact he couldn't share much and why he'd disappear for days at a time. He didn't find he cared enough to let them in—it was easier to hold them at arm's length, especially after the last woman. Yeech!

But with Savannah, it's different. From the moment his eyes met hers he couldn't shake the protective feeling he had about her. He leans his forehead against the wall with a groan—his father said this could happen one day but he never believed it. He just wasn't the relationship type; he was married to his job. Christ, get a grip man! He pushes off the wall—he will not let this ridiculous feeling cloud his judgment. She's just another pretty face who needs help. He lets out a steady, long breath. *Stop thinking about her!* It's just that this damn woman is keeping him up at night...he needs to separate himself from her and it needs to start now. Suddenly her bedroom door opens. He takes a step forward, ready to pounce on the good doctor when instead she comes out, wiping her eyes with a tissue.

"Oh, hi." Her wide, watery eyes look up at him.

Oh shit. "Are you all right?" *What was that you were just saying?* He groans internally. She nods, forcing a smile out. Is she nervous? She's acting nervous.

"Yes—mm, I just need some fresh air."

Holy shit, she's nervous—all the signs are there. He holds up his hand to stop her but Doctor Roberts comes out scanning his notes. She slides around him and hurries down the hall. Slippery little woman. He shakes his head; she is probably rattled from her session.

"Oh, Cole," Doctor Roberts holds up his recorder. "We should talk."

\*\*\*

"So no real description of the American, just that he was there and confirmed that she was who they said she was." Cole clicks the audio recorder off, plugging it into the USB cord. He hits a key, uploading the session onto his computer.

"Only that he had flashy boots," the Doctor adds. "Honestly, in my professional opinion, she doesn't know anything. You'd have to be one hell of an actress to pull this off."

Cole agrees with the Doctor. Not that he thinks Savannah is anything but innocent—it just feels good to have someone confirm it. "Wow." He shakes his head. "This is the third case with this son of a bitch. I wonder what his connection is?"

Doctor Roberts rubs his face in thought. "I don't know, but it's still beyond me that they kept her alive all this time. Why not make the exchange? Granted, fifty grand is peanuts but they've had seven months to up it to a million. It cost them money to keep her fed, not that she ate much."

Cole's stomach turns, remembering what she said about making a promise to herself.

"I don't get it, it's like they kept her on ice. What were they waiting for? I think there's a lot more to this case then what we're seeing."

Cole taps his pen on the arm of the chair. "I think you're right. We'll keep her father in the dark. I don't trust it won't go public—there are leaks everywhere. Too many eyes on him."

"Yeah, the man sure loves the media," Doctor Roberts mutters.

"Overall what are your thoughts on Savannah adjusting here?" Cole has to ask. He needs to know what is making her nervous. Was it today's session or something else?

"I'd say she's doing well. Just the fact that she started talking after fourteen days was impressive. She's an interesting woman. She picks up on a lot more then you'd think. Watch her when you're in a group—she studies people's behavior then once she feels she understands them she'll engage. I suspect her trust in people was tested a lot while she was held captive, perhaps even before." He reaches for his bag. "I feel after some time she'll come around, but don't be taken by her feisty behavior—it could be a front. She uses it as a shield to keep people who make her uncomfortable at arm's length, though if you read her file she is a bit of spitfire at times." He stands, fixing his tie. "One thing her physician and I agree on is she was not raped. She shows no signs of any sexual assault."

Cole sinks further into his chair. *Thank fuck!*

"That being said, it sure opens up another whole box of questions."

"Yeah, it sure does." Cole leans forward shaking his hand. "Okay, Roberts, see you tomorrow."

Cole rises, looking out the floor-to-ceiling window. He tucks his hands into his pockets and watches the clouds float across the mountains. He can't wrap his head around it—no sexual abuse, no million dollar ransom. They keep her alive for over seven months, and despite her psychological state she's relatively all right. It just doesn't add up. He needs to start laying out the pieces to this growing puzzle. They're not going to let Savannah get away that easily.

\*\*\*

I decide to head to the lake in search of a canoe instead of a horseback ride. I don't know how to ride a horse, and I don't feel like learning. I've had way too much of an emotional day to tumble ass up in a bush somewhere.

I step carefully into the fiberglass boat, balancing with my hands on the sides and gingerly push off from the dock. The paddle glides through the water, sending me away from the house. It's not that I don't want to be here—I do—I just need to get away for a bit to clear my head. I feel emotionally raw from today's session and I have some things I'd like to mull over and then tuck away so I can make my peace.

The lake is large and before I know it the house looks tiny, although I know it is far from it. I was bored the other day and counted sixteen bedrooms, two kitchens—and it had eight BBQ's, I would have continued my exploring but I ran into Keith, who is also known as 'seven', getting ready to head out for his shift. He showed me some of his gear and told me that the weather in Montana is nothing compared to the heat and sandstorms they've seen in Afghanistan. I wanted to ask about his time there but the look on his face encouraged me not to.

I tuck the paddle away and lean back, bringing myself to the bottom of the canoe with my feet propped up on the seat. I stare at the clouds relishing in the fact that I can. I drift for a long time. I tune into every sound. I feel the armor around my chest slowly loosen and today's stress starts to melt away. I close my eyes. Yes, this is just what I need—me and nature.

\*\*\*

My eyes flutter open as a new sound finds me— it is almost like something is bobbing to the surface repeatedly. I can hear air bubbles. I pull myself up to a sitting position taking in my surroundings. Six pairs of eyes are staring at me through black goggles—mouths covered with oxygen masks and six massive rifles resting on top of the water. Holy shit! I open my mouth and let go with one earth shuttering scream, making it bounce off the mountains. One person makes a move toward me making me jump to my feet. The boat rocks, sending me into the water. The cold water is a shock to my system. It's freezing. My breath is sucked from my lungs in a giant whoosh, and doesn't want to come back. I feel someone wrap their hands around my waist, pulling me to the surface. I bat at their arms, kicking with all the strength I have. I scream repeatedly, and clock the nearest with an elbow, causing him to release me momentarily. I swim forward lunging for the overturned boat when I hear my name being yelled out.

"Savannah!"

My frozen fingers claw desperately at the wood but I can't get a grip. My limbs are becoming stiff and my heartbeat is out of control.

"Savannah, stop, it's us!"

"Get away from me!" I shout. "I won't go back!"

"Savannah, it's Mark." His voice finally registers.

*What?*

He swims up next to me as I'm shaking like a leaf. "It's okay," he whispers, holding his gun and his other hand in the air showing me he's not a threat. His oxygen mask is floating in front of him.

He slowly removes his mask, giving me a glimpse of his face.

I close my eyes, trying to calm myself.

"We're sorry, we didn't mean to scare you."

I nod. Being scared doesn't even begin to register how I'm feeling.

"Come on, we have to get you warm."

A speed boat shows up and Mark and someone else climb aboard with me. Mark wraps a blanket around me while the other guy moves to sit with the driver.

He keeps his goggles on but spits out the air piece.

\*\*\*

Mark rushes me inside through a door I haven't seen before, meeting Abigail who already has a bath running for me in my room. I am whisked away before I can say anything else to Mark.

The warm water burns as it thaws my limbs back to normal again. I'm still reeling with what happened and feel bad, but at the same time mad at the guys for scaring the shit out of me and ruining my relaxing boat trip.

Abigail tries small talk as I sit buried in bubbles in the tub. She keeps an eye on me as she chats away. "We are having company tonight; it will be nice having someone else for dinner. Why don't you pick something from the left side of the closet tonight?" That means something a little fancier. She prattles on. "You would look lovely in that soft sweater dress, why don't you try it on?" She fusses about and I know she is worried about me.

I give her a reassuring smile.

I stand staring at the clothes. It's strange having a wardrobe that you had no part of buying. The clothes are my style—this would normally shock me but I guess it was all part of my background check. Plus you can Google my name and a thousand images will pop up. Google…I haven't thought about using the Internet in a long time I wonder if I could get my hands on a laptop soon.

I blow dry my hair, letting it fall in waves down my back and apply some light eye makeup that compliments the pinot noir sweater dress that clings to my body, landing a little lower than mid-thigh. It would have been something I'd wear out to dinner with coworkers. It's pretty, with a touch of fun. I ponder the V-neckline. There was a time I wouldn't have but now I found myself hesitating. It dips a little low but it was still tasteful. Abigail did say pick something from the left side and she did mention a sweater dress. I leave the mirror and head back to the closet looking for shoes. I notice a jewelry box on one of the shelves I open it, finding three sliver bangles. They are beautiful! I slip them over my wrist while grabbing a pair of black heels.

*Okay, Savi, stop stalling.* I shake off my jitters as I walk down the stairs.

\*\*\*

Cole can't believe what happened this afternoon. He hadn't heard her screams as he had been on the phone with his father who was telling Cole that he was going to stop by for dinner tonight. Cole quickly notified Abigail to make his father's favorite meal, honey-glazed ribs, and let the guys know to dress appropriately for dinner. His father is still acting CEO of the company, and is well loved around here. He is a charmer to say the least. Cole's mother gave him a run for his money but he landed her in the end. Cole was sad she wasn't coming tonight but she had a prior engagement—ultimately why his father has some free time. He has a niggling feeling his father has an ulterior motive for showing up tonight—maybe he has news of a new sighting of The American.

He grabs Mark as he walks by—they are all gathering in the living room waiting for dinner to be served. His father is in a heavy conversation with Keith so he takes this time to hear firsthand from Mark what the hell had happened on the lake.

"We had just started our drill when we noticed the canoe floating out there. We couldn't see anyone in it so we swam over to see what it was doing in the middle of the lake. We approached it carefully since it's always tied up on the dock. Then she suddenly sits up and sees us. I can only imagine what was going through her head; I know how our gear looks. Anyway, she hopped up looking—" Mark's eyes flicker over Cole's shoulder, "amazing…"

Cole turns, following his friend's gaze. If his mouth wasn't already open it sure as hell would be as he takes in the view.

*Oh God, buddy, you're screwed. Fat chance you'll be getting that out of your head tonight.*

He watches as the room takes her in, guys sneaking glances here and there. At least they're being respectful.

"You know, there are times when I really enjoy my job," Mark jokes beside him.

Cole catches her gaze as Keith hands her a glass of wine. She still looks nervous; what the hell did he do? Maybe he crossed a line touching her cheek. Oh God, what a fool he can be. No it's that stupid magnetic hold she has on him. He takes a large sip of his brandy and turns to see his father grinning at him. Oh shit—just what he needs, his father inside his head.

Mark makes a quick exit as he spots Abigail walking by with a tray of stuffed pastries.

*Yeah, thanks man.* He walks over to the fireplace, needing something to do. He sneaks a peek at her talking to Paul. This is the first time he's seen her in a dress and he hoped to hell it would be the last because his eyes can't help but rake up and down her long, slim legs. The way her dress hugs her body, the way her hair hangs in long waves, all make his stomach flip. Damn this woman!

"Pretty little thing, huh?" His father whispers over his shoulder.

Busted.

"Yeah, she is," he mutters into his glass. His father chuckles, coming to stand in front of him.

"The Mayor's daughter," he says, acknowledging who she is. "Her father is making quite the shit storm with the media. When will they learn to keep their mouths shut?"

"I fear we may only have scratched the surface

of this case," Cole replies quietly. "Plus The American is involved with her kidnapping." His father flinches almost imperceptibly at the name. "So you know what that means."

"Shit, yeah. He won't stop until she's found." He swirls his drink. "Poor girl, her life will never be the same. Have you heard if they'll relocate her?" Cole's stomach sinks.

"I think its best she stays here. She's adjusting well. Witness Protection could send her backward."

"Mmmm." His father coughs as he tries to hide his smile. "Well, I'll see if I can talk to Frank— maybe after some time passes we could make a position for her or she could get a job in town. I'll get her some new paperwork lined up."

\*\*\*

"Savannah, this is Daniel Logan," Cole says, introducing her to him as they approach.

Her eyes go back and forth as she realizes she is meeting his father.

"Oh-Oh." Her smile appears. "It's nice to meet you, Mr. Logan." She holds out her hand for a shake but he wraps his fingers around hers and kisses the top of her hand. Oh lord...

"The pleasure is all mine. Please, call me Daniel."

Her eyes shift to Cole's, then to the floor.

What the hell is that? Christ, he wants to drag her into the corner and demand to know why she's acting strange around him.

"Dinner is ready," Abigail calls out. Mark makes

a beeline for the table. "Boys," she mutters, but a grin appears.

"Shall we?" Daniel asks Savannah, holding out his arm. She smiles. Giving in to his charm, she threads her small arm through his and walks toward the dining room.

"Abigail, you outdid yourself again," Daniel compliments her as he holds up a rib. "Delicious."

"Thank you, Daniel, it was my pleasure." Her face warms at all the attention.

A few more stragglers come to the table. Savannah's gasp gets Cole's attention and his head snaps up to see York sporting a black eye.

"Hello, everyone," York mutters, taking a seat. He makes a dramatic nod. "Savannah." Her hands are over her mouth, then suddenly she starts shaking. A moment later she breaks into full-blown laughter. She reaches over, grabbing Mark's arm for support and he starts laughing too. Cole's heart skips a beat; he loves her laugh. But what is he missing?

"Something funny?" York raises an eyebrow at them, clearly not impressed.

"I-I'm…" She tries to speak but she can't form a sentence. Finally, holding her stomach, she manages to get hold of herself. "Excuse me," she says to the group. "I wasn't expecting that," and points to York.

Mark wipes his eyes dry. "I thought this was the best way for you to find out."

"Thanks. I needed it." She grins, her eyes glistening. She looks relaxed. So is this what Savannah was like before she was taken?

"Is anyone going to explain?" Daniel asks, clearly ready for a good story.

"Well," Mark's grin speaks volumes. "We had a little encounter with Savi and a canoe today during one of our drills. York was trying to help her when she fell in the water but she panicked and clocked him good in the eye."

"Lucky hit," York mutters.

"Lucky like winning a game of poker with a pair of twos?" Savannah shoots back.

"Ha!" Daniel laughs out. "Oh lord, son, I wish you'd told me about her sooner. Seems I've missed out on some good times, hey?"

"I am sorry, York, truly," Savannah says after the table dies down. "I didn't know who you were and when you grabbed me, well…" She clears her throat.

"Don't sweat it," York mutters around a rib in his mouth.

"Oh, I would have paid money to have seen that, though." Abigail laughs. Savannah's mouth drops open before she joins in too. York rolls his eyes. What does he expect when he acts like the house asshole? He has to know he'll be treated like one.

# Chapter Six

I sit twirling the stem of my wine glass between my fingers, watching the red wine rise up the sides then bleed back down. I can hear the guys joking around while they clean up in the kitchen. Abigail is on the phone with her sister, excited about her coming over for a visit soon. I push the sinking feeling away of when I'd see my father next. I long to see him and Lynn.

"How do you like it here, Savannah?" Daniel asks, pulling me from my thoughts. He takes a seat next to me at the dinner table.

"It's," I take a deep breath, "all a little surreal. Don't get me wrong—I'm incredibly thankful. It's just that I went from my old life to a prison to this." He nods. "I think I feel like I'm floating with no roots to hold me down. I'm not really sure where I belong."

"Well," he rubs his chin, "you're not the first person to say that." He says, giving me a reassuring smile. "Have you made any friends yet?"

"Umm, friends? Ah—well, Mark seems friendly enough."

"Yes, Mark has been around for a long time, good man. Anyone else?"

"I guess Paul, John, and Keith." He nods, agreeing with me. "York is an interesting character."

"Yes, York is something else."

"I love Abigail. She's like mother and sister all rolled into one." I pause, knowing what he was waiting for.

"What about, Cole? Has he been friendly?"

Oh boy. I take a long drink of my wine, stalling. Truthfully I don't really know how I feel about him. I know the stories I've heard scare me to no end, but he's also the first man in twenty-seven years that makes my stomach bubble with warmth. I've had boyfriends in the past but when my father became mayor they seemed to enjoy the fame a lot more than I did.

I glance over at Cole in the kitchen. He is such a beautiful man. Once more I take in his tall, lean body, those eyes in which you could get lost and never return. Why in the world he hasn't been snatched up still baffles me. I blush when his father clears his throat, clearly I just got caught. He lets out a little chuckle.

"Cole's been—" *caring, kind, respectful, understanding, yummy. Oh lord, Savi, get a handle on yourself!* "Great," I say, feeling like an ass. Such a lame answer. "I mean he's been very hospitable." I shake my head, fumbling over my words. "I mean...he makes me feel welcome and secure for the first time in, well, a long time." I shrug, trying to explain better. "I—I don't even know what safe feels like anymore, but whatever he does, it's nice." He grins at me, oh shit. "But that's his job so…yeah I guess he does it well." *Oh shoot me now!* Why couldn't I have said fine and leave it at that?

He chuckles again, and I close my eyes, mentally slapping my forehead. I'm such a moron!

"Yes, well, Cole has always been very good at what he does. His mother worries that he's a little too dedicated sometimes. She feels he's hiding behind his work. He likes to keep people at arm's length—you know this job can be hard on the head. He was born to be in the Special Forces but that doesn't mean it doesn't screw with you." He stops himself. "I apologize, forgive me, my mouth has run away with me."

"No, it's fine. Truthfully, it's refreshing getting a little insight on these guys." Cole, mainly, but I wasn't about to say that.

"So tell me, Savannah, what did you do for fun back in New York?"

"Fun?" I almost laugh. Fun isn't a word I've used in a long time, even before my prison. "I guess that would be going to listen to live music at local pubs, I'm a sucker for the blues."

"Oh yeah?" His eyes light up. "You know there's a few places in town that have live music."

"Town?" I look at him, puzzled. "I wasn't aware we were close to a town?"

"Whitestone, it's about fifteen miles from here. You should check it out, one can go a bit stir crazy up here." Huh.

"I guess one would go stir crazy if they were here long enough." I watch his face waiting for a sign any indication that I'll be here for a while. He takes a drink but his face gives nothing away. "I feel like you're telling me to set some roots here, make some friends, and check out the night life."

His eyes flicker toward where Cole and Mark talking. "I won't be going home for a while, will I, Daniel?"

He doesn't look at me.

"That's a question I can't answer for you right now, Savannah."

I feel my stomach sink.

"But you just did," I whisper.

\*\*\*

Cole sits at his desk flipping through footage of the last known sighting of The American crossing the Texas border into Mexico, three days ago. He leans back, rubbing his face. So this man was stepping back onto Mexican soil while we were all having dinner. He wonders where he was when Savannah first came here. There's always the possibility that they were followed, though it's highly unlikely. They changed cars twice since the airport in North Dakota. Once at the border and again before they climbed the mountain roads in Montana.

A ping alerting him to an email brings him back from his thoughts. He opens the message from Frank, his main contact within the Army. He clicks the attachment and it opens to a video of Mayor Doug Fox sending out yet another media message about his daughter. Cole rolls his eyes, as he presses play.

"It's another cold New York day that I wake up and do not have my daughter to call. It's been eight months since I've last heard her voice, gave her a hug, or told her I loved her." He pauses for a breath while his chin quivers. "Please, return my sweet Savannah to me." He claps his hand over his mouth. A woman steps up to the microphone thanking the media for listening. The shaking Mayor removes himself from the crowd.

Cole flicks the screen back to The American, deciding something does not add up. The American was normally involved with high profile men, not young women. Why the Mayor's daughter? They'd get more money if they took the mayor. The Cartels normally get more media coverage then and they love to show their power. However, the mayor is doing a stellar job in that department. Cole leans into his hands letting out a long breath.

"Cole?" He looks up to see Savannah standing in his doorway. "Sorry, your door was open." She looks around his office. "Bad time?"

He'd barely seen her since the dinner with his father three days ago.

"No." He drops his hands, trying to shake his stress. "Come in."

She walks toward him, stopping when she gets to the chair. Her small fingers clasp the back of it. "What can I do for you?"

"May I?" She points to the chair.

"Please."

She sits and crosses her legs, running her hand through her hair, tossing it over to one side. A hint of apples reach his nose. Focus.

"I think we should talk." She clears her throat, as Cole's stomach twists. "I'm sure you've noticed I've been avoiding you. I thought I should explain myself."

He was not expecting this—he waits for her to go on.

"When I first met you, I called you my carrier because that's what you were to me until I heard Abigail call you Logan. Then one night when I was in the living room I heard some of the guys talking about this man Cole and how he—" She stops, fumbling with her hands.

"He what?" he asks, wanting to know where she is going with this.

"How he killed a rat by popping three between his eyes." Cole closes his eyes briefly. "They talked about how many kills this Cole had as well as the number of bare hand kills. I was terrified to meet him. I was starting to let my guard down with you and I like that you did things that—" She blushes, pushing her lips together.

He leans forward in his chair wanting to know more about these things that she likes.

"I was caught off guard when you told me your first name; I couldn't believe that Cole was you. After taking some time to think it through though, I realize I was judging you unfairly because I don't know you enough to judge you, so for that I'm sorry."

He watches her carefully, realizing it took a lot for her to come in here and tell him what she has been thinking. He leans back in his chair feeling a little annoyed at the same time.

"I imagine hearing something like that would frighten you. Sadly the guys may spill more details as the time goes on. I guess you can chose to understand what we do or you can chose not to. I won't say I'm sorry for killing those people; they're evil. In my line of work there are the good guys and the bad guys. There can be no blurred lines; it's black and white."

"Okay." Her voice is quiet.

There it is again, he thinks. This is the problem he has with people. They didn't understand his life. They judge and run away. Anger rises in him but he fights it down. How could she realize what his life is like?

"Now that we have that cleared up, is there anything else?" he asks, letting his temper ease up some.

"Yes, actually, I know the rules but can I get my hands on the Internet?"

His back stiffens, the internet always poses problems.

"I'll get Abigail to show you to a study where you can use the computer in private. Remember everything is being monitored."

She stands quickly. "Great, thank you." Her eyes drift down to his desk and narrow. "Is that me?"

He looks down and sees her file open in front of him. Shit! He snaps it shut but not before her hand reaches out pulling out a newspaper article about her disappearance.

"This was snapped the night I was taken." She runs her finger over the picture. "I remember that dress." She squints like she is remembering something. "Hmm."

"What?" He stands, coming next to her side looking over her shoulder at the picture. "Do you remember something?"

She flips her hair and there is that apple smell again.

He pauses, allowing himself to enjoy her scent—after all, he spends basically three hundred and sixty-five days a year with men, he thinks. Needless to say, Savannah smells amazing. Oh lord, there he goes again. He forces himself to concentrate.

"See," she turns to look at him over her small shoulder, "I was having drinks with Joe Might in this little pub. There was the bartender and one old man in the corner. I know because I was on high alert, watching for the damn paparazzi. But this was taken from behind Joe. I would have seen them…wait." She holds the picture closer. "There's a reflection capturing part of a hand. I wish it was clearer. Is there a way to blow it up?"

"Umm, I have the email with the attachment. I could bring it up and then blow it up larger." He sits down in his chair, opening his email. She follows standing next to him. He normally would never let anyone see his computer, but he enjoys her not being afraid of him. He quickly opens the attachment and brings the picture up and zooms in on the reflection. The hand becomes a little clearer.

"Look." Savannah leans over him pointing at the screen, causing her hair to brush over his neck. A jolt runs through him. "It's a silver bracelet with a heart on it."

Cole prints the picture to keep a copy.

She turns leaning her body against his desk in front on him. She raises her hand rubbing her forehead. "Something's there I just know it—like it's sitting on the edge of my memory."

She looks so sweet and serious trying hard to remember. Cole can feel his walls starting to crumble and he wants nothing more than to pull her onto his lap and hold her and tell her everything will be all right. Instead he reaches for her hand, *Oh, you stupid fool.* Thankfully she doesn't pull away though her eyes travel up from their hands to his eyes. His fingers flex, holding her hand a little tighter. Oh…one little tug and she'd be on his lap knowing just how much he wants her there.

"Give it time, but it will come. Your mind has a lot to process."

"You sound like Doctor Roberts," she jokes. "Thanks, though." She makes no attempt to pull away and neither does he.

His stomach is swimming laps with the occasional somersault. *Lord, I am falling fast. Get a grip!*

York comes busting through the door in the middle of a rant. He stops when he sees Savannah behind the desk. She's crossed the forbidden line Cole has. She drops his hand, leaving him feeling a loss. "Hey, Savi, didn't know you made office calls," York mutters sarcastically.

"York." She nods, turning to leave. "How's the eye?"

"Abigail will help you," Cole says to Savannah, "if you remember anything."

"I will, thanks." She smiles then turns to glare at York. "Be careful out there." She taps her eye on the way out.

God, she is fun to watch, Cole thought grinning. He turns his attention to York who is shaking his head at him.

"What do you want?"

"No, my friend, I think the question is what is it that *you* want?" York nods toward the door as it closes behind her.

***

I try to lose the grin that is tugging at the corners of my mouth but it's difficult. There is something about Cole Logan that makes all my senses stand at attention. I can't believe I didn't flinch when he held my hand, but it felt right. I put the thought aside. I need to hunt down Abigail.

After Abigail gives me the rundown on what sites were blocked, like email, Skype, Facebook, etc. I am finally left alone. I bring up Google and type my father's name. There must be a billion links to look up so I start with the newest one. I feel my stomach twist when I click on the video and watch him pour his heart out about me. I continue watching more news clips till I can't take it anymore. I wipe my eyes dry and Google my name and pictures and articles come flying at me. I click images and see Lynn and me walking at the beach together we were laughing after spending the day soaking up some sun. Oh Lynn, I miss her so much it hurts. I print off the picture.

I search my name and the date I was taken. The *New York Times* has a picture of me on the front cover with a caption 'Mayor's Daughter Disappears—Is This a Cry For Help?' I shake my head reading on; I follow my story as the newspaper and magazines gathered more information. Lynn even did an interview about our last day together, at the end asking the media to give her some space. My poor Lynn.

I read that I ran off with a biker gang that daddy didn't approve of, that I'm living with a cousin in Canada, some say I'm held up in a rehab in California. I start to feel nauseous; the stories make me look like I brought this on myself. Finally the report was released with a statement from the kidnappers asking for a ransom, however, it didn't seem to make headlines for very long.

"I'll leave this for you, dear." Abigail sits a tray down next to me. "Please try and eat it."

"Thank you, Abigail." I reach over taking a sip of the green smoothie. She smiles, leaving the room.

I go back to the articles on my father and notice that he doesn't comment on the ransom so much as just wanting to get me back. Maybe they didn't want to draw attention to it. I flip through a few pictures wanting one to print off of dad too; I need some memories to remember who I still am, or was.

I find one of dad at a fundraiser smiling at someone who was out of the shot. He was clicking his champagne glass. I pressed print when something catches my eye. It's a woman's hand holding the other glass to his and there was a silver bracelet with a heart dangling from it from her wrist. Holy crap! I start clicking like mad through the photos trying to see if I can get a better look at this woman. I realize that they were at the annual fundraiser for breast cancer we attend every year to help support the cause. It was something we did for mom. I shudder at the sudden vision of my mother having to deal with all the chemo; she looked like a different person toward the end of her life.

I guess it was nice to see my father smiling like that four months into my kidnapping, funny as that sounds, it was a good feeling knowing that he wasn't stressed at least at that moment, but the woman in the picture made my stomach knot, who the hell was she? I look up the number for the charity organizer and jot it down, hoping that I could make a phone call. I'll discuss it with Cole later.

I also search *Los Sirvientes Del Diablos* (and Servants of the Devil). I print off their history from Wikipedia as well as the Cartels. I think I should know what I'm up against. I read about other kidnap victims who got away and lived to tell their stories. They all had one thing mine didn't: a very large ransom. Most were asking for half a million. I start making a list of things that are similar or different from my kidnapping. I click on the lamp without a care about how late it's getting; I'm so engulfed in my research.

I was held captive for a lot longer than most. Seems *Los Sirvientes Del Diablos* doesn't like to keep their victims for long. They did a proof of life picture and video on me roughly five times. The stories I'm reading say they only did it twice. So why keep me longer? What purpose did it serve, especially when I was only worth fifty grand! That number still makes my gut twist.

"Savannah?" I turn to find Abigail in the doorway. "Will you be joining us for dinner?"

I glance at the time on the computer. I have been at this for nearly five hours.

"Yes, sorry I lost track of time. I'll be right down." I unfold myself from where I was sitting and gather my things. My brain feels fried. I haven't stared at a computer in a long time, plus I had a lot to take in. I drop my stuff in my room and head down the stairs.

I find Abigail hustling about the kitchen. I offer to help but she says she has it under control so I go look out the front living room window. The horses are running back and forth along the fence and a light flickers off in the distance, warning of another flippin' storm coming. Another flicker and it sends me into a flashback.

\*\*\*

*"Up! Chica apurate!" the fat man yells at me.*

*I hurry to my feet as two women enter with a tub on wheels filled with water. They have a bucket with shampoo, body soap and a large sponge.*

*"What's going on?" I ask, feeling my panic rise.*

*"Picture time," he mutters standing by the door holding a large, army issue gun. "¡Apúrate!" he screams at the women then disappears out the door. They both approach and one gives me a small smile.*

112

*"We need to remove your clothes," one whisperer, "quickly." I'm confused but am so happy to see a woman here I don't protest. She helps me into the tub and proceeds to wash me. She's mostly concentrating on my hands, neck and face. The other woman won't make eye contact as she starts roughly washing my hair. I want to cry out—it hurts—but I don't, as at least I'm finally getting clean. Before I know it I'm yanked out of the tub and being dried off. When the other woman leaves for a moment I lean into the nice one.*

*"Please, what is your name?" She looks around as her hands fuss with my hair. "Please, I'm so lonely—you're the first person who's been nice to me since I arrived."*

*"Maria," she barely whispers. "Do as they say! Don't fight them or they'll kill you."*

*A hissing noise makes us both jump the other woman has returned holding a dress and looks angry at Maria. She yanks a dress over my head letting it fall to my knees. It smells awful but it looks clean. Someone wraps a blindfold over my eyes making me start to panic. Is this it? A hand grabs my arm and drags me a few steps out of my room where I'm pushed to my knees. When the blindfold is removed I'm staring at a video camera. A bright light is pointed at me, nearly blinding me. I look off to the side, seeing legs from the thighs down and they are holding those army guns. I can't see their faces but there must be ten of them. A newspaper is shoved into my hands.*

*"Sonria," a man yells from behind a tripod holding a video camera.*

113

*"Say your name," the fat man hisses at me I look over at the video camera and see the red light on. "¡Nombre!"*

*"S-Savannah Miller," I whisper, then someone snaps the newspaper away. Shit! I want to see the date!*

*"What's your papa's name, what he do?" My stomach turns as I lick my dry lips.*

*"Doug Fox, Mayor of New York."*

*"Up!" Someone grabs my arm as someone else returns the blindfold. Just as I was being pulled out of the room I hear the boom of thunder.*

\*\*\*

"Ahh!" I shriek as I am jolted back to the present. I scream again when someone touches my arm and holds me steady. I realize it is Cole and my hands grip his biceps for support.

"Hey, what's going on? You're white as a ghost," he whispers.

"Sorry." I shake my head trying to clear the memory. "I just was remembering something." I take a deep breath, fighting the urge to cry.

"Did you eat lunch?"

"No, she didn't." Abigail gives me a shake of her head from the doorway. "I found your sandwich in the trash."

I close my eyes, feeling terrible.

"Sorry, just wasn't hungry."

She sighs, then announces dinner is ready.

"Please don't skip meals, Savi." Cole still has me by my arms.

I look up finding him looking genuinely worried.

"Cole, I need to talk to you about somethi—"

"Whoa, two times in one day guys. People might talk." York snickers, coming up next to us cocking one eyebrow inquisitively.

"Perfect timing as always, York," Cole mutters, watching me. "Let's go eat, shall we?"

I sip my lemonade and manage to eat half of my dinner. I don't engage in the conversation; I am lost in thought about the girl with the bracelet. Who is she? Why is she following me? How does she know my father? Wow, everything tilts—I feel dizzy all of a sudden and my hand flies out, gripping the edge of the table.

"You don't look so hot, Savi," Mark says from beside me.

"Could you excuse me?" The room spins slightly but I manage to head outside.

I wrap my sweater around me as I lean over the deck railing. Yes outside is a good choice. The smell of the storm is thick in the air. It is only a matter of time before the rain will start. The sky looks angry as the dark clouds roll around the mountains. I drop my head, feeling dizzy again.

Maria's face flashes in front of me. She smiled, making me want to cry. She was supposed to be my friend. She used to sneak into my room at night and sit on the floor against the wall and we'd talk about our families. It only lasted for a few days but it was something I clung to. I confided in her one night about finding a hunting knife that one of the men dropped while dragging the tub inside my room. I was planning to use it to escape. She asked to see it and when I showed her she grabbed it, shoving it in my face and calling out for Jose. She was just using me to find out information and it crushed my heart. I truly liked Maria and I thought she liked me. I was badly beaten with a wooden paddle and my ears rang for two days straight but I learned an important message that night: Trust no one.

"Gonna be a big one." I jump but don't turn around. My stomach twists like it is battling with my dinner. "Sorry, I didn't mean to scare you."

"I'm sure," I shoot back. York comes into view as he stands by my side, peering down at me through his gray, wolf like eyes.

"I'm going to give it to you straight, Savannah, now that I finally got you alone." I let out some short breaths trying to fight the dizzy feeling. "I hear The American was involved in your kidnapping."

"The American?" That's what I called him. "Does he not have a name?"

"We've been watching him for six years and no one has been able to identify him yet. He's good and runs thick with the Cartels. He's heavily protected; no one has been able to get near him. You need to try and remember every single detail of your encounters with this man—it's crucial."

"I've been try—"

"Not hard enough!" he bites. I turn my head, staring up at him for a moment. I'm seeing double.

"Not hard enough! I'm sorry, but were you held captive for seven months and treated like a dog? No—you weren't. My memories come and go. Sometimes things trigger them, sometimes they don't. I can't force them." I step closer to him. "I'm still trying to process all this. Things are so fucked up, York! So don't tell me that I'm not trying hard enough!" I stagger, feeling ill.

He grips my elbow hard and angrily pulls me out of view of the doors. "I get that you're trying, Savannah, but now that we know The American is involved it's a game changer. He doesn't lose his prisoners—ever." He lowers his voice. "His name is now linked with you and your disappearance and now that you're out of the *Los Sirvientes Del Diablos* hold, you're going to be his number one priority. Do you understand why I'm telling you to use your head and remember everything? This is why. You could fuck this whole place up." He waves his hand over the property. "Fuck, I wish we knew more about you and the situation before we came and got you out. Fucking Cole."

Okay, now everything is spinning. I reach out my hand to a chair for support. "You—you're saying you wouldn't have come for me?"

He makes a pissy face. "What I'm saying is that we should have and still should hand you over to the Witness Protection Program. All you're going to do is cause us trouble and potentially expose all that we've worked so hard for."

"I didn't ask for this York!" I spit out, feeling defensive. "Shit, what am I supposed to do with this information besides try to crack open memories locked inside my brain with a fucking deadbolt?"

"You should think about leaving," he says without missing a beat.

That sucks the wind right out of me. I turn on my

heel and make my way down the stairs to the grass. I don't want to go back inside and face everyone. If this is what's going on, maybe he isn't the only one who feels I'm jeopardizing this place. I head for the boathouse with heavy feet. I feel off balance. I collapse on a chair, trying to fight off the nausea. Jesus, what did I eat? I open and close my eyes— everything is shifting to the right. I move my hand in front of me and it blurs in its path like a rainbow. I flop forward on all fours heaving, my stomach wrenching. I lay my cheek to the cool wood staring out at the water watching the curtain of rain traveling toward me. The raindrops bounce off my face, freeing me of my sweaty forehead and feeling very cool.

They don't know who the American is? Just that he'll be looking under every rock in the US until he finds me? Wow, I'm royally fucked. How or rather why is this happening to me? Oh God, what if I ruin all this for the Logans? Three generations, and they've saved countless lives. I lean forward, emptying my stomach again. God, I feel miserable. I flop back down on the deck not having the strength to do anything else. My clothes are drenched but I don't notice anything but the violent pain in my stomach. Oh no! I roll and continue the horrible act of emptying my stomach; there can't be anything left in there. I close my eyes promising myself I'll speak with Cole about leaving.

"Savannah?" I hear Keith whisper through the rain. "What are you doing?"

I don't move. I barely find my voice.

"Need a minute."

"Can I get you out of the rain—" He drops in front of me, the brim of his hat streaming with water. "Jesus, Savi, you look horrible." He reaches out, taking my wrist and checking my pulse. I hear his rain jacket squeak as he mutters something into his radio. I can't make it out, things are going gray. "I need to get you inside."

I push away his hand letting mine fall in front of him with a smack. I feel like I'm heavy as lead. There is no way he is going to move me. If he did, I think I might black out from the motion.

"No," I whisper, concentrating on a rock. I need something to focus on that isn't moving. He watches me for a moment, then stands. Oh good, please leave me be.

# *Chapter Seven*

Cole is sipping a brandy listening to John tell a story about a flat tire he got while coming back into the US from a snatch and grab in Mexico when Mark catches his attention. He waves him into the kitchen and follows, only to find him looking distraught.

"Keith needs to speak with you," Mark says, handing his radio to him. Cole looks at him funny. Mark is on duty tonight, but if Keith requested him it must be important. "You need to take this."

"Logan to Delta Seven."

"Logan, you need to come to the boat house. I have a situation."

"Be right there." Mark was already handing him a rain coat, his face looking worried.

He jogs down the lawn over the soppy grass, his boots sinking in, making it slippery. Keith stops him a few yards from the boat house.

"It's Savannah." Cole's stomach sinks. "I found her lying on the deck of the boat house, she looks really sick and her pulse is racing. She won't let me move her. I didn't want to force her." He gives Cole a look; they all know better than to force things with their "guests." Victims of kidnapping are to be handled with kid gloves. "I just thought she'd respond better to you." Keith's hand grips his arm as he comes closer. "Cole, she doesn't look good."

"Take me to her." Cole follows him around the corner to where a drenched Savannah lies on the deck floor looking lethargic. Delta Six is holding an umbrella over her head. Cole's heart sinks as he rushes to her side, dropping to his knees seeing how pale she is. He checks her pulse; it is racing.

"Hey, Savi." He tries to remain calm and notices her eyes never shift from the horizon. "Why are you out here?"

"Tell Cole I'll leave," she barely whispers. Leave? He glances up at Keith who gives a grim nod—she is clearly out of it. He bends down trying to get a good look at her pupils; they're dilated. He glances back at Keith giving him the sign to call the doctor.

"Code one, Keith." Keith quickly calls it in.

She moans holding her stomach. "Savannah, why would you leave?" He tries to distract her as she is retching again.

"The American—his name is connected with mine—he doesn't lose hostages."

What the hell? How did she know this? What she's saying is classified information.

"I need to leave before—" Her words were slurring and her eyes look heavy. "Tell Cole not to worry. I'll leave."

Over his dead body will this woman be leaving the safety of his house.

"I'm going to pick you up now, Savi."

"No," she whimpers trying to push him away, "sick." He ignores her protests and cradles her to him. She is so exhausted her body is like mush against his.

"Keith," he calls over his shoulder, "my entrance."

Keith nods, running up ahead opening a side door reserved for Cole only. It is a direct route to his room.

Once they are out of the rain and in the back hallway he turns to Keith. "Go get Abigail and don't mention a word of this to anyone. Call in someone to replace you tonight, get dried off, and meet me back in my room."

Keith nods then glances at Savannah before he leaves.

Cole is happy it was Keith who found her and not one of the other guys. They might have moved her, thinking it was for the best.

He opens the door to his bedroom, placing her on his bed. Her hands grip his jacket, making him still.

Her eyes are closed and he knows she is barely hanging on. She moans, letting go of him. Holding her stomach, he grabs a small garbage can.

*Wow, she's really sick.*

"Oh my goodness, Savannah." Abigail comes rushing in his room with a homemade medical bag, pulling out a thermometer and sticking it in Savannah's ear.

Savannah moans again, tucking her knees to her stomach, her breathing growing shallow. "No fever. Cole, should we move her to her bedroom?"

122

"No, this situation stays here until we know what's making her sick."

"The doctor should be here any minute," Keith chimes in.

"Okay, boys, give me five minutes so I can get her into something dry, please." Cole pulls out a black T-shirt handing it to Abigail before walking into the private hallway with Keith.

"I want you to keep this whole thing quiet for now, Keith."

"Of course."

"Did she say anything to you?"

"She kept saying she needed to leave." He shakes his head. "She was talking to someone earlier but I couldn't see from my post. It got heated with whoever it was—she caught my attention when she shouted. I watched her leave the deck and walk down to the boat house. She stumbled as she reached the chair. I thought perhaps she had too much to drink, so I let her be. But then she fell forward and collapsed on the deck. By the time I got there she was vomiting hard and was white as a ghost. I'm sorry I didn't move her, but—"

"No, you did the right thing." Cole thinks for a moment. "I want to know who she was talking to, and if you hear anything at all I want to know about it immediately." Who would have opened their fucking mouth?

"Of course." Keith disappears down the hallway.

*** 

"When did the symptoms begin? Did anyone

123

notice?" the doctor asks, looking serious.

"She was fine when I brought her lunch at noon. She said she was just tired," Abigail says, looking pale.

"She seemed fine when she came to talk to me around eleven," Cole chimes in, wracking his brain trying to remember if she seemed different. "Dinner she seemed fine too. She ate a little."

"Anything to drink? Alcohol?"

"No, she's not a big drinker," Cole says crossing his arms.

The doctor draws her blood then tucks it carefully into his bag.

"Do you think it's the flu?" Abigail asks impatiently.

"No I don't think so. If I was to guess I'd say she either has food poisoning or she ingested another type of poison." Abigail gasps as Cole balls his hands into fists, tucking them tightly against his sides.

"No one else is sick." Abigail's look is horrifying. "We all ate the same thing, I made dinner."

Cole squeezes her shoulders—he would never think anything but the best of Abigail.

"Then perhaps something she drank." The doctor slides the IV into the top of her wrist. "Someone could have slipped something in it."

Savannah moans quietly as the needle pokes her skin.

"It's all right, sweetheart, this will keep you hydrated." Cole is fighting the urge to comfort her.

The Doctor looks up at Cole. "Do you have any

bottled water that hasn't been opened?"

"Yes." He moves swiftly to his mini fridge and hands him one. He watches as the doctor measures out a tablespoon of charcoal into eight ounces of water.

"In," the Doctor checks his watch, "fifteen minutes the anti-emetic shot I gave her for vomiting should kick in—get her to drink all of this." He stands placing it on the table. "I'm going to get this blood to the lab. She's stable for now but if she gets worse before I return, call me immediately."

"How long till the results come in, Doctor Rice?" Abigail moves to Savannah's side rubbing her arm gently.

"First priority, Doc." Cole gives him in a look from across the room.

"Always, Logan. I should know in a few hours."

"Use my private cell." Cole didn't want to risk anything being overheard. There are too many unanswered questions.

Abigail walks the doctor out the back way.

Cole sits in a chair watching her sleep. She looks tiny in his king size bed. He tries in vain to push the awful thoughts of *'What if?'* aside. What if no one saw her down there? What if…He'd seen people in a lot worse shape, but with Savannah it's different. Every part of him wants to lie down next to her, breathe her in, and hold her tight. He wants to bring her the comfort that she deserves. He rubs his face, leaning back in the chair. He checks his watch and grabs the glass.

Sitting on the edge of the bed, he gently moves her hair out of her face. "Savannah," he whispers, making her stir. "Open your eyes for me."

She moans as she tries to open them.

"Here, drink this. It will help your stomach." Her mouth opens slightly. He slips the straw between her lips and talks her through drinking the whole thing. "Good job, now you can sleep."

She doesn't move after that.

A knock at the back door brings Cole to his feet. He opens it, finding Keith holding a bottle of brandy and two glasses.

"Thought you might need one." Keith shrugs, stepping into the room. "What did the doctor say?"

"Possibly poison, results should be back soon."

Keith looks shocked and hands him a glass.

"What did you find out?"

"York spoke to her." Keith makes a face as Cole's expression hardens.

He takes a long sip, trying to control his anger. "He was trying to explain to her that she needs to remember everything about The American. He's pissed at you—"

"He's pissed at me?" Cole shouts they both glance at Savannah, who stirs.

"Yes, he says that we shouldn't have taken her back here. That WPP is a better choice." Keith holds up his hand stopping him from his rant about the WPP. "That's all I know, either way he was straight with me when I asked, giving me the information—he didn't seem to be hiding anything. I told him you wanted him to take my post tonight." Keith grins. "He wasn't pleased, but he went."

"I bet," Cole hisses, sipping his drink. They sit in silence for a little while listening to the rain beat against the window.

***

"Cole?" Abigail's voice comes from the doorway—neither man heard the door open. "Doctor Rice is here."

Cole glances at his watch, stunned to see three hours has elapsed. "Hi, Doc. You didn't call my cell?"

Doctor Rice checks Savannah's vital signs—everything seems to be all right. "I decided to come over and give you the news directly." He removes the IV.

Cole is quietly going mad while the doc checks her over again.

"It was tetrahydrozoline poisoning."

"What!" Abigail turns looking at Cole for clarification.

"Eye drops," Cole answers. "Every man carries a bottle—the elements are rough on the eyes. How much was in her system?"

"Enough," the doctor says.

Suddenly a dark feeling comes over Cole and he grips the back of his chair. "Doctor Rice," Cole's voice is low. "I need you to remove the test results from your database right now."

"Of course, I'll call the lab immediately." He slips out into the hall.

"What are you thinking?" Keith asks.

"I don't know, but I don't like this and I think we should keep any details about what has happened under wraps." Cole downs his drink in one swallow.

"I don't understand, Cole," Abigail says crossing her arms. "How could she possibly have been poisoned? None of our boys would do this."

"I don't want to go there either, but someone did do it. She wouldn't have done it to herself."

"Why erase it from the database?" Keith asks trying to understand.

"If they run the lab and it goes into the database, it's a pretty unusual poisoning, it might stand out and we don't need anyone taking an interest. I just hope that the lab didn't enter it online yet."

"Oh dear!" Both men look at Abigail. "She likes the lemonade I make. I made her a large batch yesterday morning, and it sat in the fridge all day. So anyone could have spiked it at any time."

Cole let out a long breath. Of course, he looks at Keith.

"Check the video surveillance footage. Let's see what we come up with."

Keith squeezes Savannah's hand then leaves.

"Abigail, could you bring me the some of that lemonade, please? I'd like to take it in for testing," Doctor Rice asks her from behind them. "Cole, I'll be back tomorrow to check on her, she should recover just fine. We caught it early and thankfully she didn't ingest enough to—" He pauses seeing Cole's expression. "She just needs rest."

Cole plops down on his chair with a sigh. This whole situation seems surreal. The mere idea that one of his trusted men could betray him makes him feel sick; loyalty is essential in this business. He'll have to fill his father in on all this immediately. He really needs the old man's advice. He wonders how to deal with York. What he the hell was he thinking opening his mouth to Savannah about anything? She doesn't need to know that her life is never going to be what it was, that she probably would never be able to go back, especially not with what he suspects is going on.

He downs another ounce of brandy hoping to take the edge off then leans back, glancing at the clock. 3:50 a.m. He finally puts on dry clothes then collapses back into his chair, unwilling to leave Savannah in case she wakes. He is exhausted as well...

*** 

"No-no-please."

Her words make Cole's eyes pop open, he lifts his head to see her twitching.

"No more! I'm sorry."

He jumps to his feet moving to the bed. "Savannah," he whispers, "wake up."

"Nooo."

He shakes her softly, making her eyes open.

She looks up startled. Her chest is heaving and tears trickle down her cheeks.

"You were dreaming," he says quietly. "You're safe."

She shakes her head 'no' slowly as she falls back to sleep. "Don't leave," she mutters, moving her hand on top of his.

"I won't. I promise." He kicks off his boots, not caring about what is right or not, and climbs in next to her, leaning his back against the leather

129

headboard and holds her hand in his as she sleeps. Yup, he is putty in her hands for sure. *Shit.*

"You smell like him," she suddenly whispers, still mostly asleep.

"Smell like who?"

"Cole."

He feels his heart speed up then let's out a chuckle. He knows it's wrong, taking advantage of her in the state she is in, but who is he kidding?

"Is that a good thing?"

She sighs. "Very."

Okay, he's in. He's about to toss all his chips on the table. She needs to be his. Now that he has confirmation that she is interested in him he feels his guard drop. The overwhelming protective instincts that he has been experiencing since she has arrived crash down around him like a landslide. Yup, he has officially fallen head over heels for this woman and it near scares him half to death!

\*\*\*

The smell of apples fills his nose. Its intoxicating warmth spreads down to his toes. He is thoroughly enjoying this half-awake, half asleep time next to her—that is until he hears someone clear their throat. His eyes flutter open to a grinning Abigail.

"Morning." She beams with a stupid grin, her eyes shifting from him to his side.

He rubs his eyes then looks down at Savannah tucked into him. He isn't sure exactly where to go with this and looks up at Abigail with a silly grin. His brain takes a moment to remember all the details of night before.

"I'll just leave your breakfast here." As she places the tray on the table he notices there are two servings. "I'll be sure not to let anyone bother you this morning."

"Abby—" he mumbles, trying to make his brain function properly.

"No, no." She holds up her hands walking backwards toward the door. "Just stay put." She continues to grin widely.

*Oh, thank God it was Abigail.* He knows he can trust her to keep his confidence. *Well actually*, he sighs, who is he kidding? He shakes his head. *No doubt she's calling his mother right now, filling her in on all the details.*

Savannah shifts next to him. Her hand moves to his stomach and her head falls on his chest.

He waits till her breathing goes back to smooth, even breaths then wraps his arm around her back holding her a little closer to him. He loves the way she molds to him. He knows he should slip out of bed before she wakes—she'll probably freak out if she wakes in his arms—but he just can't seem to move. His brain and heart are having a battle. Finally he flips off his brain and basks in her warmth, falling back to sleep.

***

His vibrating cell phone brings him out of his groggy state. He starts to move but realizes that Savannah is still draped over him. He snakes the phone free and checks the ID, seeing it's a text from

131

Mark wondering where he is. He switches the cell to 'silent' and places it quietly on the nightstand.

"Cole?" He hears her soft voice.

"Yes." He feels his stomach sink—*Oh God.*

She shifts, trying to sit up but can't.

"It's all right, Savannah," he assures her, "it's not what you think."

"Why am I in this room, in bed with you?"

His brain mentally slaps him. *Ass!* He decides to go with the truth.

"Because you asked me to." *Because I can't leave you alone.*

She shifts again, this time managing to lift herself onto her knees.

The loss of body contact makes him experience a sudden loss. He instantly misses her.

"What happened?" She looks down at the T-shirt she is wearing and gasps, quickly tucking it between her legs—not that she needs to; it is like a dress on her. "How did I get in this? And why is my head pounding?"

He sits up, leaning against the headboard. "You're in my room because it's the safest room in the house. Plus there are two ways to come and go. Do you remember anything from last night?"

She looks around taking in her surroundings her hand holding her stomach no doubt she still feels awful. "I remember getting sick, and Keith."

"You were poisoned, Savannah. We think someone may have spiked your lemonade."

Her expression suddenly changes and all the color leaves her face. She's remembering...tears pool in her beautiful dark eyes making him break in two. "What? Who would have poisoned me?" she cries, trying to understand what had happened. She wipes the back of her hand across her cheek catching a tear.

"I—I have to go." She moves to the other side of the bed.

Cole jumps to his feet catching her in time as she tumbles forward losing her balance. "Oh!"

"No you're staying here." He scoops her up, placing her back on the bed.

"No you don't understand—" She fights him, but he pins her to the mattress with his body.

She tries to push off his arms but she's too weak to fight for long.

"I do understand. I know York spoke to you."

Her eyes turn to meet his.

"I know he told you about the American and that he doesn't lose his captives. And that he will hunt you until he finds you. But, Savannah," tears are streaming down her cheeks now, "I promise you I will not let him find you."

Her lip quivers. She looks terrified.

"Please, stay and let me protect you." His face is inches from hers. He gently lifts the sheet and dries the corners of her eyes. "You have to trust me."

"I—I do," she whispers without hesitation.

He closes his eyes, letting out a sigh of relief.

"Cole." Her soft voice makes his eyes open. "Did you spend the whole night with me?"

He nods, not sure if he can speak, her trust means more to him then he thought it would.

"Thank you." She lifts her head giving him a soft peck on the cheek.

Her lips are like velvet against his stubble. Every nerve in his body stands at attention. This woman is waking up parts of him that he didn't know he had. He slowly peels his body off hers, knowing he can't hold her like this forever. He pulls her up with him, so they're both sitting up.

"Who do you think drugged me?" She quietly shifts the T-shirt around her legs again.

He clears his throat. "I don't know. I have Keith reviewing the video." He watches as she rubs her head. "Are you feeling okay?"

She nods but he can tell she is lying. "I need a shower and my toothbrush," she mutters with a tiny grimace, "and some Advil."

He opens the drawer next to the bed and hands her two Advils and a bottle of water.

She hesitates taking it.

"It's all right. The water is from my fridge, no one comes in here without a security code and only me and Abigail know it."

"I found something—yesterday I found something. I need to show it to you."

"Okay, Savi, but let me get you to your room and have Abigail help you get showered. Then you can show me."

"All right."

Cole pulls off his shirt, opening his dresser to get into something clean. He catches her gaze reflected in the mirror.

She studies the tattoo on his shoulder. "What does *De Oppresso Liber* mean?"

He had gotten it after his first year. It depicted an eagle holding two arrows wrapped in the American flag with the words written in a horseshoe shape around it. It isn't particularly large, about the size of a hockey puck. A lot of the other guys got huge tattoos wanting to make a statement but he didn't do it for anyone else but himself.

"To free the oppressed," he answers as he slides a clean T-shirt over his head. "All right, up you go."

She lets him help her off the bed and he waits until he knows her legs are steady. He wraps an arm around her waist, letting her lean her weight into him. God, she feels good against him.

\*\*\*

"Where are we?" she asks, looking around.

"The back passage through the house. It's a safety precaution if we ever come under attack." He feels her flinch as they move along the passageway.

"What's in there?"

He moves to the open door and lets her look inside the tiny room with its wall full of books and a floor filled with plush cushions. "Oh, it's so cozy," she whispers in delight.

"It's a room my mother designed when my father would work long hours and the house became too busy. She'd lock herself in here for hours, losing herself in her stories." He smiles, remembering curling up in a ball next to her as she read Moby Dick to him.

"Here we are." He opens a door and helps her through.

She looks baffled that part of her wall is actually a door.

"Can I access that passageway from in here?" she asks eyeing the door as he shuts it behind them.

"Yes," is all he offers her, and she nods, not pressing for more information.

He sits her on the bed and calls for Abigail to come up. He feels her mood change as she looks around her room—her arms wrap around her stomach.

"What's wrong?" he asks, kneeling in front of her.

"I just feel—" her dark eyes stare into his. "In your room, I feel—" She stumbles again.

"Safe?" he asks hoping he isn't wrong.

She nods, dropping her head.

He brushes her hair behind one shoulder. "8986," he whispers.

She looks up at him puzzled.

"If you pull back the panel there where the door meets the wood. The code is 8986. 8987 is the code for my door, if you're feeling scared."

Her eyes soften and she wraps her arms around his neck, pulling him to her.

His body doesn't think twice about wrapping his arms around her and burying his face in her neck. *Oh God she smells amazing.*

She rests her head on the top of his shoulder. "Sorry." She smiles against him. "I must smell terrible."

"No." His voice is hoarse.

She pushes herself back with both hands on his shoulders to stabilize herself. He is still wedged between her legs but she didn't seem to care. Her eyes flicker down to his lips—he wants her to make the first move, not knowing how fragile she might be with all that has happened to her.

God help him, he is losing his control. If he just moved forward a few inches he'd be where he wants to be. He watches as her tongue licks her bottom lip and he hears himself moan.

"Cole, I've never felt—"

"Here I am, Savannah!" Abigail bursts into the room and halts mid step when she sees the two of them. "Oh, I'm so sorry."

Savannah drops her hands and shifts back on the bed. Cole closes his eyes briefly, cursing at their intruder.

"I'll see you in a bit, Savi, ahh…after you have had a chance to clean up and get a bit more rest."

"Thanks."

# *Chapter Eight*

I feel more human after a two-hour nap and a shower. Doctor Rice comes by and checks on me, saying how lucky I am that Keith found me in time. I am also informed that the lemonade was indeed spiked with Visine eye drops. Apparently it can cause a lot of harm if ingested. If I had drunk a second glass I would be a lot worse. There are some cases where people actually died. I appreciate the doctor's explanation but it was upsetting to say the least.

Poor Abigail is in fits apologizing to me. She fusses over my pillow about six times and asks if she can get me anything. I assure her I am fine, I just want to get up and stretch my legs. I get the green light from Abigail but I have to promise to eat and if I felt tired to get rest and not fight it. I promised more for Abigail's sake than for me and seeing her eyes light on up on the way to the kitchen is well worth the promise.

"I'm thinking oatmeal with sliced almonds? It's healthy and will stick with you."

"Sounds good, thanks," I say, sitting on a stool at

the breakfast bar.

"Don't worry, dear, Cole gave orders that all food was to be tossed out and replaced so everything should be fine." My jaw drops.

"All the food? Are you kidding me? You had enough to feed an army!"

"We are the Army," Mark chimes in ignoring my eye roll. He looks me over. "How bad was it?"

"Let's just say I felt like I was knocking on death's door." I shudder at the memory. "But I'm better now."

"Glad to hear it," he says, leaning over and plucking a grape from the bowl. He lowers his voice, "Cole, Keith, Mike and I are the only ones who know what happened and we want to keep it that way until we know what we're dealing with, okay?"

"Okay—sure, but who's Mike?"

"Delta Six. Keith had him watch you while he filled Cole in on the details."

"Oh, have I met him yet?" I try to remember.

"No, but you won't forget him after you do." He smirks. "Let's just say I'm glad you were out of it when he was watching you, he's one scary looking son of a—" Whack! A tea towel hits Mark in the face.

"Mouth, Marcus." Abigail scowls pointing a wooden spoon at him. He laughs as she sets the bowl of oatmeal in front of me along with a glass of orange juice.

\*\*\*

139

Cole doesn't show his face again for the rest of the evening. I am disappointed because I still haven't shared what I found with him. I realize it isn't that important in the general scheme of things. I am feeling pretty beat and pass out around seven, not waking until eight the next morning. Feeling restless, I am told that Doctor Roberts needs to take some personal time off and that we'd pick up where we left off when he returns. In the meantime there was someone on call if I needed to speak with them. I don't.

I spend the next day lounging around my room under Abigail's watch. She won't let me do much— I know she is making sure I'm feeling all right.

The next day my body is more than ready to get back to my daily routine.

"Hey, Savi." Mark appears in the kitchen. "What are you up to today?"

"Oh, you know, got a meeting at eleven, client lunch at noon, presentation at two. Same old, same old."

"Bored are we?"

"I just need to move." I bite into an apple.

"Well, we're running drills up and down the mountain. We're dressed in blue and we'll be firing paintballs so don't go giving any of us black eyes again, all right?"

"No promises," I joke.

"Well, if you are in the mood, give it to the guys with the red arm bands. I'm green." He winks.

\*\*\*

I take the longer path up to the see the horses. I enjoy this route, at one point it gives you the most beautiful view of the lake. I wish I had a camera. I'll have to see if Abigail knows where I can get my hands on one. Perhaps there's a place in town. I take a seat on the grass soaking up the cool mountain air. I lean back on the ground closing my eyes. I love the way the wind blows making a soft wispy sound and how it grows louder as it gets closer.

"Savi." I squeeze my eyes shut. No, they will not break my happy Zen moment.

"Savannah," Mark hisses my name again.

"Can't hear you," I hiss back. I feel the vibration of him crawling up next to me.

"You know how to shoot?" My eyes pop open to see his blue helmet flipped up in the front. "You up for a bit of fun?"

"Hell yeah."

\*\*\*

Before I know it, I am pulling on John's dark blue camo outfit. Thankfully I wore my dark hiking boots, but it doesn't matter because John's pants cover them almost completely. I can see why they picked John he is the only one who is only slightly taller than me. I notice the name tag reads Agent Black.

"Are you still training?" I ask as John shoves the gun in my hand—*Holy hell is it heavy.*

"We're done. Now it's play time. We need someone who can fit down in that gully and into the hole there in the barn." He points at a building. I

141

wouldn't call it a barn exactly. "Once you're in there you need to capture the flag and tuck it in here." He points to a pocket on the vest. "Then run like hell on wheels back to me so we can fly it first."

"Seriously, the US Army plays capture the flag for training?" I laugh.

"It's a great training tool. Trust me, you'll see." He holds the gun up to my eye. "See that right there? Line it up with your target then shoot." I line it up with the can and squeeze the trigger. Pop! Pop! I actually hit it! I jump up and down giving myself my own high five. I look to see Mark smirking. "Great job, it's actually a little scary that you hit that target."

"I play a lot of video games." I shrug.

"If you get shot, you go to a room in the far corner of the building where you'll wait for five minutes than be released out a side door. Meet back here if that happens."

Oh my, there is a lot to take in. "So who else is on our team?" I ask, hoping for Keith.

"We're green. They won't shoot at you. Lean your head forward."

Yeah…that's the green team what about the red? He scoops up my hair and pulls on the helmet.

"Do they know I'm not John?" I start to feel uneasy.

Mark pulls my visor down. "No, it's better this way. Just stick with me." *Wait! What?* "Oh and Savi, don't get shot."

John gives me a thumb up and runs away.

Mark grabs my arm and pulls me low and down

along a path. "Whatever you do don't take your helmet off."

I nod, knowing there isn't a chance in hell that's going to happen.

He gives me quick instructions then points me at the hole in the building. "Heads up and don't shoot green." He pats my back easing me into the opening.

It is a little hard at first with all the clothing but I manage to get in.

*Holy shit!* This is no barn! I just walked into a training room for the friggin' Green Berets! I drop down behind a metal shield. *Okay, Savannah, you can either chicken out or live a little. There are no paparazzi and no daddy to disappoint. Perhaps you'll get a in shot at York.* Oh yes, that did the trick.

I move to my knees and take in my surroundings. I see the flag but I also see a guy with an orange band shimmying down a pipe on the far wall. *Really? A pipe?* Good lord I'm in trouble, and Mark never mentioned a third team! I rest the gun on the top of the shield awkwardly aiming at orange and take the shot. *Shit!* I hit right above his shoulder.

He drops the last fifteen feet and rolls under a stack of crates.

I duck hoping he didn't see me. Okay, think! I see some old scrap metal and make a beeline for it, I hear shots being fired but luckily none hit me. *Okay, keep moving, Savi.* I scan the debris and spot a long cement tube—I run to the side of it and peek inside. I see a flash of an arm and I wait watching his reflection in an old hubcap. I see a blurry

143

movement and make my move.

*Hello, Red.* I grin, raising my gun and popping two in his back.

He turns in disbelief, raising his gun in the air as he walks out of sight.

*Hell yeah!* What a rush this is! My heart is pounding through my chest. *Okay, back in the game, Savi!* I crawl along the side wall, keeping my body low. A series of loud pops pierce my ears. Looking up I see orange splatters. I freeze holding my hands over my head. *Shit, shit, shit, shit!* Thankfully the noise and my helmet muffled my scream. I open my eyes seeing a set of black boots in front of me. Oh shit! I look up seeing the tip of a gun staring at me. I have to fight the flashback that is coming on full force. Then a quick pop hits his shoulder and he is out. I nearly burst out in glee! I give him a little wave as he walks away and notice he's on the red team.

He flips me the bird over his shoulder.

So that makes two red down and one orange that spread nine bullets at the wall. I keep moving. I finally look over and see I'm just a few feet from the flag. Screw it! I jump to my feet and sprint toward the flag, I leap and my hand just brushes over it as I feel three pops to my lower stomach. Noooo! I fall to the ground, now thankful for all the gear. I feel the paintballs but it doesn't hurt. I jump to my feet—I have to look like I do this all the time.

Oh no, I'm supposed to know where to go. *Damn it!* I hear some laughter off to my left, *Thank God.* I walk in seeing the guys with their visors up cracking jokes about how they got shot. I take a seat against the wall, fighting the urge to cross my legs. I look around and try to sit like them. I spread my legs and lean on an elbow. I feel ridiculous—this is not comfortable. Someone on the orange team comes and sits next to me, his arm and chest dripping green paint. I wonder if Mark shot him. He holds his fist out to me. *Oh, right. Fist bumps.* I bump him back and give a nod. I notice he doesn't remove his visor either. I wish I knew who he is but his name tag is now covered in green. I glance up at the screen where the times are counting down for each guy. This place is seriously cool—scary as hell—but frigging cool.

"You have fun last night Black?" I feel an elbow to the ribs by orange, who points at Keith.

I nod hoping he won't ask me another question.

Keith looks at me strangely then shrugs as he stands.

"Heads up guys, Lopez says he saw Savannah by the stables." I freeze. "So stay clear of that area."

Everyone nods and I find myself mimicking them. I feel a little loved that they are watching out for me.

"Is she wearing a dress or pants today? I want to know if I should be on high or low ground," York calls out, making me tense again.

"When will you learn, York? She's just not into you," Keith shoots back with a sigh. "Leave the poor woman alone."

I jump to my feet when I see my time is up. I race out of the room, not wanting to hear anymore. Just as I'm crouching under a table a loud siren goes off and people start walking out of the building.

\*\*\*

As soon as I'm outside I see why the siren went off. No way! I see that the orange team is flying the flag. They are all cheering, holding beers in the air.

Everyone comes together removing their helmets. I almost lose it when I see that the orange teammate with the dripping green on his arm and chest sitting right next to me is Cole.

"Game's over, Black," York shouts. "Helmet." He knocks on my head.

*Oh shit, oh shit, oh shit.* Finally Mark comes to my side with John. Everyone stops and looks at me, then John, then me some more…

"I recruited one more." Mark laughs, nudging me to remove the helmet. I unclip it, pulling it off slowly making my messy hair fall all around me. The looks on their faces are priceless.

"Hi." I beam at them.

"Wait," Keith holds up his finger at me, "was that you on the ground right before I got shot?"

I smile and repeat the wave.

"Oh my God." He starts to laugh but stops when he sees Cole's face.

"That wasn't smart, Mark," Cole bites out. "We'll discuss this later."

Mark moves in front of me, blocking Cole's stare. "He just has a job to do. Don't worry, he's not mad at you." He grins. "Well fuck me sideways, how much fun was that?"

"It beats a day at the office." I laugh high-fiving him. "I have to admit I was going to kill you when I saw the inside of the 'barn.' You sent me to war!"

"Pretty cool though, right?" I burst out laughing again.

"Yeah, it will be something I'll never forget. Oh wow. Thanks, Mark. I kind of needed that."

"Anytime. All right, I'm going to go face the heat." He hands me a beer, then leaves to face the music with Cole.

I see Keith coming to my side. "How much trouble is Mark in?" I ask.

"Cole and Mark are tight. Normally he'd get watch duty for a night but now—" he stops himself, "he may get a little more."

"Why?" I fumble with the beer cap maybe it isn't a twist off. He takes out his wallet and removes a sliver looking card. No, it's actually a bottle opener? Cool. He flips the lid off with a smile.

"Handy little thing," he says, tucking it away but not before I notice the letter S engraved on it. I wonder if they all have one. He waits till it stops foaming and hands it back.

"Thanks."

"We're cracking down on the rules now." He gives me shrug.

"Ah, I see. Because I'm luring the American closer." His face flinches. "It's okay, Keith. I get that I'll be here for a while and I'm on the top of 'the American's most wanted to re-kidnap list.'" I sigh, taking a sip of the beer. "Any word about the poison?"

"Cole is the one you should be talking to about that. Sorry, Savannah, but we have rules."

***

The conversation around the dinner table is pretty interesting tonight. Cole has yet to join us.

Abigail is floored that I had participated in 'the battle,' as they call it.

"You think that was a wise idea, Mark?" She narrows her brow at him.

"It was worth the punishment." He winks at me.

I love that Mark took one for me so I could have a little fun. I'll have to make it up to him somehow. I heard that he also took all the heat not wanting to John to get in trouble as well.

"What you get anyway?" Keith asks, chewing on a roll.

"Three nights at the peak." He shrugs.

"Shitty," Keith responds.

"The Peak?" I ask, not following.

"It's the worst post to be at and it's normally reserved for the rookies," Keith explains, "especially this time of year with the wind and rain. Makes my bones ache just thinking of it."

"Oh, Mark, I'm sorry."

"Don't be. The look on the guys' faces when you took off your helmet is worth every minute up there on that cold, cold hill!" He holds his beer up at me. "To Agent Black, someone not to turn your back on." He eyes Paul, who I had hit two times in the back. Everyone raises their glasses to me as we all start laughing.

"So, when is the next battle?" I'm joking but everyone grows quiet. "Come on, you said I could shoot."

Cole comes to the head of the table looking less than impressed. "Sorry I'm late, Abigail. Dinner looks great." He glances around the table. "Please don't stop the conversation on my account."

"Tell me, Savi, how to did you manage to pop me in the back?" Paul bravely asks.

"Hubcap. I could make out your movements in the reflection."

"Impressive." He chuckles.

"Paul," Cole wipes his mouth with his napkin, "tell Savannah how you hurt your neck."

Paul sighs loudly. I guess I won't like this. "Keith dropped from twenty feet above me, slipped a disc in my neck. Hurts like hell when it rains."

"Keith, tell Savannah about your knee." Cole turns to where Keith is sitting.

"I got plowed from the side by Mike. We both fell ten feet off a beam; he landed on my knee."

Cole points to Mark. "Left shoulder."

Mark turns, pulling up his shirt revealing a jagged scar across his shoulder.

I gasp, covering my mouth. It looks terrible.

"Fell on a metal peg, got dragged a few yards. Tore right through my gear."

Cole focuses back on me. "My point, Savannah, is all this happened during our training in paintball. We didn't know it was you in Black's uniform today. Any one of us could have seriously injured you. There will be no other battles that you will be involved in."

# *Chapter Nine*

Cole watches everyone go their own way after dinner. No one seems up for socializing tonight. He is fine with that. He is still reeling from what happened at training.

John appears and drops his duffel bag at the door next to Cole's and signals he is ready.

Cole nods at him and heads for the stairs, knowing that what he is about to say isn't going to be easy—at least not for him.

Savannah's door is open. He peeks in and sees her sitting in front of the fireplace, the glow of the flame casting shadows on her face. Her hair is in a messy bun held up with a pen. A few pieces have come loose and she looks sexy as she is leaning over, studying a photo.

"Savi," he says quietly so as not to scare her.

She glances up, giving him a sexy smile.

"May I come in?"

"Sure."

He walks in, seeing papers and photos fanned out in front of her.

"Is this what you wanted to show me before?"

"Yes, I found something." She hands him the picture she was just studying. It is of her father at a charity event. "Look who he's toasting with." She points to the bracelet. "He knows the girl who took my picture in the pub."

Well he'll be damned, she found something.

"This was taken four months after my kidnapping. They must be close because my father doesn't smile like that with just anyone."

Huh—interesting.

She tucks a piece of hair behind her ear. "I tracked down the number of the charity event coordinator. I've met him before. I thought I could call him."

"No, Savi—"

"I won't give my name or anything, but I could get the guest list. I've been to these things enough times to know who's who and I could start the process of elimination."

"I'll get you the list," he says a little harder than he intended to.

"Fine." She dismisses his tone.

"What's this?" he asks, picking up an article about a woman who was kidnapped.

"Well I been researching *Los Sirvientes Del Diablos* and found a few stories of the victims that were actually returned unharmed. Shocking how few there were." She rubs her stomach. "Their ransoms were huge—like a couple million. One woman was only gone a month and they got one point five for her." She sighs. "Cole, my ransom just doesn't make sense. Their pattern changed with me, why? I'm wracking my brain—why was The

American involved in my case?"

"Okay, slow down. This is a great find," he says holding up the picture studying it. "I'll make the call and get the guest list. This is all one giant puzzle and you'll go mad asking all the questions at once. You need to pick one and start there. If you hit a dead end, put it aside and pick up another. A path will soon start to show itself, then a picture will start to form. Have you had any more flashbacks?"

She bites her lip, debating telling him.

"I remember my first proof of life," she finally whispers, "when I first met Maria." She looks really uncomfortable. She bends down picking up a small piece of paper. "Here's the number for the charity." Her face looks flushed and her eyes are watery. "His name is Gary, he's really friendly."

"Hey, what's wrong?" he asks, stepping toward her.

She shakes her head, handing him the paper. "Some flashbacks are harder than others." She lets out a shaky breath.

Before he could ask any more questions John sticks his head in the door. "Hey, Savi." He grins at her, "Logan, the chopper will be here in fifteen. We're good to go."

"You're leaving?" She looks up quickly, her eyes startled.

"We got a lead that needs to be followed in TJ."

She shakes her head stepping away from him. He doesn't like it when she does that.

"Who's all going?"

"John, Paul, Mark and I."

"For how long?" She looks unhappy, almost nervous.

"Three to four days at the most."

Her eyes go wide as she processes his words. "Savannah, it's—"

"I don't want you to go," she blurts out making his lungs freeze. "I-I don't want you to go, Cole."

He reaches out, pulling her to him.

She goes willingly into his arms.

He can feel her trembling as her arms tighten around him and he breathes in deeply, her apple shampoo making his heart ache.

"Don't go," she whispers.

"Ahh, Savi, I don't want to but I have to," he whispers into her hair.

"It's not safe, what if—"

"We don't use what ifs. We check in once in the morning and again at night. I'll be back in a few days."

She pulls away slightly, looking up at him. "Promise me you'll be back."

He knows he shouldn't, he never would have before, but looking into her eyes—feeling the way he does—he cannot stop the words.

"I promise."

She closes her eyes, leaning her head on his chest.

He reaches up, removing the pen from her hair, and runs his fingers through it. "You have no idea how hard it is to walk away right now."

"Then don't."

Oh god, she's killing him. His brain is firing off so many things but he cares about only one.

She lifts her head almost like she can hear him. "Cole."

"Yes."

"Kiss me."

He dives down, pressing into her soft lips.

She wraps her arms around his neck pushing her body into his. The first swipe of her tongue makes him dive in deeper and she moans as she becomes jelly in his arms.

He can't get enough of her. She tastes so sweet. One hand travels down to her waist. His fingers run along her velvet skin, making his knees weak. She feels so tiny in his arms; he has to remember to be gentle. His hands slide around to her back, then down over her ass, giving it a firm squeeze.

She nibbles at his lower lip, making him painfully hard. "Cole," she leans back letting her hands travel down his stomach.

He shivers, pulling her back to his lips—he needs to taste her.

"Logan, choppers are here," John shouts from down the hall.

She doesn't stop the kiss, so he puts everything he has into it until finally finding the strength to pull away, leaving her off balance.

"See you in a few days." He kisses her once more, quickly, unable to hang around any longer. He knows he has to get away from her. She is like a drug, sucking him backwards.

"Be safe," he hears her whisper. Damn it, he turns, giving her a smile than leaves.

*You've crossed the forbidden line, asshole!* He smiles a little though as he rushes down the staircase, her taste lingering on his tongue. His head is swimming as he squints, making his way toward the chopper, flinging his bag inside, and jumping into his seat.

Mark gives him a questioning eyebrow then joins his grin like he just figured out where he was.

Cole closes his eyes, letting himself have a moment relishing the past ten minutes.

***

I flop down on my bed, staring at the ceiling. I want to laugh, cry, and scream—my body is firing sparks all over. I have never been kissed like that before—or was it that I've never felt like this about a man before? Either way it is amazing. Now he has four days to think about it. What if he realizes it is a mistake? I'm technically a client. *No, don't go there, Savi. Enjoy your high.* I cross my arms over my head, smelling him on my clothes as I close my eyes and drift off to sleep.

***

Autumn Ball, Manhattan, 2014. I hit enter and my fingers strum the desk. I have decided that my first task is to find out who the silver bracelet woman is, why she took my picture, and why she was following me. Everyone is a suspect, so I wonder if it was a coincidence that she was there the same the day I was taken? I decide to Google the events that I know my father would normally attend. The Autumn Ball was a few days ago. I click on images, scrolling through six before I spot my father. He's shaking hands with some people in one photo, in another he is standing at a podium, in a few pictures he is with the Chief of Police who is making a speech.

I keep clicking and clicking and it becomes pretty tedious but I decide to keep at it. Just as I am about to give up and try another tactic, something catches my eye. I lean in, trying to get a better look. I click on the image to make it bigger, then click print, grabbing it from the tray the minute the machine lets go. Holding it under the light I'm able to make out my father's table off to the right of the picture. He is sitting beside a woman. His body is blocking hers, but I can see her wrist and there it is—that bracelet again. I rub my head, trying to take in what I'm seeing. Not only did this woman take a picture of me, but at two different events since I was kidnapped she's been photographed with my father. What the hell? I need a break to clear my head. I know something isn't right here and I'm not really sure what to make of the whole thing. I need time to mull it over. I scribble down the number for the event coordinator and leave the room.

\*\*\*

I find myself in the kitchen measuring out ingredients for my mother's famous chocolate chip cookies. I tripled the batch, knowing one would hardly be enough. I love baking; I love how my brain goes into idle mode and lets my hands do all the work.

"The guys mentioned that they smelt something good, but I think I may have died and gone to heaven." Keith snatches a cookie off the cooling rack, shoving it in his mouth. "Mmmmm, warm cookies."

I laugh, pouring him a glass of milk.

"Thanks." He takes a swig. "Damn, those are good, Savi!" He takes another.

"Thanks, I love to bake."

"I love that you love to bake." He grins.

I transfer the last twelve cookies to the rack, not looking at him.

"Any word from the guys?" I ask casually.

He nods, setting his empty glass in the sink.

"Checked in this morning; they crossed the border and are heading to the location now."

"Cole said they check in twice." I want him to know Cole spoke to me about it, so I showed him I know about the check-ins.

"Yes, they'll check in again when they're back at the safe house." He pauses, watching me. I pretend not to notice then he clears his throat. "Should be around seven our time." He grabs a few more cookies. "I got to go get some stuff done, I'll see you later."

\*\*\*

The dinner table has a few new faces. I'm assuming they step in when Cole's group is gone. I notice York takes over Cole's seat at the head of the table. He can't possibly be in charge while Cole's away, can he? The thought makes me ill.

"Savi," York greets me with a superior tone, "meet Two, Three, and Four." He waves at the new guys at the table.

Two rolls his eyes. "We also have names. I'm Adam, this is Dell, and that is Quinn. Nice to finally meet you; we've heard all good things."

"Yeah like you rocked it at paintball," Quinn says winking. "Heard Cole was livid though."

"It was fun." I grin remembering the rush. "He was pretty upset, but he cooled off."

"You're not scared of him are you?" Adam asks, amazed. I don't want to act like I know about Cole's background story. I know there is a lot more to him than that.

"Of Cole? No, why would I be?"

Adam sits his fork down. "I've watched him snap a man's neck as he strolled by like it was nothing." I close my eyes at the image. "He's not exactly warm and fuzzy."

"I spent seven months with men that made me beg for my next meal and beat me so I could hardly walk. So no, Cole doesn't scare me at all. He's been nothing but nice to me."

"Point taken," Adam adds quickly. "If it counts, I really like your cookies."

I laugh, seeing York look a little irritated. I ignore him.

"Thanks. So what is it that you guys normally do?"

"We're normally traveling and aren't often at the house," Dell answers. "So it's nice to have a break. We step in when Team Blackstone is called out."

Blackstone…"How often is Blackstone called out?" I ask, sipping my wine.

"Depends. They're the Alpha team here at Shadows. They handle the high risk stuff and they're called out, oh, maybe once or twice a month." Dell takes a swig of beer. "We're at a level five because of your case. Things are a bit tense along the border. *Los Sirvientes Del Diablos* are stirring up a lot of dust since you dropped off their radar."

"I still don't understand why I'm such a big deal to them. You'd think they'd cut their losses and move on. Christ, it's just fifty grand!"

"No, Savannah, you're worth more to them than just fifty grand. I mean they are blackmailing—"

"Dell!" York snaps, making me knock over my empty water glass.

*What the hell?*

"Sorry, Quinn, ah…did you catch the game last night?" Dell tries lamely to change the topic.

"Oh no," I hold my hand up to York, "you don't get to shut him up. This case involves me and I get to hear all the details. Dell—out with it!"

"Not a word, Dell," York warns.

"Stop, York," I hiss. "Who are they blackmailing? My father? Lynn? Why? With what?"

Dell shakes his head. "I'm really sorry, Savannah, I shouldn't have said anything—"

"Like hell you shouldn't"

"Savannah, enough." York stands, placing his hands on the table, staring me down.

I stand, meeting his stare. I can feel my hands

vibrating with anger.

"Shut your mouth."

Abigail suddenly leaves the table.

"Pardon me?" The table grows silent. "Why are you angry? Because Dell's didn't trap me on the patio to tell me this?"

His eyes narrow down at me as he clenches his fists.

"Stop, or I'll make you shut up." He bites out each word carefully.

I raise my chin feeling my emotions change. I need to pull off a huge lie.

"You. Don't. Scare. Me." I say as I hold my eyes steady on his.

"I should." A few of the guys rise to their feet ready to step in if need be.

I smile sweetly. "You'll never fill that chair the way he does." I toss my napkin on the table. "Excuse me, guys."

I make way down the hallway—my high is quickly being replaced with the fear I said I didn't have. I look down at my wobbly legs and run smack into something hard. I snap back but I get jolted forward into the arms of the biggest, scariest, tattooed man I've ever laid eyes on. His arms are huge; he looks like he bathes in steroids. He is tatted up from his smoothly shaved head to I'm guessing his toes. Holy mother of shit.

"Umm," is all I could get out before I find my voice. "I really, really hope you're Mike." He grins widely.

"Yup." He helps me steady myself. "I got word York was at you again."

I roll my eyes at him. "That man hates me. I bet he'd buy me a plane ticket to The American himself if he could get away with it."

He laughs loudly. "You really get under his skin, and we all love it." His face goes serious. "Did he threaten you?"

I look down. The last thing I need is this getting back to Cole.

"Look—we had words. He'll cool off, and tomorrow's another day." I can see him thinking.

"You know Cole can watch the security tapes of the house from where he's at right?"

"Let's not give him a reason to lose focus on the job he's doing, okay?"

He nods his head—seems like he agrees with me.

"There's a radio in the kitchen by the intercom. If you change it to our numbers you can get us directly. Seven is Keith and I'm six. You need us, you call us, deal?"

"Okay, deal. Thanks Mike."

***

The next day I avoid York as much as possible. I hear Cole's team finally checked in at eleven the night before. I can tell things aren't going exactly to plan by Keith's tone when I enter the kitchen this morning. He and Abigail both look stressed, although they assure me everything is fine. I don't press it.

Abigail and I decide to have dinner in the entertainment room and watch some of our favorite

161

movies.

"So when does your sister arrive?" I ask, stabbing a piece of lettuce with my fork.

"In two days. She'll be here for Thanksgiving and stay for a few months. That's pretty normal for her; we're really close."

Lynn flashes in my memory. I quickly tuck that emotion aside. "Cole's parents will be here too and you'll get to meet his mother, Sue. She's lovely, warmhearted, and a pretty smart lady. She's quick and sees a lot."

"Living here you would have to be," I joke. "How did you even start working here, Abigail? I mean, it's not like a position here would be listed in a local employment ad in the newspaper."

"No, definitely not," she laughs. "I started working for the Logans when Cole was six. As he got older and didn't need a nanny anymore they moved me here. I love it, these boys are like the kids I never had."

"Mark's your favorite isn't he?" I ask, knowing I'm right.

"I do have a weak spot for Mark mainly because he and Cole have been best friends for about twenty-three years. Mark's mother wasn't around much and his father left when he was born so he always looked at me like a parent." She sets her plate on the couch and turns to look at me, grinning. "Can you keep a secret?"

"Of course." I'm excited for a little girl talk.

"Mark met a girl a little while ago. They've been talking. Her name is Melanie. She works in town so one day I decided to check her out, you know, make

162

sure she's good enough for my boy. Well, I found her working at the coffee shop. She's tall, slim with red hair—sweet little thing, and I did something." She stops, giving me a guilty face.

"What did you do?" I can barely wait to find out.

"I introduced myself to her we ended up talking for twenty minutes after her shift and I invited her to Thanksgiving dinner." She cups her mouth. "He's going to kill me!"

"Oh my God." I burst out laughing. "That's classic! Do you think she'll show?"

"I do." She wipes a tear away. "Oh lord, Savi, what do I do?"

"Maybe Mark will invite her and you'll be off the hook."

"She did mention he was hinting around—"

"Wait! Back up a second." I shake my head. "I don't understand how you are able to invite someone to come here to the house for dinner?"

"Oh no, sorry, Daniel's best friend, Zack, has a restaurant and bar here in town. They have great food. Plus it's a huge break for me."

"Oh, I see. Well maybe we can blame John." We both burst out laughing. Poor John. He got in some shit too over the paintball game. Guess Mark didn't take all the blame.

"Perhaps." Her face shifts expression. "These boys work really hard and they do a lot of the things that average person can't. Holidays, no matter how big or small, I try to make sure that they are celebrated because they deserve to have some down time to just be themselves." She raises her eyebrow at me. "I think that's why I invited Melanie. I want

Mark to find someone that he can someday come home to. So I'm just giving him a little push." She chuckles. "Isn't that what parents do?"

"I think it's sweet." Oh, I just love Abigail, and I can't wait to meet her sister June.

# Chapter Ten

A pounding headache wakes me out of a dead sleep and I crawl out of bed feeling lightheaded. I make my way to the kitchen knowing Abigail has a stash of Advil in her personal cabinet above the stove. I down three and drink two glasses of water then sink into a chair, propping my head on my hands. A movement to my left has me fully alert.

"Well, if it isn't Savannah Miller, case number 22571," York mutters, leaning against the wall holding a beer. I immediately get the impression it isn't his first.

I'm not in the mood for him, so I stand and move toward the hallway, but he slides over, making me change route to the living room instead.

"You're pretty quiet now, aren't you, pretty lady?" He follows behind me then steps in my way. I stop trying to go around him and head for the stairs, going down two at a time.

I don't know where I am going; I just don't want to be alone with him. I slip into an office, shutting the door behind me, but his shoe stops it from closing and he slams it open. "Oh, Savi, you don't

165

seem so brave now."

"Move, York," I order, raising my chin and squaring my shoulders as he steps toward me at the same time, taking a sip of his beer.

"Or what? You weigh a buck fifty soaking wet. I could blow and you'd fall over."

I hold up my hands as I feel the desk hit the back of my thighs. "Not so brave when you don't have your knight here, hey?"

"I don't know what you're talking about," I whisper, feeling like an ass. What a stupid line that is.

"So you're saying that you and Cole aren't fucking?"

I cringe at his tone.

"Well, that changes things then." Before I know what is happening he yanks me to him crushing his lips to mine.

*Oh yuck!* The mix of beer and his cologne nearly brings my dinner up. I push, pound, and kick trying to get him off but he has me pinned. His hands start to roam. O*h shit*. I shove my knee up and drive it in his crotch just as I bite down hard on his lower lip, he cries out as he falls backwards. I leap over him and dash for the hallway not getting three feet before his arm snags around my waist slamming me to the wall. Air rushes out of my lungs from the impact.

He grips the top of my arms hard, lifting me off my feet looking angrier than I've ever seen him before. Blood drips from his lip, I got him pretty good. "You're fair game, Savannah. There hasn't been a woman like you here before—young and real pretty. I rather like it." His grip tightens on my arms and I can't help but cry out. It only makes him squeeze tighter. "I think I'm going to claim you as mine."

*Oh, what? Seriously? We hate each other!*

"Get your hands off of me!" I cry.

He laughs as he drops me to my feet pressing his erection into my stomach.

"Screw off, York!" I hit his chest hard but he reaches down, ripping my shirt open as he traps my arms at my sides, slowly running his gaze down my body. I am so thankful I wore a bra to bed tonight. He lets go with one hand to undo his belt.

"Stop it! No, York!" I start to cry when I realize he actually intends to follow through. "Please, York, no, don't do this."

He is fumbling with the buckle, cursing at me to shut up.

I take the moment and knee him again, hard. This time he falls backward, tumbling into the wall. I run in a full sprint up the stairs across the living room to the other set of stairs in the entryway. I wrap my ripped shirt around me when I get close to the bedrooms and hear Abigail's door open just as I reach my door. I slam the door, locking it behind me, sliding down to the floor sobbing and out of breath. Unable to think straight, I don't know what to do. I haven't been that terrified since I was back in my prison room.

"No," I hiss squeezing my eyes shut. *Not now. I can't go back there. Stay in the present!*

"Savannah," York whispers from outside my door.

My eyes pop open and heart pounds in my throat.

"Open the door." He rattles the door knob. "I can hear you breathing." His voice is oddly calm, considering he has had two hard blows to the crotch. "You know I can pick this lock in a heartbeat." I scramble off the floor, hopping to my feet and frantically feeling around the wooden panel for the key code. I hear the door handle rattle again. Finally the panel flips down and I punch in the code in 8986 twice before I get it right and the door pops open and I slip into the darkness.

My trembling fingers feel my way around the wall there must be a light switch but I don't want to chance anyone seeing me. I find the little library room that belongs to Cole's mother. When the door closes behind me a tiny glow shines from a light in the corner and I flop down on the pillows, curl into a ball, and cry myself to sleep.

***

"Ouch," I whimper as I roll onto my back. My eyes feel dry and puffy as they adjust to the soft glow. Gold lines make a beautiful Indian pattern along the ceiling. I gasp, realizing I'm not in my room as the memories of last night come rushing back to me. I lift my hands to cover my face and feel the pain in my arms. Looking down at the pair of black and blue hand prints—one on each arm—I can't believe that I escaped him. Shit! I scramble to stand on shaky legs, My head is fuzzy, making me retch as I try to let the dizziness pass. I sneak out of

the library and stand at the door to my room. I put
my ear to the door listening to hear if anyone is in
there. It sounds clear, so I punch in the code and
slip inside.

Everything looks okay. Nothing has been moved,
my unmade bed reminding me of what almost
happened. My stomach drops when I see the time—
ten thirty! Oh God, I hope Abigail hasn't come up
to check on me yet. I rush into the shower after
grabbing a blue tank top with a grey sweater that
tied in the front. Knowing there will be no blow
drying my hair today because of my arms, it will
have to dry wavy. I stand in front of my door trying
to convince myself to go downstairs and face
everyone. I am beyond mortified that someone
might see the security tapes. I need to figure
something out.

"Good morning, Savannah." Dell smiles as he
reaches for the OJ in the fridge. "Sorry about last
night."

"You have nothing to be sorry for, Dell," I
reassure him. "Where is everyone?"

"If you mean, York, he's been in Cole's office
all morning. I think he's nursing a hangover
because he's hurting today." He laughs. "Serves
him right. He gets such a power trip whenever
Cole's gone."

Good. I hope his balls are swollen to the size of
grapefruits.

"Yeah he sure does," I mutter. "Hey, do you
have any pain medication that's stronger than
Advil?"

He stops mid bite.

169

"Why, did you hurt yourself?"

I look away not wanting to lie but my arms are really starting to ache.

"Isn't there any goddamn ice in this place?" York yells from down the hall.

My stomach turns as fear kicks in.

"You know what, never mind." I head for the stairs and up to my room. Once my door is locked I start to shake. *How am I going to live in this house with him?* I crawl onto my bed and concentrate on my breathing.

*** 

"Savi." Abigail shakes my arm.

"Ouch," I cry out my eyes pop open seeing her puzzled face.

"Sorry, but it's time for dinner."

I roll back over wincing in pain. "I'm not hungry."

"Savannah Miller," she whips out her mother tone, "I know for a fact that you haven't eaten a thing today. I don't know what's going on with you, but I will not leave this room unless you are with me."

I sigh pulling, myself up quickly before she can touch me again.

"Care to share," she asks as we walk down the hallway her expression questioning.

"Not really," I whisper, pulling my sweater tighter around me. "Sorry." I feel badly not being able to share what happened but it's still too raw and God knows what she would do.

170

We walk into the living room to find Dell and Quinn talking to Cole. My stomach jumps; they're back! Abigail winks as she walks by—oh man, she's good! But as my excitement rises my nerves do too.

"Hey, you." Mark leans in giving me a peck on the cheek as he hands me a martini. "You look like you could use something stronger than wine tonight."

I took a long sip of the heavenly drink.

"Guess I was right," he states.

"When did you guys get in?" I ask watching Cole's back he still hasn't spotted me.

"Thirty minutes ago." He shakes his head. "It was a rough trip. Glad we were able to come home early."

"Rough?"

"Honestly, you don't want to know."

I nod. I probably don't.

"Come on." He tugs on my arm, making me flinch as he walks me over to Dell, Quinn, and Cole. My eyes scan the room for York.

Cole looks tired but when he catches sight of me the smile that runs across his face makes my stomach warm. "Hey." His eyes dance over me.

"Welcome back."

"As promised," he whispers so only I can hear him. I can't help the smile that sneaks out as I take a drink.

"You." Keith points at me rushing up to our group. "You want to explain how you dropped off the radar this morning?"

Fuck! I shake my head, looking around. Luckily

no one is paying attention. Abigail has turned some music on and it drowns out his voice.

Cole looks at me then at him.

"I-I got up early and went for a walk by the lake."

"You're a shitty liar, Savi."

"Look, can we not do this now?" My eyes plead with him to drop it. I feel my goddamn eyes starting to water. Really, can someone throw me a fucking bone here?

"Just be thankful Dell said he saw you, or there would have been a search party looking for your ass." He suddenly steps forward giving me an unexpected hug.

"Don't do that again, or I'll put a tracking chip in your arm." I let out a long breath, then he pulls away eyeing me, then huffs and walks off.

"Seems we missed some action while we were away," Mark chimes in. I look up at Cole who is watching me carefully.

"You don't even know the half of it," Quinn mutters. I shake my head at him. God, why won't people talk about something else?

"Hey, boys," Abigail calls out, "could you help me?"

Cole doesn't leave; instead he moves a little closer he bends down and his mouth hovers at my ear.

His hot breath makes me shiver.

"There wasn't a moment when I was gone that I didn't think of you, Savannah. You're like a goddamn drug that's making me weak at the knees." My breathing catches as my heart beats away doing a happy strum. "It's taking every ounce of my self-control not to kiss you right now."

"I wouldn't stop you," I say before I can even think about it.

He steps away shaking his head smiling.

"Umm, Cole I need to—"

"Heard you were MIA, Savi," York's voice makes my blood run cold. "You want to explain where you were?" My entire body is locked in place all I could do is stare at my drink.

"What happened to you?" Cole asks, moving the attention off me.

"Tripped; fucking cat."

Ha! I want to knee him again for blaming poor Scoot but my body betrays me and I stand immobile listening to his lies.

"How'd everything go while we were away?"

"Same shit, different day, right, Savi?" He wraps his arm around me pulling me painfully to his side grinning. "We had one of our little spats, but we made up. Didn't we, pretty lady?" He makes my skin crawl.

"Well, good," Cole says, taking a drink of his brandy, but I see him look at York strangely. "Glad to hear it." I try to move away but York's fingers dig into my hip.

"Cole," Mike calls out, "a minute?"

"Be right back." Cole replies heading off to join Mike.

*No! I don't want to be here. I want to go back to my little safe spot in the library.*

York leans in. "You speak a word of what happened last night and I'll personally hand you over to The Cartels myself." He kisses my temple and walks away.

I wrap my arms around my stomach, downing the rest of my drink.

Mark shows up handing me another, he just watches as I finish half of it in one swallow. "Mark," I whisper, "do you have any idea when you're going away next?"

"Possibly next week but it's not set in stone."

I feel the blood drain from my face.

"I don't think I can stay here."

Mark drops down to my eye level. "What? How can you say that? What are you talking about?" His eyes are searching mine, but I feel numb. I'm shutting down.

"Dinner is ready," Abigail announces.

I turn walking toward the table.

\*\*\*

Everyone is deep in conversation. Paul is talking about the men they encountered at a house they cleared out.

I, on the other hand, am very aware of York sitting directly across from me.

Cole finally joins us sitting on my right. Abigail was on my left as usual.

Mark replaces my empty glass with another.

My head is swimming; no food and two martinis cause quite the head trip.

"What number is that?" York asks, pointing to my martini glass.

I lick my dry lips, picking up my glass and

174

taking a long sip, keeping my gaze on his as I give him a silent 'fuck you.'

Cole looks between the two of us trying to understand what is going on. Cole's smart enough not to ask me in public.

"So, Abigail, what time does Aunt June arrive tomorrow?" Mark asks.

"Seven." Her face perks up. "You're picking her up at the bus stop right?"

He nods.

I want to ask if I can go along but I decide not to push my luck considering later on that evening we'll be heading into town for Thanksgiving dinner anyway. I'm excited to see some of the town. Hell, I just want to see past the first set of gates.

"Aren't you feeling well?" Cole is leaning over when I look up. "You haven't touched your plate."

I glance down. "Just tired," I fib, picking up my fork and popping a green bean in my mouth.

After the table is cleared everyone moves out to the living room for drinks. I spot Dell by himself pouring a drink and I want to make my move and corner him for more details about the possible blackmail comment he let slip when Mark steps in my path.

"You care to explain yourself?"

"Not really."

"Okay, what happened while we were gone?" He waits but I can't find the words. I can't even think up a good lie. He grabs my arm and pulls me to Cole's office closing the door behind us then he stands crossing his arms. "I've got all night."

*Ouch!* "I don't want to be here anymore," I blurt

out.

"Bullshit," he tosses back.

"I don't feel safe."

"Yes, you do." His eyes narrow in on mine. "At least you did right up till we left. So what happened while we were gone?"

I shake my head. I don't know what to do.

"Savannah, did someone hurt you?"

I let out a sob and put my hand over my mouth, wanting to spill everything but scared to.

He stands in front of me holding my arms.

I flinch, looking away.

"The men in this house are part of a tight group. We all have to be able to trust one another. If there is something we need to know you have to tell us before we bring any more people to this safe house."

*Oh God.* I start to cry harder.

"He told me he'd hand me to The Cartels if I tell anyone." The words are out before I can stop them.

"Do you think Cole would ever let that happen? He's my brother, and I can honestly say this is the first time I've seen him head over heels for a woman."

I feel myself blush.

"He is one scary guy and knows a lot of dangerous people. No one in their right mind would cross him."

I nod but can't help thinking, *York did.*

"Okay, so that being said—" his voice suddenly changes, "who hurt you?"

I breathe in a sharp breath. "I'll tell you, but you need to help me erase the tape. I don't want Cole to see it."

"No deal, Savi, I'd get fired for that."

My anger rises. "Then show me where they are and I'll do it."

"I can't let you on his computer. Besides, Cole has the tightest security system you can buy and he has a ridiculous number of passwords."

Well, that I believe. "I don't want Cole to see me like that. He may not want me—" I stop myself, shaking my head.

"Savannah." He grips my arms.

This time I cry out.

He lets go as he eyes narrow in on me. He quickly tugs at my sweater but I step back. "Savannah," he says again and reaches over, yanking it off my shoulders.

I try to cover up the marks, but he bats my hands away.

"Holy fucking shit!" he snaps. He turns me to the side getting a better look at the perfect handprints then steps back running his hands through his hair and covering his mouth as he thinks. Suddenly he moves to Cole's computer and starts typing away.

"Please, Mark," I beg him, "don't." I pull my sweater back on as I race up to the front of the desk. I knew he knew the passwords! "Mark!" He isn't listening. "Please, please, please, stop." Then I see his face drop. I watch in horror. It's like watching a train heading for a car full of people who can't get out. I know when he gets to the part where York throws me up against the wall, the color drains from his face. He slowly stands and walks toward the door. I throw myself in front of it.

"Mark, please, I promise I'll tell Cole. Just wait until after tomorrow."

"Savannah, please move." His tone is eerie.

I stare up at this 6'2" man who could easily pick me up and move me aside in the blink of an eye but he doesn't. He's asking me to move. I place my hands on his shoulders just as he did mine.

"Mark, Abigail is so excited to see her sister. This will ruin the mood in the house and I'm so tired of the attention being on me. Please do nothing until after Thanksgiving dinner. Do it for Abigail and the rest of the house. They deserve a break."

His eyes squeeze shut while he thinks.

I think he's going to say no but his eyes flicker open showing me he understands.

"You have until tomorrow night. If you don't tell him by then, I will."

Oh thank God. I drop my head. "Okay, yes. Thank you."

"Are you hurt anywhere else? Anywhere at all?" He looks so upset that I want to hug him.

"No, I promise." I wipe my cheeks dry wanting to reassure him. "It's just my arms. He was drunk."

"So he didn't trip over Scoot and bite his lip," he mutters more to himself than to me.

"No. Do you believe that he would hand me over to The Cartels?" He runs his hand over the back of his neck.

"Fifteen minutes ago I would have said 'Hell, no,' but now after seeing that tape, I don't know."

"Oh God." I feel sick.

"York knows all the ins and outs of this job. He knows which lines you don't *ever* cross. I don't care

178

if he was drunk; he wasn't too drunk to throw you against the wall or to form a complete sentence."

"Wait? Could you hear us?"

"There's no audio yet but we all lip read. I could make it out some of it." Oh God.

I try to let all of this sink in. "What's going to happen to him?"

Mark moves back to sit on the couch while I stand not knowing if I'm coming or going. Fuck, I'm so scattered!

"Well, if Cole doesn't kill him, which I suspect he will, he'll be sent back to Army headquarters for a psych check. They'll want to review the tape to see if you want to press charges."

I feel a chill race up my spine. That is the last thing I want to do, I just want him gone.

"This is going to be a big blow to the house, although I always knew there was something wrong with that son of a bitch."

"I don't understand why he'd risk his career? He knows the cameras are all throughout the house."

"Cole has been upgrading the entire security system, and right before we left they were working on the cameras downstairs. They were having trouble getting them to connect to the server so they were offline for six hours. He probably thought they were still down. Fuck, I want to rip his head off right now."

A knock at the door had us both jumping. Keith pops his head in.

"Is there a party I don't know about?" When he sees my face he comes in, shutting the door behind him. "Okay, what's going on?" I shoot a look at

Mark who is standing up.

"Nothing that can't wait for a day," he says, walking me to the door.

Keith doesn't buy it but doesn't push it either, and the three of us walk back to the living room where only a few people were left.

Cole's face relaxes into a smile when he saw us walking over to him. "Hey, where did you two run off to?"

"Just got chatting and lost track of time," Mark says, looking around the room. Oh God, there was York a few feet away.

I could practically feel the rage building in Mark's body as I see him watching York. I begin to feel even more nervous when I notice Cole watching him too, I need to think fast.

"I'm really happy you're all back." And that's what I come up with? *Smooth, Savi.* Cole looks down at me smiling. *Well that was worth the dorky line.* My stomach flutters. "I bet you're all beat?"

"Very." He downs the rest of his drink.

"Me too."

"Come on, I'll walk you upstairs." We say goodnight to everyone.

Mark gives me an extra-long, soft hug.

\*\*\*

The walk up the stairs is quiet it isn't until we are alone that he put his hand on my back. Such a simple act makes me feel so much better. He checks my room, like he always does, and turns on my fireplace. I close the door quietly and then join him at the fire and he stares down at me with that smile that reminds me that I'm a woman with needs.

"You're so beautiful," he whispers, tucking my hair behind my ear.

"Thank you for keeping your promise." I close my eyes, feeling his hand running up my neck.

He cups the back of my head, tilting it to the side so my neck is exposed. "If I get to come home to this," his hot lips kiss me just under my ear, "I'll promise you every time."

My body goes limp as his words sink in.

He presses his lips back down as his tongue twirls in circles, chuckling between his kisses. "You have a wild heartbeat."

"I can't imagine why," I breathe. My hands move under his shirt running along his stomach. I no longer register the pain in my arms.

His breathing changes, giving me some much needed courage.

I let my fingers explore. Jesus this man has zero body fat! I run my fingernails around to his back making him pull back with a hiss.

"You're testing my self-control here."

I grin, happy he's feeling as weak around me as I am around him.

He wraps his arms around my waist pulling me to him. "I don't want to screw this up with you. I've already crossed a line I should never have crossed. Call me weak, but I'm drawn to you and I've never felt this way before."

I feel like I might burst but for a good reason this time. "I haven't either," I whisper and pull back slightly. "The way I felt when you left and again when I saw you downstairs—well it isn't something I've ever…I mean, I understand that you're risking your reputation being here right now and I respect, well, not going public with it."

"Problem is," he reaches down, lifting me into the air, pulling me against him as I wrap my legs around his waist, "I want everyone to know you're mine."

I grin raising an eyebrow. "Am I now?"

He nips at my neck playfully.

He leans in giving me a long deep kiss.

My legs tighten around him as my body coils with lust, then he pulls away leaving me breathless.

"I want you to be," he whispers looking up at me with his deep dark eyes.

"I want to be too," I confess, feeling lightheaded. I lean my head back against the wall as he licks the length of neck. I moan, tilting my head to the side and squeezing his erection harder between my legs.

He slams his hips into me growling as he sucks where my collar meets my shoulder.

"Fuck me, Savi." He groans as he slowly lowers me to the ground taking my hand to his mouth kissing it softly. "Get some sleep, baby."

My insides melt into a pool in my stomach. This man positively has me wrapped around that smile of his. God, am I really ready to start a relationship with someone? Maybe I just need to stop overthinking things and let myself live a little.

# Chapter Eleven

I change, then begin to pace the room, suddenly feeling guilty for not telling Cole what happened with York. I just need one more day. God, I hope Mark keeps his word. Hearing footsteps outside my door makes me stop pacing and I can see a shadow on the floor. A soft knock makes me shiver. What if it is Cole? Maybe he can't sleep either. Am I ready for this? I slowly make my way over and open the door.

Two glossy eyes stare down at me. Shit! His eyes rake over my nightgown.

"Evening," he purrs as I try to slam the door but he puts his foot in to stop it.

"Move your foot, York!" I hiss, swallowing down a lump of fear. Footsteps coming up the stairs make him look away and I shove him backward, slamming the door and locking it. Screw this! I grab a blanket off my chair and slip into the back hallway.

\*\*\*

J.L. Drake

Cole wakes to banging on his door, then it bursts open.

Abigail is madly running around his room, he squints trying to catch up.

"Where is she? Tell me she's with you!" She's talking a mile a minute racing into his bathroom.

"Who?"

"Savannah! She didn't sleep in her bed again last night and I can't find her anywhere!"

That wakes him up. He jumps to his dresser, pulling on jeans and a black T-shirt.

They both run to her room to confirm it is empty. Hearing voices coming from downstairs Cole runs out the door. Abigail on his heels, he flies down the stairs and races into the kitchen.

"Wow, where's the fire?" Paul asks, holding up his coffee mug.

"Have you seen Savannah?" Abigail asks breathily.

"Yes, she's out on the patio." Dell points outside. "Everything okay?"

Cole doesn't answer. He moves through the dining room, his stomach in knots. There she is— dressed in a white sweater and light pink tight-fitting pants sipping a cup of coffee. Her hair is hanging in big curls around her shoulders. Christ, she takes his breath away. She must have sensed him watching because she turns to look at him. Her eyes light up then drop quickly after looking over his shoulder.

"That girl is getting a goddamn tracking device in her neck this time!" Keith shouts, storming into the dining room. "Cole, this is the second time she's

184

done this," he complains.

"Calm down, Keith," Abigail says just as she hears Savannah open the door behind them. She is biting her lip looking guilty her eyes downcast.

"Why are we shouting?" Mark hisses, looking like he got two hours of sleep.

"Sweet boxers, man." Cole points to his Ironman underwear. Mark flips him the finger.

"Savannah, I warned you." Keith points a finger at her. Her eyes flip to Mark's. He catches the look and suddenly looks more alert.

"I'm so sorry. I fell asleep in the entertainment room. I couldn't sleep."

"Wrong answer, Savi, I watched the tape." She runs her hands through her hair as Mark mirrors the same action. *What the hell is going on here?* Keith wonders, looking from one to the other.

"Keith, I'm here. I'm okay." She starts looking nervous again her eyes shifting over to the kitchen.

"That isn't how this house works."

"Keith," Mark whispers, "give her a free pass just one more time, okay?"

Keith looks at him shaking his head. "Last time, Savi, so help me God." He holds up his hands stopping himself then turns and leaves muttering into his radio.

"T minus fourteen hours, pretty eyes," Mark mutters to Savannah.

"Anyone care to fill me in?" Cole asks crossing his arms sitting on the edge of the table. Both of them stare at the ground but say nothing. "Well here's the problem. Mark, you don't make eye contact with me when you're hiding something.

You've been doing that since you were a kid and Savi—" She looks up at him, running her fingers through her hair. "You do that," he points to her hand, "when you're not being honest or you're scared." He sighs when they both look at one another. "What happens in fourteen hours?"

"Cole," Savannah steps closer holding up her hands, "you asked me a little while ago to have trust in you and I do. Could you have a little in me when I ask you to just give me today? Please?" Her eyes hold his for a moment. God, he's falling hard for this woman but this secret feels like it is going to end badly.

"This isn't going to be good is it?" Her face flushes as she looks over at Mark. "Do I need to be worried about anyone's safety?" Savannah's face flinches.

"I've got this for now," Mark says. "Savannah has her reasons for keeping quiet and though I don't quite agree I respect her wish to wait until tonight to share it with you or I will."

Okay, this sounds big. "Mark—can you give us a minute?" Cole waits until they are alone then angles his back to block the security camera, watching her as she nervously plays with the candle on the table. "Baby," he whispers. She looks up at him her face wanting to tell but she won't. "I won't push this issue. I feel like Mark's got it handled for right now but you have to tell me where you go at night." She sits the candle down, turning it between her fingers and thinking. "What if something happens and I need to get to you? You almost killed Abigail with worry this morning."

She slowly nods her head. "Your mother's library," she says quietly. "I feel safe there."

He let out a sigh, a little surprised that he was unsure for an instant. He didn't know what she was going to tell him. For just a moment he thought it was another man's room, and immediately felt guilty for even going there in his head.

"I'm sorry for using that back passage but I just really feel safe in there," she repeats. "It's been a rough few days, and I overslept. I was hoping to slip in and out without anyone noticing. I really am sorry, Cole." He reaches for her hand settling his on top.

"Don't be sorry, I'm just relieved it wasn't someone's room you were seeking out. It makes me happy you feel safe in there. Use it anytime."

"Truthfully," she moves a little closer, "I wanted to go to your room." He inhales sharply, her eyes lock with his. "Lie in your bed, smell you all around me," she whispers as a corner of her mouth goes up, looking damn sexy.

As she stands in front of him smiling he shifts, feeling his temperature rise. His fingers curl around the edge of the table. She is making him painfully hard.

Straddling one of his knees and leaning to one side, she reaches for her coffee cup and continues. "Sleep in nothing but one of your T-shirts."

Her breath against his neck has his hands in a death grip on the table.

She pulls away chuckling into her mug. Oh she is good, she knows he is about to burst!

"Savi," he growls, "left top drawer—my T-shirts." He hears her laugh as she heads into the kitchen.

"Two can play this game, baby." She smirks over her shoulder with a sway in her step.

God damn, that ass.

\*\*\*

A scream from the entryway has him hopping to his feet and out to the dining room.

"Ahh! I can't believe you're finally here!" Abigail shouts into her sister's shoulder.

Cole shakes his head, rubbing his chest. What is it with women and shouting when they greet each other?

"Coley!" Aunt June grabs his face smacking a kiss right on his lips. "How's my handsome young man doing?"

He grimaces at her nickname for him. "Fine, thanks."

"So I've heard." She winks at him. "Oh my!" She looks over his shoulder. "And you must be Savannah."

"I am; nice to meet you."

June pulls Savannah in for a hug, making her wince slightly. Her face quickly recovers but Cole still catches it. June steps back to get a good look at her. "I bet you're a nice change of scenery for the guys, huh?" Savannah's face reddens.

"Oh June, leave the poor girl alone. Come on, Savi, let's find you something to wear tonight." Abigail links arms with Savannah pulling her toward the stairs.

"Must be some girl to put a look on your face like that." June elbows him in the ribs.

Cole smiles. He has no intention of lying to her. *It's not like he can, anyway,* he thinks wryly.

"That she is." Aunt June is always so observant.

***

Cole sits at his desk. He doesn't even get his email open before a knock at the door interrupts him. He glances at his second monitor seeing Keith.

"Come in."

"Look, we need to talk about this whole Savannah disappearing act—."

"She's been going to the private library," Cole interrupts while studying his computer screen.

"What? How does she know about that place?"

"She saw it when I was bringing her back to her room after she got poisoned."

"And you're okay with that?" Keith's tone makes him look up.

"Something happened while we were gone, she felt nervous, and went to a place where she felt safe. She only knows the code to her own room." He leaves out the fact that she knows his too. "She can roam all the hallways in this place, but she can't access any room without the codes. You know that."

"What if she finds the door to the bottom floor?"

Cole leans back in his chair. He doesn't like being questioned so much. "Then she sees a door that looks like every other door in the hallway. No codes, no access."

189

Keith nods and takes a seat.

Cole sighs, seeing this is going to be a long day. "What do you know about what happened?"

"All I know is that she and York got into it over dinner. She was talking to the new guys and Dell slipped up admitting that *Los Sirvientes* were blackmailing someone."

Cole's jaw clenches. He needs to have a word with Dell.

"I guess that got Savi upset and she pressed on for information, but York had a power trip moment and the two of them got into it."

"How badly?"

"Bad enough that York actually threatened her."

Cole instantly gets angry. *Christ, York needs to tame it down*, he thinks.

"A few more words were exchanged and she left. Abigail came and got Mike. He caught Savannah in the hallway—nearly scared the poor thing to death. She seems a bit rattled but other than that she was all right. So I don't know if the blackmailing thing is playing on her or if it was the dinner fight. She just seems different. She's been hiding away from us till you all came home." Keith rises. "Look, Dell felt terrible about what he said. Don't be too hard on him. It's York's power trip that needs to be brought down a few pegs. That man is a loose cannon and I swear he has it out for Savi."

"Sounds that way."

"Anyway it's all on the tapes so you can see it for yourself."

Cole runs his hands over his face. "I can't do anything until I get this report finished and sent over."

"I'll leave you to it."

***

Cole fusses over his tie in the mirror. He prefers army boots and camo gear over a suit and tie any day, but it has been a long standing tradition to go to Zack's restaurant in town for Thanksgiving.

Zack had worked for Shadows many years ago. When he retired, he didn't like the idea of leaving the area so he opened a restaurant and bar with his younger brother. Cole's father and Zack now live two doors down from one another, best friends attached at the hip since they were kids. Abigail now teases him and Mark for having the same kind of friendship. She's right, he laughs at himself. He couldn't imagine not having Mark around.

Normally the "guests" that stay at the house are kept at arm's length. Forming a relationship with one of them like his with Savi simply doesn't happen. They certainly have never had one included at their own off-site holiday dinner. Zack doesn't shut down his restaurant completely for them but with the number of Agents going tonight he isn't too worried about taking Savannah out in public. "Though you can never be too careful," he mutters to himself, tucking his gun into the holster on his hip.

He shrugs on his jacket, inspecting himself. He wears a black suit with a red tie; his hair is gelled down slightly and slicked back. He shakes his head. "I look like a fucking attorney from Wall Street." he curses. "Fuck!" He knows he can't handle the city life. He wonders if Savannah misses it. If they did end up together, would she want to go back to New York? The thought makes him uneasy, so he pushes it aside.

Cole heads downstairs to find Keith and Mike waiting for him. As they hurry outside he notes the temperature has dropped dramatically. His cell phone shows it's twenty-six degrees out.

Paul opens the door letting him hop in the Escalade.

Savannah is in the back and he makes his way directly toward her, purposely ignoring his two grinning aunts until he is beside her.

"Ladies, you look lovely this evening."

"Same to you, Logan." June winks.

His grin widens as he takes in Savannah's appearance. A long, white fur coat is wrapped around her small frame. Sparkly earrings peek through her curled hair and that heavenly apple smell is lingering around her. "You look lovely, Ms. Miller."

"Why, thank you." She smiles making her eyes dance. "You look quite handsome yourself."

"It's the tie," he grunts, tugging it away from his neck.

They drive in a convoy of four—two Escalades and two spotter cars. He doesn't like driving the mountain roads at night. There are too many high areas where a sniper could sit and wait. Cole doesn't notice Savannah is picking up on his vibe until he sees her face. Reaching for her hand he threads his fingers through hers, figuring since they are in the back no will notice. June is keeping the conversation going with Paul and Mark up front. She squeezes it but he can see she's anxious. He leans in and points with his free hand.

"See over there, those lights—that's the city. Not much further."

"You're nervous," she whispers.

"Not nervous, just alert." He leans in until his lips brush over the shell of her ear. He breathes in her scent as her grip tightens. "I like having you tucked away on my mountain where I know you're safe."

She looks up at him with worry but before he could ask his phone begins to vibrate.

"Logan."

"It's Keith. We're at the restaurant in position. Place looks busy but Zack is ready for us. Your parents are here along with a few of their friends."

He glances at his watch. "Copy that, six minutes out." He snaps it shut and gives Paul a nod, letting him know everything is a go.

"Savi—what do you say if someone you don't know approaches you?" Mark asks from the front seat.

"That my name is Nicole and I'm here with family on a ski vacation."

"Perfect, and if you feel uncomfortable or nervous in a situation tonight, what's your safe word for us to step in?"

"Blackstone."

Cole looks down at her and hears Mark turn around too.

"Okay, Blackstone." Mark glances at him

puzzled. Cole hops out the side door, scanning the parking lot first then helping everyone out. He keeps close to Savannah as they walk into the restaurant. His parents sit at a very long table with Will, a guy he grew up with—it is great to see him—and as they all exchange greetings his mother gives him a nudge as she meets Savannah. Good lord is everyone aware that he has feelings for this woman? Or was Abigail just on the horn again?

He gasps as he helps Savannah take off her jacket; her black dress is so tight it is like a second skin. The sleeves hit right above her elbows, the length a little lower than mid-thigh, and it has a deep V-neck. Scowling at Abigail, who is avoiding his stare, he realizes he is clutching her coat still. He smoothly tries to wrap it back around her.

"You should keep this on! You'll freeze!"

"I'm all right, thanks." She waves a hand, taking her seat.

He grumbles as he hangs the coat on the rack. He sits next to her, watching the guys at the table take in her beauty—or her chest—which York is gawking at. He has to fight with himself to not wrap his arm around her chair and claim what's his.

Drinks are served and Cole's father rises to deliver a familiar holiday toast to friends. After dinner arrives everyone dives into various dishes and conversations.

"So when are you guys heading back to TJ?" Kyle asks. He is one of Cole's childhood friends who joined the Army the same time Cole did.

"Possibly next week." He sighs, seeing Mark glance at Savannah. "But I—ah, I'm not sure if I'll be attending that trip." He wants to see who is listening to them.

"I've never known you to skip out on a chance to snap someone's neck," York comments, taking a bite of his turkey.

"York!" Cole's mother hisses. "That's totally inappropriate."

York shrugs, seemingly unfazed by her recriminations. "No secret you have more kills than any of us."

Cole can't believe he is hearing this. His mother pointedly looks at Savannah who is downing the rest of her wine. He stabs his finger at York. "One more word like that and you'll be finding your own way back." He doesn't shout but his clipped tone says it all. The guys are all good buddies but there is still rank in his house, and he will be damned if he is going to let York forget that.

Cole shakes his head looking back at Kyle. "I have a lot to catch up on. Frank is breathing down my neck."

"Yeah I get that," Kyle says, moving his attention over to Savannah. "So." She shifts slightly. "Tell me something about yourself."

She leans forward, resting her forearms on the table, her bracelets making a pretty noise as they clink together. She pulls her dark hair off one shoulder, showing off her slender neck that his tongue is begging to taste. "What do you wanna know?"

He shrugs. "Something that none of these guys know yet."

Cole leans over letting her know she can be

honest with these guys—they've all signed NDA contracts.

She presses her lips together taking a moment to think. "I love the blues. Give me a local pub with bad food and live music and I'm a happy girl." She smiles as she remembers. "My friend Lynn and I would spend every Friday night at this little hole-in-the-wall pub in Queens just to listen to a musician named Flat Street Tony. He played the cello and had a voice that would make your soul dance." She let out a little laugh. "One night Tony came over and gave us a signed copy of one of the first vinyls he ever recorded. I have it mounted—" she stops herself, "had it mounted in my living room." Her mouth twists as she looks down at her fingers. "No paparazzi, no daddy to disappoint, no one cared who I was. It was my little slice of heaven." She looks up seeing the entire table is listening to her story. "So to answer your question, I like the blues." She runs her hands over her lap.

"A girl who likes a dive pub, bad food, and mellow music. Jesus, Savannah, you're like every man's dream." Kyle laughs into his beer bottle. "Don't let this one leave."

"Didn't you hear Kyle?" Savannah says leaning toward him lowering her voice. "I'm taking over Agent Black's job."

Cole turns to look down at her only to find her grinning ear to ear her eyes sparkling. It takes some major self-control not to grab her, throw her up against the wall, and take right then and there.

"Savi, are you trying to get me in more trou—" Mark laughs stopping mid word. "Melanie?"

196

Savannah's head whips over to Abigail, who looks like she's just seen a ghost.

"Who is this?" Cole whispers leaning into Savannah, knowing she knows something.

She turns so that their faces are almost touching. "The girl Mark's been seeing."

Really? That might explain why Mark's been so eager to do the runs into town lately.

Melanie looks at Abigail. "I was just grabbing something to eat and saw you. I thought I'd come by and say hello."

"Well that's nice of you, dear. I'm Abigail. Please, won't you join us?"

June is already grabbing a seat and wedging it between Mark and Savannah.

Mark shoots Cole a look, mouthing he's going to kill Abigail.

Savannah has to squeeze into him—luckily for him most of the action is on her side so now he has an excuse to wrap his arm around her chair. She seems to like this; as she settles in next to him she quickly runs her hand over his thigh. He lets out a puff of air fighting off the nasty thoughts that are flashing through him.

"I don't want to intrude," Melanie starts to say, but Abigail is pushing her into the seat.

"Nonsense."

Cole catches his father's gaze. He's smiling at both him and Mark, and his mother is beaming too. Well at least his father seemed all right if something was going on with him and Savannah. He needs to speak to him about it though.

"Do you work here in town?" Savannah asks

Melanie.

"Yes, at The Cliff. It's a coffee shop my parents own. I'm helping them out while I go to school. I'm getting my marketing degree."

"Oh, I have a degree in marketing. I used to work for—" She catches herself. "So how did you and Mark meet?"

Melanie doesn't seem to notice Savannah change the topic.

"Yes, how did you two meet?" Keith asks, clearly loving this situation.

"Agent Black's job?" Cole whispers over Savannah's shoulder. His lips just brushing over her warm skin she chuckles. He can tell she enjoys getting a rise out of him. "I hate your dress."

"No, you don't."

He can't help but smile. Damn woman is good, but he can play this game. He looks around seeing most of the attention is on Mark and Melanie. The restaurant is loud and very busy.

"I want to run my hands up your thighs and find out what you're wearing under that ridiculously tight dress." She stiffens. Yes, at the moment he has the power. "Push you up against the wall, bury my face in your neck and show you just how fucking hard that dress is making me." He gently traces circles along her smooth inner thigh. "Find out if you're as ready for me as I am for you." She swallows hard as her cheeks start to blush. "I want to taste—"

"Savannah, come with me to the bar?" Abigail asks, pulling his attention away. He wants to scowl at her again, but she doesn't know what he was just up to.

Savannah nods. Pushing back her chair, she leans in pretending to point to something in the far corner.

"Nothing," she whispers, "to answer your question. I'm wearing nothing underneath."

Poof! The power shifts back to her as his eyes widen, running down her body.

"Excuse me." She gives him a sexy smile.

"I don't know how you guys get any work done with that walking around the property," Kyle jokes.

"What, is that what you all do?" Melanie asks Cole, who is trying to drag his eyes off Savi.

"Army."

"Really? I've always heard there's a group that trains somewhere around here, but you never see them in their uniforms. Is that you guys?"

"Yes, we train all over the country."

"Well, it's kind of nice knowing there's more protection up here. Seven policemen is hardly enough to handle this whole town, especially with the amount of tourists we get. They should bring more cops in."

Cole has to agree with her. The town is understaffed but the police are well trained and work well with his company. No locals have ever stumbled upon their location because there are three separate armed gates spaced three miles apart and you have to have a level five clearance to get through any of them. If anyone spots the house the rumor they put out is the property belongs to a Kent Cuttingham who made his millions in the green air industry. The Army and his father have every angle covered when it comes to the Shadows house. So far there's never been a problem.

"Cole," Abigail places her hand on his shoulder, "either Savi has been recognized or she has an admirer."

He looks over to where she shifts her gaze. At a small table by the window sit three men and a woman. "Navy sports coat, blond hair," she says through a smile as she notices Kyle watching them. "I didn't want to hurry her away from the bar as she and June are talking, but he's been watching her since we walked over. I notice he's been pointing to her and he said something to his friend on his left. They were looking at their phone and nodding."

"Another round?" Cole asks the table as he stands cheerfully. "Mark, you want a scotch, neat?"

"Yeah, that sounds good." He nods. 'Scotch, neat' is their code for possible threat.

"Melanie?"

"Nothing for me, please. I'm driving."

"Very well." He turns to Abigail. "Go have a seat. I'll check it out."

Cole slowly heads toward the bar while watching the table by the window out of the corner of his eye. He catches Zack's arm as he goes by.

"Table of three men and the woman, who are they?"

"Out of towners. Sounds like they're from Chicago."

"All right, can you do a sweep? Find out what they're talking about."

"Of course." He moves off toward the kitchen.

Cole makes his way over to Savannah and slips

in behind her. "Nicole, can I get you another?" She flinches but quickly recovers.

"Please." She pushes her half empty wine glass aside. "Let's make it a martini this time." Cole orders while June finishes her story then leaves, saying she needs to go hound Melanie.

"Here," Cole slides the glass to her, "just act normal, baby."

"My legs are shaking." Her trembling hand moves for the glass but stops to shake it out.

"Hey man," Cole says to the guy next to her, "would you mind shifting down one so the lady can have a seat?"

"Oh yeah, sure." The man moves down a seat. Cole helps Savannah onto the tall bar stool.

"Thanks, I thought I might fall."

"I'd never let that happen."

She smiles but he can tell she is nervous.

"How did you know who Melanie was?" Hoping to distract her while he watches the table of four.

"Abigail found out he was talking to her so she introduced herself and ended up inviting her to dinner. You think Mark will be mad?"

"No," Cole laughs, "it's not surprising that she's playing Cupid. It's not the first time she's tried this. Abigail wants grandbabies more than anything."

"Yes, I got that impression." His eyes shift to hers as she chuckles. "She asked if I was on the pill." His mouth drops open. "Even though she knows I am, it was one of the first things your physician spoke about to me. He said it's a smart move since I live in a house full of men." She laughs. "Yeah, that was fun to wrap my head

201

around, but after my conversation with Abby I think I may need to start hiding them."

Cole lets out a laugh of his own. Oh, that Abigail is a trip sometimes.

"Well she should be flattered," Zack says, leaning into Cole. "They think she's Megan Fox. I think at most they'll ask her for an autograph. They were going to approach her until you showed up."

"Okay, thanks, Zack."

"Anytime." He looks over at Savannah. "I hope you enjoyed your dinner."

"I truly did. You have a wonderful restaurant, Zack. Thank you for having us."

He leans in so she can better hear him. "You are welcome anytime. Get Cole to bring you to dinner some night. I'll reserve you the booth in the corner no one will bother you. I'll cook you something special myself."

"Well that's an offer I can't refuse." Cole nods. "We'll have to set that up soon." An evening alone with her sounded perfect.

"Wonderful!" He claps his hands together. "All right, I must go. Enjoy the rest of the night."

Cole watches Savannah sip her martini. She seems to be a little more comfortable now. She peers at him over the rim of her glass, her eyes holding his making him swallow hard. "Have I been spotted?"

"No, they think you're Megan Fox."

She coughs on her drink, laughing. "Well now, that I'm all right with. Bring 'em on, I can talk about Optimus Prime and Autobot Drift."

Cole burst out laughing. *God, she is funny.*

"Sorry, you're out of luck. They won't come over because I'm here."

She raises her eyebrow.

"Over my dead body, baby."

She gives him a playful smile.

As long as they don't snap a picture of her he doesn't care what they think. Social media is a real bitch. "Let's go back to the table."

\*\*\*

"We'll see you for breakfast, dear." Cole's mother kisses his cheek before she gets in their Land Rover.

"Drive safe," he says to his father, shutting her door.

When Cole reaches the SUV he walks up to Abigail and June laughing at Mark about the look on Mark's face when Melanie arrived.

"No, no, please, laugh away. I'm glad my stomach hitting the floor and rolling out the door was so entertaining to you," he scoffs from the front seat, only making them laugh harder.

Savannah looks out the window, off in her own little world.

He sits next to her fixing the vent to blow warm air on her. "You see something?"

"No, just thinking."

She seems far away, so he leaves her be and signals for Paul to leave and they start their drive home.

"A little music, Paul?" June asks. He turns on some music and the Beatles' *Hey Jude* fills the car.

Savannah's hand rests on his thigh.

He looks down to find her looking troubled. He wraps his arm around her pulling her into him.

She runs her hand along his waist, jumping when she feels his gun.

He kisses the top of her head, holding her tighter. He doesn't care if Paul sees him in the mirror, he wants to hold her. She has something big to tell him tonight and it is obviously playing on her. He's been patient but she's suffering and it bothers him.

She tucks her head into his neck and relaxes a little.

His phone vibrates in his pocket he reaches down seeing it's a text from Keith.

***Green Land Rover - since Zack's - branching off - see who he follows.***

"Paul," Cole's voice is sharp through the music, "keep on course."

Paul nods looking in the mirror.

Savannah sits up looking behind them out the window.

"Look forward, please, Savi."

She stares up at him, sensing his mood change. "Is there someone following us?" Her voice is shaky and she starts to rub her hands over her lap her nerves getting to her, "Cole, say something please."

"Besides the blues what other kind of music do you like?"

"I'm not five, Cole...your attempt at a distraction is a little insulting. Keep me in the loop or the panic that's about to surface will be the least of your worries."

He has to fake a cough to stop from laughing. *She's so feisty.*

"Keith noticed a Land Rover following us."

"So, couldn't they just be going somewhere?"

"Not on this road."

"We have company," Paul announces.

Savannah reaches for his hand. He loves that she looks to him for comfort.

"How far are we away from the house?" she asks.

"Ten minutes to the first gate," Cole answers while texting Keith back.

Just as they approach the turn off for the first gate the Land Rover slows down then suddenly speeds around them.

Paul flashes his card to the first guard and gets waved through.

Once the gates close behind them Savannah puts her hands over her face. "I hate this." Her words are muffled.

"I know," Cole says rubbing her back, wishing he could make it better.

Savannah heads straight into the house before Cole gets a chance to see if she is all right.

"Give her a moment," Abigail says, looping her arm through her sister's. "This is a reality check for her tonight."

"We got the plate number, let's go run it," Mark says as they walk to Cole's office.

# *Chapter Twelve*

I flop on my bed after changing into a tank and yoga pants, wrapping my sweater around me, needing to feel safe. The drive home played on some buried emotions that are surfacing quickly. I close my eyes falling asleep immediately.

"Savi." I stir. "Savannah," Abigail whispers loudly, "wake up, please!"

I pry my eyes open, seeing her looking frantic.

"What's wrong?"

"You need to go down to Cole's office before he kills him!"

I sit straight up, feeling like the room is tilting to one side. "Oh no!" I cry, jumping out of bed and running down the hallway, taking two steps at a time. My heart is pounding in my ears as I shove the door open to his office. Cole has York by the neck against the wall. Mark is loudly saying something.

"Cole!" I scream. "No!" I run over to him. "Please don't do this."

"How could you hurt her?" Cole is yelling at York, ignoring me.

York is struggling to breathe.

I reach up touching Cole's arm; it's like steel.

"Cole, please look at me!" I beg.

"Savannah, get out of here!" Cole yells, barely hanging on to his temper.

Keith blows into the room. "What the fuck?"

"No, Cole," I cry, trying to get his attention. "Look at me. I'm fine, I'm not hurt."

"Mark!" Cole barks out, making me jump.

Mark comes over quickly, pulling my sweater off my shoulders.

"Mark!" I shriek. "What the hell?"

Cole's eyes flicker over at me taking in the bruises on my arms. They instantly grow dark and angry. He quickly punches York in the gut, doubling him over.

York collapses, gasping for air and clutching his midsection.

I yank my sweater back up, tears streaming down my face. "I trusted you. I can't believe you told him!" I scream at Mark.

"He didn't." Cole's voice is like ice. He's standing perfectly still, staring down at York. "I watched the tapes."

"Savannah," Mark's says, ignoring my last comment, "tell Cole what York threatened you with."

What is Mark doing? Is he trying to make the situation worse? "Mark, stop." I'm shaking, feeling my emotions are shot all over the wall. I just want this to end.

"Savannah." Cole doesn't sound like himself, and it's borderline scary.

I look at York, who is giving me the nastiest

look I've ever seen. My mouth dry, I run my trembling fingers through my hair, feeling sick.

York pulls himself up to his feet, standing like he is getting ready to fight.

I step back as he shakes his head at me.

He moves his hand up to his lip, wiping off the blood. "Aww, Savi, we could have had something beautiful," he smarms. "You should've kept your fucking mouth shut. Bad move." He chuckles then starts coughing.

Mark moves in behind me.

As I stand frozen he hooks an arm around my waist holding me tightly. What the hell? "The sick son of a bitch threatened to hand her over to The Cartels himself if she said anything," he says to Cole.

Cole launches himself at York, sending him hard into the wall.

"No!" I scream, trying to get away, but Mark wraps his other arm around me. I thrash all around as the two of them fight. "Let me go! Keith, stop them!"

Keith shakes his head at me; it feels like I'm watching a movie and I have no control of the outcome. "Cole, stop! You'll kill him! He's not worth it!" Nothing is getting through to him. I'm shaking so violently that I start losing focus. Then it hits me.

"*Blackstone!*" I scream at the top of my lungs, making the entire room freeze.

Cole's fist is inches from York's bloody face, his breathing heavy and his look that of a madman. He drops York's limp body on the ground, stepping away.

Mark's death grip on me loosens, freeing me, and I sink to the floor sobbing.

"Get him out of here," Cole whispers.

Mark and Keith pick York off the floor. York starts laughing like he's delirious. "Watch your back, Savannah."

My hair is blocking my view of him but I can feel his eyes on me.

Mark jabs him in the ribs making him cry out.

"Go!" Cole orders. The three disappear through the back door.

I stand on my shaky legs, feeling like I might pass out. My head is swimming with everything that just happened. I open the office door but it is pushed shut, his arm above me.

"Savannah," Cole's voice is bleak, "please stay."

My hand falls away from the handle.

He lets out a heavy breath, takes my hand, and leads me out of his office through the back door.

His room is just how I remembered, big and open. He doesn't speak a word as he strips off his bloody shirt and dress pants. He disappears for a few minutes in the bathroom.

I stand completely unable to move. Suddenly he's in front of me pulling off my sweater. He inspects my arms as I look away feeling raw.

He bends down and gently kisses the bruises on each arm he drops to his knees in front of me wrapping his arms around my waist pressing his head against my stomach.

"I'm sorry, baby. Please forgive me." His words nearly break me.

"Don't apologize. You didn't hurt me," I whisper, feeling such sadness that he thinks I'm upset with him.

"If I had been here, I could have protected you."

"You told me you don't do what-ifs." I cover my face and start to cry. "I just want it to all go away but he wouldn't leave me alone."

Cole gets silent.

I wipe my cheeks dry trying to get hold of myself.

"I almost killed him. I wanted to," he confesses.

I drop my hands with a heavy thud. "Me too."

"Thank you for stopping me," he says, looking up and holding my gaze while he gets to his feet. "No one but you could have."

I sigh, feeling exhausted. "Come on."

He pulls back the covers, letting me crawl in. He wraps his arm around my stomach pulling me to him. His chest expands as he blows out a long breath—I know he's worried about what I witnessed tonight so I lift his hand off my stomach and kiss his battered knuckles. He leans in giving me a kiss on my neck.

"Who told you about 'Blackstone'?" he asks.

"Dell."

I hear him mutter something as he pushes a button on his side table turning off the light.

"Thank you for protecting me," I say into the darkness.

"I always will," he whispers, his words making my heart thump louder. I'm falling fast for this man and it's more than a little scary.

I wake to a steel cage around me—we didn't

move an inch last night. I wiggle, trying to stretch and his grip loosens so I slip off the bed and head to the bathroom.

"Holy…!" I exclaim with a smile when I walk into the world's biggest bathroom. A deep red and gray runs throughout the whole room right down to the tile in the four-person shower. It has eight jets and three shower heads. A large oval tub sits in the corner with a view of the mountains; it's gorgeous. I stop gawking long enough to use the restroom and steal Cole's toothbrush.

"Ew!" I hiss when I notice dried blood on my pants and on the hem of my shirt. It's probably Cole's but the idea of it being York's has me tearing my clothes off and throwing them in his hamper. I spot double doors and decide I need something to wear.

Rows of T-shirts, shirts, heavy knit sweaters, and pants line the walls. Clearly this is his military closet. Everything is so perfectly placed I'm almost intimidated to touch anything. I realize I'm taking too long, so I grab the closest T-shirt and shrug it on. It's dark green and has ARMY written across the front and LOGAN on the back. It's huge and comes down to my knees. I roll one side up and tuck the knot under the shirt keeping in place so it isn't like a tent on me.

I open the door to find him propped up in bed reading off his phone. He looks sexy with his messy hair and the sheet covering one leg. He looks up and does a double take. A lazy smile runs over his lips.

"Morning," he says, his voice raspy.

"Didn't mean to take so long. I took a wrong

turn in there," I joke.

He chuckles as his eyes rake over me.

"Sorry." I look down at his shirt. "There was blood on my clothes."

"Don't be, I never thought that shirt could look sexy until now."

I smile, running my hand through my hair not sure what to do now. Last night was intense and our emotions were high.

"Come here, baby." He holds out his hand. He pulls me onto his stomach making me straddle his waist. His fingers run through my hair as he watches my face. "What are you thinking?"

"Honestly?"

"Always."

"I'm nervous what happened yesterday might affect us."

"How so?"

"You're losing a man who's been with you for…how long? You guys have a great thing here, I don't want to be the reason something bad happens." I fumble with the hem of my shirt. "I begged Mark to erase that tape." I feel him flinch. "He told me he couldn't, that he could lose his job."

"Smart man," he mutters.

"I saw the look on his face when he watched it." I look up. "I didn't want to see that on yours."

He twirls a piece of my hair around his finger thinking. "I'll be honest with you. It took me to a dark place I haven't been before. Mark walked in with York right as I finished watching it. I don't remember how I got my hands wrapped around his neck or how I got him against the wall." I swallow

212

remembering it. "I could tell York didn't give a damn about the consequences for doing what he did—it happens to some of us. We see things in our business that harden you. Some deal with it differently than others. The signs were there though—all his comments to you, his lack of respect for rank. I'm just sorry I didn't see it until it was too late."

"Honestly, I'm fine."

"You weren't fine, Savi, you were being threatened in a place that's supposed to be safe. You had a man who you were supposed to be able to trust force himself on you, hurt you." He closes his eyes struggling with his words. "Christ he was going to—"

"Please," I plead, placing my hands on his bare concrete slab of a stomach. "I don't want to talk about this anymore. Other than being a little sore and frightened I'm fine and he's gone." I lean over, feeling like I need some more contact with him and kiss his chest. "This is where I feel safe, whose hands I want on me, whose lips I want to taste…" I feel him shiver at my distraction.

"Savannah," he moans.

"He may have hurt me, Cole, but you saved me."

He reaches down, grabbing my hips and flipping me over, devouring my mouth. His nails run down my thighs and around my behind.

He yanks my hips off the bed and grinds into me. "Feel what you do to me?"

I do—it is digging into me hard. "I can help with that." I lean forward pulling off my shirt and unhooking my bra tossing both aside. *My…I'm bold*

213

*this morning.* I think I need to feel something, something that will push aside the fear that's weighing heavily at the back of my brain.

"Oh baby," he moans, savoring the view. He runs his hands along my sides, then along my stomach and finally over my breasts.

I bite my lip to stop from crying out—it has been too long since I've been touched.

"You're fucking beautiful, Savannah." He leans down, leaving hot trails with his tongue.

My fingers find his hair and grab on, making him kiss harder.

"Mmm, you taste so sweet." One hand slips into my soaked panties running a finger between my folds.

I arch my back, wanting more. "Ohhhhh…"

He closes his eyes. "I love how responsive you are." Just as his finger is going to make a pleasurable dive, there's a knock at the door. We both jump.

"Go away," he calls out between kisses.

"Logan, your parents just arrived and Dan is looking for you," Paul says, instantly sucking all the fun out of the room.

Cole squeezes his eyes shut, cursing. "Yeah, all right, thanks."

I sit up pushing him back. I need to get back to my room and have a cold shower. I grab the army shirt, tugging it over my head.

"I totally forgot they were coming," he sighs, hands on his hips.

I step up on my tippy-toes giving him a playful kiss. "To be continued," I tease, smacking his butt

214

and giving him a grin.

He hooks his arm around my waist pulling me back to him. He turns me to face him, asking "Are you really all right?"

I run my hands over his shoulders. "I am."

He leans in, giving me a quick kiss.

\*\*\*

I pull off a piece of my muffin, popping it in my mouth while listening to Cole's mother, Sue, discuss her Christmas plans.

"Savannah, you should see what the town does for the week of Christmas. All the businesses decorate their stores and each night for five days one place holds a party," Sue explains, beaming.

"It's a really big deal if your store is selected to hold one of the parties," Abigail adds. "Of course Zack's was picked. He is every year."

Mark appears at the patio door, asking, "Savi, would you mind grabbing Cole for me? I would myself, but—" He points to his soaking wet boots. It had been raining all morning.

"Of course." I hop up from the table to find him.

"Yes, Mark, you stay right there. I just had the floors cleaned," Abigail warns as he pretends to move his foot inside, laughing.

I make my way down the hallway toward Cole's office and hear voices when I get closer.

"Where is he now?" I hear Daniel shout. I freeze outside the door.

"Downstairs," Cole answers. *York is still in the house! Where downstairs?* "He's not talking, just

215

says he wants to talk to her." My stomach twists.

"No way. He's crossed a line that he can never come back from!" Daniel pauses. "Does Savannah have any idea about her father?"

I step closer to the door, not caring I'm eavesdropping.

"No, and there's no reason to say anything until we are absolutely positive we are right." I feel the hair on the back of my neck stand up.

Daniel clears his throat. "This is bad, Cole, not only for the reputation of this house, but he knows the details of her file. He could easily leak what—"

A chair scraping on the floor makes me miss what Daniel says, damn it!

"...plus the blackmail, and God forbid The American gets wind of her whereabouts. She'll be plucked out of thin air so quickly we won't have a chance in hell of getting her back—not this time. With his reputation, he'll send her back one limb at a time using the local news station, just like the last one."

The walls start to shift as I process his words. Suddenly the door opens and Daniel jumps, staring down at me horrified. "Savannah!"

Cole runs up behind him.

"Mark," I feel like I'm having an outer body experience, "is-is looking for Cole." My voice is barely above a whisper. I turn on my heel and walk down the hallway each step feeling heavier than the last, Daniel's words "one limb at a time" bouncing around my head. *Then there was the comment about something being leaked? What was that?* I sink into my chair at the table.

"You look like you've seen a ghost, dear," Sue says, reaching out, touching my hand, "you're freezing."

"Savannah," Cole makes me jump. He looks visibly shaken. "Can we talk?"

Mark peeks his head in the door, "Hey Logan, I need—"

"Savi, please," Cole cuts him off.

Everyone is staring at me. I need to get some space just to process what I heard. I can feel myself shutting down and my walls building up.

"Mark needs you right now," I say finding it hard to look at him…or anyone at that moment.

"What if I need you?" he counters, making his mother turn her head back and forth between the two of us. What was he doing? He's risking his career and his reputation right now.

"Son, deal with Mark," Daniel says, resting his hand on Cole's shoulder. "Give her a moment."

Cole doesn't move right away, not until his father gives him the nudge toward the door. As soon as he is out of hearing range Sue looks at Savannah with an inquisitively arched eyebrow, to which she can merely shrug slightly.

"Savannah," Daniel starts to say, but I stand, needing some space.

"Excuse me." I take off toward the door grabbing a jacket on the way and head out into the pouring rain.

I don't know where I am going but the forest looks inviting. I walk for a while weaving in and out of the trees. The sound of the rain on the leaves sooths my aching head. I grow tired of the constant battle with the slippery ground—flats are not made for hiking. The rain starts to taper off as I come to a small clearing by a brook. I tuck my raincoat under me and sit down to rest under a tree, finally allowing myself the freedom to cry as I let my brain go over what I heard.

\*\*\*

Cole sits at his desk watching the live feed into York's cell. He's sitting on his bed, strumming his fingers on his thighs. What happened to him? York's a known ass but he'd never hurt anyone before. Fuck, what if he had succeeded in raping Savannah? The thought is crippling to him. Cole rubs his face, feeling drained.

"You're in love with her aren't you?" his father says from the doorway.

Cole's hands drop away. "No." Was he? He cared for her a lot, but love?

His father grins, shutting the door behind him. "Son, I had that same look on my face when I first fell for your mother."

"I've only known Savi for what, a month?"

"Sometimes it only takes one look to fall in love."

"Yeah, well, I know we shouldn't even be talking about her like this."

His father sighs as he crosses the room taking a seat in front of him. "Normally I'd say no, we shouldn't be, but I know you'd never step over the line for just anyone. I see the way she looks at you too; it's not a one sided feeling. Christ, you could see her visibly relax when you wrapped your arm around her chair at dinner last night."

Cole leans forward resting his arms on his desk. "What am I supposed to do? I love the way I feel when we're together. Her smell lingers on my clothes and it drives me mad throughout the day. I love who I am with her. Her words were the only ones that got through to me last night. If she wasn't there, I think I would have killed York. She can bring me to my knees with one look, and her lips..." Cole stops, seeing his father's expression.

"Welcome to being in love, son," he chuckles. "Good fucking luck!"

Cole shakes his head. *Oh shit I'm screwed.*

"Even if that's true, how am I supposed to be with her here in this house? The guys will lose respect for me getting involved with one of our victims, I mean 'guests.' It's a huge violation."

"Yes, but if you truly are in love with her, then you have to take the risk. Don't let your job stop you from living your life. But that's a decision only you can make. As for the guys, they'll see you're not in it for a quickie—never been your style and we raised you better than that." He smiles.

"You both have some huge obstacles to overcome when she finds out the truth. It could be a game changer. What if she wants to go back to New York? This—" he indicates waving his hands, "isn't for everyone."

"I know." Cole tosses his pen aside. "For the first time, I'm totally lost on what I should do."

"Take some time and think about it. It isn't something you can decide right away. You've got a lot to deal with right now and she's not going anywhere."

Cole nods and picking up his radio and changing the channel to seven. "You have visual?"

"Ten-four. She's two point four miles west of the house."

"She's a little wanderer," Daniel says, chuckling.

"What's she doing?" Cole asks, wishing he could see her.

"Sitting by the brook, been like that for the past thirty."

"All right, stay with her, but keep your distance."

"Copy that."

Daniel stands, tucking his hands in his pockets. "Come on, let's go find your Mom. She needs her Cole fix."

Cole follows him out of his office. "So tomorrow, Frank will be arriving with a few others to take statements. They believe York is tied into the poisoning but they don't have enough evidence yet to charge him."

"What time tomorrow?"

"Thirteen hundred."

"Maybe we can get your mother to take the ladies into town to help get Savannah through this."

"Yeah," Cole says, shuddering at the idea of Savannah leaving the house again, but it would be good for her to have some girl time.

\*\*\*

I close my eyes, feeling the thumping of my head inside my skull.

*Why was my father being blackmailed?* Maybe he was involved in buying weed? If so, big deal, who isn't? Christ, most of the people in politics have a hook up.

The American's history is something I can't even process yet.

Then there's York. Where is he downstairs? I thought I had seen the bottom floor. Would he really sell me out? He couldn't hate me that much, could he? Maybe he was in it for money? Either way, I wish I could talk to him, find out what's going on in his crazy mind. Was he the one who poisoned me? I never did hear if they found the how or why of it. I feel myself going into shutdown mode. I want to stop thinking at all, but I can't help that this is what I do when I suffer an emotional overload. I fight it, but there it's no use and I feel myself drifting off to sleep.

I awake suddenly shaking. I'm frozen to the core. Snowflakes prick my cheeks like tiny needles, one by one bringing me out of my fog. When my eyes adjust I see it's getting late.

I have no idea how long I slept after mulling everything over. I'm still confused. I now realize that there is way more to what happened to me than meets the eye. Problem is—I'm not sure I want to know all the details. Along with the truth comes many lies and I think it might be more than I can handle.

A rustle in the trees sounds to my left. I tense and then remember.

"Which one of you has he sent to babysit me today?" I call out, leaning my head back against the tree. Snapping twigs and heavy footsteps become louder as the tall dark figure soon comes into view through the falling snow. "Ahh, are you here to slap a tracking device on me now?" I half joke, feeling a little drunk off my emotions.

"Come on, Savi, it's starting to snow harder," Keith says, holding out a hand.

"I don't want to go back yet."

"You'll freeze."

"I'm not cold."

He raises his eyebrow obviously not buying my protest. He then pulls out his radio, "Delta Seven to Logan." He waits with a smug look on his face.

I roll my eyes.

"Go ahead, Keith," Cole's voice creaks over the radio.

I don't break my stare with Keith. I'm not scared of him.

"Ms. Miller is refusing to come back to the house, despite the fact she's soaking wet and it's starting to snow. Permission to use Code Forty-Five?"

*Forty-Five? What the hell is that?*

There's silence for a moment then it crackles. "Give her the radio." Keith hands it to me.

I sigh taking it out of his hand. "Good afternoon Cole," I say calmly.

"Savi, please go back with Keith before you freeze to death."

"I like it here, I was rather enjoying the silence before you sicced you're watchdog on me," I tease, looking up at Keith and grinning. "No offense." He bites back a smile.

"Savannah, you see Keith's left shoulder? Well if you don't get your backside off that ground and start walking toward the house you're going to be hoisted over it and carried out."

My jaw drops, my temper rising fast. I hand the radio back to Keith wrapping my arms around my knees and stay perfectly still on the ground. Yeah, I can be one stubborn ass sometimes.

"Well?" Cole hisses impatiently.

"Permission to use code forty-five?" Keith asks through a grin. He's loving this!

"Permission granted."

Everything gets blurry as Keith scoops me up, tosses me over his shoulder, and starts marching through the woods. I start to protest, hitting his back and shifting all around but all this it does is make his death grip tighter. After a few minutes I am suddenly struck with how I must look. I start to crack up and before I know it I'm in a full blown laughing fit and struggling to breathe. When we get to the clearing he drops me to my feet. I stumble backwards rolling on the ground. I have to hold my sides they hurt so badly.

Keith looks down then joins me in my laughing fit as he pulls me to my feet. "Was that fun for you?"

"Yes, it was, thanks."

He rolls his eyes as we start making our way back to the house. "I'll deny this if you ever repeat it, but I really like how you are with Cole. No one else would ever dare talk to him the way you do."

"People have mentioned that before. Saying they're surprised I'm not scared of him. What is it that I'm not seeing?"

"Cole is normally all business; that's what makes him so great at what he does. People have nothing but respect for the guy and his family. He's a great friend to have—he'll be the first to take a bullet for you. But I've seen what happens if you cross him and it's not pretty."

I look up at him feeling slightly nervous about what he'll say next.

"Is that why you didn't step in last night with York?"

"Yes. York knows the consequences of betraying Cole and this house. York got off easy. If you weren't there to stop it I have no doubt he would have left in a body bag."

I shake my head at that thought. I know he is right.

He sighs. "So, you overheard Dan and Cole talking?"

A knot in my neck begins to tighten. "There's a lot I don't know about my, ah, case. I feel like I won't be overly pleased with the outcome, will I?"

He pushes his lips together. "I'm thinking not," he whispers. "I'm really sorry about what York did. I wish you told me but Mark explained to me why you didn't. It was really sweet of you to think about everyone else." We walk in silence for a bit, listening to the freshly fallen snow crunch under our feet.

"Keith." He looks down at me. "What if I don't want to go back to New York after this is all over?" He pulls me into his side.

"Then we'll make you our chef," he says with a

grin. "Speaking of baking, Abigail just got a shipment of apples in. You think you could make another apple crisp for me? After all, I did have to babysit you all day."

I elbowed him playfully. "Fine."

# Chapter Thirteen

Cole taps his heel repeatedly into the ground, waiting "patiently" for Keith to return with Savannah. The snow is starting to pick up, leaving a thick layer on the ground. *Christ! What is taking so damn long!*

"I see them," Abigail calls out from the window.

Cole hurries to the door and out onto the porch. His parents follow while Abigail and June stay in the window.

Savannah's arms are wrapped around her middle and she has Keith's gloves on, looking like she's freezing. As he walks down to meet them he sees her blue, shivering lips muttering something.

"Did you have to carry her?" Cole asks, glancing at Keith.

"Yeah," he replies with a chuckle. "She laughed the whole time, so it wasn't as effective as I hoped."

"Cold yet?" he asks her. "Go have a shower, before you freeze to death." He's feeling so many emotions; he knows he is coming across as angry.

She looks up at him no doubt confused by his tone and shakes her head leaving.

"I don't think that's a good idea Savi—" Keith starts to say as Cole gets hit with a snowball in the back.

He spins around finding Savannah making another one. She stands back up and chucks it at his shoulder sending pieces of snow down the front of him. Both his parents have their hands over their mouths waiting to see what he'll do next.

"Don't be crabby with me, Cole Logan," she shouts through the snow flakes. "You see Keith's left shoulder? Well if you don't get over your cranky mood you're going to be hoisted over it and carried to the lake for a refresher." She crosses her arms, throwing his words back at him.

Keith bursts out laughing as she turns on her heel heading for the stairs mumbling something to his parents making them laugh too.

"Oh dear, I just love her," his mother calls out.

Yeah, he can see that. "All right, Keith," he says, fighting his smile—*Christ, she is something else; he was not expecting her feistiness*—"Thanks for bringing her back. You can go inside."

Keith twists his mouth trying hard not to laugh again. "At the risk of stepping over the line, my friend, that girl is perfect for you." He slaps Cole on the shoulder as he runs inside.

\*\*\*

I crawl onto the couch burrowing under the blanket that Abigail wrapped around me and am handed a cup of coffee. Daniel is lost in thought and Sue is sitting across from me, grinning.

"I'm sorry." She chuckles. "I just keep picturing Cole's face when you hit him with the snowball."

"It was pretty funny," June chimes in holding a plate of brownies in front of me. "Try one."

I take one off the plate and bite into it. "Oh wow." I savor the taste on my tongue. "June, these are delicious."

"Savannah, were you dating anyone before?" Sue blurts out.

"No."

"I'm surprised a beautiful woman like you isn't married with a possible child on the way."

"Let's just say I didn't meet Mr. Right back in my old life." I see her glance at June and stare down at the piece of brownie in my fingers. It was slowly melting.

"Perhaps you'll find him in this life," Sue says, smiling.

"Perhaps what?" Cole asks, taking a seat. He drapes his arm around the back of the couch behind me. I see Sue beaming again.

"Girl talk, dear," his mother says quickly.

Cole looks at his father. "Sorry, Dad."

"Yeah," Daniel sighs.

I glance at Cole. "Do you still need me to enforce Code Forty-Five? Or are you out of your crabby mood?" I grin as he shakes his head, grabbing my hand with the brownie in it and nipping it out from between my fingers. "Hey!" I laugh.

"Mmm, warm brownie," he moans, rolling his eyes back.

"Perhaps she already has," Abigail whispers to

Sue, but I catch it.

"Oh, I think I can hear Christina's heart breaking from here." June chuckles.

"Aunt June!" Cole's face suddenly goes serious.

"Who's Christina?" I ask, wondering why she mentioned her.

"She's been in love with Cole since she moved here four years ago." Sue shrugs. "She's a bit on the crazy side."

"Please don't start, ladies," Cole warns.

"Why would her heart break?" As soon as the words come out of my mouth, I feel like an ass.

"Because I'm not interested in her," he answers quickly. "One date and she was practically making wedding plans and naming our babies."

"What was the name for the boy again?" Abigail laughs to her sister.

"Fritter." June slaps her hand over her mouth to hide the smile.

"As in apple fritter?" I ask, barely containing myself.

"Exactly!" Sue and Abigail chime at the same time.

I look up at Cole. "Fritter Logan, sounds like a character from Lord of the Rings!"

Daniel bursts out laughing. "Oh my God, it does!"

"Any time you're all finished." Cole flops his head back against the couch.

"Ohhh," I pat his leg. His hand falls on top of mine holding it there for a moment.

"Obviously, if I had known she was that crazy I wouldn't have agreed to the date in the first place.

Last time I let Mark set me up on a blind date."

"Hey man, she's hot," Mark chimes in sitting next to Abigail. I try to pull my hand away from Cole's but his grip tightens. I look up at him wondering what he's thinking but he doesn't look down. "I didn't know she was bat shit crazy!"

"Mouth." Abigail swats his arm.

"All I saw was a fine ass and a pretty face," Mark says, earning two swats.

"Hey," he complains, "you're always telling me to be honest, so here I am and what do I get?" He jokes but leans over, giving Abigail a kiss on her cheek. You can see how much he adores his adopted mother.

"I ran into Christina yesterday," Dell says, joining our conversation. "Cole, I guess you left your coat there Thursday."

Thursday? The day they arrived home from their trip? I felt a strange pang of jealously, and what made it worse was Cole flinched. This time I pull my hand out quick enough that he can't stop it.

"What's with her keeping it so bloody hot in there? I swear she does it so she can wear those skimpy outfits. Don't get me wrong, I'm not complaining—"

"Dell," Sue holds out her glass, "could you get me a refill, please."

"Oh, of course," he says, scooping up her glass. "Anyone else?"

"Scotch, neat," Cole blurts out.

Mark's grin grows a little wider, making me wonder if that means something.

"So, Savannah," Sue says brightly, "would you

like to join the ladies and me in town tomorrow for a spa day?"

"Umm…" I fumble with my words having mixed feelings about leaving the house, but it's not every day I get a chance to be pampered. "That sounds nice, thank you."

"Keith and Paul will join you," Cole states to his mother.

"Of course, son." She nods like she's used to him speaking this way. "We'll take good care of Savannah."

I sigh, wishing I didn't have to be treated like a child. Cole's fingers start rubbing my neck and I'm confused by his public display of affection. I catch Daniel's eye…he grins then looks away. *Maybe they're fine with it?* I wonder what was said between the two of them. I would love to have been a fly on the wall for that conversation.

Dell hands Cole his drink and perches on the arm of the couch next to me.

Mark checks his watch and smacks his hands together. "Puck drops in five minutes guys!" he shouts.

"Who's playing?" Sue asks.

"Kings and Blackhawks," I answer, not really thinking about it. Mark and Cole both stare at me. "What? I have male cousins. It's embedded in me to catch the highlights and knows who's playing." I shrug.

"Who's your favorite team?" Mark asks, quieting down the group. He shifts forward on the couch looking very serious.

"Penguins," I say, feeling strong loyalty toward

231

my favorite team.

Mark jumps in the air, shouting. He pulls me up wrapping his arms around me.

"Listen up everyone!" he shouts with his arm over my shoulders. "Miller is a Penguins fan!"

The entire room breaks out in cheer. I laugh and shake my head. I have to admit it feels pretty damn good being in a room full of people who generally like me for me.

Dell grabs my hand before I can sit. "I think I just fell in love with you," he says, deadpan. "Marry me!"

"Well, with a proposal like that," I joke. "Hell yeah, Sugar, I'll marry you."

"One condition." He points at me. "We get married in our jerseys."

"Oh, Dell," I fan my face, using a southern belle accent, "it all sounds so classy."

"Oh, I know." He winks.

It doesn't take much convincing for the boys to have me join them to watch the game. Nine of us sit in the entertainment room watching the seventy inch TV. The announcer blares from all around us—I count six surround sound speakers.

I'm in the back corner with Cole feeling pretty beat after the day, sipping a stiff Dell-made drink called Tale of the Devil.

"Please know," Cole says, squeezing my hand under the blanket, "I just went to pick up a package at Christina's store. It was hot and she made me wait, so I removed my jacket and forgot it there, nothing more."

"Cole, we weren't together then anyway," I

whisper, downing the last of the drink.

"I thought we were."

"Logan, phone call," John interrupts us from the doorway. "Line three."

"Shit." Cole rubs his face. "I have to take this...be right back." He squeezes my hand then leaves.

"Another, Savi? It will help you sleep," Dell says with a wink.

I nod, loving the idea of sleep.

I remember seeing the score 2-0 Kings near the end of the third period. I stir to Mark trying to wake me. It isn't happening. "I'm fine here," I mutter.

"Come on, you." Mark scoops me up.

"You don't have to carry me," I mumble. "I can—I think...nope, I can't walk—thingsssss are blurry."

"You're slurring your words." He laughs. "You sound like a hissing cobra with those dark eyes of yours." That makes an image flash in front of me.

"Cobra, cobra," I pronounce the word carefully. "I've seen a gold cobra."

"Wow, you really don't drink much, do you?"

"Two cobras, after he hit my face." I feel Mark stop.

"Who hit your face?"

"American man." My head flops to the side I'm so tired. "I remember now, I've seen him before." Mark sits me down on the bottom of the stairs. He pulls out his cell and calls someone. I lean against the wall watching the stairs blur together as another memory comes to me. "He has a ring that has—" I tip forward but Mark grabs my shoulders, stopping me.

"What has she had?" Cole's voice booms in front of me.

"A tail," I answer very matter of fact. "Wait, now, that's not right."

"She's had two Tale of the Devils." Mark moves over as Cole comes into view.

"And I saw two cobras," I remind Mark.

"Yes, Savi, gold, right?"

"Mmmhmmm." I nod. "With black eyes."

"Where did you see this?" Cole asks.

"Right after he hit my face. It hurt a lot."

"The American," Mark adds. "She said she's seen him before, something about a ring."

"Yes, a ring," I look at my fingers, trying recall which finger it was. Cole takes my hands in his.

"Where else have you seen him, Savi? The American."

Memories start flashing in front of me. They're all going by so fast. "Baby, look at me." I do, trying to focus, I hate when these flashbacks come…it stirs so many emotions.

"It's okay, I'm here," he reassures me.

"Once at a restaurant with Lynn. He was at the bar watching me," I say quietly, trying to concentrate. "And at the market." My head turns to one side as I remember something else. "His boots made a sound that was different, like nails tapping on tile." I lower my voice. "He came to my prison one night." I swallow, remembering. "He stood over my bed staring down at me." I raise my hand to my lips. "He whispered something in Spanish and kissed his two fingers and pressed them to my forehead."

"Do you remember what he said?"

"Yeah, he said, '*Pronto serás mia, mi amor*'.

Cole's eyes widen and fear runs across his face.

"Are you sure that's what he said? Think, Savannah."

I nod a bunch of times. "Yes, I wanted to know what it meant so I could research it, but forgot about it till now." I run my hand through my hair so it is out of my face. "I think I might be drunk. Wait-wait! What does it mean?"

"I'll tell you in the morning." He scoops me up and carries me up the stairs.

My head is spinning like a Ferris wheel. "You don't have to carry me!"

I hear him laugh as I open my eyes and squint focusing on his jawline. He has a five o'clock stubble that's begging my fingers to trace along the outline. "You're very handsome, you know that?"

"And you're very beautiful."

"I'm engaged," I joke.

"Oh, baby, the only guy who will ever have a ring on that finger of yours is me."

My heart stops—did he just say that? I decide to see if he did.

"Mmm, Savannah Logan, I rather like the sound of that."

"Me too." He pulls back the blankets and sits me on his bed.

*Huh, I guess he did.* "You're very confident," I say with a grin.

"I'm confident when I know I'm right about something."

"Wait, you just walked me through the front door of your bedroom." I look around. "Someone will see!"

"I don't care. Arms up."

I do, falling forward. "I think I might be really drunk, which is bad because drunk girls are not flattering."

He pulls off my top, replacing it with one of his T-shirts. "Well, I kind of like you like this." I smile at his words. He leans me back and starts undoing my pants.

I grin, lifting my hips off the bed.

"I know that look." He smiles back at me. "And trust me, baby, there's nothing more I want to do than to sink myself deep inside you. But I will not have our first time end with you passing out on me."

I moan. "I love that you're such a gentleman." He pulls my pants off, looking down at my panties.

"Yeah...it feels great right now," he says sarcastically, closing his eyes and taking a moment. "Come on, under the blankets you go," he says as he tucks me in.

"You're still dressed." I yawn.

"I am." He sighs. "I still have some work to do."

The room is spinning. I watch him shake two different looking pills into my hand. "Take these." He supports me, helping me drink some water. Way too out of it to even ask what they are, I close my eyes, feeling him stroke my hair.

"Will you come to me later?" I mumble as I drift off to sleep.

"I always will."

\*\*\*

Cole pours himself a fourth cup of coffee, feeling beyond beat. He only got two hours of sleep on his office couch while going over reports for York's case. Frank is arriving in twenty and he needs to get his head in the game. He looks out the window, sees the guys heading up the mountain for their morning training and wishes he could join them and burn off some tension.

Checking the time to ensure he would catch Savannah before she leaves for the spa, he hurries down the hallway finding her pulling on her jacket in the entryway as she chats with his mother.

"Hey, I thought you were training with the guys." She smiles up at him.

"I wish," he mutters. "Can I speak with you for a moment?" She follows him into a room.

"What's wrong?" She runs her hand across his morning scruff. "Did you get any sleep last night?"

"I want you to stay in touch with me today," he replies, ignoring her question. "My mother has a phone, so send me a text when you get settled at the spa, okay?"

"Okay," she says, looking at him. "But, Cole, you're kind of scaring me."

"I just don't like the idea of you driving through those mountains without me. I don't like you being away from me period," he admitted.

"Me either." She sighs, making him happy hearing her words.

"However, that being said I want you to have fun, don't let the ladies pry too much. Mom adores you and will want to know everything." She looks up smiling her eyes holding his.

"I should go," she says, wrapping her arms around his neck and kissing him deeply.

He squeezes her to his chest not wanting to let go.

She pulls back. "Try to get some rest, baby."

He loves how she cares for him like they've known each other forever.

"Okay, you need to go or you'll never get out of here." He kisses her one last time.

\*\*\*

I think I've died and gone to heaven as I sink further down into the brown goo.

"Who would have thought mud would feel so heavenly?" June moans, sipping her champagne.

"Who would have thought I could stomach this," I hold up my glass, "after Dell's mad concoction last night?" I laugh, thinking about something. "Sue, is Dell York's replacement?"

"No, he's just filling in until they bring in someone else."

"Ladies," Carlos interrupts us, "time to move on."

We spent the next three hours being pampered to the nines, everything buffed and polished. The girls encouraged me to add some honey highlights to my hair, saying it will help brighten my mood, and I am stunned with how much I love the look with my huge curls draping down my back. We all decide on complete makeovers after that.

I feel amazing. As we take our seats for a late lunch at Zack's restaurant I'm thankful the lunch rush is over...there are only two tables occupied besides ours.

"Ladies!" Zack calls out hurrying over to our table. "You all look beautiful!" He turns to the male host, clucking his tongue. "Adam, you should sit them in the window they would draw in more customers."

"I agree." Adam winks at me and I smirk finding his boldness funny.

"Please, let me make you something special." He snatches the menus, giving them back to Adam. "You all just sit back and let Zack take care of you. Wine." He nods at Adam.

"Thank you, Zack," Sue says as Zack leaves.

Abigail grins at me. "Looks like someone likes the way Savi glows today."

I smile moving the attention over to Abigail. "Speaking of liking the way someone looks at someone, care to give the dirt on Doctor Roberts?"

This makes June perk right up.

"As in the house psychologist?"

"Yes, June," I grin, "that one."

"I'm not sure what you're referring to." Abigail tries so hard not to smile but it doesn't work with three people waiting to get the goods. "We kissed once," she says, picking at a piece of bread.

"What?" The three of us yell at the same time.

"Why do I not know this?" June snaps her at sister.

"I didn't want you to say anything to him. Besides, it was a one-time thing in the summer. We both haven't spoken about it since." She waves her hand. "It was nothing."

I shake my head. "I sit in front of that man for an hour a day," I say. "I see the way he looks at you. He likes you, Abigail."

She smiles back at me.

"Let's plan to have him over for dinner this week."

"Yes, let's!" June chimes in.

I beam at June then turn to see Abigail blush. "Don't let someone good slip through your fingers, Abigail, you deserve to be happy."

"Speaking of deserving to be happy," Sue sits back in her chair looking at me. "What's going on with you and my son?"

Oh shit. I lean over, pouring myself some more wine…making her laugh.

"Ladies, bon appetit," Zack announces as he and Adam serve our lunch. "Chicken Souvlaki with roasted potatoes and grilled asparagus," he says with a flourish.

It smells amazing. Everything looks so perfectly placed on the plate you almost don't want to touch it.

Adam leans over my seat, whispering, "You must have come from the spa…you smell of vanilla."

I nod, fighting the blush I feel rising in my cheeks.

"Can I get you anything else?" I notice he isn't asking the rest of the table.

"No, thank you. I'm fine." I glance at Sue, who is chuckling.

We are all pretty quiet as we start eating. I'm hoping to god they don't bring up Cole again but I know it's highly unlikely.

"What do you miss most from home, Savannah?" June asks throwing me with her question.

"I-I'm not sure," I stammer, thinking. "I mean I miss a lot of things, but my life was so different." I lean back letting Adam clear away my plate. "It wasn't exactly going the way I thought it would. I was becoming less and less connected to the outside world because of the paparazzi. I was trying so hard to be what my father wanted and so hard not to be what the press was convinced I was, that I lost who actually I was."

June nods. "So who is the real Savannah, and what does she want out of this life?"

"Umm…" I hadn't really thought of it. "I guess I'm still figuring out who I am. As far as what I want out of life, it would be just to find someone who loves me for me." I tilt my head giving it some thought. "Someone to curl up with on a stormy night, holding me till it passes; someone who no matter what kisses me hello and goodbye." I think of Cole. "Someone who can melt your heart with just one look, make your knees weak when they say your name. Make your breathing stop when they reach out to touch you." I look up to see three women staring at me with dreamy eyes like I'd been singing a love song. I cough and we all sit up a little straighter. "I'm tired of putting my life on hold. I just want to be happy. I know I have a long road ahead of me and a lot more hurdles to get over, but the fact that I know I will be doing it with all of you makes it a little easier," I confess.

"That's a lovely thing to say dear." Sue reaches for my hand, giving it a squeeze.

God it feels nice opening up and letting them in, even if it's just little baby steps, I smile to myself. Something else pops in my head and makes me feel happy all of a sudden.

"The piano, June." I smile, glancing at Abigail who gives me a wink. It means so much that she's never spoken about me playing it when I first arrived...I know she understood it was a private moment for me. "I've only played twice since my mother passed, but I love to play the piano."

"There's one in the living room dear," June says. "You'll have to play for us some time."

"We have piano here!" Zack booms coming toward the table.

*How the hell did he hear us?*

"You want to play?"

"No, no, I'm too rusty." I hold up my hands. "Perhaps another time."

"Okay, but I'm holding you to that," he says through a grin. "Ladies, I hope you enjoyed your lunch, we'll see you soon, right?"

"Of course." Sue stands giving him a hug.

We say our goodbyes as Adam races ahead of us opening the door.

"Have a good afternoon," he says with a bow. "I hope to see you again real soon, Nicole."

"I'm sure you do," June jokes on the way over to the SUV.

Keith is on the phone with someone watching me

as I come toward the car. "She's fine. We're about to head home. Okay."

He smiles. "You got the boss in a knot because you didn't text."

"Oh shoot!" I hit my forehead. "I forgot."

"No worries."

"Sorry."

# Chapter Fourteen

Abigail and June sit in front of Sue and me. June is prattling on about Doctor Roberts, wanting to know all the juicy details. I notice Sue is quiet and looks like she is deep in thought. I decide I may as well give her something since she's been so incredibly generous and loving toward me.

"I really care a lot about your son, Sue," I say quietly so the guys up front don't hear. "I've never felt like this before. It's a little new to me, and a little scary." I drop my gaze to my hands, suddenly wondering if maybe I have too much baggage for her son. "We may not be the perfect fit but he makes me feel alive when we're together."

"Savannah," she says, "you and Cole fit perfectly together. I can't tell you the last time I've seen my boy truly happy." Her eyes gloss over. "He cares for you deeply too, I can tell."

"Tell me you want children," Abigail hisses over her shoulder, making me throw my hands over my face.

"We want a little fritter!" June laughs.

"Well I don't know about 'Fritter,'" I say, "but

yes, I've always wanted kids." Abigail and June both turn to look at me.

"Don't toy with us Savannah." Abigail gives me a look. "Our boys need to have babies—we've been waiting too damn long."

"Oh my!" I laugh as I look over at Sue who is nodding in agreement with them.

Later as Abigail and I start dinner, I realize I haven't seen Cole since I left this morning. There seems to be some tension in the house and I recognize that Mark and John also seem a little on edge.

"How was your day?" I ask, trying to feel them out.

"I've had better," Mark mutters, grabbing a beer from the fridge popping the top off with one of those credit card openers with the S logo. "You may want to make extra...looks like our company will be staying for dinner."

"Company?" I ask surprised. "Who's here?"

"I just don't understand why they'd put oil and water together in the same house," John hisses as Mark ignores my question, and tosses him a beer.

"Oh no, they're not!" Abigail stops stirring the soup shaking her head. "When's Dell leaving?"

"Already gone." Mark shrugs at me, seeing my face fall. "It's how it works here."

I feel badly I didn't get to say goodbye.

"I'll be damned if he joins Blackstone. I don't trust that man."

"I assure you I have no interest in joining Blackstone," a tall guy with short brown hair says, coming into the kitchen. "The less of Logan I have to see the better," he says as he steps in front of me, blocking me from the salad I'm working on. "You must be Savannah Miller."

"I am." I wait for him to move—I don't like the way he spoke about Cole.

"I'm Derek Rent." He holds out his hand, so I give him a quick shake and move around him. "Looks like we'll be housemates."

"So I've been hearing." I try to sound friendly, but if Cole, John, and Mark don't like this guy, there must be a good reason. "Welcome."

"Don't listen to these guys," he says as he takes a seat at the island, stealing a chopped mushroom from my pile. "No one likes the new guy."

"New guy would imply we don't know anything about you, unfortunately that's not the case," Mark says as he downs his beer.

"Ah, Mark, are we still going to do the same old song and dance?"

"Where's Cole?" I ask changing the subject, wishing he was here.

"He's talking to Frank, in his office," Derek says with a long sigh. "Things got pretty heated earlier."

"Is everything all right?" I ask tossing the mushrooms in the bowl.

"Not when I left the room."

The usual large crowd doesn't join us for dinner tonight but Mark, Paul, John, and Derek are at the table and as I sit down Keith slips in to my left telling us that Cole, his father Daniel, and a man named Frank Brandon will be joining us shortly. Abigail, June and Sue try to lift the tension at the table.

"I still think it was priceless when Carlos tried to get Keith in for a seaweed wrap." June laughs, continuing. "The look on your face, Keith—"

"Was like confusion mixed with disgust," I finish for her, the girls and I start laughing.

"Why would anyone wrap themselves in something you eat between two sticks or avoid in the ocean?" Keith says, shaking his head. "I'll never understand why women do the things they do."

"Amen." Mark raises his beer.

"Sorry we're late." Daniel leans over giving Sue a kiss on the cheek.

"Savannah." Cole grabs my attention. "This is Frank Brandon."

I stand to shake hands with him. With his green camouflage pants, black heavy knit sweater, and his hair in a crew cut over intense dark eyes, he is the ultimate definition of an "army guy".

"Nice to meet you." I smile at him simultaneously noting that Cole and Daniel look exhausted.

"It's a pleasure to finally meet you, Ms. Miller." He moves around the table to sit directly across from me.

I slip back into my chair watching Cole's face. Something seems off.

So, Ms. Miller, how are you adjusting to the house?" Frank asks, digging into the scalloped potatoes.

"Please, call me Savannah. Just fine, thank you. I feel safe here, something I didn't think I'd ever feel again."

He nods while chewing. "That's nice to hear.

Savannah--have you ever been to Washington?"

Cole stands, scraping his chair loudly on the floor, and disappears out of the room.

"Umm, yes once when I was a child. I don't remember too much though," I reply as Cole returns with a glass of brandy, "so please don't quiz me."

He chuckles. "I won't." He looks over at the ladies asking, "How was your trip into town today?"

I think it's strange he knew we were out.

"It was very nice and relaxing, nice to be pampered sometimes. Mix that with a little girl talk and you have a great day," Sue answers him, giving me a smile.

"Your hair looks nice," Cole says.

I smile at him happy that he noticed.

"Adam thought so too," Abigail says, laughing. "We went to lunch at Zack's and that poor boy was tripping all over himself making sure she was well taken care of."

"Oh, I bet," Cole mutters.

"Can you blame him?" Derek chimes in giving me a smile and a shrug.

"He was only doing his job," I protest shooting a look at Abigail, "it was nothing."

As the dinner dishes are cleared away Frank asks if I will join him in the living room for drinks. I look over at Cole making sure he's joining us as well. He nods at me and follows us with Mark and Daniel right behind him. I notice Keith and Paul are hovering around as well; something's up.

Scoot pounces on my lap demanding his normal belly rub. He wedges between Cole and I and presents himself rather shamelessly. I start rubbing while being handed a Mark special, which concerns me, considering he knows firsthand how drunk I was last night. The presence of the martini tells me I'm probably not going to like what I am about to hear.

"Savannah, I want to talk to you about your case," Frank says leaning forward in his chair, "but first I want you tell me what happened between you and York."

And so it begins.

I fill him in on as many details as I can remember and answer a ton of his questions, including a few that I wasn't comfortable with.

"So you didn't give him any signals that would prompt him to come on to you?"

"No!" I snap, feeling angry. "I told you we didn't get along since the moment we met."

"Can we get on with this?" Daniel asks, looking annoyed.

"Was York involved in my poisoning?" I ask.

"I can't really answer that," Frank says, shifting on the couch.

"Well, I guess I can't really answer any more of your questions," I reply, folding my arms and feeling my temper rise.

Scoot bats my hand but Cole takes over the rub so I can focus.

Frank lets out a long sigh pressing his lips together thinking. "Yes, we believe he was."

I nod letting that information sink in. "Why? I haven't done anything to that man—why would he try and kill me?"

"He wasn't trying to kill you—"

"Says you," I cut him off.

"He was trying to send a signal to The American as to where you are. If you went to a hospital they would have entered your file online and it would pop up to anyone who knows where to look for a case of poisoning by tetrahydrozoline. Thankfully, Logan was able to figure this out and stop the Doctor before he entered it."

I look over at Cole. "I guess that's two times you've saved my life."

His face looks so troubled I want to ask him what is wrong but I can't.

"Savannah, we have a problem," Frank says bluntly. "It was bad enough when we found out The American was involved in your abduction, but now to know that he's in love with you, that's—"

"Wha—What!" I set my drink down heavily on the table. "What are you talking about?"

"*Pronto serás mia, mi amor.*"

I look at Mark then Cole, suddenly remembering my conversation from last night.

"Soon you'll be mine, my love," he clarifies for me.

My blood pressure drops onto the floor as I stand up, feeling suddenly chilled. I awkwardly sit on the stones next to the fire.

"I'm sorry, I thought you knew what it meant," he says, seeing my reaction.

"No." I shake my head and look at Cole, feeling confused.

"You were in no state to hear what it meant," Cole explains, looking worried. "I couldn't risk you disappearing into the woods again."

"Savannah," Frank says, pulling my attention back to him, "we know York has connected with someone who has ties to the American. There's a chance he may have given up your location. I feel its best that you come with me to Washington until we get this cleared up."

So many things run through my head at once, all I can do is hold on until my brain catches up.

"I know you're comfortable here, but if The American is on his way—"

"So you don't know for sure," I manage to whisper.

"No. York won't talk to us," Mark says stepping toward me. "He'll only talk to you."

"Mark!" Cole snaps making me jump.

"I'll do it."

"No!" Cole snaps again.

"Where is he, Mark?" I ask.

"Downstairs."

Cole jumps to his feet lunging at Mark sending Scoot hissing under the couch.

Daniel jumps up getting between them. Downstairs! Where?

"Cole, sit!" Daniel pushes him backwards.

"Even if we did allow you to speak to him it wouldn't matter. We need to get you out of here," Frank says standing.

I stand too, shaking my head. I head for Cole's office where I know he keeps my file, having seen where he put it on the day I first met with him. I return with it a few moments later. I hand the file to Frank; he looks puzzled but opens it.

"If you are saying I need to leave here then you can toss out my agreement and I'll go home."

"No! Savannah!" Cole shouts coming over to me, I hold up my hand to stop him.

"If you're saying that me staying here is going to make it unsafe for these guys and the location of this house might be compromised, then I want to go New York."

"I don't think you understand how big this is," Frank says, surprised by my reaction.

"You're right, I don't. I'd love some answers if you're willing to provide them."

"Frank, give her some." Cole looks pale. "She needs to understand how serious this is."

Frank looks over at me, tossing the file down on the table as he sits. "Please Savannah, take a seat."

Cole reaches out gripping my arm and pulling me down next to him.

Frank lets out a deep breath, leaning his arms on his legs looking at me. "Someone contracted to have you kidnapped. We're not entirely sure who yet, but we have a few theories. One being your father's right hand man, Luka."

I kept shaking my head. Luka has been like an uncle to me forever.

"The others?"

"I don't want to go there yet."

I feel like I was hit in the stomach by a hammer, my meal is threatening to shoot up my throat like one of those high strikers you'd find at the carnival to test your strength. "My father's one of them, isn't he?"

"Savannah, everyone is a suspect right now,"

Cole says quietly.

Frank sighs, "After you were taken by *Los Sirvientes Del Diablos* they found out something and decided to flip the tables. They were ordered to kill you after the first day; that's when we realized you weren't involved."

I jump to my feet feeling pissed. "Pardon me?"

"There was the possible thought that you and your father planned this. He's up for reelection and it gave him a ton of attention with the press, but—"

"Are you fucking kidding me?" I hiss turning to look at Cole. "Did you believe that too?"

Cole shakes his head. "Savi, your case just keeps growing. Yes, before we got you, it was a possible thought. Once we had confirmation you were still alive and still under their watch we realized there was something more going on." I feel sick. "We are sure they're blackmailing your father with something."

"Oh my God," I whisper, fighting the spins.

Frank clears his throat. "We're not saying your father is involved with you being taken, but they have something that they're using to blackmail him, threatening to expose it if he doesn't pay."

"Wait!" I pace the floor trying to catch up. "When did they start blackmailing him?"

"Over a month ago."

"You mean right before I was rescued?"

"Yes."

"Why start then?"

"We don't know."

"Maybe York gave them the heads up on your plans to rescue me?"

"That's something we're considering." Frank nods. "Look, we don't know who set up the kidnapping in the first place. We don't know where *Los Sirvientes Del Diablos* or the rest of the Cartels are, but they have something they are using against your father. We don't know where The American is, but he's a damn smart man and always gets what he wants, and he wants you. If you go back to New York, you'll be taken."

I run my hand through my hair, then grab Cole's drink off the table, downing the brandy in one swallow. *Holy Christ that's strong!*

"I'll take my chances," I mutter, making both Cole and Mark jump to their feet.

"No, I won't let you," Cole says. grabbing my hand and pulling me to my feet, he wraps his arm around my waist holding me tightly. "Frank, she's just scared."

"Frank," Daniel says in a calm voice, "my father built and created Shadows. As of two days ago, I signed my company over to my son. I believe that if everyone who's employed in this house is behind having Savannah continue to stay here then she should be able to stay, if that's what my son wishes."

"I do," Cole answers without missing a beat.

Frank ponders the idea. "If everyone is on board then fine, we'll stand behind you. But think about what you're risking if they find her or this place."

"No, guys." I swallow the lump in my throat. "Daniel that's incredibly kind of you but I don't want them risking all this just for me." I can't help the tears that are threatening.

"Savannah, stop please," Cole whispers, gripping me harder.

"Call a house meeting," Frank says watching the two of us.

Cole no longer cares who sees his affection for me?

"Frank, may I have a word with you in Cole's office?" I ask, feeling Cole flinch. "I'll be right back," I say. "*Please trust me*," I beg him with my eyes.

"Of course." Frank waves toward the hallway.

# Chapter Fifteen

Cole feels such a loss when she leaves his side. Watching her walk away, he wonders what in the hell they're going to discuss.

Daniel calls over the radio to ask everyone leave their post temporarily for a house meeting in the living room—ASAP.

Mark grips Cole's arm pulling him off to the side. "I wanted Frank to tell her about the blackmail. It might trigger something for her, plus we don't want her going back to her father yet. Something still isn't adding up there. I'm sorry about the York comment; I thought maybe she'd stay if she could help with the York investigation."

Cole nods. He knows Mark is trying to help but he hates the idea that Savannah might go looking for answers from York.

"You're up son," Daniel says, nodding at the crowd now gathered in the living room around them.

Cole moves to the fireplace and everyone stops talking—waiting to find out what's going on.

"Thank you all for coming in so fast. Here's the

situation. As of right now we've discovered that York may have been in communication with The American's people. We now know that The American had other plans for Savannah," Cole swallows the bile in the back of his throat and continues. "It seems he was planning on taking her for himself and has stepped up the hunt for her. Frank Brandon is here and wants to take Savannah back to Washington for her own protection but Savannah won't go. She wants to go back to New York rather than put Shadows at risk." A light roar sounds among the crowd.

"No! She'll be killed!" Abigail shrieks holding her stomach.

"Here's my plan." Cole holds up his hand getting their attention again. "Frank will allow her to stay here as long as everyone is in agreement and understands the consequences that come with protecting her here at Shadows. This could get bad so if you're not okay with it please let me know and I'll lay you off temporarily until this is over—no judgment passed. With a show of hands, who is not all right with Savannah staying here?" No hands are raised.

"I think I speak for all of us when I say Savi isn't going anywhere." Keith's voice booms throughout the living room.

Cole gives him a nod, feeling relief spread over him. Now he just needs to convince Savannah.

"If you don't mind," Mike tugs at his jacket, "I'm sweating in my gear and I would like to get out there and watch for that sick son of a bitch."

"All right, go. Thanks guys." Cole waits for the

crowd to leave and then leans his forehead on the mantle taking a breather and wishing this would end.

"Oh dear," Sue says rubbing his back, "your father just filled me in. I'm sure she's just scared and worried about all of you—give her some time. You know this is a lot for her to process."

"I don't know what I'll do if she leaves," he whispers.

His mother comes around to face him.

"We had quite the talk in the car on the way home. She really cares about you, Cole."

"Mention the part about the Fritters, Sue," June says as she eavesdrops while walking by.

Cole looks over at his mother who is trying to hide a smile. "Yes, well, the aunts," she nods toward Abigail and June, "got confirmation that she does want kids."

Oh lord! Poor Savannah; he could only imagine the firing squad of questions that were thrown at her. Although the idea of having a little one running around wasn't as scary as he thought it would be. He shakes his head. *What the hell is happening to me? I've only known this woman for two months!*

"Son." Daniel nods toward the hallway where Savannah is shaking Frank's hand.

"I'll see you all tomorrow," Frank calls before he disappears out the door.

Savannah walks into the living room and he can see she's been crying. He can't help but wonder what is going on in that pretty little head of hers, but knows he has to give her some space. He doesn't say anything.

"I have until tomorrow to decide," she says, not looking at him.

"Come and sit, Savannah," his mother says as she puts her arm around Savi's shoulders and walks her to the couch. Draping her favorite blanket around her, she says, "Can I get you anything?"

"No. I'm all right, thanks."

"What did Frank say?" Daniel asks, watching Mark leave the room to answer his cell phone.

"He just filled me in on the risks if I stay or leave. He answered a few more questions and in turn I answered a few for him. I will not go to Washington...the idea scares me more than going back to New York. Trusting people doesn't come easily for me anymore. I'm just really confused." She rubs her head. "I don't think of New York as my home anymore and after what I learned tonight I feel like I can't trust anyone there." She starts to cry. "The worst part is I have mixed feelings toward my father. What does that say about me? I'm a horrible person. I'm sorry," she says, standing. "I really just need some time to think this all through." She looks over at Cole. "I promise—no woods." With that she turns and heads upstairs.

Cole jumps to his feet, pacing the room and ignoring the low hum of voices in the background. He knows he can't let her leave. Needing to prove how much he cares for her, he takes off toward her room with his mother's protests to give her more time ringing in his ears.

Marching down the hallway, he throws open her bedroom door locking it behind him. The shower is running; he strips off his clothes and heads toward the bathroom. He does not hesitate as he opens the shower door and steps in.

"Cole!" She jumps letting her gaze travel down his body. "Oh!"

He grabs her around the waist lifting her up and against the wall.

She lets out a squeak as her legs wrap around him.

He likes her this way…she can't run and he has full access to her long, slender neck. He leans in, kissing her below her ear feeling her pulse quicken. He brushes his lips over her ear. "What is there to think about, Savi?" he whispers hoarsely.

She runs her hands through his wet hair, letting out a sigh. "Cole, I can't stay."

Oh, hell no. He positions himself at her opening and slams in.

She screams, gripping his shoulders.

He nearly doubles over she is so tight and ready for him. "Does that feel good?"

"God, yes! Again!" She wiggles her hips. Her chest pushes into his face. Sweet lord she's beautiful! He pulls out and slams in again nearly buckling. Christ, she feels amazing. He takes a minute, needing to control himself—it has been a long time since he has been with a woman. He slams again making her shoot up the wall.

"Yes!" she shouts, clawing at his skin like she is starving for him.

He slows the pace teasing them both, making short little thrusts.

"Cole, please," she begs, wiggling, trying to get more friction. "Please."

"If you leave, I'll never see you again. You told me you were mine." She starts to whimper as he thrusts up hard. "This is where you belong, baby, with me—nowhere else."

She leans forward sealing her lips over his, kissing him deeply.

Oh, this woman is going to kill him. He returns to his rough movements, giving her everything he has. He's completely lost in her...his mind is spinning with all her gasps and moans.

"Cole!" she calls out. He can tell she's close.

"Give it to me, baby, give in."

She screams as her entire body shakes and squeezes him like a glove. His vision goes cloudy as he loses all control, emptying himself into her.

They are both panting as they come down from their high. She's like jelly in his arms, completely spent. He washes her, basically having to hold her up with one hand. He wraps her in a towel and puts her to bed. He quickly dries himself off, chucks the towel in the basket, then crawls in behind her, their naked bodies giving each other comfort.

It's pitch black but he can tell she is still awake...her breathing is uneven. He kisses her shoulder, letting his lips linger on her silky skin, "I'm not letting you go Savannah," he whispers. She doesn't say anything but she pushes herself tighter against him.

\*\*\*

*I tap my fingers on the railing, watching the numbers light up one by one; fifteen more to go.*

"*Savannah!*" *Luka calls out as I step out of the elevator door on the twenty-sixth floor of the Maxwell building. "What are you doing here?" He gives me a hug.*

"*I'm meeting Dad for lunch.*"

*He looks at me funny, and I know what's coming.* "*He must have forgotten. He left about ten minutes ago.*" *I curse inwardly.*

"*Third time in two weeks—a girl could get a complex,*" *I joke, giving him the best smile I can muster.* "*I guess I'll head back across town.*"

*Luka squeezes my arm.* "*Sorry, sweetheart. I'll let him know you were here.*"

"*Thanks.*" *I click the button a few times then decide I'd rather write my dad a post it and stick it to his monitor so he would see it when he got back. I race off toward his office. Margo, his receptionist, is away from her desk so I slip inside grab a pen and quickly write, 'You forgot again...you owe me three lunches- S'*

*I post it to the monitor and let myself out.*

"*Oh, hello,*" *a woman with straight blonde hair cut in a bob greets me.* "*Savannah. right?*"

"*Ah, yes.*" *I smile.* "*Where's Margo?*"

"*Her father is sick...she had to go visit him in Philly.*"

*Later on that evening, my father finally calls me.*

"*Hey, Dad,*" *I say rubbing my eyes.*

"*Savi, sorry I forgot about today,*" *I hear a woman's voice in the background.*

"*Dad, do you have company?*" *I grin.*

"*Don't be ridiculous, Savi, it's just Margo. She came over to drop off a file.*"

*"Right." I laugh, walking over to grab a blanket off the chair.*

*"We'll reschedule for another day. Got to go. Good night, Savannah."*

*"Have fun, Dad." I'm still laughing as I hang up. I stop suddenly when my eye is drawn to someone standing across the street. He seemed to be looking directly at me. He was holding what looked like a folded newspaper, when he turned away I noted how the light reflected on his boots...they look odd, like they flipped up at the tips. How strange.*

My eyes pop open as my heart pounds out of my chest. I look at the time: four thirty. Cole is wrapped around me so I gently try to move his arm but it locks around me.

"Why is your heart racing?" he whispers in my neck. Crap.

"Bad dream. I'm sorry I woke you."

"You didn't." He rolls on his back, pulling me into his side so my head rests on his chest.

"You haven't slept?" I feel terrible.

"What were you dreaming about?"

I sigh as he dodges my question.

"I remember another time I saw The American. He was outside my condo watching me."

Cole doesn't say anything he just stares at the ceiling. What I wouldn't give to know what he is thinking. When I can't take the silence anymore, I roll on his stomach and straddle him. The only light is from the full moon so it's hard to read his expression. I trace paths down his stomach with my fingertips…it flexes when he folds his arms behind his head. I know he is upset with me but I haven't had time to really think since I passed out after our shower encounter. I shiver when I remember the feeling of him inside of me. I push my weight on top of my knees to get the angle right then sink down before he has a chance to stop me.

"Savannah!" He jolts forward, grabbing my hips, "Fuckkkk."

I shift my body around adjusting to his size. He lays back down as I start a slow, lazy pace.

His hands press over his face as he sucks in a deep breath. He gasps, "Christ, woman!" He grabs me, holding me still as he flicks his hips up trying to get deeper, faster.

I push his hands away, smiling. I am in control this time.

He shakes his head, groaning, as I set the pace, again running my hands down his front, stopping in all the right places. Payback is going to be fun.

I pull him almost all the way out, but only take him back an inch.

He hisses out a puff of air.

I pull up again and slam down knowing I could barely take much more.

Suddenly I am on my back and my legs are hiked up over his shoulders. He pushes into me, taking me hard. My eyes close and I smile—I love how dominating he is in bed. Ha! He's dominating outside the bedroom too. I do love how I got him to this point, knowing he would take over.

"Look at me, baby."

I open my eyes—he's inches above me, his eyes

showing me how worried he is. "Right here is where you belong," he says as he slams hard, making his point and taking me over the edge.

I'm lost in a sea of colors as I scream out his name, my orgasms coming in waves.

He covers my mouth to muffle my screams as I feel him quiver, finding his bliss right after mine. He flops down, resting his head on my stomach as I run my fingers through his damp hair. "I want to do that to you every morning," he says as he kisses me above my belly button right before he rolls off, pulling me back onto his chest. "Next time I want to take it slow, make it last for hours."

I don't have any words for the way I feel. Instead I lean up, kissing him once on under his chin.

I wake again at seven. This time Cole doesn't budge when I slip out of bed. I pull the blankets over him making sure he's warm before I jump in for a quick shower. I manage to get dressed without waking the poor guy.

"Good morning," Abigail says, handing me a cup of coffee. "You get any sleep?"

"A little." I sigh feeling a bit sore; two times with Cole and I should be sitting on a donut ring. "Cole is still sleeping. He's really tired. Can you make sure no one wakes him?"

"Of course. And Frank arrived twenty minutes ago. He's outside with Daniel if you want to speak with him."

"Yes, I do. Thanks."

She comes around the island, giving me a hug. "Please don't leave us, we all love you," she sniffs, letting me go.

My eyes prickle. "I love you too, Abigail." And I do…wow I really do care a lot for this woman.

I pull on my coat and boots and head out. It's lightly snowing as I make my way over to Frank and Daniel at the stables.

"Good morning," I say, coming up behind them.

"Hello, Savannah," Frank says. "Have you made your decision?"

Daniel takes off his knit hat, slips it over my head, then grants me a Logan smile. "I'll see you indoors."

\*\*\*

Cole opens his eyes, feeling like something is off. His hand quickly does a swipe of the bed and he jumps when he notices she's gone. Shit! It was quarter to eight, and Frank was arriving at six thirty. He flips down the panel on the wall, enters the code, and races toward his bedroom. He needs to get some clothes.

Running down the stairs and into the kitchen he finds his father and Abigail looking worried.

"Where is she?"

"Out by the stables," Abigail says. "They've been talking for over an hour."

Cole moves over to the window and spots them. Savannah has her back to the house; Frank is nodding his head.

"Why didn't someone wake me?" he asks trying to think clearly.

"Savi wanted you to sleep."

Of course she did. He flops himself on a stool,

thinking he can barely remember the last time he slept past seven am.

"There's nothing you can do, but wait," Daniel says from behind him. "Looks like they'll be a while…go have a shower. You look like hell."

After taking his Dad's advice and grabbing a brief shower he joins them back at the kitchen table. His mother hands him a plate of bacon and eggs. He rubs his head. This waiting is killing him.

"How did she seem last night?" his mother asks, sitting across from him.

"Confused. I can tell she doesn't want to go."

"She doesn't," Keith states, joining them. "She told me when we were walking out of the woods. She asked what if I don't want to leave, what happens then?"

Cole sags into his seat.

"She's leaving because we're all in danger," Daniel says into his coffee mug. "She cares about us that much that she's willing to risk her own life just to make we're all right. She's a pretty amazing woman."

"We're always in danger," Keith huffs. "Never stopped us before."

The front door opens and they all stop talking. Savannah comes around the corner first, looking frozen.

Cole quickly pours her a cup of coffee. "You didn't wake me," he whispers, handing it to her.

"You needed to sleep," she says reaching out and squeezing his arm—her fingers are like ice. Just as she takes the mug Frank enters the room.

"Well, your girl puts up one hell of a fight," he

says, pulling off his hat and sitting at the table. "I'm mentally fried!"

Cole leans back holding onto the island as his stomach bottoms out again.

Frank makes a show of checking his watch saying, "I have to run into town. I'll be back this evening with my men to transfer Agent York back to Washington."

Savannah steps forward, shaking his hand. "Thank you."

Everyone is quiet. After they hear him leave all eyes are on her.

"Well," she sighs, "I guess you're stuck with me."

Cole sags into the counter as everyone jumps to hug her...it feels like his feet are welded to the floor.

She turns and pushes up on her toes, whispering into his shoulder, "I didn't want to leave this house, these guys, or you."

The corners of his mouth go up as he leans down. "I wouldn't let you even if you tried."

She turns her head toward him. They were so close he can feel her warm breath on his cheek. Cole glances around and sees everyone is busy. He leans in, giving her a light peck on her lips.

She tilts her head, surprised, but grants him a smile that reaches her eyes. He's fallen.

# Chapter Sixteen

I push the cart slowly through the aisle.

"Okay, so silver and gold?" Abigail asks me as we enter the third Christmas store in a row.

Since I decided for a second time to stay at the house, I thought it was about time to decorate.

Abigail and June normally do a Christmas tree, but that's about it. Not this year...if I'm staying, then we are decorating just like Lynn and I did back in NY. Winter wonderland.

"And red," I add as Abigail holds up a package of white sparkly snowflakes. "Now those are prefect, how many in a package?"

"Umm, twelve—oh, look, gold ones too."

"Perfect! Grab three of each."

She laughs, dropping them into the cart.

"So do you know how Melanie and Mark are doing?"

Abigail holds up some thick red ribbon, I nod while grabbing boxes of ornaments and a red velvet tree skirt. "They're doing really well actually." She beams. "He's even talking to me about her now. He wants to invite her to the light show in town when we all attend."

"Wow, kind of like meeting the family officially…again!" We break out laughing.

After three more stores I am more than impressed with what we got. Paul shakes his head each time we came out with a cart full from each place.

"I'll take you to Zack's once I know you're settled," he says. "I'll take off over to the grocery store to save some time."

"Okay…" I hesitate giving him my list.

"What?"

"Just don't substitute things."

He smirks at me—we've been down this road before. "When it says—"

"I know." He snatches the list out of my hand. "When it says sharp cheese don't get medium cheese. Oh, I remember." He chuckles, waving me into the SUV.

Zack is more than happy to see us. Our impromptu shopping trip didn't allow us to give him a heads up that we were coming and he falls all over himself with glee. Adam, remembering last time, sits us by the fireplace.

"Ladies! What an unexpected pleasure," Zack says warmly. "Are you in town to do a little shopping?"

"Savannah wants to spread some Christmas cheer throughout the house so we needed to buy some decorations," Abigail informs him, smiling as she removes her coat.

"I think we bought the town," I joke.

"Well isn't that fun!" He snaps his fingers at

Adam. "A bottle of my personal favorite." Adam rushes off toward the back. "You two sit back and let Zack take care of you."

I smile that seems to be his line with us. I am more than willing—he always makes the best food.

"Can I ask you something personal?" Abigail takes a sip of her water

"Sure."

"Who taught you how to play the piano?"

I clear my throat feeling the lump that comes whenever anyone mentions the subject. "My mother."

"I thought so."

"Why's that?

She thinks for a moment. "You have a lot of emotion when you play. Tell me about her?"

"She was wonderful." I shrug, then seeing she's really interested, continue. "She was the kind of mother that would drop anything and play with you. She taught me how to bake, how to ride a bike, how to sing." I couldn't help but let out a chuckle. "She wass the singer in the family; I just play the piano."

"What about your—" she starts, turning red and fanning herself.

"Abby?" I start looking around.

"No, look at me," she says. "We're just talking."

"Yes, that's what we are doing." I laugh, puzzled. Then I realize what's putting her into a state.

"Hello, Savannah, Abigail, you both look lovely today."

"Thanks, you too," I say. "What are you up to today Doctor Roberts?" I eye Abby, whose face is finally starting to go back to her normal shade.

"I had to pick up some packages then decided to have a bite of lunch."

"Please say you'll join us," I ask as Abigail's eyes widen.

"Thank you, that sounds nice."

Adam rushes a chair over for him—he must have been watching us.

"It can get lonely eating every meal by yourself," he admits, settling in and glancing at Abigail who has yet to say anything. "That's a lovely blouse, Abigail, it makes you shine."

"Thank you." She smiles coyly. "And I see you're wearing your red tie."

This time it is Doc Robert's face that blushes. "Yes, well, it is my favorite," he whispers.

My jaw nearly drops when I realize what they must be referring to last summer's romance.

"So, Doctor Roberts, do you have any plans tomorrow night?" I ask, feeling badly that I'm breaking up their moment, but I am about to grant them another.

"I do believe I am free."

"Wonderful. Please join us for dinner. It's Abigail's night off—" She looks at me puzzled— "And I am in charge of cooking. Her sister, June, is in town and I understand that you've never met."

"You have a night off?" He smiles at Abigail. "Well, how can I refuse?"

I have to press my lips together so not to yelp with joy! "Well that's great! Be there at five?"

He nods and I see Abigail trying not to smile.

"Can you excuse me a minute? I need to use the

restroom." I decide these two could use a little private time.

I head for the restroom but get sidetracked by a newspaper sitting on the bar. I glance at the cover then begin reading the local news about the light festival. A chiming noise outside has me looking out the window as I notice someone across the street; there is something familiar, but then he is gone. I freeze in place. Pushing the newspaper away from me I squint, but it's bright out with the snow. The moment I think I see him a trolley comes by and he hops on turning so his back is to me. I open the front door stepping outside. My mind is racing...his blue coat, red hat, blue coat, red hat. Continuing down the narrow, snow-filled sidewalk I round the corner and see the man getting off at a bakery. I hurry across the street so quickly a car has to slam on its brakes. The driver shouts at me but nothing registers in my urgency to follow this man. I slip into the bakery looking around at all the faces then I see a blue coat draped over a chair but the guy isn't there. "Umm, did you see the man who owns this jacket? Did you see what he looks like?" I ask the couple at the table next to the coat, they both shrug, shaking their heads. I turn to two women behind the cash register. "Where is the man who owns that jacket? Has he ordered yet? What does he look like?" I repeat urgently.

"Umm," the young women stumble, "I-I'm not sure, I'm sorry."

"Don't be sorry, just think, where is he?" I nearly shout at her. The whole place is looking at me when the bathroom door opens and a man comes out checking his belt.

"That's him," the girl at the table calls out.

"It that your blue jacket?" I ask the man.

"Yes," he answers. *Oh God.* I rub my head. *What the hell was that, Savi?* Talk about freaking out, I shake my head feeling stupid.

"I'm sorry, I thought you were someone else." I start toward the door but look back at him.

"Excuse me," I call back out to him, "are you wearing a red hat today?"

"No, green." He holds it up.

My stomach drops when I look at his jacket again. It's different, it's a pea jacket. The other guy's was a ski jacket. Shit...I push the door open as someone steps in front of me. I hold the door for them but they don't move. I look up and see Paul peering down at me. *Oh, shit...*

"What do you think you're doing?"

"I'm sorry, I thought—" I shake my head. I don't want to say I think I saw Jose Jorge. I'll sound crazy and they'll probably add an extra hour to Doctor Roberts's sessions. "I'm sorry."

"You are damn lucky I found you when I did. Cole is—"

"You called Cole?" I snap. "I've been gone what, five minutes?"

"No, I called Keith, and you were gone fifteen."

"Keith!" I toss my hands in the air as I walk around him "That's even worse!"

"How is that worse?" He hurries to catch up. "Look you can't run off on me like that."

I stop to look him. "I didn't run off on you, I just thought—" I shake my head. "Look it won't happen again. I'm sorry. Can we just forget about this?"

"Fine." He nods.

Lunch goes fairly well after I dodge twenty questions about what just happened. Doctor Roberts wasn't buying it but at least he left it alone for now. He and Abigail seem much more relaxed with each other and they both seemed to be looking forward to tomorrow night's dinner. I slowly come off my adrenalin rush, but the image of blue coat, red hat guy is burned into my memory. Somewhere deep down inside there's a part of me that thinks it could be him.

Abigail fills me in on their conversation while I was away from the table. I guess he's wanted to see her for a while now but wasn't sure if she felt the same way. Her face is positively glowing. I've never seen her so happy before. She hugs me as we walk to the car, thanking me for tomorrow night. The rest of the drive she prattles on about this and that. I keep catching Paul watching me in the mirror.

Sinking into the couch while Abigail fills June in on our day I glance at all the bags thinking I should probably get started with the decorating, but I don't get up. Instead I close my eyes, needing a minute to think. I hear someone clear their throat, and open my eyes to find Keith looking down at me. His arms are crossed and he has the look of death on his face. I hold up my arm saying, "Go ahead. Chip me." He rolls his eyes.

"Oh boy, would I love to," he snickers. "Are you insane?"

"Possibly." I sigh covering my face with my

arms. "Does Cole know?"

"Yes." *Of course…* "He was there when Paul called."

"And on a scale of one to ten?" I ask peeking out.

"It was ten, but now I'd say an eight."

I sigh again. I seem to be doing that a lot these days.

"He's on a conference call but I'm sure he'll want to see you afterward."

Oh, I bet.

\*\*\*

Cole stares at the speakerphone. Frank is giving him the play-by-play on what happened after they left the house this afternoon. Reaching over for the crystal bottle of brandy he pours himself a double…this shit is getting out of hand. He takes a drink, setting the glass down and flexing his hand—the hand that has been gripping his pen since Frank started his story.

"That's un-fucking-believable!"

"Yeah well, it was pretty intense." Frank clears his throat. "I got to go. I'll be in touch."

"All right." He rubs his face feeling exhausted when Abigail's text comes up alerting him dinner is ready. He lets her know that he won't be joining them. He needs to make some calls—the first one to his father.

Cole doesn't come out of his office until close to ten. Faint music reaches him as he walks down the hallway. He comes to an abrupt stop when he steps into the living room. *Holy shit...*

"Pretty amazing, hey?" June asks, handing him a rum and eggnog. "She's been working on this all evening."

Savannah is up on a ladder putting a star on top of the Christmas tree. It is decorated in silver and gold with thick red ribbon wrapped all around it. A red velvet tree skirt lies underneath. The fireplace has garland outlining it, with lights strung through and more red ribbon. A huge, tastefully lighted, matching wreath hangs above it. Silver and gold sparkly snowflakes are hung at different lengths in each window. Candles are placed throughout, tying the whole room together. June points to the banister going up the stairs which is covered in garland to match the fireplace. A big vase sits on the entryway table containing a huge poinsettia...she even gave it a light dusting of glitter to make it sparkle like the rest of the place.

"Wow," is all he can get out.

"Is everything all right dear? You look stressed."

He shakes his head. Now isn't the time to get into things.

Savannah looks over at him, giving him a smile that nearly has him running to her. "What do you think?" she calls out.

"It's amazing." He winks, watching her grin widen.

Mark walks by holding a bag of trash and stops next to him. "What's going on?" he asks quietly.

Cole shakes his head watching Savannah climb back down the ladder. Derek is, of course, ready for her in case she falls.

"Don't fuck with me. Your face is telling me something big is up."

"Later." He glances at him then his eyes narrow in on his chin. "Nice glitter."

"Oh, come on!" he hisses, rubbing his chin. "This shit doesn't come off." Cole tries to hide his smirk. "Oh, fuck off!" Mark storms off toward the bathroom.

After everything is put away everyone comes together for drinks and sweets. Mark is hovering by the table. Every once in a while Cole will look at him funny just to screw with him. He loves messing with him. He looks for Savannah but she's disappeared…he finds himself drifting back to his conversation with Frank and his stomach twists, making his thoughts go dark.

"You care to tell me what's going on now? Or do I need to call Dad?" Mark asks from beside him.

"Downstairs." He motions with his head.

He starts to tell his story but hears Savannah whispering with someone around the corner. He holds up his hand to Mark.

"That's the thing I don't know," her voice trails off.

"Well, that's the deal," Derek says.

What the hell? Cole steps around into view, making Savannah jump.

"Cole," she starts to say, but he cuts her off.

"What the hell is going on?" He shakes his head, making eye contact with Derek. "Go upstairs, Rent," he orders. Derek looks at Savi.

"Will you be okay?" he asks her. *Really?* She nods, running her hand through her hair.

"Why are you here with him?" Cole nearly shouts at her. "Do you know how this looks?"

"What are—?"

"First you run off at Zack's, leaving Paul to hunt you down, leaving Abigail unprotected just because what, you wanted a fucking pastry? Then I find you down here with Derek whispering in the dark. What the fuck is going on?"

"No! It's not—"

"You know what, never mind, I don't want to fucking hear it, Savi! Start using your fucking head, and think about someone else for a change."

Her face flinches as her gaze drops to the floor. "Can I speak now?"

"No." His jaw twitches as he tries to hold back his anger. "You should probably go upstairs now." He watches her turn on her heel and head up the stairs.

Mark comes around the corner. "Wow," he whispers.

"Shut up."

"That was harsh, Cole. She's one of the most selfless people I know."

"Fuck!" Cole rubs his face. Today's events have his emotions all over the place.

\*\*\*

I head up through the dining room and out to the patio. I need some fresh air badly. As I pace the snowy deck trying to catch my breath and soothe my hurt feelings, the last ten minutes loop over and over again in my head making me breathe harder and I soon start to see spots. My hands clutch at my stomach as I try to calm myself—shit, shit, shit!

"Savi?" Derek calls out slipping out the door. "You okay? What's happening?"

"I just need a minute." I hold my hand up. Between Cole's words and possibly seeing Jose today I am about to toss my dinner. I squat down into a ball covering my head with my arms as a vivid memory hits me.

*"Eat, perra!" the fat man shouts at me, jamming a roll at my mouth. "Eat or you'll get my fist again."*

I shudder…was that really him in town or am I losing my mind?

Derek's footsteps echo as he comes closer. He doesn't speak but simply puts a hand on my shoulder, a friendly gesture letting me know I'm not alone.

I take the comfort and let my stomach settle. After a few moments he goes back inside and I stand breathing through my nerves and head for the door.

I find Keith talking to John.

"Keith," I say, "can I speak with you?"

"Sure thing," he replies, and we walk off to the side.

"Since Cole is too busy yelling at me to listen, will you let him know the reason I walked off today is because I thought I saw Jose Jorge?" Keith's face falls.

"Yeah, okay," he replies. As he shoots off toward his office I make my way up to my room.

\*\*\*

My eyes pop open at five. It takes me a moment to realize I'm not back in my prison. I shower and get dressed and head downstairs, lighting the fireplace, and lying down on the floor near Scoot. He curls into my stomach as I lay on my side, my head resting on my arm. He must have been up late because I'm not getting hounded to scratch his tummy. Closing my eyes and listening to his soft purr relaxes me.

"What do we know so far?" I hear someone talking as I drag myself from my sleepy state.

"Just that he was standing outside of Zack's." Cole is speaking from the kitchen.

"Okay, where is she now?"

"Her bedroom."

I awkwardly move to my feet feeling a little sore from sleeping on the floor.

"Did she get a good look at his face?" I recognize Daniel's voice as I round the corner.

"Somewhat," I answer, making them both jump.

"Where were you?" Cole asks, eyeing my fur-covered shirt. I don't answer him...I'm still pissed. Instead I reach for a mug and pour myself some coffee.

"You should have told someone," Daniel says, giving me a small smile.

I stop at the island and turn toward him still ignoring Cole.

"I was going to," I mutter. "I need to change."

"When you're done, please find us in Cole's office."

"Sure." I nod walking upstairs.

\*\*\*

As Daniel holds Cole's office door open for me and I take in the room I note that Keith is sitting across from Cole and both look as tired as I feel.

"Come and sit down, Savannah," Daniel says pointing to the open seat. Keith gives me a smile as I sink down next to him and everyone stares at me. I'm not sure if I'm supposed to talk or what?

Daniel is the first to speak. "So tell us about yesterday."

I sigh, trying to hold back the emotion that is twisting inside me again.

"I went to use the restroom," I begin, "when I saw a newspaper on the bar and stopped to look at it. When I looked up, I glanced outside and saw a man looking my way. He looked so much like Jose Jorge, I was really shaken up. I couldn't believe it so I started to follow him. I needed to be sure. Jose—" I stop myself.

"Jose what?" Cole asks leaning forward in his seat.

Oh God, I feel sick. "Jose was the one who used to whip me," I wipe a pesky tear away. I could almost hear the tension thicken. "If it was him, I needed to know. I couldn't lose sight of him. I wasn't thinking—"

"Yeah, you sure weren't," Cole hisses, making me turn to him.

"You don't need to remind me again, Cole! You got through to me last night," I toss at him, making him flinch.

"Then what?" he asks tersely.

"So now you want the details?" I blurt. I can't help myself; he hurt me.

"Yes." His jaw flexes.

I look away. "I followed him to the cafe. I went inside but he wasn't there. I lost him." I leave out the part where I harassed a poor employee and a customer.

"What was the man who you thought was Jose wearing?" Daniel asks.

"Blue jacket with a red hat and jeans."

"Why didn't you tell someone right away?" Cole asks.

"Because I felt stupid! I thought I saw a man who I hate more than anything in the world and I went off chasing him...to what? Confront him? He overpowered me for seven months so I don't know what I was thinking. I was going to tell you, Cole. I just hadn't seen you all day other than when we were decorating, but you disappeared again." I gulp and continue my tirade. "When I went downstairs to grab some ice for Abigail I ran into Derek. He saw I was upset and asked what was wrong but I told him I wanted to talk to you about it first. That's when you came down and saw us. I wanted to tell you then but you never gave me a chance. You just tore a strip off me and accused me of frigging around with Derek. I'd never do that to—" I stop myself, remembering we aren't alone.

Looking at Daniel, I feel the need to apologize. "Look, I'm sorry for running off. I realize how dangerous it was; not just for me, but for Abigail too." I glance back to Cole. "It was selfish of me, it won't happen again."

Cole shakes his head, looking down at his desk. Everyone is silent.

"Are we done here?" I ask.

"Yeah, Savi, you can go. Thanks," Daniel says, rising to his feet.

\*\*\*

Cole leans back in his chair watching her leave as his father takes her seat rubbing his head.

"Am I missing something, or is Savi in a bad mood today?" John asks coming into the room and making himself a cup of coffee. Realizing the tension in the room, he turns. "Ahh, did I just walk in on something?"

"Savannah thinks she saw Jose Jorge," Cole says, rubbing his face.

"Do you think it was him?" John asks, looking around the room.

"I don't know, but she thought it was him enough to risk her safety. She followed him two blocks before Paul found her."

"Holy shit."

"Keith, I need you on this. Get the security tapes and find out what you can."

"Sure thing," Keith says pulling out his phone.

Cole's e-mail alerts him to an incoming message and he sees it's from Frank. "Shit!" He quickly opens the attachment and hits print.

"Trouble son?" Daniel asks, seeing Cole's face.

Cole hands the paper to John who takes one

glance at it and lets his head drop. Keith snatches it out of his hand and reads it with Daniel over his shoulder.

"Shit, boys…this is huge." His father's words are haunting.

# Chapter Seventeen

I need to burn off some serious tension. Prepping dinner just isn't cutting it. I head downstairs in my workout gear. My neon yellow soled sneakers squeak as I hit the polished hallway heading to the gym. Abigail had done well buying the newest gym clothes. My black spandex capris have a matching yellow stripe up the side that pairs nicely with the black top that hits right about my bellybutton. I open the door and find Paul and Derek working with weights.

"Hey, Savi," Paul calls out between a rep. "Come to sweat?"

"That's the plan." I look around trying to decide what I want to start on first and my eyes catch a door over on the back wall. Remembering that Keith mentioned there was a boxing ring here somewhere, I make my way over and peek in the window. An instructor is showing John some moves. I slip inside, curious to learn more.

I watch as John lays a series of punches into the man's glove.

He turns and does a kick in the air.

"Okay, good, but take five and try to get your mind clear, you seem off today," the instructor says, tossing him a towel.

John sees me and looks around the room. "Oh, hey, Savi."

"Hey. You don't sound happy to see me?"

"Sorry. Interesting day. Has Cole found you?"

"Not since this morning, why?"

"Just wondering," John says as he downs some water. "What are you doing here?"

"Just thought I'd check out the ring."

John's phone rings and he steps out to grab it.

"I'm Mario," the instructor says, leaning on the ropes.

"Savannah."

His eyes narrow. "You've never boxed before?"

"Nope."

"You want to be able to say you have?"

"Sure." I smile, taking his hand as he pulls me up and holds the ropes apart for me.

"Put these on." He hands me a pair of red gloves. "First, you need to know the proper stance." He tells me to put my right heel and left toe on the centerline because I'm right handed. My weight should be even on both feet and my knees slightly bent. I'm told to keep my feet diagonal, more than a shoulder width apart and raise my back heel slightly. Hands up, elbows down, eyes just about the tops of my gloves keeping my chin tucked in.

"And, breathe." He grins. "Okay, I won't go over the basic step drag right now because John will be back soon, but for now, let's see how you toss a punch. Have a little fun."

I smile at that. I shove my fist forward, meeting his glove.

"Good, but this time breathe out as you toss the punch and don't flex your fist and arm until you hit your target."

"Okay." I nod, trying to remember everything. I go back to my stance and try again, this time remembering to breathe.

"Nice!" He grins. "Again." After a few rounds of this he starts doing it back, showing me a few blocking moves.

"Oh, what?" Derek says coming into the room. "Mario got Savi in the ring?"

"Yup." I toss a punch at Mario's shoulder but he blocks it at the last moment. "Better watch your back, Derek, I'm learning some mad skills over here." I laugh, trying to avoid a punch but get hit in the arm instead.

"Oh, really?" he jokes, "Thanks for the warning."

"Oh no!" Paul whines loudly moving Derek from the doorway. "Savi, really?"

"What?" I ask, seeing John coming back from his phone call.

Derek laughs on his way back out.

"You know what." Paul gives me a look.

"Savi, you're asking for trouble," John mutters taking a seat as he pulls out a protein bar. He downs it in two bites.

"I'm a twenty-eight year old woman." I throw another punch harder than I thought I could. "If I want to learn how to box, then it's my right to do so." I send two quick punches at Mario. "So if you all don't mind..." I look at John, who holds up his hands letting me know he'll shut up.

"Okay, so," Mario says eyeing everyone, "what am I not getting here?"

"Nothing," I mutter tossing another punch.

"You're sparring with the boss's girlfriend," Paul yells out.

"Paul!" I shout holding my hands up. "What the hell?"

"Seriously?" Mario's face drops.

"Seriously!" Cole says standing inside the door. We all turn to look at him.

*Shit.*

"Oh sorry, Savi." Mario shakes his head he starts removing his gloves.

"Savi, out of the ring." Cole waves his hand at me.

"Why would I do that, exactly?" I ask feeling my temper rise yet again.

"Savi," he warns me.

"It's not against house rules for clients to use the gym," I look around, "and I'm in the gym."

"Oh boy," John mutters grabbing his bag and moving toward Paul who quickly follows him out. Mario steps out of the ring and runs to catch up. Great, now I'm alone with Cole.

Cole runs a frustrated hand through his hair as he walks toward me. "You're right Savannah, clients are welcome to use the gym." He jumps up ducking under the ropes. In two strides he's in front of me. "But as my girlfriend, I don't want you sparring with anyone else in this house."

"Cole," I huff, removing my gloves tossing them

aside.

He hooks an arm around my waist pulling me to him. I struggle with the fact that I long to be in his arms but am still hurt. "After last night—"

"I'm sorry, Savannah." He cuts me off. "I didn't give you a chance to explain yourself, I just jumped to conclusions and I'm sorry."

"Yeah, you did, but you also said some really hurtful things." I step back out of his hold. "Honestly I think we need to step back and take a breather. My head—"

"I'm not letting you go, no matter how hard you push me away. We had a fight, couples do that—"

"Couples also trust one another," I point out. "You obviously don't trust me."

He moves in front of me again. "I do, it's just that yesterday was pretty awful along with you running off. Then I find you downstairs with Derek. I took my whole day out on you. It was wrong and I am sorry, baby." He leans forward kissing my forehead. "Please say you forgive me."

I sigh, wrapping my arms around his waist as he rests his cheek on my head. "I do." We stay like that for a few minutes both just needing one other. "Can I still play in the ring?"

"No."

"Why?"

"Because I don't like seeing someone hit you, even if it is just for fun."

"Fine." I mean, how can I argue with that response? It's sweet how much he cares for me.

"What are we doing about the Jose situation?"

"I'll be discussing that over dinner tonight." Oh

no.

"Can you do it after dinner?"

He pulls back to look at me. "Why?"

"Because you'll dampen the mood. I need it to be light and fun tonight."

"Why?" He pulls me back to his chest.

"I'm giving Abby and Doctor Roberts a push toward each other." I feel him shaking his head then a slight chuckle follows.

"Okay, but I have to talk about it afterward."

"Deal." He helps me jump out of the ring, and through the gym. His eyes lower to my mid-section.

"I hate your top."

"No, you don't," I laugh.

***

June hands Abigail a large glass of white wine.

Abigail frowns. "You know I like red."

"Not tonight, Abby," June scowls. "You never drink red on the first date, do you want your teeth turning dark?"

"No, you're right."

I hide my smile as I put the lid on the feta cheese salad and place it in the fridge, thinking about the list of things I need to get done. Okay, so salad is done, chickens are prepped, veggies are chopped and ready to go. Okay, now for dessert.

"You look pretty, Abby, in your pink wrap-around dress," I say trying to help her with her nerves.

"It's June's," she replies, smoothing the fabric. It doesn't surprise me. June is the younger sister and has a taste for fashion. She looks at me. "Thanks, dear. You look lovely, too."

I smile, looking down at my purple V-neck top and black leather leggings paired with heels.

"So this weekend is the light festival in town. Are we all planning on going?" Mark asks coming into the room. He stops dead in his tracks when he sees Abigail's outfit. "What are you wearing?" He looks at me. "What's going on? Why do you three look so dressed up?"

"Calm down, Mark," June says. "Doctor Roberts is coming for dinner."

"Oh, okay," he says as he heads to the fridge but stops again. "Wait," He looks at Abigail. "But why are you so dressed up?"

"Oh, so close," June laughs into her glass.

"Are you? Is this?" He shakes his head. "Are you dating the Doc?"

"No," she shoots back, "we're just talking." Poor Abigail can't hide her smile.

"Am I the only one that doesn't know?" He looks to me. "Does Cole know? Of course he does." He tosses his hands up. "I don't know how I feel about this. I mean, I haven't had time to think this through." He sinks onto the stool, rubbing his head. "I mean the Doc's a good man, but is he good enough?" He's now talking to himself, June rolls her eyes laughing. The doorbell rings and Mark suddenly stands and fixes his shirt. "I'll get it."

"Be nice," Abigail warns while June and I are holding onto the counter laughing.

"Okay, that was quite possibly the one of the funniest moments I've had yet," I say dropping my hands to my knees trying to catch my breath.

"He's so protective," June says wiping the tears away. "It's so sweet."

"It is." Abigail nods downing her drink. "Okay." She stands, smoothing out her dress. "Come on, ladies."

"I need to finish up, you go on. I'll be there shortly," I say, filling June's glass before they head off toward the living room.

I set the timer and pop in the potatoes in. When I stand back up I feel a set of hands wrap around my waist. "Hi."

"Hi," Cole says, resting his head on my shoulder. "You look nice and you smell like dessert." I can tell he is stressed; he sounds tired.

"Are you okay?" I wrap my arms over his, holding him closer to me.

"Not really," he admits, "but we'll get to all that later." He kisses my shoulder. "I just needed this." He sighs, nuzzling in my neck.

"Happy to help," I say leaning back giving him a peck on the lips. "Doc's here and Mark is freaking out." I laugh. "It was really funny when he found out why he's here."

"Ha, I bet."

Derek's voice booms through the house, making Cole grimace.

"What happened between you guys?" He groans.

"About five years ago he was trying to be a hero and didn't have my back when we were trying to clear a house. I nearly got my throat slashed by a Cartel who had a knife tied to the end of his rifle."

I gasp covering my mouth.

"It wasn't even what actually happened, it was how he was afterward—like we look out for ourselves instead of as a unit. That's why he'll never be in Blackstone. I don't trust him."

"I understand."

Derek's voice is getting closer so I started to move but Cole doesn't let me go. "Cole?"

"I'm not ready yet."

I smile. "How about you hold me tonight?"

I feel his chest rise and fall heavily.

He kisses my shoulder again and steps back.

"Hey ya, Savi," Derek says entering the kitchen. "What's for dinner?"

I turn to the fridge pulling out the chicken breasts. "Chicken stuffed with feta and roasted red peppers."

"Mmm, sounds good." He leans over taking a look.

"I should get these on the barbecue," I say, about to walk over, but Cole takes the dish saying he'll do it.

"He's in quite the mood," Derek comments as he takes a seat at the island.

"Well, I can't imagine you'd be happy having to deal with what he does in the run of a day." I go to pour myself some wine but his hand grabs the bottle before mine does.

"Allow me." He smiles. "So tell me something, Savi, were you dating anyone before—" He pauses.

"No." I answer truthfully, knowing where this is going. He shifts a little closer.

"Well, I was thinking that you should let me take you out. You know, like a date." And there it is…

"Oh buddy, you're so blind." Keith laughs coming into the room. Clearly he heard my awkward moment. Cole walks back in from outside setting the dish on the counter. He looks at me, then Keith. I'm sure he's wondering why the air in the room is so charged.

"So what do you say? Friday, six o'clock?" He pushes on, not caring about our audience or the fact that it's against house rules. Keith leans against the fridge grinning back and forth between me and Cole, loving every minute of the show.

"What's going on?" Mark whispers as he joins Keith.

"Savi just got asked out on a date."

I glare at the both of them.

"Oh!" His face suddenly brightens. "Oh. Okay, continue." He waves his hand like this is a live performance.

"There you are, Savi," June says coming to my side. "Come say hello to Doctor Roberts. You did, after all, invite him."

"Sure," I say, trying to smile. "Excuse me." I want to throw my arms around June and thank her for getting me out of there when she did. She winks at me and I guess she must have overheard too. I mouth 'thank you' and head for the doctor.

Cole keeps his word over dinner, not bringing up work. He helps keep the topic light, even though I catch him and Mark exchanging looks. Doctor Roberts and Abigail are hitting it off nicely. June seems thrilled to see her older sister gushing over a man. Not that Abigail gushes, but she certainly is glowing.

"I can't believe you did all this," Doctor Roberts says waving his hand around the room. "It's stunning. You certainly have an eye for decorating."

"Thank you." I smile. "Christmas is my favorite time of the year."

"I love that you love Christmas and it's your favorite time of the year." Keith laughs, picking up a cookie. "So good."

"Is that cheesecake?" Mark asks, bloody well knowing it is. He leans to the side taking it off the table behind him.

"I swear, you sit there just so you can be close to the desserts," I laugh.

"I do," he claims, laughing and plopping a huge piece of cheesecake on his plate.

The conversation picks up again and we soon retire into the living room for drinks. Cole is speaking with Doctor Roberts and it looks serious so I don't go over.

"You never answered my question," Derek says from behind me. *Shit*...I turn and attempt to smile.

"I'm actually seeing someone, but I'm flattered you asked me."

"Sure," he says slipping his hands in his pockets. "I'm  sorry; I wouldn't have asked if I knew."

"It's okay."

"Can I have everyone's attention? I have some information to share with all of you," Cole calls out over the chatter. "Please gather round. I would like to get this over with."

As we make our way over Keith tugs on my arm so that I sit next to him and June.

"Are we late?" Daniel asks coming into the

living room with Sue.

"No, you're right on time." Cole nods as they take a seat.

I notice he doesn't give them his normal warm greeting. Sue seems a little off but I pretend not to notice as we all gather waiting for Cole to start.

"All right," he says as he put his hands on his hips. "At approximately seventeen hundred yesterday, Frank, along with Agent Bridges, left to transport York to Washington. Thirty minutes into the flight York got hold of Agent Bridge's gun, killing Bridges and during the altercation a stray bullet hit the pilot, wounding him." He pauses as everyone starts whispering, then continues. "In the ensuing struggle, Frank shot York and killed him. I won't share all the details but the pilot was able to fly on to Washington. He's okay, just going to have to use one wing for a while." He seems to realize he almost made a joke and looks stricken.

"Poor Agent Bridges. Did he have a family?" Abigail asks quietly.

"A wife but no children. She has been contacted," Cole chokes out.

"Why?" I ask, trying to make sense of it all.

"York admitted to Frank that he had been selling certain information to the Cartel." He looks directly down at me. "And to poisoning Savannah."

I shake my head in disbelief.

"He swore he didn't give up the location of the house, but he knew it was only a matter of time before they forced his hand, and he wanted out. Seems he got in over his head, thought he could be selective as to what he would tell them. He was wrong."

"So Frank is all right?" Mike asks from behind me.

"Yes." Cole looks around one last time. "I've known York for ten years. I truly believe he didn't give up the location of Shadows. He got greedy, but even his moral compass wouldn't allow him to go that far."

A few people start to get up but Cole clears his throat. "One more thing." He looks at me. "This morning, Blackstone got word that we are on standby."

My heart rate drops. I know this means when they get word they will have to leave almost immediately.

"Frank has confirmation of the American's location. We have the green light to take him out dead or alive." *Holy shit.*

"Did Frank give you any indication of when you might leave?" His mother asks holding onto his father's arm.

Cole takes a drink. "It could be any time. We're waiting to get a visual before we leave." His eyes flicker over to mine again but I break our connection, feeling too raw.

"For now we keep on doing what we're doing. I don't believe the house is in any immediate danger. That's all for now. I'll keep you updated as we know more."

It takes everyone a few moments to start to move. I, on the other hand, fly off the couch needing some space. I make it to the kitchen before I hear him.

"Hey, hey, hey," Cole says reaching for my arm, "don't run."

"I'm not." I close my eyes, hating that I just lied. "Okay, yeah I was."

He moves closer sliding his hand down my arm lacing his fingers in mine. He brings our hands up to his mouth giving mine a kiss.

"Everything is going to work out."

"How do you know that?"

"Because fate would not have brought you to me just to take you away." He smiles, kissing me on my lips once. "And now that I have someone to come back to, I'll have to be extra careful." He kisses me again.

I try and clear my head remembering that he could be leaving at any point. "Can you promise me something?"

His jaw twitches but he nods.

"Promise me that whenever you get the call, no matter where you are or what you're doing, you'll see me before you leave." A tear slips down my cheek; he catches it with his finger.

He runs his hand along the back of my neck kissing me with such passion I forget to breathe. He backs away just slightly. "Oh God, baby, I promise."

I nod as he backs up reaching for a tissue for me. I dry my cheeks and take a deep breath.

"There you are." Derek says. "I wanted to see how you're doing."

"I'm fine." *Please go away.*

"You know what fine stands for right?" he says with a grin.

"Freaked out, insecure, neurotic and emotional," I reply nodding. "I'm an Edward Norton fan." Derek throws his head back and laughs.

"I heard you were funny but you're quick too, I like you."

Cole, who is leaning across from me, against the island, rubs his face with both hands. I know Derek is getting on his nerves with the flirting.

"So who are you dating anyway?" he asks boldly.

"Me," Cole says, dropping his hands. My mouth drops open but I quickly recover.

"You?" Derek's eyes pop. "You're dating Savannah?"

"Yes."

"Isn't there some house policy?"

Cole glares at him. "My house, my rules, remember."

"How convenient for you," he snickers. "Nice that the boss is sticking his hand in the honey pot."

"Weren't you just trying to do the same, Derek?" I ask.

"Remember your rank, Agent Rent." Cole stands pointing his finger at him. "We might live together under one roof, but you will still treat me as your superior."

Derek shakes his head but clenches his jaw. "Yes, sir," he says smartly as he turns and leaves the room.

"Cole," I say stepping close to him and grabbing his shirt in my hand so he'll look down at me. "Take me to bed?" He smiles down at me.

"Sure, baby."

Cole still seems annoyed when we get to his room.

I sit in the chair in front of his window watching the snow fall, hit the window, and slowly melt, trickling down the glass in a hundred different paths.

"Crash into Me" by Dave Matthew's Band flows through the room as the light dims. Cole moves in front of me and my eyes drag lazily up his body. His dress shirt is open, tie removed, sleeves rolled up, hands tucked in his pockets. I feel my lips turn upward; this man is pure perfection.

Bending down, he squats in front of me gripping the back of my calf sliding his hand downward till he hits my ankle where he gently removes my shoe. He repeats this for the other one.

I watch his stomach muscles flex as he moves about.

His dark eyes lock with mine and blaze as he hooks his arms under my legs and behind my back.

I wrap my arms around his neck and I feel myself lifted into the air.

As he looks down at me with hooded eyes, his expression unreadable, he hesitates.

"Cole?"

His grip tightens right before he lays me gently on his bed. Peeling his shirt off and tossing it on the floor, he climbs over me. His lips find mine and he slowly and softly swipes his tongue along the inside of my mouth.

"Let me love you the way you deserve." He brushes my hair back from my face, tilting his head slightly. "You are the most beautiful woman." He kisses along my jaw, up to my ear, stopping as a long moan escapes him. "It's like someone got inside my head, found my deepest desire and created you."

"Cole," I whisper feeling pure emotion take over, "no one has ever made me—"

His lips capture mine before I can finish. His hand travels down my side to unbuckle my pants. He pushes them down chucking them over his shoulder.

I lean up removing my sweater, desperate for his mouth back on me.

He whips his pants off in a flash, kissing my stomach. His hands travel up to my breasts gently massaging them through my lace bra.

"You're so soft," he breathes between kisses, "so perfect." His hot fingers release the clasp exposing my breasts to his hungry lips.

I lean my head back into the pillow as a shot of lust bursts through me.

Spreading my legs apart and settling in between them he lines up and nudges forward ever so slightly. He flattens his chest to mine, his hand cupping my face, staring down at me with such adoration. "It scares me how much I need you, Savannah."

I hold my breath as his words hit me. "I physically hurt when you're not around to touch." I run my fingers along his jaw as he leans into me closing his eyes.

"I'm right here, yours to touch whenever," I reassure him.

He lets out a sweet breath as he slides his long

thick length into me, deliciously, painfully slow. His eyes lock with mine holding me captive until he's fully in.

I tune into the sad voice of Sam Smith singing "Not in That Way". My eyes close as my emotions play tug of war. My heart is incredibly invested in this man, tangled in a web of love that almost makes it difficult to breathe.

He is pouring out his feelings, opening his heart, and exposing his soul to me. All that is running through my mind is he'll be leaving soon.

"Don't, baby," I hear him whisper over my cheek as he moves at a gentle pace. "Don't go there now, I'll come home."

I press my lips together letting a few tears leak out.

He kisses them away. "Stay with me, my sweet Savannah."

My eyes flutter open.

"Fall with me. I promise I won't let you go."

All I can do is nod as he kisses me breathlessly.

The slow pace is making my head spin. A ball of fire grows quickly in my stomach. My legs are restless so I wrap them around his waist feeling his back muscles twitch and my hands grip the sheets as he whispers my name.

"Cole!" I beg, knowing I'm so close.

He starts kissing along my collarbone.

The mix between his hard breaths and his hot lips tip me over the edge. I free fall into fireworks losing my ability to think. I can only feel. I'm tumbling, spinning, twisting inside. I'm vaguely aware that I'm screaming something incoherent.

Cole's shaking and gripping my legs, getting deeper. It's all too much but I don't want it to stop! Sweat bursts out along my skin, my hands hanging on for dear life as we both reach the peak together, his body convulsing along with mine. I feel myself floating back to earth, like a feather taking its sweet time to land.

Sinking back into the mattress, I feel like I'll never move again. Cole wipes the hair out of my face as he smiles down at me. At the same time he slides out, making me flinch at the loss of him.

He gets a warm facecloth to clean me, then chucking the cloth in the general direction of the bathroom he crawls back in, making the bed dip. He tugs my limp body into his chest, running his fingers up and down my spine.

I close my eyes, giving into the utopia that's rushing through my veins. Being in Cole's arms has never felt more right. He owns every part of me. Just as I'm walking the thin line to blissful sleep I feel Cole's chest vibrate against my cheek.

"You can always fall, Savannah, because I will be the one catching you."

# *Chapter Eighteen*

"Savannah!" I feel my shoulder being shaken roughly, "Savannah wake up!" Cole shouts through a whisper.

"Okay, I'm awake. What's wrong?"

Cole is tossing clothes at me.

"Get dressed," he says pulling on his pants. "Quickly, we don't have time!"

My mind scrambles as I tug at my clothes and pull on my boots.

"Here!" He hands me my jacket. "Follow me." He grabs my hand and opens the bedroom door, checking to see if it's clear. "Come on!" He hurries down the hall. Why aren't we using the back stairway I wonder?

"Where are we going?"

He doesn't answer, stopping as he unlocks Abigail's room. Abigail, June, and Sue are huddled on her bed looking terrified.

"Stay here, no matter what. Don't open the door. I'm the only one with a key." Cole holds my shoulders as he bends down to eye level. "You'll be safe; wait for me." He kisses me then instructs June to lock the door behind him.

"No, Cole, wait!"

"Savannah, stay!" he orders.

I look back toward the women, feeling completely confused since I was woken out of a dead sleep. My mind is madly trying to come to terms with what is going on.

"Come here," Sue says, patting the mattress beside her. "Tell me, Savannah, when you guys were coming down the hallway, did you hear anything, see anything?"

"No." I shake my head. "I don't think so."

"Oh God, this is bad," June cries. "I always knew this day would come, but now…" She reaches for her sister's hand and starts to pray.

"I don't understand. What's going on?" I ask.

"The Cartels," Abigail says in a straggled voice. "Mark said there's at least twelve of them."

"Oh my God," I say, starting to shake, "this is all my fault."

"No, dear," is all June says.

Pounding on the door has us all screaming at once. Someone yells something in Spanish then the door blasts open. Wooden chips fly all around us and we're momentarily stunned before Abigail starts screaming at the top of her lungs.

All I see is a black AK-47 rise out of the dust and flash three bright bursts of light followed by a thud.

June flies to her sister's side as two more flashes of light appear and then June flops to the floor on top of Abigail. I feel Sue fling herself on top of me, pushing me back on the bed as her body gives four violent shakes, then goes limp. Her blood drains all around me covering my face and hair as I struggle to get free. When she falls to the side I see The American standing in the doorway wiping his hands with a white handkerchief.

"Time to go," he says like nothing has happened. Like he hasn't just killed three people I love! I ignore him, rushing to Sue—holding her cooling body in my arms as I try to bring her back, but she's so pale.

"Please," I cry, sobbing loudly, "wake up!" There is so much blood. I feel The American grip my arm and pull me toward the door.

"I said, time to go!"

"No!" I scream. "Please!"

"Savannah! Savannah!"

My eyes pop open as I leap out of bed, still screaming for my friends. I run for the door when a strong pair of arms wrap around me. "How could you kill them?" I sob, "They're my family."

"Savannah, stop, it's okay. You were dreaming." Cole's chest vibrates against me. "It's okay, it's okay."

"Cole?" I whisper.

"Yes, baby, it's me."

"Cole." I turn in his arms, sobbing into his chest and collapsing as he lowers me to the floor with him. I hold onto him for dear life until the nightmare wears off and I'm left to deal with its hangover. After a while I finally calm. As I rest my head on his leg, his fingertips run along my arm—back and forth.

"You want to talk about it?" he asks softly.

I shake my head no. Even just him asking brings on more tears.

"Okay, when you're ready then."

After some more time goes by I decide to ask a question that's been bothering me. "If the house was to be attacked, is there a safe room?"

"Yes, there is," he replies gently.

I let out a long breath.

"Under the entertainment room there's another level. It's where we kept York. There are four jail cells and beyond that is the safe room. More like a safe floor, it's huge—the size of the kitchen, living room, and dining room combined. It's untouchable from the outside. If we ever were to get attacked you would use the back hallway and follow whoever is taking you down to that room where you will stay until it's safe." I shift so that I'm looking up at him.

"Would you come with us?"

He plays with a piece of my hair between his fingers. "The captain doesn't jump on the lifeboat."

A few more tears slip down into my hair. "But what if he has a reason to?" I counter trying to grasp for straws.

"Baby, I know it's scary, but I'll protect you."

"I'm not worried about you protecting me, Cole, I worry about something happening to you." I move to sit up, feeling my head clogged from crying so much. I wrap my arms around my drawn up legs, resting my chin on my knees.

"This is my job, Savi, and I'm good at it. If it means anything, I'm not scared. It's what I do." His mouth twists as he looks at me. "What are you thinking?"

I shrug, feeling tired, but now I'm nervous of falling asleep. "Sometimes I feel like this is one big dream. I mean this kind of thing doesn't happen every day. I feel like I'm stuck, helpless, and taking up the Army's time and resources. I know this isn't my fault but it doesn't make me feel less of a burden to you all." I let out a long sigh. "I just want answers. I want to know who's behind this whole thing. I want my life back."

"I know you do." Cole pulls me to my feet and lays me back in bed. He wraps his arm around me, tucking me against his side. "You're not a burden Savi, you're one of the best things that's ever happened to this house. Not just for me, but for everyone." He moves my hair out of his way and kisses the side of my forehead. "Try and get some sleep; you're not alone. I'm here."

I close my eyes counting his heart beats till I finally pass out.

\*\*\*

*Five days later...*

We walk hand in hand down the decorated street, colored string lights hanging in rows along both sides. Christmas trees stand outside every shop beautifully trimmed with every imaginable ornament and decoration. Carolers dressed in historical costumes sing "Carol of the Bells" as they stand next to a hot-chocolate booth. A horse-drawn carriage is pulling a family of four down the street with sleigh bells ringing as they pass. Sue was not kidding. This town certainly is in love with Christmas. This is truly amazing. It looks like a scene right out of a Thomas Kinkade painting. I glance up at Cole who's looking very classy in his black wool button up coat and gray scarf. I search his face, trying to see if he's here with us or thinking about what's ahead.

The tension in the house has calmed down some since Cole held a house meeting the other night after dinner.

Keith could not confirm if it was Jose Jorge or not the day I thought I saw him in town.

But like Cole said, there's nothing we can do but be prepared. He was wary about this outing but Daniel convinced him that we have to keep on living as long as we take the proper precautions.

I had a wig and glasses on, about to head out the door, when Cole stopped me.

"How do you feel?"

"Honestly, a bit funny." I hold a piece of the wig up. "I never pictured myself as a blonde."

He smiles and pulls it off.

"I think if we're careful enough, you won't need this," he chuckles adorably. "Here." He tugs on a light pink knit hat. "That's better." He fingers one of my curls. "I like the sexy-librarian glasses though," he jokes.

I bat his arm but keep the thick rimmed glasses on. They really do change my appearance.

Spotting Mark and Melanie walking together up ahead makes me smile, seeing that she has linked arms with him, her fire red hair peeking out of her green hat. They look happy; it's refreshing to see everyone enjoying themselves. We really needed this.

A jewelry shop window causes me to stop—who could resist! I press my hands on the frame to get a better look. "Oh, it's beautiful," I whisper, causing the glass to fog briefly.

Cole leans over my shoulder to get a better look. It's a small crystal tear drop with a real snowflake preserved inside, hanging in the middle of a delicate chain. The way the crystal is set helps magnify the tiny flake.

"Really does make it one of a kind." He smiles as he says it.

I have to laugh thinking how true that is. We continue walking to meet up with the group—we've fallen a bit behind.

Cole doesn't seem to be in a hurry. He suddenly flinches, then mutters something. He stops and leans down close to my ear. "Please go with what I say next."

I look up at him and he shakes his head then I hear what's making him uneasy.

"Well, well, Cole Logan," says this long-legged blonde with unbelievably white teeth.

"Hello, Christina," he says back through clenched teeth…oh the bat-shit crazy ex! She looks over at me, then down at our joined hands.

"Who's this?" she asks him, not acknowledging me.

"This is my fiancée." He smiles down at me and I play my part well by stepping up on my tippy-toes giving him a rather long kiss.

311

"You're engaged?" She looks like a trout with her mouth hanging open. "Well, that's a pity."

I roll my eyes.

"Yes, we are and we have to meet up with the family so...ah, take care, Christina." He nods, stepping around her.

"Happy Holidays, Serena," I say sweetly.

"It's Christina," she huffs behind me.

We round a corner before Cole says anything. "Well..."

"She seems nice."

He starts laughing then pulls me into him giving me a hug.

"So, your fiancée huh?"

"It's not far from the truth baby," he mutters into my hair but before I can get him to clarify exactly what he means by that, he's tugging my hand in the direction of Zack's restaurant.

Dinner is just being placed in front of us when Cole's cell phone rings.

Mark looks over at him with a worried look as Cole excuses himself from the table and steps outside.

"Could be anything," Keith whispers in my ear.

Watching Cole through the window gives up nothing, as his back is turned to me, so I can't read his face. Twenty long minutes go by and everyone at the table attempts to draw my attention away from Cole. Finally it's Sue who comes and sits in Cole's chair who gets me to focus on her.

"Hey," she says gently running her hand over my forehead. "Are feeling all right? You look a little pale."

I shake my head and think about this morning and over the last few days I have been feeling a little off but it's to be expected with all that's been going on.

"I'm stressed and my stomach's been a bit off."

Her eyes narrow watching me then finally she nods. "Have you been getting much sleep?"

"Surprisingly, yes," I reply. Minus the horrific nightmare at the beginning of the week, I have been getting lots of sleep. "I even took a few naps."

"Well, that's good." She smiles.

I think I've convinced her I'm all right but it makes me wonder how bad I must look. I glance over at the window but Cole is gone. Looking around at everyone I see he's not in the room. Just as I'm about to get up and look for him he returns, putting an icy hand on my shoulder.

Mark looks at him and I catch some kind of emotion run across his face but nothing happens.

Sue gives him back his chair and heads over to her seat whispering something to Daniel and his eyes flicker over to mine.

*Really guys I'm all right.*

"Cole?" I say, turning my attention to him.

"Savi, you should eat, your food is getting cold." He is looking at my untouched plate.

*Seriously? You want me to eat?*

"Was that Frank?" Mark says, looking past me to Cole.

"Yes," he whispers.

"Are we being shipped out?"

Cole glances around the table then shakes his head.

313

*What does that mean?*

"So Mark, what are your plans for Christmas?" Melanie asks, breaking the tension. Mark takes long deep breath before replying.

"Umm, I'm leaving tonight actually for my cousin's cabin."

I stare at him, unmoving.

"Oh yeah, when will you be back?" she asks.

"Not sure yet," he says with a smile plastered on his face, "but when I get back we'll have to go on that ski trip we talked about." He looks very uncomfortable.

I shove my plate away while Mark's words hit me like a blow to the head. "Excuse me," I say, rising out of my seat.

Cole stands up signaling his mother.

"Savi," he says, sounding worried.

"I just need the restroom," I whisper not looking at him.

Sue comes along, acting like she has to go too.

My head is spinning. I begin to feel a little dizzy, and Sue helps me to the leather couch in the powder area of the restroom.

"Here," she says, holding a cool towel to my face as she sits next to me.

"They got the call," I whisper. "They ship out tonight."

Sue takes my hand but puts her fingers over the inside of my wrist.

I look at her, thinking this is odd. "I'm all right, I just feel a little dizzy."

"Mmhmm," she hums, continuing to check my pulse.

"How do you deal with it?" I ask, feeling desperate for some help.

She sighs, letting my arm go.

"It took a while to get used to it," she says quietly. "I just found things to keep me busy until he came home. Luckily for you, you have me, Abigail, and June, until she goes home, and the rest of the house."

"I'm scared," I admit to her.

"I know," she says, giving me a comforting hug. "So am I."

\*\*\*

Cole is trying everything in his power to concentrate on the meal and the guests but his conversation with Frank has him very uneasy. He nods to his father to meet him at the bar. They both excuse themselves and make their way over.

"Two brandys," Daniel orders as Cole runs his hand through his hair. "All right, son, what did Frank say?"

"Blackstone is shipping out tonight at twenty-three hundred."

His father hands him his drink. "Target destination?"

"Mexico City."

"That far south?"

"Yeah."

"Hmm," Daniel says, rubbing his neck. "Are you thinking—?"

"Yeah, I am."

"Should I make the call to Agent Joel?"

"Definitely."

"Cole," his father says, placing a hand on his shoulder, "we'll protect her. I'll bring in my guys and make sure it's Fort Knox up there. You need to focus on this trip and you need to do whatever it takes to focus and get your head in the game."

Cole looks up and sees Savannah is back at the table.

"I hear ya, Dad."

\*\*\*

I watch as Mark says goodbye to Melanie. I feel torn wondering which side I would like to be on. Maybe there's something to being kept in the dark about their work. But at the same time not knowing would kill me. Oh Christ, I'm my own worst enemy.

I feel Cole come up behind me, he slips his arm around my waist and ushers me out into the cold air. Sue and Daniel decided to spend the night to say goodbye to the guys before they leave. When Cole broke the news to Paul and John I was surprised by their reactions; they acted as if they were just given an updated weather report. I, on the other hand, am feeling tired—very tired. I lean into Cole, wrapping my arm around his waist.

"You cold?"

I shake my head no. The Christmas thrill I had earlier is long gone now. I wish the holiday would pass so I don't have to think about the fact that our first Christmas together will now be spent apart.

We all walk quietly back to the cars. Cole's body

language has changed. He seems like he's lost in thought. I want to ask him what's on his mind, but that seems silly considering they're shipping out in four hours.

The ride home is painfully quiet. Cole holds me close stroking his thumb over my hand.

I can tell he's scanning the horizon. I wonder if he ever gets tired of being alert all the time.

Cole grabs my hand after I hop out of the truck. "Take a walk with me?"

"Sure."

He holds my hand and leads me to a path in the woods. We walk in silence—the only noise the sound of the snow crunching under our boots. Arriving at a clearing on the top of a hill we look down at the lake. The moon is bright and it casts a bright path through the ripples in the water.

"Wow," I murmur softly, not wanting to break the mood. "It's so pretty."

"Savannah?" Cole says quietly.

I turn to him finding him staring at me.

"I want you to be extra careful when I'm gone. No trips to town, no running off into the woods. Please, keep someone with you at all times, promise me?"

I nod, understanding how serious this is.

He steps toward me. "I need to be able to focus while I'm away. I need to keep a clear head."

"I promise, Cole. I do understand. Don't worry, I won't run off, I—"

"I'm in love with you Savannah." *Oh.* "I couldn't go away this time without telling you that I am in love with you. This is a first for me. I've never felt or said those words to any woman before."

I feel my eyes brim with tears. "Cole." I clear my throat. "I hate that the first time I'm saying this to you, you're leaving me, but...I love you too."

He closes his eyes breathing out a shaky sigh.

I cup his face with both my hands. "It's a first for me too." I kiss him softly. "Promise me you'll come back to me."

He wraps his arms around me tighter. "I promise, baby."

\*\*\*

I wake with a start, my eyes feeling puffy. Reaching behind me, I remember he had indeed left me last night. It seemed like only moments ago we were tangled in the sheets together showing one another how much love we had to give. Glancing at the clock, I see it's nine thirty already. I jump out of bed and head to the shower. I can't believe I slept so long.

"Hi, Savi," Abigail says handing me a cup of coffee as I take a seat at the island. She slides me a red box with a bow. "Cole left this," she smiles waiting for me to open it.

I pull on the bow and slowly open the lid. My hand flies to my mouth as my eyes fill and overflow with tears.

"Well?"

I turn it around to show her the crystal tear drop with the fortified snowflake inside.

"Oh, Savannah it's beautiful," she exclaims,

clutching her hands together over her chest in a moment of joy.

"I saw it last night in a shop while we were walking to Zack's. Cole must have slipped away after his phone call." I pull out a note stuck on the bottom as she helps me clasp it around my neck.

*To remember the day we spoke*

*those special words,*

*Yours – C*

I hold it to my chest as a lump builds in my throat. "Abby?" I sniff, then feel a huge wave of nausea. My head spins so hard I almost fall off the stool. "Whoo."

"Savannah?" I see Abigail call out but I barely hear her. Sweat breaks out across my neck and my stomach turns. Oh my God, have I been poisoned again?

She shoves a bucket in my face just in time for me to loudly empty my stomach.

"Oh my," Sue says from somewhere behind me. "Let's get her to bed."

# *Chapter Nineteen*

I wake a few hours later.

Sue is sitting with someone at the table by the balcony door.

"Hi?" I say, feeling groggy.

"Savannah, this is Doctor Brown. She's an OB/GYN."

I move to sit up better in the bed.

"Okay." I shake my head. "Why is—?" Then it hits me—no appetite, nauseous, emotional, tired— "Am I pregnant?"

Doctor Brown steps toward me. "I believe you are, Ms. Miller."

What? "But I'm on birth control!"

"No birth control is one hundred percent effective. Sometimes these things just happen. I'm assuming you know who the father is."

*Really?* I blush when I look at Sue, oh God, I know she wants grandbabies but it's too soon! What if she thinks I'm trying to trap her son? Hell, we only *just* announced that we loved each other last night.

"Savannah." Sue smiles at me.

"Yes, I do, it's Cole." I lean my head back wondering what the hell Cole is going to think.

"Well, that's good then." Doctor Brown smiles down at me. "Do you remember when your last menstrual cycle was?" I think back but am drawing a blank.

"I honestly don't remember."

"All right, I will need you to come by my office in a few days. I don't have the equipment here, but I want to perform an ultrasound examination. We want to make sure the baby is off to a good start." She opens her bag saying, "For now, start taking these." She hands me a bottle of prenatal vitamins. *Oh God.* "Have Sue contact me when you can make it in. Please get lots of rest and eat." She rises to leave.

"Thank you, Doctor Brown," Sue says, walking her to the door. "I'll be in touch."

Sue turns to me with the biggest smile on her face that I've ever seen. "Oh, Savannah!" She tosses her hands in the air. "I've never been happier!"

I feel like asking for a time out so I can process what the hell I've just been told.

She crawls on the bed next to me. "Are you all right?"

*Not really.*

"I don't know," I answer honestly, suddenly remembering her behavior at the restaurant. "You knew, didn't you?"

She smiles. "I had a feeling, but I was waiting to see if I was right. This morning confirmed it; that's why I called Doctor Brown. She's the best in town and I've known her for years."

I nod trying to keep my head on straight.

"He told me he loved me last night," I say, fingering my necklace. "I love him, Sue, I really do." I hear her sniff than she reaches for my hand. "What do you think Cole will say?" I ask nervously.

She laughs, slightly wiping her cheeks, "He's going to be so happy, Savannah!"

"You think?"

"I know."

"It's terrible timing; it wasn't planned."

"That may be, but everything will be fine, Savannah."

"Sue," I look up at her, "can we please keep this between us?"

"Daniel knows."

"That's fine, but just the three of us, okay? I don't want Cole to be the last to know."

"Of course, no one but us three."

I let out a long sigh and try not to panic about what's growing in my stomach. Then I think of Cole and the idea of a little part of each of us in one little body makes me smile. I find myself rubbing my stomach as I fall back to sleep.

\*\*\*

Cole holds the satellite phone to his ear while he separates himself from everyone. They're all exhausted from the day. They had a run in with a group of Cartels and their camp was discovered. They had to grab what they could and haul ass to a new location. He glances at his watch—it is just past midnight.

322

"You guys good?" Keith asks.

"Yeah, just barely," he says as he briefs Keith on the day's events and current situation.

"All right, well, everything is quiet on our end."

"Good," Cole says, hesitating…

"Savi's got the flu," Keith says.

Cole could hear the smile in his voice. "So if you start feeling sick—good luck because she's been in bed all day."

Poor Savannah, he had planned to call earlier and hoped she was close so he could speak to her. The fact that it was against his own house rules to use check in time for anything personal was totally beside the point. Since Savannah came into his life all his rules went out the window.

"You want me to wake her?"

Keith's question throws him; was he thinking out loud? "No, it's late. We're watching the house, early tomorrow or rather today so this is my check in for…" he looks at his watch again, "last night and this morning."

"All right, stay safe."

"Will do. Raven out."

\*\*\*

"I see seven men on the east side," Mark whispers, "five on the west."

"Copy that," Cole replies moving his binoculars confirming same. "Seven on the east and five on the west." He shifts, reaching for his radio when it crackles to life.

"Fox one to Raven one," Paul's voice cracks

over the radio.

"Go ahead Fox one."

"We have a green Hummer heading toward the house approaching from the northeast."

Cole spots the truck and follows it. "Copy that Fox one, I have a visual. I want to know who's in that vehicle."

"Ten-four."

The Hummer passes through the gate without any problem and stops in front of the mansion. Two armed guards open the door and pull out a man in a navy blue business suit wearing a cream-colored cloth bag over his head.

"Hum," Cole says, "interesting that his head is covered but his hands aren't tied."

"Yup." Mark nods.

"Seems our mystery guest might be doing business with The American."

"Guess they don't trust him to know the location." Mark squints. "You think it could be the mayor?"

"No, this guy is taller and slimmer."

They watch as the suit and one of the armed guards disappear inside and the Hummer takes off back the way it came.

"Guess he'll be staying a while," Mark says, rolling onto his back stretching out his neck. He checks his watch and pulls out a protein bar. Cole inches backwards then leans against a rock out of view. He spits his gum out and opens his water.

Mark pulls at his vest, shifting. "Fuck, I miss the snow."

"Me too," Cole says, thinking of Savannah.

"I know that look."

"Yup, you have it too," he shoots back, making Mark grin.

"All right," Cole says putting the cap on his water then pats his side looking for…

"Here." Mark tosses him a piece of gum. Ever since they joined the Army together, they've been chewing gum. When they are out on duty it helps them relax. Cole pops it in his mouth while he studies the map.

"Ahhh, yuck, what the fuck is this?" Cole asks, making a disgusting face.

"Hubba Bubba."

"What are you, a twelve year old girl?"

"It makes for a better chew." Mark shrugs.

"It's disgusting."

"No, what's disgusting is your old man cinnamon gum."

"I can literally feel my teeth sticking together. What shit flavor is this?"

"Sweet and sassy cherry!"

"I…I," Cole shakes his head, "I don't even know what to say right now." He spits out the gum and replaces it with one of his own. They both lay back on their stomachs and inch forward back to their post.

\*\*\*

I sit on the living room couch holding my purse on my lap, completely lost in a memory.

*"I didn't even know you were seeing someone,"*

*I say sitting next to Lynn on my father's couch. Lynn had arrived on dad's doorstep looking like she'd just seen a ghost.*

*"I'm not seeing someone, Savi, I just hooked up with someone and now I'm late."*

*"How many days late?"*

*"A week," she says, drying her eyes.*

*"So," I quickly do the math then my mouth drops, "was it someone from..." I inch closer seeing my father in the kitchen, "from the Charity event we went to last month?" She closes her eyes for a moment, taking a deep breath. "Oh my God, was it Jones, that smokin' hot blond guy from Dad's office?"*

*"Luka's 'Assistant'? No, not Jones!" She shakes her head in disgust. I ignore her bitchiness toward his title, as I know for a fact that Jones works his ass off for my father and everyone else in the office.*

*"Then who? And was he not wearing a condom? Not trying to sound holier-than-thou, but come on, Lynn, even I have a sta—"*

*"Have a what?" My father asks giving me a stern warning not to finish my sentence. He hands Lynn a bottle of water and takes a seat across from us. "So you're pregnant?"*

*Lynn's eyes pop open she looks to me for help but I'm just as stunned that he heard us talking.*

*"Umm, I don't know," she says, turning three shades of red.*

*"Who's the father?" he asks like he has a right to, but I don't stop him because I'm dying to know too.*

*"I'd rather not have this conversation until I*

*know for sure."*

*My father slams his glass down on the table. "How could you be so stupid?"*

*"Dad," I shot back. "Don't."*

*"Be quiet, Savi." He scowls at me, waving a finger in my face. "I swear if I ever find out you're pregnant before you're married, consider it aborted. You will not shame my name." He looks at Lynn. "You should consider the same thing or get a ring on that finger before the press finds out." He leans forward narrowing his eyes on us. "Figure this situation out before I do." He stands leaving the room cursing under his breath.*

*I reach for Lynn's hand giving it a squeeze. My stomach turns. If my mother could hear him now she'd be devastated. Thankfully, later on that night the pregnancy test came out negative. I'd never seen Lynn so relieved and I never did find out who the possible baby daddy was.*

"Ready?" Keith asks, standing next to me.

I didn't even hear him come in the room.

"Yes."

Keith held his ground when Sue and I told him I needed to go into to town, but once Sue said the letters OBG he backed off, not asking anymore questions. I'm sure he thinks I have some kind of infection. Normally I'd be embarrassed but today I find I'm a little too excited to care. I would love to share this with him but I want to tell Cole first. Besides, Derek is in the SUV with us and he's been a little distant ever since he found out Cole and I are dating.

"Hood up, hair tucked in, and glasses on, okay, Savi?" Keith says from the driver's seat. He glances at me in the mirror.

I nod doing all the things he told me.

Mike is two cars behind us. He's the spotter for today.

We pull up to the curb and wait for Keith to get out and open my door.

Derek opens the office door for me and I see Sue standing in the waiting room.

She rushes over and wraps me in a hug. "Thanks guys, I can take it from here," she says to Keith and Derek.

They both take a seat by the door, looking around at all the women. They look very uncomfortable, which makes me smirk.

With Sue's arm still around me she walks me through to the back.

I'm guessing they know her pretty well since they all wave and let us go on through.

I change from the waist down and wrap a paper sheet over me which rips twice as I try to get comfortable.

Lying back, I'm feel a little nervous as Doctor Brown explains what is about to happen. A very long cold probe up is shoved up my "wuha" and I breathe out, staring upward and counting the flakes on the ceiling. A tiny gasp from Sue makes me look at her; she has her hand on her chest.

"See that right there?" Doctor Brown says, tapping her finger to the screen. "That little round circle is your baby."

I look back up to the ceiling, crossing my arms

over my face, and start to cry.

"Oh, Savi," Sue says, coming to my side, "don't cry, everything is going to be okay."

"I know." I sniff trying to catch my breath. "I just wish Cole was here for this."

"I know, dear," she whispers. "Me too."

I wipe my cheeks and look back over at my baby. My heart thumps loudly as I watch the little circle pulse along with mine. "Wow," I whisper with a hitch in my voice. My whole body floods with emotion.

"Heartbeat looks perfect," Doctor Brown says with a smile tapping away on the keys. "And I'd say you're about five weeks."

I press my lips together trying not to smile at my dirty thoughts of Cole and me in the shower, in his bed, my bed, my—.

"Here you go." She hands me a picture.

"Can I get one more?" I ask.

"Of course." She prints one off. "Get dressed then we'll go over all the do's and don'ts."

She and Sue start to leave but I call Sue back as I sit up.

"You need to share this with Grandpa," I say, handing her one of the ultrasound pictures.

"Thank you!" she cries giving me a hug. "I can't wait to."

I tuck the goody bag the Doctor gave me in my purse and meet Keith at the door. He sees my red eyes and gently reaches for my arm.

"I'm not sure if I want to know the answer to this question, but I promised Cole I'd watch over you like a hawk, so I need to know, are you okay?"

"I am actually." I grin. "I really am." My stupid eyes water again.

"So why are you crying?"

My heart plays tug a war with feeling unbelievably excited but yet terrified for Cole. "I miss Cole," I admit to him. "I just wish I could speak with him myself, hear his voice—" I sigh, feeling sappy. "Sorry."

"Don't be," he says and gives me his famous Keith side hug. "When I spoke with him last night I could tell you were on his mind." He leads me to the truck.

\*\*\*

"Eggs or waffles?" Abigail asks, handing me a cup of coffee.

I look down at the cup and remember I shouldn't drink it...*Oh shit, I have to break up with coffee too!* I look down at my beloved drink and make a promise I'll return as soon as I can. Oh, this is going to be hard to hide.

"Just toast will be fine," I say. Abigail whirls around with a concerned look.

"Savannah, what's wrong?"

*Shit*..."Nothing, I'm just not that hungry." And the idea of eating eggs or waffles makes me want to puke.

"What are you not telling me?"

Oh lord, I feel awful not letting her know there's a little Fritter on the way.

"Savi?"

"I think I still have that flu."

Her eyes soften at my lie as she heads toward the toaster.

"Savi?" Keith calls from the hallway, "can you come here, please?"

I follow him to Cole's office and he points to the landline, smiling as he shuts the door behind him.

I sit in the massive, leather chair and pick up the receiver.

"Hello?"

"Hey, baby." His voice rasps over the phone, sending off about a million butterflies in my stomach all at once.

"Hi," I choke out, trying to keep my tears at bay. "Are you all right?"

"God, I miss your voice."

"I miss you, too, Cole. When are you coming home?" I know I sound desperately needy but dammit, I am.

"As soon as I can possibly get there, I will. Right now we're doing surveillance, making sure we know as much as possible before we make our move." He pauses for a second then chuckles.

"What?"

"You called the house *home*."

I smile. He's right, I guess I did. "Yes, well, it is my home now."

"Hmmm," he hums into the phone, "it sure is."

I bite my lip and am about to tell him about our little creation when I hear him let out a long sigh.

"What's wrong?"

"It's a first for me to be struggling with being in the field. Normally I do my job with no distractions, but knowing you're there without me...it's hard to concentrate."

Oh God. I try and think quickly.

"Cole, listen to me, I am not leaving this house for any reason. I'm not running off and I check in with Keith as often as possible. Please, please don't worry about me, I'm fine. I just want you to concentrate on what you're doing so that you can come home to me safe and sound." I squeeze my eyes shut. The topic of our baby is on the tip of my tongue, but I can't do it. He'll stress out that much more. "You made a promise to me, Cole."

He clears his throat, "I did." I hear someone talking in the background. "Savi, I have to go." He pauses. "I love you."

"I love you too, Cole." I feel the tears spill over as the line goes dead. "...and I'm pregnant," I whisper into the dial tone.

"Savi?" Keith asks sticking his head in the door. I hang up the phone but don't get up. He moves in the room watching me carefully.

"I need you to do something for me, Keith."

"Okay."

"Don't tell him about me going to town today."

"Savannah, he hasn't asked yet, but if he does, I can't lie."

"You can't tell him, Keith. He told me he can't concentrate because he's worried about me. I told him I'm not leaving the house. If you tell him it will only make things harder for him."

He shakes his head. "I can't. You're my friend, but he's my boss. I—"

I stand, pulling out the ultrasound picture from my pocket and handing it to him.

He takes one look then glances at my stomach.

"Five weeks." I smile, rubbing my stomach.

"Oh my God," he whispers.

"Keith, if he finds out I went to town, he'll want to know why, and I can't—not while he's in danger out there."

"Okay, I agree with you." He suddenly comes around the desk giving me a huge hug—picking me right off the ground. "I'm really happy for you guys. Wow."

"Thanks," I wheeze. "Can you put me back down?"

\*\*\*

Cole folds his arm under his head and stares out the window of the abandoned house outside of town. His team has been holed up here all night since being forced to withdraw from their primary position. They are hunkered down to avoid detection, which leads to gaps in perimeter security. Through one such gap wanders the Cartel scout.

The boy is maybe ten years old and seems as surprised as Cole and his men when he comes upon the camp without warning.

Paul spots him first, but by the time Cole figures it out the boy has already given the signal.

Three minutes later the headlights of a Land Rover race toward them. Luckily they are next to the river, and manage to slip away unmolested.

Cole has never slipped up like that before and is angry with himself, but he couldn't seem to get his mind off Savannah. Damn it, he is worried something is going to happen to her. It's the first time he's really had a reason to get back, and God does he want to go home…He finds himself missing so much about her, even the way she looks at him, like he's the only one she sees.

Ahhhh! Focus! He squeezes his eyes shut, trying to clear his head. Nothing is working. He looks over at Mark who is passed out in the corner, taking advantage, as only an experienced combat soldier can, of any spare moment to grab some zzz's.

Paul is propped up against the wall, using the handle of his weapon as a pillow. … John is at the door leaning on the window frame on first watch. Cole jumps out of bed grabbing his gun.

"John, I'll take the first shift. I'm wide awake and there no sense in neither of us getting any rest."

"Thanks, but if it's all the same, I'd rather not," he says, not leaving his post.

Cole nods his understanding not being able to turn off a bad feeling. These situations are high stress and The American is someone they've been up against before; the man is ruthless. Cole rests his weapon on the wall next to him and sits on the ground angling himself so he can see out the back window. They sit for a long time tuning in to every single noise that finds them.

"How's your sister?" Cole whispers. John's sister was hit by a semi in an intersection four months ago. It was touch and go for a while with the swelling in her brain but she somehow came out of it all right—well somewhat all right. It was really hard on John considering she's his twin and they are really close.

"Better, physically. They say she should be able to walk again," John whispers. "As for her mental state, she's still missing most of her childhood. She doesn't know anyone but Pops, so that's hard. At least they caught the driver. He was eighteen hours over his log book. "

"Oh, man, I'm sorry."

"It is what it is," he mutters. They both go back to comfortable silence.

Cole looks at his watch. It's seven thirty in the morning. He and John never left their posts, neither getting a wink of sleep. They often work on less in situations like this. Cole grabs the satellite phone.

"Checking in at oh seven thirty five," Cole says as the call connects and Keith answers.

"Roger, Raven One. What's the plan today?"

"We're going to hit the house. They had company yesterday so we want to get in there and see who it is."

"All right, copy that, going ahead with plans to move in on the house today." There's a pause. "Daniel and Sue decided to stay here at the house. Agent Joel and three others arrived this morning, so the extra backup is here. Sue has been keeping Savi busy, so—"

"Good, that's good." That makes him feel a whole lot better. "All right, I'll check back in with you tonight."

"Stay safe."

"Will do. Raven One out."

Cole tucks the phone into his vest pocket, downs a protein bar and a few chocolate covered coffee beans. He takes a deep breath clearing all thoughts out of his head and finally focuses on what's to come.

"All right," he says as he walks into the room where the guys are packing their gear. "Let's go get 'em."

# Chapter Twenty

I roll over when I hear a knock at the bedroom door. Keith stands there with his hands tucked in his pockets.

"Hi, Keith," I glance at the time. It's four in the afternoon. I've been hibernating in my room all day. I've been canceling my appointments with Doctor Roberts until Cole comes back. I'm just not in the mood to talk about my feelings. I just want to feel the way I feel. I know this has everyone concerned, but for once I'm being selfish and not caring.

"May I come in?"

"Of course," I say moving to sit up against my headboard as he sits on the side of my bed.

"This," he takes my ultrasound picture off my bedside table, "deserves to be in something nice." He pulls out a small silver frame with a swirly design and slips the picture inside. He sets it back down, angling it toward me. "There." He smiles.

My lip quivers and tears leak out and drip down my cheeks. I lean forward and give him a hug. "Thank you, Keith, for so much." When I pull away I see his eyes are glossy and we both pretend not to notice.

"Right, well come on downstairs. Daniel and Sue are here with luggage so I'm assuming they're staying for a while."

Smiling at him and loving that idea, I agree and hop off the bed.

I felt Abigail watching me all dinner long. I wasn't eating, but it wasn't because of the baby. I had caught a news clip about my father while I was getting out of the shower. The reporter asked if there was anything new about my disappearance and my father said no, but he seemed a little different. I wonder what is going on there. I wonder if he paid the ransom money and then realized he wasn't getting me back. Just merely seeing his face brought all sorts of emotions to the surface.

"Savannah?" Sue says bringing me back to the here and now.

I look up and see everyone has left the table.

She and Daniel are both standing watching me. "Is everything all right?"

"Yes," I nod then look down at my barely touched plate. "Sorry, I'm just tired."

Daniel looks at Sue and they both walk me into the living room and sit me on the couch, Sue makes me a cup of chamomile tea while Daniel hands me a light green gift bag.

"What's this?" I ask, sitting it between my feet.

"Something for you now, and something for the little one later."

"Oh!" I pull out the white tissue paper and reach in, feeling the softest little nose and a smile breaks out. I nearly cry when I sit the teddy bear on my lap, he's brown, with black eyes and a black nose. He has an Army hat with Army boots and a little jacket, Logan Jr. is sewn in green thread making my heart burst. "It's perfect, thank you," I whisper, rubbing its little ear.

Daniel leans forward kissing my head. "No, Savannah, thank you." He smiles, sitting back down as Sue returns with a tray full of fruit and cheese along with the wonderfully smelling tea. Taking a few sips, I soon find myself relaxing.

We chat about everything, my past life, my new life, what names I like for the baby, etc. By the time I head to bed I'm mentally fried, but for the first time in ages I'm feeling positive about my future. I reach down and rub my tummy. "'Night, little one."

\*\*\*

Cole slams his body up against the wall, closing his eyes listening to the footsteps around him. Two upstairs and three coming from the east toward him. His radio clicks two times; it's Mark letting him know he's still okay. Paul checked in moments ago but John hasn't yet. He clicks his radio once, checking in himself. A reflection in a picture, he waits until the man steps into the bedroom. One… two… three…he counts, then reaches out, wrapping his hands around the guy's neck and twisting violently, snapping it. Lowering the former threat to the ground, Cole rolls him under the bed and waits for the other.

"Raven Two, what's your position?" he whispers into the radio.

"Two-Three west," Mark replies. Perfect, he's on the second floor, three doors from the stairs.

Cole sneaks a look out the door. "Ten-four, Raven Two. Raven One inbound."

"Copy."

Cole raises his gun and checks to ensure it's clear. He spots the two men upstairs and sees two across the hall. The lights are dim and with his black gear, camouflage, and face paint he should be hard to spot. He moves fast and makes it to Mark's room in a matter of seconds. Mark is crouched behind the door.

"Just a graze to the shoulder," Mark quickly informs him.

Cole checks it out. It's deep and bleeding and he'll need a few stitches, but all things considered, Mark's okay. Cole makes fast work bandaging the wound, then hands Mark a few of the caffeine chocolates to help keep alert.

"John?" Cole asks, worried.

Mark shakes his head no.

"Okay. Paul?"

"First floor hall closet was where I saw him last."

Cole shakes his head bitterly. He doesn't want to use the radio unless he has too. He's not sure where John is or whether he's been captured or killed. Either way there's a good chance they'd have found John's radio by now, and would be listening. Bad enough they possibly just gave out their own location.

"We need to move," Cole says, looking out the window. "Have you seen The American?"

"No, but he's here. The Hummer and Land Rover are still parked out front. No one has left."

"Okay, I'll head downstairs. I'll signal for you to come when it's clear." Cole moves in front of Mark. "You wait, understand?"

Mark's face is pale and drenched in sweat, but he nods.

"Remember our pact?" Cole says, grabbing his brother's face so he'll look at him. "We joined together—"

"We retire together," Mark huffs out.

"Right. Stay with me 'cause if anything happens, I'll tell Melanie you died skiing on the bunny hill." Cole grins quickly.

"You would, too."

"Right, so stay with me."

"Yeah, I'm here with you."

Cole gives him a nod and slips out the door into the darkness, moving down the staircase. A quick glance at his watch shows him they should all be checking in again in ten minutes. Where the fuck is John? His hand runs along the wall till he finds the hall closet door handle. "Green Fox One?" He whispers.

The doorknob turns and Cole sees Paul sitting on the floor nursing a blood-soaked leg. *Shit*! He moves in getting a better look. He quickly unties the soaked bandage and his fingers feel how deep the wound is. He curses when he sees how much blood Paul's lost. His face is growing paler by the minute.

They need to abort the mission. "Stay here, I'm sending Mark for you then the both of you get out."

Paul starts to argue but Cole shakes his head.

341

"That's an order, Agent."

Cole peeks out the door and clicks his radio signaling Mark to come down.

"Any sign of John?" Cole asks as he rewraps Paul's leg.

"No, the last time I saw him was in the dining room," he replies, huffing through the pain. "We got separated and I got knifed and ended up here."

"Okay, set your watch for ten minutes. Start the clock after I leave. If I don't return with John get out. That's a direct order."

"Yes, Colonel." Paul nods and wipes the sweat from his forehead.

Cole helps him to his feet, propping him up against the wall.

Cole slowly opens the door. Seeing Mark coming down the stairs he moves across the hall and signals all clear then covers Mark until he's safely inside the room with Paul. Staying low, weapon raised, he moves carefully through the living room, then the dining room.

He feels something hit his shoulder. He turns and sees John crouched down between two lion sculptures. *Thank fuck.*

John points to his radio that is dangling in pieces around his chest.

Cole checks around and gives him the hand signal to get up and move to his position.

John nods and joins him at his side.

"We're aborting the mission. The others are hit we need to get them out of here. GF One and R Two have both lost a lot of blood. If we get separated, meet back at our command post."

John nods and they start to move toward the front entryway. A man comes into view on John's right.

Cole lunges forward, covering the man's mouth while wrapping his arms tightly around the startled target's neck, cutting off his airway. He orders John to move on.

The man elbows Cole in the stomach but Cole squeezes harder until the man stops struggling and goes limp. Cole sees his men making for the door when he spots another two men heading toward them from deeper within the residence.

Cole quickly pops a bullet in the first man's head and is about to do the same to the second when he feels a hard blow to the back of his head. He drops to his knees, a loud ringing sound taking over his brain right before his vision goes dark. His face hits the ground with a heavy thud.

\*\*\*

I roam the property, soaking up the sun even though it's still freezing out. Derek stays close. We've managed to get past our awkward moment in the kitchen and have started to build a friendship. I am thankful for that since living under one roof with so many people can take its toll.

He's still flirty but I think it's all in good fun. We chat about music as we approach the front of the house.

"Other than blues, what else do you listen too?" he asks, tucking his hands in his jacket pockets.

"Umm, Beck, Radiohead, Weezer, and I fell in

love with this Canadian band called the Tragically Hip." I grin, remembering one of their songs called "Ahead by a Century." I must have played it twenty times in a row one day. "They started in the early eighties. You should check 'em out, they're an alternative rock band."

"So you like alternative rock then?"

"I like all music, but yes, that would be my second favorite." I smile, then spot Keith watching us from the porch. A slow chill runs up my spine as he slowly starts to walk our way.

"Savannah, can you come join me inside?" Keith asks looking white as a ghost. I feel the panic form and it grows inside my stomach, making its way to my heart which is now beating at a rapid pace. I look at Derek, seeing him make eye contact with Keith.

A moment later Derek takes me by my arm, walking me toward the front door. I don't want to be indoors.

I want to run far away from what they're about to tell me. I don't want to think the worst, but it's there teeter-tottering between the good and the bad. One moment I'll be okay then the next I'm looking for an exit.

Keith opens the door to Dr. Roberts's office.

I feel the tension in the room and a rush of goose bumps breaks out making me shiver.

Daniel's arm is wrapped around Sue. Her eyes are glossy and her hands are clenched into fists.

Oh God, I look around at everyone's face feeling the haunting prickle that's dancing along the back of my neck.

June holds out her hand for me to sit next to her. I do, nearly falling over my shaky feet.

Abigail joins us a moment later dabbing her eyes with a tissue. Doctor Roberts gives her shoulder a quick squeeze. Everyone is painfully quiet as Daniel gives Keith a nod to begin.

"Fifty-four hours ago team Blackstone entered the house known to be The American's main residence." He clears his throat as mine closes over. "Things didn't go according to plan. They had to abort the mission. While attempting to retreat they came under fire. Everyone got out, except Cole."

Everything stops. Time; movement; brain waves; breathing; heartbeat—you name it, it just stops. I barely hear his next words, but they eventually find me. "We do know he's alive."

"How?" Sue cries out, reaching for her husband, who grips her hand tightly.

"We've received confirmation from Washington that the satellite camera picked up an image of Cole being transported to an unknown location by The American and the Cartels."

My lungs beg me to take a deep breath. Finally I do, letting out a horrible sob.

Abigail leans over rubbing my back as I fall forward onto my thighs.

"We don't know all the details, but the guys are in pretty bad shape and have been ordered to return to the house once they've been checked out by the medic in Washington."

"They-they left him there?" I whisper feeling the heat from the tears that course down my cheeks.

Keith looks at me pressing his lips together.

345

"Frank is now in charge," Daniel says in an eerie voice, "since Cole isn't able—" He stops himself, taking a deep breath. "They're coming home, that's an order from Frank. They don't have a choice, Savannah."

"Yes they do!" I shout through my tears. "What about Cole? What if they—" My hand covers my mouth. Another loud sob escapes as I stand, feeling sick and light headed. "Please make them go back," I beg. I turn to Keith crying out every word. "Please, please, Keith, please, make them go back and find him. I want him back, he needs to come back!"

"I'm sorry, Savannah, it's out of my control." Keith's eyes plead with me to understand.

I start to back up toward the door. I feel claustrophobic—the walls closing in and the ceiling lowering. I need to get away. Everyone is watching me. Some stand and approach, but I hold up a hand warning them off. I just want Cole back. I bump into Derek who's now standing in my path. I hear Sue say to Daniel that I should calm down. How can I calm down when they are telling me that Cole is being held captive, not when the father of our baby is being held against his will…no, I need to get out of here…*Now*.

The look I give Derek makes him move aside. Doctor Roberts calls out for me but I hear nothing but the door handle turning. I move without thinking up to my room, punching the keypad on the wall and dropping onto the pillows in Sue's private library. I curl up, passing out immediately. My thoughts quickly return to when I was held safe and sound in his arms. Yes, it's only a dream, but I'll take what I can get.

*\*\*\**

Sue finds me some time later with Keith's help. She slowly lowers herself to the floor.

I'm awake, facing away from her. I ache too much to move.

She lies behind me wrapping her arm around my mid-section holding my hand in hers.

I sob, desperately needing a mother and she sobs, desperately needing a child to hold.

She holds on while we both go through a roller coaster of emotions. We both fall asleep and wake several hours later feeling drained, and in need of some water.

We decide to go for a walk, neither wanting to be alone.

Keith and Daniel are working away in Cole's office.

Not wanting to disturb them, we head outside for some fresh air. We don't talk about anything important just mindless jabber when the pain becomes too much. I'm really thankful for Sue needing me as much as I need her. She's is fast becoming my rock. Thank God for her and Abigail. I don't know what I would do without them.

I flinch when she does. We hear it before we see it, the noise of the rotor makes my heart pound. I turn to see the black helicopter flying low over the mountains behind us. As it descends, it kicks up snow, making it swirl around us. I squeeze her hand knowing how hard this is going to be.

She tugs my arm heading back toward the house.

We're almost to the porch when the SUV stops next to us. I feel Keith come to my side.

The doors open and Paul gets out first. He's struggling to stand up straight.

John is next coming to Paul's side, grabbing his bag then wrapping his arm around Paul's waist to stabilize him.

Mark keeps his head down as he comes into view. His body language makes me uncomfortable. I notice not one of them has made eye contact with me.

Keith motions for us to come inside.

Sue never lets go of my hand as we slump down onto the couch waiting for them to join us.

They drop their bags and carefully make their way in. Daniel helps John sit Paul on the couch. His leg is in a small brace making it hard for him to move around.

Mark's arm is in a sling tied tightly to his chest, he's like a robot making his way to his seat. He sits staring at the floor I'm not even sure if he knows we are all here with him.

"Here." Daniel sets Mark's drink on the table and stands by the fire. I notice Mark doesn't reach for it. We all wait while the guys gather themselves.

"Nothing went according to plan." Paul's voice is quiet. "The moment we entered the house, it all went to shit."

My stomach is in knots. I want to yell out what the fuck happened? Where is Cole? But I don't. Instead I sit and stare at Mark who still hasn't looked up.

"A maid caught us as we moved through the kitchen. She dropped her tray and one of their men saw us."

"There were so many of them," John says clearing his throat. "My radio got busted when three of them jumped me. I managed to get away and went to our next location but no one came so I went back to the last spot I'd seen Paul in the dining room. I found a safe spot and tried to fix my radio but it was done."

"After I got a knife to the leg I found cover in a closet. Thirty minutes later, Cole found me," Paul says.

I break my gaze from Mark and look at Paul.

"He saw my leg and told me that Mark had a bullet wound. He said we were to abort the mission. That's when he left looking for John."

John rubs his head. "We got stopped on our way over to get them. Cole got one man down and sent me ahead to get the guys out. I met Paul and Mark in the hall and we headed for the door. The last thing I heard was a gunshot and a Cartel falling down the stairs. I glanced back when we were running for our check in point. I-I—" He shakes his head. "I couldn't see him."

My head starts to prickle, my eyes are feeling fuzzy, and my hands go cold as I listen.

"We waited for him." Paul takes over because John is barely holding it together. "We waited all night and into the morning. We fixed each other up as best we could and called in for support. By the time they came the place was cleared out. We were ordered to return here until further notice."

My eyes shift around the room trying to absorb what we're being told. I want so much to yell at them to go back but I can see they're just as raw as I am. They had to leave a man behind, their Colonel, their friend, and brother. I can't imagine. Suddenly, I feel a horrible cramping pain in my stomach, one that matches the pain from the gaping hole in my heart. I wrap my arms around my mid-section as my face breaks out in sweat.

"Savi?" Keith is kneeling in front of me. "You need to calm down."

"Calm down? Calm down!" I repeat feeling the anger burn through me. I stand, feeling the pain wrap around my middle.

"Yes, Savannah," Daniel warns, but I'm not realizing what they're getting at.

I back away running both hands through my hair, tears streaming down my face. My chest feels like it's going to explode. I raise my arms up wide. "You want me to calm down while Cole is sitting in a prison somewhere or six feet—" I stop, closing my eyes. I feel everyone staring at me. I drop my arms hitting my legs with a thud and turning on my heel I head for my room. I curl up in a ball to ease the pain in my stomach and cry myself to sleep.

\*\*\*

Cole huffs out as one of the men sticks his finger in the large gash across his torso. Over the last two days, he has been tortured by some very imaginative assholes. The electric shocks, waterboarding, and whippings haven't broken him yet. The two rats in front of him seem to be growing bored. They leave him hanging by his wrists from a chain, his feet a foot off the ground. His shoulders have lost any feeling long ago. The pain he should be feeling is blocked by long hours training to turn that part of the brain off. He watches as they walk down the hallway forgetting to shut the door. He takes the opportunity to listen to all the sounds in the little house. He concentrates on trying to remember the steps from when he arrived. Eleven steps from the Land Rover, three steps past the doorway, fourteen till the bedroom. He hears a TV turn on and the opening of twist-off beers. He closes his eyes, slipping into meditation mode, taking this time to get some rest so he will be mentally strong enough when they decide to come at him again.

\*\*\*

A bright light burns into his closed eyelids. Cole senses he's not alone.

A shadow moves in front of his face and the sound of nails on tile sparks a memory for him. Savannah's description of The American's boots. Cole plays like he's passed out, hoping to gather something from him.

"So, this is the famous Colonel Cole Logan," The American says in perfect English.

"*Si señor*," a man's voice answers.

"How many men did his team kill?"

"*Veintiocho*"

*Yeah, motherfucker. Twenty-eight down, a*

*billion more rats to go.*

"And he's not talking?"

"No."

"I think I may know how to fix that."

Two footsteps later and he gets a hard punch to the stomach. "Time to wake up, Colonel," The American says sharply.

Cole coughs, trying to catch his breath, then leans forward taking in what the man is wearing: his signature, black and white suit, a cowboy hat, and his ridiculous looking cowboy boots with the gold-headed cobra sticking out at the tips.

"At last, we finally meet after all these years," he says.

Cole keeps silent, watching him, studying his movements. He has a slight limp in the right leg and he keeps tilting his head to the left like his neck is hurting.

"So, I'm going to ask you a question and you're going to answer it. Where is my Savannah?"

It takes everything in Cole's body to not to react.

The American nods his head fixing his left shirt cuff. "So short term physical torture doesn't seem to bother you. I wish we had more time, but sadly we don't." He taps his mouth with his finger. "I wonder how strong you are mentally." He smirks. "Mr. Donavan, would you please join us?"

Cole gaze moves to the door when he hears footsteps.

It only takes a moment to realize who it is. A wheel of photos flicker through Cole's memory the most recent from when they were doing surveillance on the house and this guy shows up. A navy blue suit with a cream-colored cloth bag over his head with his wiry body is hard to forget.

"I'll take it you recognize me?" he asks, smirking.

"I do," Cole grunts out.

"You see, Colonel, we have a problem. You screwed up a very important business deal for me." He moves closer. "This can be very easily fixed if you would just give me Ms. Miller."

Cole takes a minute, trying something. He rotates his shoulder and flops his head around like he's losing consciousness.

Mr. Donavan looks at The American. "Can you at put him in a chair or something?" He points to Cole's stomach. "This is offensive to me. I don't need to see this all stretched and bloody."

The American shakes his head slowly, annoyed, but calls for the men to come. "Don't try anything," The American says, sticking a 40mm in Cole's face as the men release the pulley system lowering him into a wooden chair. They keep his hands and feet bound but don't actually tie him to the chair. He notices one of them is wearing a longhorn belt buckle. The horns look more like a weapon than a decoration. A dull ache runs through him as he starts to feel the beating his body took but relishes in the fact that his plan worked and he was released from the ceiling. His mind slips back into survival mode as he sits, his body starting to build strength as the seconds tick by.

"Now," Mr. Donovan says as he takes a seat in front of him, "where's the girl?"

Cole moves his tongue around his mouth.

Tasting tin he spits to his side…yup blood. He looks over at the man, taking his time answering, "Why the girl?"

"Do you know who I am?" He leans forward in his chair, "I mean really know who I am?"

"Luka Donovan, the Mayor's assistant."

"Correct. I've known the Mayor's daughter for a long time," he says, smiling at Cole.

Cole smiles back but for a very different reason, his much more violent.

"You see, the Mayor is up for re-election. The numbers are good but due to his daughter's constant fuck-ups they're not great. So a change was necessary." He leans back shaking his head. "I never would have been able to pull it off if it wasn't for Lynn."

Cole always suspected Savannah's best friend, but could never connect the dots. "Savannah trusted her more than anyone," he continued conversationally. "So when Lynn and I met for dinner and she agreed she could get a customer of hers to pose as a prospective client who could lure her 'friend' down to the parking lot at the right time, it was perfect."

"Joe Might?" Cole interrupted.

Luka nods with a shrug. "You see, Colonel, much like in your profession, I, too, meet a lot of shady people. You start to learn things. Like money doesn't always buy you what you want, but a pretty face and a smoking body like Savannah's can."

Before Cole even thinks about what he is doing he lunges forward, plowing Luka off his chair into the wall.

Luka cries out as the wind is knocked out of him.

Cole elbows him in the face and knees him in the stomach just as he feels a hard crack between his shoulder blades. He drops to the ground and sees the butt of the gun as it collides with his temple. The pain doesn't register as he tries to get back up but The American sticks the gun in his face making him freeze.

"Make one more move and I'll blow your head off," he hisses closing his eyes, teeth grinding loudly, no doubt trying to calm himself. "Get him out of here!"

Two men grab hold of Cole and another keeps his gun in his face.

He sees Luka in a ball on the floor moaning holding his stomach. He tries to force himself to control his thoughts as the deadly violence in them would probably get him killed if he didn't. Handcuffing him to a water pipe in a small closet and slamming the door closed, they leave him alone in the dark. Cole shifts, leaning his head against his hands using pressure to stop the bleeding from his temple and letting out a long sigh thinking of all the ways he could escape. He just needs to get his hands on a weapon.

A small breeze of cool air next to where the pipe meets the wall gets his attention. He lines his eye up with the one-inch hole and he can see outside— there's lights about twenty yards away. He must be in a small town. He turns back around when he hears footsteps, then muffled voices and a loud crack, followed by a thump. He sees the light under his door go dark as something is being dragged outside the room. Shaking his head not wanting to know, he pulls at the pipe testing it's strength. He leans back, kicking at the base of it but it's no use. "Fuck!" he whispers to himself resting his head against the wall, needing sleep. He closes his eyes, but all he can think about is Savannah. She must be beside herself right now. His chest hurts thinking about her. He knows she will be devastated to find out Luka and Lynn are behind her kidnapping.

# Chapter Twenty-One

"Wake up!" Luka kicks him in the ribs. "I said wake up!"

Cole opens his eyes, even though he's been awake most of the night. He dismisses the pain in his ribs and smirks when he sees Luka is sporting a black and blue goose egg over his eye.

Luka glares down at him. Closing the door he pulls up a chair and sits watching Cole. "I heard you were one tough Green Beret. Hell, you became a Colonel at thirty; you must really be something," he croons. "But you see, Colonel, everyone has a weak spot." He leans back, crossing his legs. "And last night you showed me yours." He smirks back. "She's beautiful, isn't she? Her long, silky hair, her tan skin, those dark eyes that seem to pull you in, that slender body with *just* the right amount of curves, mmm, so lovely." He shakes his head like he's remembering something. "I don't think there's a man in that office that didn't think about screwing her."

Cole's jaw muscle twitches as the adrenalin rushes throughout his body.

"I can see that you've fallen under her spell too, which explains another reason why you won't give up her location. Don't waste your time." He laughs. "She has a pistol personality, a gatekeeper guarding her heart, and she doesn't open her legs for anyone."

The wave of emotion that hits Cole is something unreal. He actually finds himself grinning on the inside and the corners of his mouth tugging on the outside. Yes, he had found his way to Savannah's heart. Now he just needed to get back.

"Sounds like you're interested too?" Cole murmurs, hoping to get more detail about the kidnapping.

"Nah." He shakes his head. "I like my job too much to touch that, so I settled for the best friend."

Cole rolls his eyes; what a prick. "Tell me something, Luka." Cole shifts, resting his forearms on his bent knees. "How did you locate someone to kidnap Savannah?"

Luka laughs a little. "You'd be surprised how easy it is to find someone willing to remove my little problem, a word here, a word there and soon I had a few offers but when *Los Sirvientes Del Diablos* approached me, we soon had a deal. She was nabbed and taken to Tijuana. She was supposed to be killed within a week, but then this guy," he points over his shoulder and out the door indicating The American, "got in touch with them and made his own deal. He wanted Savannah for himself but agreed to wait until the ransom money came through." He pauses, leaning forward. "There are rules, you know. You can't just come in and take her. He had to wait until it was a done deal."

Fuck, this guy is a talker and a real asshole. Cole is going to enjoy fucking up his face.

"But then *Los Sirvientes Del Diablos* got greedy. They got in contact with the Mayor saying they have his daughter and that someone else was interested in her so whoever pays the most gets the girl." Luka removes his glasses, rubbing the bridge of his nose. "The Mayor didn't react the way I thought he would. I swear he was relieved she was gone. His own daughter! His votes were climbing. He started dating a woman." His voice softens. "Don't get me wrong, Colonel, he loves Savannah but she just wouldn't climb aboard the campaign wagon and a man has his priorities." He sighs loudly.

"Hey!" The American yells, suddenly bursting through the door. "What the fuck are you doing?"

"Just chatting," Luka says calmly.

"I didn't bring you here for a fucking meet and greet. Get out so I can get this done." The American slips a pair of brass knuckles over his fingers, making a fist.

"Is that really necessary?" Luka asks, making a disgusted face as he stands up. "May I have a word with you outside?" He touches The American's shoulder jumping back when the man turns on him grabbing his arm, twisting it.

"Don't fucking touch me, ever!" The American hisses. "Outside!"

Luka nods as he rubs his arm, following The American out the door. It slams behind them leaving one man with a machine gun alone with

Cole.

Cole tilts his head staring at the man. He's so young, maybe early twenties. His face is sweaty and his body is shaking, making his fingers flex on the gun.

The kid tosses the strap over his head. "You move," he says in a thick accent. "I blow your head off."

Cole smiles at him and whispers something under his breath, waiting for him to come just a little closer, sure enough the kid takes two steps toward him. Cole suddenly grabs the side of the pipe as he kicks the barrel of the gun so it shoots up slamming the kid in the eye. He falls backwards with a scream and scrambles to the other side of the wall away from Cole's reach.

The door flies open and The American sees the kid on the floor, holding his head and groaning in pain. He looks at Cole, walks up to him and punches him in the side of the head once with the brass knuckles.

\*\*\*

It's dark again when Cole comes to, a tiny crack in the wall providing a cool breeze. His skull feels like he was hit by a Mack truck, probably fractured. It hurts like hell just to open his eyes and he's thankful the light is off. The door opens as another wave of nausea hits hard. He leans over, vomiting. *Fuck*. A water bottle is dropped at his feet. He looks up to find Luka standing above him. *Oh Christ, here comes good cop-bad cop again.* He moves his hands down the pipe using his foot to slide the water bottle toward him. He opens it and takes a drink awkwardly, the cool water like liquid gold. His stomach feels immediately better—if only he could get some painkillers. He chuckles a bit at the thought.

"Something funny?" Luka asks, sitting on the floor across from him.

"Not really," Cole huffs as he drops the empty bottle on the floor.

"She hated the press, you know." He starts his story like they never got interrupted. "Savannah hated her father for choosing his job over her so she'd get drunk and parade around town disgracing herself."

Cole bends down and reaches for his throbbing head, feeling the blood trickle down his neck. Luka tosses his water bottle at him, hitting his leg.

"You paying attention? 'Cause this is where it gets interesting."

Cole glares over at him, dropping his hands and straightening up.

"One night I found the Mayor drinking in his office. He confessed that someone contacted him with proof of life for Savannah but since he didn't pay right away, now they were blackmailing him saying he'd set the whole thing up. I knew *Los Sirvientes Del Diablos* told him I was behind the whole thing. I could tell by his look. I thought it was all over but instead he asked for my help. I was shocked…after all she is his daughter, but I just dodged a major bullet. After all, we both want to be at the top and we'll do whatever is needed to get there."

He claps his hands together making Cole's head pound. "So a new plan is hatched! We start to use the media as much as possible. No one could accuse us of not caring about our missing Savannah. We ignore the ransom demands and hope they'll dispose of her. Everything was running smoothly. There was no contact with them, everything was good. But then, a few months later, I'm at a bar, and boots here," referring to The American, "approaches me, saying we better pay up, or they're going to release a recording they have with the Mayor on the damn phone discussing the ransom deal. They were going to prove that he did know his daughter was alive and he didn't give a shit. So we started low balling. We started with fifty grand just to buy us some time to think but before we got the chance she vanishes into thin air."

Cole leans back, trying to get his aching head to absorb all the information Luka is throwing at him.

"Hang on." Cole stops his babbling. "You thought ignoring a group with ties to the Cartels was going to make them go away? Had you even heard of the Cartels before you got involved with them?" This guy is seriously stupid.

"They got paid for taking the girl. As far as I was concerned our deal was finished. They were the ones who didn't fulfill their end of the bargain."

"You're playing stupid in the Devil's backyard," Cole says in disbelief, not caring if it pisses off Luka. "Hell, you made a deal with his God-damned self-proclaimed servants!"

Luka rubs the back of his neck. "Yes, I

understand that now," he agrees, nodding sadly. "They accused us of taking her and started sending reminders that we owe them two million or they'd release the tape." He raises his voice. "They threatened my family, and Lynn, and they tried to set my car on fire. Boots or 'The American' as you call him finally realized we had no idea where the hell she was or what was going on. After a lot of money and time we found out the fucking US Army has her hidden away!" He leans forward again staring right into Cole's eyes. "You see Colonel, I did make a deal with the Devil, and I have to see it through. So this brings us to you. I need you to give the girl to The American, I need to pay the two million, and the Mayor needs to win this election so we can all go and live our lives the way things were meant to be. It is a very easy fix."

Cole's mind is blown. So many lies, so many deceitful people. He can't believe that her own father could give her up so easily. God, this will kill her if nothing else does.

"How stupid do you think I am?" Cole asks. "You think with all that you told me that you're going to let me go? Luka, I didn't become a Colonel at thirty because of my fighting skills."

"I really don't like repeating myself, but considering all that I told you, I'm sure your mind is spinning. So where is she?" Luka sighs, ignoring Cole's comment.

Cole decides he needs some more information before he makes his move.

"Why would Lynn betray her?"

Luka seems to consider. "I'll answer you, and in

return, you answer me." He straightens his tie. "Lynn and I became involved a few years back. She didn't seem to mind that I was eleven years older. We kept it quiet, no one knew, especially Savannah. Lynn despised her. She was jealous, she couldn't understand why Savannah didn't want to be a part of the campaign and involve herself in her father's life. Why couldn't she see that we would all benefit. We would all be taken to the top with him." He shakes his head. "Lynn had a bad childhood. She resented Savannah had a good one, and was now throwing away Lynn's chance at finally getting what she deserved."

"Watching your mother disintegrate over four months hardly makes for a happy childhood." Cole shoots back, feeling his anger bore through his veins.

"It really was for the best, although her mother was not a supporter of Doug going into politics." Luka shrugs rolling his eyes. "Apparently Savannah takes after her."

Cole starts to laugh, his patience with the man has run out and his vision is clouding. "You're so fucked."

"That may be so," Luka says getting to his feet, "but I'm not the one handcuffed to a water pipe in a house full of men who want me dead. He opens the door and signals for someone to come in. He turns looking at Cole. "Last chance." The American walks in, looking pissed off and stressed.

"Well?" he asks Luka.

"Fuck you," Cole says, making the two of them look at him.

"What?" The American's face twists.

"I said, fuck you."

The American studies him for a moment then takes out a handkerchief, dabbing his brow as he considers. "Okay, Colonel, we're done here." He nods at two men to come in while he points his gun at Cole's head.

One of the guys is the kid from earlier, his eye painfully swollen shut. The kid removes one of the handcuffs freeing him from the pipe. He slaps it back on Cole's wrist, pulling him to his feet. Normally, he would make a move, but he is outnumbered and can hear more men in the other room. No, for now he'll wait for the perfect moment before he strikes.

"We could still get it out of him." Luka starts to protest, but The American shakes his head.

"He won't talk. He has too much pride. Don't you, Captain America?" He laughs. "I know you care for the girl in the same way I do. We both love her. I can see it in your face when I mention her name."

Cole's face hardens.

"I can't wait to feel her under me, Colonel. I can't wait to hear her whimper and beg when I—"

Cole shoots forward, head butting The American, sending him backwards. The guard with two working eyes knocks Cole in the head with the butt of his rifle, bringing him to his knees.

He cries out as his ears ring, pain exploding in all different directions throughout his head.

The American's boots clink on the floor as he comes closer. "Take him to the tub. I think the

Colonel needs a little reminder who's in charge here." He looks at Longhorn. "I need to make a trip into town. Give him ten, then cuff him back to the pipe."

"*Si, señor.*"

Cole hears the American leave the room, the door shut behind him, and the roar of an engine.

"Change of plans," Longhorn says to One Eye. "Get the back room ready, *esé*." He smirks down at Cole. "Time for some fun, Colonel."

***

I've been a mess for the past three days. I just lie in bed and watch the time tick by wondering where Cole is. I catch myself slipping, thinking the worst, but then I feel guilty for giving up hope. I cry a lot and barely eat. June and Abigail take shifts watching me. Sue has been curled up on my bed most of the time. She needs comforting as much as I do. We both take turns being strong for each other while Daniel and Keith work frantically with Frank, trying to use their contacts in México to track down Cole. Mark, John, and Paul try to help, but they are all ordered to stand down. It's now personal for them and two of them are still recovering from their wounds.

Derek is in charge of the new men that Daniel brought in. Everyone seems to be busy doing something but me. I feel stuck between moving forward and wanting to stay in the past when Cole was with me. I hum quietly to my stomach. I find it soothes me and hopefully it soothes the little one too.

Needing a change of scenery, I head downstairs. When I hear shouting from the entertainment room I head that way. I peek around the corner to see what is happening. Everyone in the room seems to be waiting for a video to start.

"All it says is that it's a message for Team Blackstone," Daniel says, looking pale.

The video comes into focus and I reach for the wall for support. Cole is on his knees, beaten, shirtless, and sweaty, a nasty cut running along his torso. Blood drips in trails over his face from a gash on his head. His mouth is gagged and his wrists are cuffed in front of him. He looks up into the camera making my heart stand still. Everyone gasps and cries out. Mark stands, moving closer to the TV.

A man stands next to Cole; his hands are crossed in front. Then I see it he's holding a large machete. I freeze not breathing. My brain begs me to look away but I can't.

"All you had to do was return her," the man says as the camera moves up to his face. "Blackstone killed twenty-eight of our men. Now I will kill one of yours and will continue killing until you give us what we want." The camera zooms in on his face then slowly moves down his body to the knife held over Cole's neck.

Cole is breathing hard, his sweat beads obvious in the close up zoom.

Suddenly the flash of the machete moves quickly. The force of the cut sends Cole's body in a twist and it slumps to the ground. Blood sprays everywhere including onto the camera lens.

Everything goes silent. People are moving in slow motion around me. I lock eyes with Mark who has heard me gasp and discovers me watching them.

He looks horrified and frozen, staring at me, making everyone turn to see me standing there.

Daniel cups his mouth in horror while Paul and John gasp, rising to their feet. A sharp cramp in my lower stomach has me crying out and I fall forward as pain grips me in a vice.

Mike is standing nearest, and he leaps toward me cradling my head before I hit the floor.

The physical pain is overpowering. I gasp, trying to catch my breath. My fingers claw at my stomach, *What the hell is happening?*

"Call the doctor!" Keith shouts as he flies to my side.

I see the horror in his face when his eyes flicker to my stomach.

Daniel pushes Mike out of the way and bends down toward my ear.

"Shh, sweetheart," he whispers through a sob, "Just breathe." He strokes my hair murmuring something to Keith.

Everything goes black.

\*\*\*

"Her HCG levels are low," a nurse says as I stare at the wall, expressionless, everything numb. "Twenty-six forty. I'll go check the results of her urine test." She nods to the doctor as she leaves the room.

"Savannah, do you feel any discomfort?" I feel

so much pain the idea of pinpointing a single one seems impossible.

Daniel touches my hand tears streaming down his face as he bent down to my eye level.

"Savannah?" he whispers.

I close my eyes and nod once.

I feel the unwanted pressure as the probe is inserted, the odd noise like you're standing too close to a speaker while holding a microphone fills the room. A tear rolls down my face as I see Cole standing in front of me. It's only for a moment—then he's gone. A sob hits me. I want to curl into a ball but I can't. I have to wait till they find out if the only tiny piece of Cole I have left is still alive inside me. I close my eyes. This is all too much.

# Chapter Twenty-Two

## *The next night*

I feel Sue slip off the bed. Her steps are quiet as she shuts the door behind her. She only leaves when she thinks I'm asleep. I open my eyes, seeing it's still dark out. My head is pounding but I don't care. I don't want to be alone, but I don't want anyone with me except Cole. Keith has permanently taken up residence on the couch in Cole's room, saying he won't leave until I do.

Rolling over, hugging Cole's pillow, breathing in his scent, I sob, not just because I lost the one person I love more than anything, but because I will never hold our baby. My only comfort is that Cole will. I never believed in heaven or hell but right now I just want to picture them together, happy, and waiting for me to join them. I imagine Cole holding our little one. Telling him how much I love him, kissing his soft, deep-brown hair, and looking into his sweet dark eyes—so much like his father's. I reach for the Army teddy bear bringing it to my chest. I feel so empty, so lost. I've felt pain before but that was nothing compared to this. How am I supposed to move forward when everything in my body is telling me I can't? I'm over this life; I want a redo.

My eyes focus on something taped to the back of Cole's nightstand. I shift, pretending to pull the cover over me more. I see what it is and feel like fate is finally on my side. Taking a deep breath and closing my eyes I make a silent promise to myself for the second time in my life that I will make it back to my family. There's a difference between living and surviving, but this right here is neither. I lean up slowly to look at Keith; he's fast asleep. I reach for the handle, slipping it out of the holster, my hand slippery with tears. Still clutching the teddy bear in one hand, I raise the pistol to my temple with the other. For the first time in a long time I finally feel like I'm at peace.

*** 

Major Mark Lopez - 01:52 am

Mark sits at Cole's desk, sipping his brother's brandy. He's finally gotten his hands on the DVD the Cartels sent. He had to convince Frank to let him have it before he left in the morning. He feels strongly they are missing something—he just doesn't know what.

He presses play and watches the tape again and again when finally something catches his eye. He backs up the tape and watches frame by frame. "What!" Mark whispers in disbelief, setting his drink down so quickly it splashes over his hand. He shifts forward, watching the last scene before Cole slumps to the floor.

"Holy fucking shit!"

## The End

# Acknowledgments

A huge thank you to Corporal George Myatt and Officer Darcy Wood.

## About the Author

J. L. Drake was born and raised in Nova Scotia, Canada, later moving to Southern California where she now lives with her husband and two children.

When she is not writing she loves to spend time with her family, travelling or just enjoying a night at home. One thing you might notice in her books is her love of the four seasons. Growing up on the east coast of Canada the change in the seasons is in her blood and is often mentioned in her writing.

An avid reader of James Patterson, J.L. Drake has often found herself inspired by his many stories of mystery and intrigue. She hopes you will enjoy her books as much as she has enjoyed writing them.

# *Note to my readers*

Thank you for reading the first book in my Broken trilogy. This story came to me in a dream one night. When I woke the next morning I started writing as fast as I could as the story flowed out of me. I completed the book in about two months. It was never meant to be a trilogy, but even after the second book I realized that I still needed more of Cole and Savannah. Their story just kept unfolding and growing. These two characters hold a very special place in my heart. As in my first novel, *What Lurks in the Dark,* there are some scenes that I have pulled from my own life. I truly hope that you will fall in love with Cole and Savi as I have.

If I was able, I would release this book like a TV series—a week at a time just to make the story last longer and savor their journey together.

Please keep in mind that this is a fictional story and that I do understand that in real life, unlike fiction, things happen much more slowly than they do in the book. The story moves along quickly and takes place in only a few months.

"Shattered" Book Two, and "Mended" Book Three of the Broken Trilogy will soon be released by Limitless Publishing.

What could be worse than being broken? Shattered.

Jx

## Novels by this author:

What Lurks in the Dark
Bunker 219 (Found in the
Unleash the Undead Anthology)

## Upcoming releases:

Shattered (2nd in the Broken trilogy)
Mended (3rd in the Broken trilogy)
Darkness Follows (The Dark Series)
All In (Tragic Anthology)

## Facebook:
https://www.facebook.com/JLDrakeauthor

## Twitter:
https://twitter.com/jodildrake_j

## Goodreads:
http://www.goodreads.com/author/show/8300313.J
L_Drake

## Website:
http://www.authorjldrake.com/